NINE SECONDS

ALSO BY VINCENT DEFILIPPO

The Leftovers Club

Book One: JoJo's Story

Catch a Falling Knife

Braking Point: *How Escalation of Commitment is Destroying the World (and How You Can Save Yourself)*

NINE SECONDS

Vincent deFilippo

ViennaRose Publishing LLC
Copyright © 2024 by ViennaRose & VJ DeFilippo
All Rights Reserved

Cover and art design by
ViennaRose Publishing LLC

http://www.vincentdefilippo.com

Print Paperback ISBN: 979-8-9883420-9-0

Printed in the U.S.A

PROLOGUE

Staten Island, Present Day

Morning sunlight poured through the rolled-up window of the Lamont family sedan. Mary Lamont, age thirteen, sat in the back seat, peering out at the southern facade of Fort Tompkins from the parking area along that end of the old fortress. The gray, block-built face of the aging granite building on Staten Island was overgrown with grass and weeds, unwelcoming and cold despite being warmed by the sun.

"Fuck. It's closed," Mary's dad, Hal, said as he gripped the steering wheel and scowled back at the old fort.

"Most of these places are closed on Mondays, Hal," Mary's mother, Samantha, said as if she hadn't mentioned that several times before they'd even left the house. "And watch your language."

Hal glanced at his phone. "I couldn't find the hours online. Damn. Came all the way from Jersey for this. It used to be open on Mondays." His voice was edging toward a whine.

Samantha popped her phone back into her purse. "Funny. I found them easily enough. They're open Friday, Saturday, and Sunday." She shrugged. "We'll just come next weekend."

1

"I work next weekend—I've got that two-day planning meeting with Delafield, remember?"

"Then we'll come for a lantern tour when you get off work." She rested a hand on her husband's knee and gave him a thin smile that told him she'd not remembered. "It's okay, Hal. We can just go have a walk along the river, then get an early lunch somewhere nice. It'll be good. Won't it, Mary?" She tipped her head so she could glance back at their daughter.

Mary couldn't understand why her father was so intent on showing her Fort Wadsworth's decrepit military facilities—Fort Tompkins and a scattering of artillery batteries with weird names like Weed and Bacon. Yeah, he'd been a park ranger once upon a time, and had given tours of the place, but that was ages ago. He'd made sure she understood that Fort Wadsworth was the name of the whole park and that Fort Tompkins, Battery Weed, Battery Bacon, and others were areas within the military park. He sold pool supplies now. And, while he waxed poetic about his days working at the old fort, Mary failed to see the charm. Maybe if the place was full of happy tourists. But empty like this it was just . . . creepy.

Mary leaned forward between their two seats. "A walk and lunch sound good to me. Let's go."

Hal turned back and smirked at his daughter. "You scared?"

Mary leaned back and crossed her arms. "No."

"Yeah, you are. I saw that expression on your face." His smile deepened and took on a conspiratorial gleam. "I bet I can get us inside. I'll give you a tour."

"I don't think that's a good idea, honey," said Samantha.

"Come on, you two wimps."

Hal got out of the car and slammed the door, grinning at them through the windows. Samantha rolled her eyes before following suit.

Mary sighed. The old fort was creep central, but if the alternative was sitting out here alone in a hot car . . . She climbed out. To her right loomed the Verrazzano Narrows Bridge. This early in the day, its shadow reached toward the fort like the long arms of a skeletal monster; it still had two of the smaller batteries in its evil grasp. Mary smiled a little. The

Verrazzano Shadow Monster was eating Bacon. She wondered if the Shadow ever smoked Weed.

Trying not to giggle, she followed her parents into the grassy gap between the fort and a big old retaining wall that seemed to run the whole length of it. Some yards down the gap—which was wide enough to drive a car through—was a tall iron fence with a padlocked gate. In front of the fence was a historical marker that displayed the requisite maps and oldie-moldy photos.

Mary stepped between the immense stone walls, giving a last glance toward the beckoning shoreline where Battery Weed hunkered on the rocks, glowering across the Narrows at Fort Lafayette. Built to defend against the British, Battery Weed was an imposing, three-story affair set in a crooked N shape; each of its three sea-facing sides sported three rows of nine windows, which at one time housed a cannon each. Rust stains seeped down from each of the windows to the one below, reminiscent of tears.

Hal cleared his throat as he stood in front of the historical placard. Its main feature was a grainy black-and-white photo of troops lined up in rows inside the fort. "Ladies, thank you for joining our tour today. I'm Hal Lamont, and I'll be your guide. Please stay with the group at all times during our tour."

Samantha laughed. "Okay, enough with the play-acting."

"Shh. I'm taking you on a trip down haunted memory lane." Hal put his hands on his hips and puffed out his chest, ignoring his wife's eye roll.

Dad can be so awkward, thought Mary. At least none of her classmates were around to witness the spectacle.

"Fort Wadsworth is a former United States military installation here on Staten Island. It's situated on the Verrazzano Narrows"—Hal swept a hand toward the water—"which divides New York Bay into its upper and lower halves. During the Civil War, it was thought to be the perfect point for the defense of Manhattan."

Mary covered her face with her hands. "This is so embarrassing, Dad."

Hal spread his arms and looked around. "Who's there to be embarrassed in front of?"

"The universe? The bats? I'm sure there are bats," replied Mary.

Hal cleared his throat again and continued. "This was the longest continually garrisoned military installation in the United States before it closed in 1994. Now, the grounds are divided into smaller units, including Fort Tompkins and Fort Richmond. Fort Wadsworth is now maintained by the National Park Service."

"Can I ask a question?" Mary raised her hand. "Why do people even come here?"

Her dad put on a maniacal grin. "Because it's scary as shit. *Bwahaha!*"

"Hal, language," said Samantha, with a glance at Mary.

"And let's not forget this is one of the places Cropsey's ghost likes to hang out."

"Hal!" Samantha shot her husband a judgy, *don't you dare* expression, but he was on a roll and ignored her.

"I thought he only haunted the old Seaview Hospital and Farm Colony," Mary said, her interest in the old fort suddenly piqued.

"Don't forget Willowbrook Mental Institution," her dad threw in, much to Samantha's chagrin.

"Yeah, they told us all about it at school. It's actually called the Willowbrook State School."

"What are they doing teaching you about sick stuff like that?" Samantha snapped. "It's wholly inappropriate."

"It's local history, Sam," Hal said. "Cropsey is as big a part of Staten Island's history as any one of its other notorious spooks. Did I ever tell you about Polly Bodine, the infamous Witch of Staten Island, who supposedly killed her sister-in-law and niece and then burned their house to the ground?"

"Enough!"

"Oh, come on, hon. It's the kid's rite of passage, their Staten Island baptism. Everyone loves a good boogeyman story—I remember your grandad Den telling me they used to scare him shitless at Boy Scout camp back in the day with tales of how Cropsey the axe murderer would kidnap kids to torture and butcher them. It's become a campfire tradition at every sleepaway camp in the Northeast."

"He snatched them when they were alone, or from their own beds while their parents were in the next room," Mary added; she was enjoying watching her uptight mother squirm.

"Cropsey was nothing more than a myth, and the name was used like people say boogeyman nowadays to stick a label on the unexplained," Hal added, clearly relishing his role as ghoulish tour guide. "Until, in 1972, the first of the children disappeared."

"I think that's quite enough now." Samantha turned to walk away.

Mary stayed put.

"Five Staten Island kids disappeared between then and 1987," Hal continued. "It was as if Cropsey had stepped right out of the stories to punish those who told them to successive generations."

"My teacher said they caught two different Cropseys, though," Mary said with a glance around the damp walls. "And they are both still in prison."

Hal gave a sage nod. "Your teacher is right. They caught a guy called Andre Rand who worked at Willowbrook back when it was open. But they say it's the evil that dwelled *within* him that haunts the places he murdered his victims. Rand was part of a satanic cult and took the kids for human sacrifices to appease the devil. But. . . kids still mysteriously vanished after he was locked up and labeled Cropsey—finally the myth had a face." Hal gave his daughter a sinister grin.

"Then, about ten years ago, Robert Cox was arrested for attacking kids—some newspaper called him Son of Cropsey and it just stuck. The police figured they'd gotten all the Cropseys and the terror that had haunted Staten Island was over." Hal upturned his flashlight beneath his chin. "Or did they...?"

"That's enough, Hal!" Samantha barked. "You're scaring her!"

"No, he isn't, Mom."

Mary's protest fell on deaf ears, and Samantha stormed away. Hal gave his daughter a resigned shrug and wry smile, and the two followed dutifully on.

Getting back into his flow, Hal gestured down the grassy sward behind him as he and Mary trotted to catch up with his petulant wife. "We are currently standing in the southern end of the fort's drymoat, which is an ingenious defensive feature."

Mary glanced up at the two sheer walls and realized both were wearing a frilly green cap of trees and shrubs. An uneven fringe of overgrown grass stuck out along the top of the wall. Curious, she asked, "Why are there trees growing on top of the fort? Did they do that on purpose?"

"They did," said their guide, "for several reasons. One was to conceal the fort from the air, and because it would cut down on the effectiveness of any ordnance dropped from the air. It also filtered rainwater down into a series of cisterns that provided the fort with water."

If the sun had been higher in the sky, Mary thought, the atmosphere would have been quite pleasant, but this early, the man-made canyon was clogged with shadows. The place reminded her of Fangorn Forest from *Lord of the Rings*.

Mom had gone to peer through the iron gate, gamely playing tourist. "This couldn't have ever been filled with water, could it?"

"No, ma'am. This moat was never intended to hold water. It was meant to hold enemy soldiers. Once they found their way in here, thinking to attack the rear wall of the fort, it was like shooting fish in a barrel because that," Hal said as he made a sweeping gesture at the high outer wall of the moat—"isn't just a wall. It's the wall of a stone gallery that our forces would fill with riflemen. And the riflemen would fire through those gun loops there."

Hal then pointed at one of the narrow, almost invisible apertures in the outer wall, before he did a 180 and pointed to a similar slit in the inner walk. "And there. Two men would be at each loop. One fired at the enemy while the other reloaded."

As he spoke, Samantha moved to the outer wall and put a hand to one of the gun loops. She quickly pulled it back. "Terrifying. It looks like an old castle . . . or a prison."

"It is creepy, isn't it?" Hal beamed down the grassy green sward sandwiched between the two granite walls. "Imagine guarding this place on your own at night or leading a lantern tour. I've got stories."

"I know," said Samantha wryly. "I've heard them all."

Hal grinned, then began walking vigorously back toward the southern end of the fort. "Let's go!"

"Hey, slow down!" Samantha struggled to catch up with her husband.

Mary hung back and watched as they got farther away. Every instinct told her to get back in the car and wait or park herself in the shade of the old battery across the street—Battery Duane. She might have rolled her eyes at the silliness of the name, but she didn't like the way Fort Tompkins looked or felt. The place did scare her. She tried to tell herself it was because of all those stories her dad had told about the fort and the strange incidents that were rumored to have happened during the lantern tours they did on summer evenings.

With a last, longing glance at the car, Mary ran after her parents.

Against her better judgment, she drew close to one of the fort-side gun loops she passed by and peered in. Beyond was pitch black. She thought she saw movement in the Stygian gloom and pulled away. Probably one of the park staff, she told herself. Which meant that her dad, being a big old showoff, was probably going to blow up in his face. She was almost looking forward to that.

Mary eventually caught up with her parents on the southeast side of the narrow fort where her dad was inspecting an iron door. She was relieved to see that it was secured with an aging Yale padlock.

"Aw, it's locked," said Samantha, sounding not the least bit disappointed. "Guess we'll just have to come back when they're open."

"No, we won't. I kept a little souvenir." Hal pulled a key from his pocket.

"You carry that around all the time?"

He shrugged.

His wife fixed him with a stinkeye. "You knew. You knew all along the fort was closed today. You meant to sneak in."

He grinned and fitted the key into the lock. "Let's see if this still works." He turned the key and grinned even more fiercely when the lock clicked and sprang open. "Here we go," he said and ushered them into a dark tunnel, closing the gate firmly behind them. "Right this way, folks. Go down to the junction and turn left. And no wandering off now."

Said junction was several yards of gloomy, dark tunnel. Mary followed her parents through it toward an intersection that appeared hopefully several shades of black lighter than the passage they were in. As she stepped into the junction, she glanced to the right. Some yards away, a wide double doorway was outlined with a gleaming ribbon of blessed, lovely sunlight. Mary reflexively started toward it.

"Left!" her dad commanded from behind her. "I said, go left. The sally port there leads back out onto Hudson Road. It was added to the fort when it became necessary to bring in the newer military vehicles."

"Sally port?" repeated Samantha. "That's a funny name for a garage door."

"It's not a garage door," said Hal.

Samantha laughed and poked him in the solar plexus. "What kind of attitude is that for a tour guide? I might have to report you."

"Sassy baggage," he said and kissed the tip of her nose before steering her to the left.

Mary gave the gleaming sally port a last longing glance and followed them. The broader gray passage led into a long sandy courtyard, at the center of which was a small cluster of trees, their crowns now lit by the sun. They had been planted in the middle of a stone-bordered swath of grass that ran down the center of the yard.

"This," Hal announced, gesturing toward the far end of the space, "is the parade grounds where the troops assembled before battle."

Mary dashed onto the grass, where she had a great view of the fort, and spun in a circle. The upper level was lined with doorways and windows; the ground level had those, plus what appeared to be corrugated metal garage doors. The walls were thick, with doors and windows set deep. Everything seemed abandoned, decrepit, and silent. Piles of bricks, pallets of wood, and other construction materials sat ready for a forgotten renovation. She imagined renovations were ongoing in a place this ancient.

"Feels like a concentration camp," Samantha shivered visibly.

"They slept ten soldiers to a room," Hal told her. "In the early 1900s, they deemed the place unfit for living."

"What was their first clue?" mumbled Mary.

Hal went on, undeterred. "As you can see, they've blocked off access to the upper level, so we can't go up there." He sounded wistful.

Mary tried to imagine what the fort would have been like with living, breathing human beings there . . . or even an actual tour group. Much less oooga-booga. "I guess it was a lot better back in the day, huh?"

Hal laughed ironically. "I doubt it. Now they mow the grass and rake the leaves. I doubt that happened in times of war. Now, if you'll just follow me."

As if they had a choice.

As Mary left the green island in the middle of the parade grounds, a raven fluttered down from the tallest tree to peck at something in the grass. She didn't want to know what it was.

Hal led his family farther down the courtyard and back into the fort proper. There, he opened an iron gate buried in the gloom beneath the second-floor gallery.

"This," he promised. "Is where the fun starts." He ushered them into a dark, narrow corridor with a vaulted ceiling that had no welcoming light at its end. Then, he closed the gate and took the lead, resuming his tour guide routine. "Now, watch your footing through here, everybody. This passage will begin to dip downward as we go, and will also get narrower. Stay close!"

He turned on his phone light and forged ahead.

Mary kept her eyes on the beam of light as she scurried along behind her parents, trying not to notice the oppressive granite and brick walls; trying not to feel the crypt-like, chill dampness that had already begun to press against her face and cling to her skin; and trying not to believe that Fort Tompkins—or its inevitable ghosts—were watching her from the places she couldn't see.

She caught up with her mother and tucked her hand through the crook of her arm.

"You okay, sweetie?" Mom asked.

"Just cold. I didn't dress for spelunking."

"Hal," called Samantha. "We can't explore this place on just our phone lights. It's too dark."

"Yeah, well, the lights are usually on. We kept them on all the time when I worked here."

"Well, they're not on now."

Samantha paused to tap something on the floor with the toe of her shoe. In the light of her dad's flash, Mary could see it was a floodlight set into the floor along the left-hand wall.

Dad gestured with his phone, making the shadows flail and flap. "I'll see if I can't locate one of the switch boxes. I want to show you the counterscarp galleries behind the outer wall. There'll be light coming in through the loopholes if nothing else." He continued straight ahead.

Mary trailed behind, realizing that the ground beneath her feet was sloping downward; they were going beneath the moat. She took a deep breath, trying not to imagine the increasing weight of rock and dirt over her head. The damp filled her lungs with the smell of wet earth and mold. Why would Dad want to bring them to this nasty place? She wanted the tour to be over.

She thought she heard something shuffle behind them and turned. Her heart beat rapidly in her chest, and a frisson of cold coursed down her back. "What was that?"

Her father's voice echoed in the narrow black tunnel. "What was what? Ah! I found it!"

Light leapt up the dank walls and across the curving ceiling.

"Oh! Good job, honey." Samantha pressed a hand to her chest.

"New switch, but in the same old place."

Mary's voice was shaky. "I . . . thought I heard something."

"That's because this place is haunted," her dad said.

"Stop it, Hal. You're scaring your daughter. Hell, you're scaring me."

"Sam, language! There's nothing to be afraid of. Tompkins was built to keep people safe."

"Yeah, if you consider mold safe." Sam wiped her hands on her jeans.

Mary whispered, "It's still so dark in here."

Hal pushed forward, "You gotta see the counterscarp galleries. They're just ahead."

Mary walked faster, placing herself beside her father.

"Is the roof getting lower?" her mom asked from behind them.

"The tunnel narrows as it goes under the moat. Think of it as a funhouse."

"I hate funhouses," said Mary. "They're grossly misnamed."

The roof lowered until it nearly touched the top of her father's head. The shrinking tunnel led to another hall. Mary turned to glance back and caught the flash of a soft light from the corner of her eye. She gasped and told herself she was seeing things. It didn't help. She wanted to cry.

Just ahead were several gaps in the walls on either side. Doorways, Mary guessed, and did not want to walk past them.

"They stored ammunition in these rooms," Hal gestured into the black-on-black gloom of the chambers on either side.

Mary's skin crawled and her heart beat so loudly, she thought surely her parents could hear it. "I hate this. Daddy, we shouldn't be here."

Hal smiled tentatively at her, as if he couldn't believe she didn't find this as much fun as he did. "Come on, kiddo. You afraid of the ghost of G.I. Joe?"

Mary stopped walking just short of one of the gaping, black doorways. "Dad, please. Let's go."

"We're almost there."

Without any warning, the floodlights shut off, plunging the corridor into darkness. All three of them froze. In the silence, Mary heard the drip of water from the doorway she could no longer see.

"Hal?" Sam whispered her husband's name.

"Hold on. Don't move. Lemme get my phone."

"Oh my God," said Sam. "I'll bet the groundskeeper found the lights on and turned them off. D' you think they know we're here?"

"I don't know. Give me a second. Damn it. I think I dropped my phone. Do you have yours, Sam?"

"It's in my purse. Which is in the car."

Mary's body went cold. She couldn't move. She was equal parts shocked and comforted when a hand wrapped around her wrist. Relief flooded her with warmth.

"Mom? Dad?"

The hand pulled her forward a foot or so into the old munitions chamber—deep into the munitions chamber. Any relief she'd felt fled as the hand was replaced with the cool steel of a handcuff.

She screamed, but the sound was cut off when another hand clamped itself over her mouth in a merciless grip. The room was spinning. Mary's entire body shook. Everything was black; there was no light anywhere in the world—no light anywhere in the universe.

"Mary?" Her mother's voice cried out in the darkness. "Mary, where are you?"

She couldn't answer. She wanted to, but she couldn't.

Hal's voice reverberated down the hall. "Mary!"

Her unseen kidnapper pushed her face-first against a stone wall, pressing his body against her back, pinning her. A hand came to her fore-head, its fingertip tracing a circle there, just above the bridge of her nose, drawing it over and over before rubbing back and forth across the center as if trying to erase it.

He whispered into her ear, "Good girl."

Footsteps entered the black room. "Mary?" Her mother was frantic. "Mary?"

The pressure against Mary's back was gone. She tried to pull away from the wall. She couldn't. The handcuff was attached to something. She was trapped. The restraining hand left her mouth and she cried out.

"Mama!"

Mary saw a sudden flurry of movement, followed by the sound of flesh hitting flesh and someone dropping to the floor.

"Mama!"

The single light of a cell phone pierced the darkness. By its light Mary saw the horrified face of her father as he entered the chamber. "Sam?"

A dark figure arose out of the shadows to wrap an arm around Hal's neck. The phone cast its beam of light uselessly in all directions as Hal struggled, choking and spitting, arms flailing. It illuminated damp walls with deep, arched recesses, a floor that glistened with water.

"Daddy!" Mary screamed. She tried to wrench her hand out of the cuff but to no avail.

The assailant spoke, his voice low and crooning, "One . . . two . . . three . . ."

Hal continued to struggle. He dropped his phone. It hit the concrete floor, its light sending up a beacon next to his wife's motionless body.

Mary whimpered.

"Four . . . five . . . six . . ."

"Please, stop," Mary pleaded. The man turned toward her, but in the darkness, she could not make out his face.

"Seven . . . eight . . ."

Hal made one gurgling cry before going silent.

The assailant sighed. "Nine." He released Hal, who collapsed to the wet floor.

Mary felt as if her spirit was leaving her trembling body. Water continued to drip in the corner.

The man approached Mary, slowly, casually, wet clay squelching beneath his feet. Her knees gave out before he reached her and she slumped against the wall, her imprisoned wrist held aloft by the cuff. The man knelt beside her and Mary shut her eyes tight. His breath smelled of acid.

Please, God. Don't let me die. Please, God.

"It's all right, Mary. You won't remember much."

CHAPTER ONE

MONDAY, ONE WEEK LATER, CEDAR GROVE BEACH

Standing on the corner of Ebbitts Street outside the entry to Cedar Grove Beach in Staten Island, Davina Speers felt a mixture of nostalgia and dread. "When I was a kid, I used to hop this fence after dark with pot and a six-pack."

"Always a rebel," said Millie, Davina's roommate and Narcotics Anonymous friend, as she held up a hand to protect her eyes from the piercing July sun.

"Joy was the rebel. She was always the first one hopping the fence. How the hell could she be dead?"

Davina saw a white sign with red letters on the Friends of Italy Reception Hall building across the street. It read: HALL AVAILABLE FOR RENT. Beside it strung a banner with the words: *Join us to celebrate the life of Joy Sheridan.*

A couple of people were smoking outside. An American flag and the flag of Italy rippled in the warm breeze. Off in the distance, Davina saw sparkling blue water, golden sand, and beach umbrellas in every color. The hot July day was perfect.

Except for Joy being dead.

The block hadn't changed much on the outside from when she was a kid. It was still a row of attached and semi-attached brick houses with cement steps and stoops. But upon closer inspection, the change was dramatic. No Italian parents hung out of windows yelling in broken English to their kids. Gone were the Italian grandmothers sweeping their steps, like Davina's grandmother used to do. The language shouted now was Spanish.

Davina knew she should go inside. Millie was growing impatient, but Davina wouldn't budge. The dream that had awakened her early this morning was playing on an endless loop in her head. A man was holding her down, his weight crushing. She struggled to escape, able to emit only the crippled sounds of nightmare. But there was no escape. None. Davina had awakened to a racing heart and sheets clammy with sweat. Several minutes passed before she felt like she could breathe again. A terrible way to start the day before going to a dead friend's reception.

A dead friend. Was that what had triggered the dream? But Joy hadn't been murdered.

A bead of sweat rolled down her back, and Davina wasn't sure if it was from the nerves or the heat. Millie stared off into the distance like she was considering whether to bolt. Davina closed her eyes and took five deep breaths, something that she was used to doing in the face of panic and confusion. She pressed her fingers to her forehead, rubbing at the spot between her brows. *What the fuck is wrong with me?*

"D, if we stand out here much longer, I'm gonna need SPF 50." Dressed in black jeans and a purple T-shirt, Millie adjusted her dark Dior knockoff sunglasses. "My skin may be brown, but it doesn't mean I won't burn. If I end up matching my shirt, it'll be your damn fault."

"Give me a sec. I can't explain it. Something doesn't feel right.

"Is it the drinking in there that's bothering you? Because you know I got your back with that shit."

"No, I'm cool with the booze, semi-drunks, and general stupidity."

"You sure you're okay?" Millie knit her brow.

There was an unspoken understanding between them. Even though

Davina kept some of her secrets from Millie, she was still the kind of person that Davina sensed could see right through her. She found that comforting. Millie's particular brand of sass always lightened things up when Davina felt like her world was impossibly dark.

"I'm okay." She counted five more breaths. "I need to do it as much for Joy as for myself. Everything has been so fucked up the past couple of years that I can't remember the last time I've been in a crowd."

Getting off the streets, rehab, cleaning up my life. I don't want to see anyone from my past.

"You're here to pay your respects. It's a reception, not a wedding. Half an hour. We'll be in and out. You're strong enough to do this."

"Yeah, I know." Davina rubbed her slim, muscular upper arm, her fingers gliding over the barbed wire tattoo on her left bicep. She watched people meandering in and out of the meeting hall. Most would remember her, but few of them would have anything nice to say. She shuddered to think of the messed-up girl that everyone remembered her to be. "What if somebody asks me what's new? What am I supposed to say?"

Millie shrugged her shoulders and pulled a pack of Marlboro Lights from the handbag dangling on her arm. "You can always say 'none of your fucking business.' But smile when you say it."

Millie demonstrated the appropriate smile and drew a cigarette from the pack, offered one to Davina, who accepted, and lit both from a Bic lighter with a Yankees logo.

"I can't believe they blew it in the eleventh last night." Millie took a slow drag, tossed the pack and lighter back into her bag, and blew out a long stream of smoke.

"I'm serious," Davina insisted. "What the hell do I say?"

"You have to say something?"

"It will be awkward if I don't."

"You tell them the fucking truth," Millie said, pointing her cigarette toward the front door of the hall. "Tell them you cleaned yourself up, got a good job, a handsome man, and you could non-metaphorically kick every one of their asses if you needed to."

"You're cracking me up," Davina was grateful for the laugh.

"See, I gots you to smile," Millie brought her cigarette to her lips. "Besides, you pretty. Folks will forget anything if you pretty."

"Oh, stop with the Wisdom of the Bayou, Mil. You're about as Creole as I am."

Still, Davina considered Millie's words. She had been told in the past that her red hair and green eyes were pretty, but for so long she'd disguised her eyes with smoky liner and her hair with black dye.

Black, like my soul.

Without the semi-Goth exterior, she felt more exposed than ever. She drew two short drags from her cigarette. She'd been trying to quit, but her efforts weren't going so well.

My last vice.

Davina shuffled from side to side, her tan ballet flats scraping along the cement. She watched as a few people filed through the front door of the meeting hall. The men wore suits, and the women seemed like they lived in a daytime soap opera—or at least shopped in one.

"It looks like Italy is still alive and well on Staten Island."

"Damn straight. I *love* it when the ladies dress up for me," Millie clapped her hands together.

Davina recognized a woman entering the reception hall: Fia Mahoney, the youth choir director at St. Margaret Mary's. Joy had given her the nickname "Fee-Fi-Fo-Fia" because of the woman's annoying ability to sniff out adolescent misbehavior. Davina vividly remembered when Mrs. Mahoney had caught her and Joy smoking in the ladies' room behind the vestry and demanded they explain why they would do such a dreadful thing.

Joy had responded with feigned bemusement, "Because we're not allowed to smoke in the boys' room?"

That had required scores of Hail Marys in atonement. Plus, detention in the church basement, which often ended prematurely with a mad escape through a window well to the beach a mere four blocks east.

Davina glanced up at the sky. She had many good memories of Joy, a rebellious companion who had taken the younger girl under her wing and gotten her accepted among her posse of 'hood rats. Well, "under her wing" was probably not quite the right description of what Joy had done. She'd been the one who introduced eleven-year-old Davina to many of the toxic substances she had spent the better part of the last three years trying to escape. Before Joy, Davina's idea of substance abuse was raiding the cupboard for whatever alcohol her mom had squirreled away. Brown Bacardi rum became her liquor of choice.

Even though Davina hated what her mother had become, she had charged headlong into the same behaviors. Escaping alcohol and drugs had been a hell of a lot harder than shimmying out of a church basement and hopping a fence onto the beach to smoke pot in the warm sand.

Now Joy was dead, and Davina wished she was more surprised. People had always commented on how alike the two were. Davina had to wonder how true that was and how deep that likeness went.

Millie flicked ashes to the street, "Well, what's the deal, D? I been standing here half my life."

"This is going to be painful," Davina took a final drag from the cigarette and tossed it. "They're all going to think I'm such a fuck-up."

"You're just fine. You're coming up on your first anniversary. Ninety-nine percent don't even make it that far. I'll bet you most in there wouldn't."

"You're probably right."

"I usually am." Millie dropped her cigarette to the ground and crushed it out with the tip of her shoe.

Davina tucked the hem of her white T-shirt into her jeans. "I appreciate you volunteering for moral support, even if everyone in there is drunk, stupid, and lily white."

"You know White people don't scare me. Besides, I'm proud to be the first Black woman to step into an Italian banquet hall." Millie made a flourish with her hand. "And probably the last."

"It's not so much this," Davina waved a hand in Millie's face. "You know how Staten Islanders can be with outsiders."

Millie grinned along with her friend. "You got me there, D. All I can do is apologize for my Grammy and Grandpa coming over the bridge back in '61."

"Goddamned second-generation immigrants," Davina laughed, her mood lightening a tad.

"They came from fuckin' Queens!"

The two giggled together, and Millie took the first steps toward the hall. Davina followed. The flags were still waving in the breeze on either side of a black awning stained with bird shit. The arrhythmic sound the awning made was dry and hollow, as though its fabric were paper thin. Seagulls screamed at waves rolling onto the distant shore, making some kind of weird jazz. The smell of hot pavement and saltwater filled Davina's nostrils.

I wouldn't do this for anyone but you, Joy.

CHAPTER TWO

MONDAY, FRIENDS OF ITALY RECEPTION HALL

PEOPLE WERE PACKED SHOULDER TO SHOULDER INSIDE THE hall. The place reeked of smoke, sweat, and pungent Mediterranean cuisine. Davina and Millie jostled their way through the claustrophobic reception hall with its dated green, white, and red decor. On the pine-paneled wall behind the food-laden tables was a map of Italy with framed pictures of Pope Francis and Cardinal Dolan hung on either side. "Christ —I can smell the Elizabeth Taylor White Diamonds from here." She nodded toward a gaggle of older ladies, all dressed in their Sunday best.

"How do you know it's White Diamonds?" Davina asked.

"I once worked a month at Perfume Mania."

"All I smell is cigarette smoke and body odor—it's worse than the gym. And the booze, of course," she crinkled her nose.

Millie shot her a side-eye, "You good, D? Takin' it one day at a time, remember?"

"I'm all good, Mil. Somebody needs to tell them to crank up the air conditioning in here, though." Fanning herself with one hand, Davina fought back the wave of nausea that crawled through her guts.

"I didn't know White people got *this* crazy around a buffet," Millie said loudly. "I tell ya, nothing brings folks together like a table full of free food."

Throughout the spacious room, the din of conversation was interspersed with laughter, some crying, and the sound of metal folding chairs being dragged over the aging hardwood floor. "It looks like half of Staten Island turned out for Joy," Davina said.

Millie snorted and adjusted her knockoff Dior sunglasses atop her dreadlocks. "Turned out for free food, more like. Who'd have thought death would give folks such an appetite?" She tipped her chin toward the back of the room; there, people three deep squeezed around the buffet that spanned five tables.

Close to the buffet, Davina and Millie passed by a table occupied by two women and a man. Empty beer bottles littered the table. The sour, all-too-tempting reek of alcohol made Davina anxious.

"It's just *so* shocking to think it might be true, Angela," one of the women said. She was a mid-fifties bleached blonde that Davina didn't recognize; she stabbed aggressively at her limp salad with a fork in one hand and a lit cigarette in the other. "That's all I'm saying." Her New York accent was as thick as the smoke.

Across the table from the blonde sat a woman Davina did recognize. She was Angela Donato, the trauma counselor who'd helped Davina deal with what happened all those years ago. It was nice to see a familiar friendly face. Thanks to Angela, Davina had been able to pick up and carry on with some semblance of a life after the assault.

Being counseled by Angela was also something else Davina shared with poor deceased Joy; the memory brought fresh tears to Davina's eyes.

Next to Angela sat her husband, Carlo, who mirrored his wife in nodding politely as the tactless blonde trash-talked Joy at her own damn funeral. It was obvious to Davina that neither wished to be drawn into their tablemate's disrespect. She wondered how come Blondie hadn't picked up on it.

Davina knew Carlo from the gym. He was one of the regulars at Dobson's, and she knew him at least well enough to say hello. He was something in the construction business; strictly blue-collar, the kind of guy who wore a yellow hard hat with his two-hundred-dollar suit on the construction site. He was a diligent student and worked hard at the self-defense moves Gerry had devised to prevent him from getting too doughy as middle age crept up on him.

Throughout Davina's many sessions, Angela had shared a few innocuous tidbits about herself—all part of the process of getting the client to open up, she guessed. She'd learned both Angela and Carlo were third-generation Italian American, whose lineage had spent their entire lives on Staten Island. The Donatos were cornerstones of the Staten Island Historical Society; they even ran the haunted bus tour together. Angela had tried her best to get Davina to come on the tour to see all the famously haunted landmarks—she and Carlo loved to dress up and scare rapt schoolkids and tourists with dark tales from the Rock's colorful past.

Although Davina had faithfully promised her counselor she would do that for definite, it never happened.

As Davina and Millie walked by, Angela nodded politely at the blonde's diatribe; far too professional to be drawn in badmouthing an old client, she shook her head and quietly sopped up the traces of marinara sauce on her plate with an end piece of Italian bread. For a split second, Davina contemplated pausing by the table to say hello, but a frosty look from the blonde woman persuaded her otherwise. As it was, Davina's eyes met briefly with her former counselor's, and the two exchanged a wan smile.

From a corner of the room at the far end of the buffet, Davina scanned the room for Joy's mother, Doris Sheridan. She was fairly certain she'd recognize her, assuming Mrs. Sheridan still had her faux flame-red hair. But in the sea of faces, making out individual ripples was nearly impossible. Davina and Millie reached the front of the buffet line when Davina spotted someone she did not want to see standing next to the bar: Detective Thomas Riley. From certain angles, Davina thought he resembled the guy who'd played the robot playing the cop in the second *Terminator* movie—the actor with two first names, Robert Patrick. From most angles, though, Davina reckoned Riley looked like what he was—just another asshole cop who thought his badge came with impunity.

A flash of panic hit Davina hard in the solar plexus; she and Riley had a long history, which stretched back to when Davina was twelve—none of it good. Even when she was on the streets, the cop never cut her any slack; he took any opportunity, valid or not, to cuff her and haul her in. If he didn't have a reason, he or his cronies concocted one. The asshole still gave her the creeps.

She found herself unconsciously rubbing her brow again and pulled her hand down.

"Why you so quiet?" Millie asked as they wedged their way into the chow line.

Davina spoke softly, "Riley."

"Asshole."

"The last time I saw Joy was about the time my life . . . started to go to shit," Davina said to distract herself from the cop. "Joy began to get distant around then, cutting ties with everybody she knew. I'd see her around the neighborhood, but then her family moved and she changed schools."

She became a ghost. I understand the impulse.

"Pardon me." A man behind Millie pointed to a tray of bagels. "Would you mind handing me that cinnamon raisin on the end?"

Davina grabbed the bagel with a napkin and handed it over. The man was older and had a round, doughy face, and kind brown eyes. He had on a crisp, clean zucchetto and robe. Davina felt like she ought to know him, most likely from church.

"Is something wrong?" he asked.

Embarrassed to have been caught staring at him, she replied, "You look familiar."

"I'm the minister at Saint Joseph's—Father Stephen."

"We went to Saint Margaret Mary."

"I made the rounds as part of the youth ministry. Perhaps you remember me from then? You can't be more than—what—twenty-four, twenty-five?"

"Twenty-two."

The priest smiled at her with self-deprecation. "I'm always taken to be younger. It helps with the youth ministry, but adults have trouble taking me seriously. I'm afraid I just have one of those faces."

A woman in line behind them called out. "Excuse me, Father. Can you keep the line moving, please?"

The priest smiled, waved his bagel at the impatient woman, and sauntered off into the crowded hall.

"*Finally*," Millie said, eyeing the hot dishes.

The squat, broad-shouldered guy in front of them turned around, his breath sour with the stink of cheap booze, which wafted out behind the eye-watering reek of his aftershave. "There's plenty of food—don't you worry about that, babe. Sadly, it's a cash bar, though." He feigned a sad face and checked out Davina, breasts to toes.

"No drinks for us. We're on our lunch break," Millie gave the man a polite smile.

"Well, at least the soda's free," the guy grunted. "I'm George, by the way. I'm your local, friendly fire chief."

Ignoring the outstretched hand, Davina looked on as Millie took George up on the offer and introduced both of them by name. Davina knew damn well who George Modica was—she'd seen his smiling, square-jawed face on the front page of the *Staten Island Advance* often enough. The guy was a modern-day hero, best friend to politicians and voters alike, even though he seemed to do more PR and personal appearances at the Historical Society than putting out fires. George also gave Davina the creeps; he was giving her the same look she'd seen dozens of times in the papers whenever he was in the presence of young women—it made her feel like he was sizing her up, much like a salivating wolf eyeing its next meal.

If George saw the repugnance in Davina's face, he ignored it. Grabbing paper plates and cellophane-wrapped plastic utensils, he handed a set each to Millie and Davina.

"So, what brings you two lovely young ladies to . . . this?" He pointed at the gathered mourners with his spork.

"I was friends with Joy." Davina was reluctant to give the letch even that much; his type rarely needed a lot of encouragement to make a clumsy move —as if she or Millie would be remotely interested in some balding, middle-aged man with a paunch, even if he was the fire chief. He'd obviously set his sights on her. Perhaps his instinct had warned him of Millie's preferences, and he wasn't about to waste his time and charm on a Black dyke.

Someone save me.

Millie stepped in, "Is that pepper steak down at the end there?"

"That?" George nodded at the steaming dish at the end of the table. "Yes. It's very good. Courtesy of Stavros. Y'know, Boro 5 Diner? I heard he just opened a new restaurant. This stuff is all Greek. You look like a gal who enjoys *Greek*, eh, Davina?"

Davina shuddered at the fire chief's lascivious double entendre; Greek was street slang for anal sex. She wondered what about her gave George the impression she took it in the ass—the maroon hair, perhaps?

"Look, Mil. Fried chicken wings," Davina spoke across George, hoping he'd take the hint and leave her alone. "I guess Stavros must've known you were coming."

"No need to be racist, D!" Millie faux-chastised as she piled her plate high with wings.

Oblivious to Davina's disinterest, George leaned in, his breath and cologne assaulting her nostrils. "I'm not one to spread gossip, but . . ." He gave a theatrical glance around before whispering, "I heard Father Stephen was sleeping with Joy's mother—along with half the women in the neighborhood. Some of the men, too—if you want to believe *all* the rumors." George shrugged. "You know how the Greeks are."

Davina nodded, wanting the conversation to be over. It was hard to imagine the shapeless old priest sleeping with anybody. "Where *is* Mrs. Sheridan? I need to pay my respects." She scanned the room over George's shoulder.

George spooned a heaped dollop of mozzarella balls onto his plate. "You didn't go to the funeral service? Poor old Doris held up pretty good for most of it, but right at the end, she just lost it. Detective Riley took her outside for some fresh air. I reckon she'd hold up better if Joy's old man was still alive."

Mercifully, one of Davina's high school classmates approached. Davina recognized her instantly as Elena Royce. Dressed more for a wedding than a funeral, Elena wore a black-and-white maxi-sundress, which was slit high to show off a lot of gym-toned, salon-tanned leg. In her five-inch stilettos, Elena dwarfed Davina's more diminutive five-foot-five. Inserting herself between Davina and the fire chief, she took a moment to give her old classmate a barely disguised expression of utter disdain, scrutinizing the tattoos that peeked out beneath the sleeves of Davina's T-shirt.

"I suppose you've heard?" As appalled by Davina's appearance as Elena was, she obviously had a juicy tidbit to share.

"Heard what?" Davina heard herself saying; she was beginning to miss George's creepy attention—he'd wandered off to chow down on his meatballs and leer over another of the young female mourners.

"I just heard from Melissa, who heard from Ashley, that Joy actually committed suicide." Elena paused, a self-satisfied smile playing at the corners of her thin scarlet lips.

Davina was overtaken by anger, "You shouldn't spread that kind of crap—especially not here, not now."

Undeterred by Davina's admonishment, Elena adjusted her stance to make the most of the high slit and went on, "You know the poor girl was never the same after . . . what happened. How long ago was it again? Nine, ten years? Remember how her parents pretended like nobody knew when *everybody* knew."

Millie whispered to Davina, "I'm gonna go sit down."

Davina gritted her teeth, staring daggers at Elena, "Find us a table. I'll be there in a minute."

"Suit yourself," Millie shrugged and walked off.

"Imagine if she did commit suicide and Father allowed her a Catholic service," Elena pointed across the room to Father Stephen. "He *must* know what Joy went through."

"What are you talking about, Elena?" Davina felt her patience wearing thin—*very* thin.

"Joy was assaulted her freshman year," Elena postured, hand on hip. "You must be the *only* person who doesn't know—I thought you were supposed to be her friend?"

"Assaulted?"

"Joy was *raped*, Davina," Elena said. "She was never the same after that, bless her heart. You ask me, I think Dr. Fidanza did it."

"What?" A sequence of dark, viscous thoughts tumbled through Davina's head. She tried to shake them away.

Relishing her moment, Elena raised a hand topped with long, pink acrylic nails. "That doctor is so slimy. He's Staten Island's answer to Larry Nassar—the Olympic medic who felt up all those poor gymnasts. My mother says all the cops go to Dr. Fidanza when they get the clap from whores."

Dr. Fidanza was my *doctor.*

Caught in a tidal wave of dark, clammy recall, Davina didn't realize she'd dropped her plate until she heard it hit the floor with a splat.

"I guess you didn't know," Elena glanced down at the paper plate Davina had dropped and lifted her brow. "I'm so sorry, my dear."

Painfully conscious of every eye in the room staring at her like she was some freakshow exhibit, and with Detective Riley bristling, Davina reached down to pick up her plate and scattered food. She struggled to process Elena's revelation. She remembered Joy had disappeared from their secret haunts toward the end of the school year. And yeah, she'd seemed moody the few times Davina had seen her after school let out, but when the family moved over the summer—ostensibly because her dad had gotten a new job—she figured the move itself had made her friend miserable.

But how could Joy have been raped and Davina not know? She would have said something to a best friend . . . wouldn't she?

Would you?

"How do you know she was . . . ?" Davina forced the words out.

Elena's perfect brows rose. "Raped? Why else would the family move off the island?"

"Her dad got a job—"

"No, he didn't. Joy's mom said as much. She said they needed to get the poor girl into 'new environs.'" Elena made air-quotes. "Nine years on and Joy still couldn't deal with it."

"You don't know shit, Elena." Davina felt the anger bubbling up inside; if she didn't extricate herself, she knew she'd be likely to land a fist in Elena Royce's immaculately made-up face. And she didn't want that for poor Joy.

With a grunt, Davina dumped her scraped-up food in a nearby trash bin and walked away. Her appetite had evaporated and, lightheaded, she navigated the thick crowd. The smell of booze, the babble of voices—it was all suffocating.

At the far end of the hall, Davina found a bench near the wall and sat. She pressed her fingers hard to her forehead to try to hold back the racing thoughts.

Five paces away from Davina's refuge, Sean Delafield clutched a clear plastic cup filled to the quarter mark with cheap scotch. Delafield, the local real estate developer running for an open city council seat, was pontificating to Father Stephen and George Modica about how Staten Island needed to be brought into the twenty-first century.

Davina had no interest in the man's ideas, but she could cope that if he was there, maybe his son, Nick, was too. Davina hadn't thought of Nick in forever and was surprised by how much she wanted to see him. She looked around the room for him.

George Modica's voice rose above the hubbub, "What's with the gun, Sean?" Laughing, he pointed at the Glock nestled into the waistband at the back of the developer's pants. "Planning on killing a Historical Society member, or just intimidating one for kicks? You usually conceal that thing."

"Open carry permit, courtesy of the NYPD. Makes me feel powerful," Sean replied with a smug grin.

George scratched his head. "Coming up with an actionable plan would make you *actually* powerful."

Sean sipped his drink. "Listen, George. The plan is simple. I will make Staten Island *relevant*. We have the last of the wide-open spaces in New York—we're sitting on a goldmine of prime real estate. Once I'm elected, I'll force the City to build that subway line straight to the mainland they've been talking about for fucking decades. No more talk. I'm the man to get it done. The Verrazzano Narrows Bridge is chicken shit compared to what I'm proposing."

"Build that line, eh?" George mocked Sean's well-worn campaign slogan. Taking a bite of his meatloaf, he dribbled gravy down the front of his pink shirt. "That plan has been on the books a hundred years already. It's never getting done. And besides, we already have a subway."

Sean snorted his derision. "It goes from one end of Staten Island to the other, George, and it's not even underground."

George shrugged and took another bite of his meatloaf before saying in return, "Nobody here wants a subway off the island, Sean."

"Sure, there's opposition here," Sean fanned a hand toward the crowd. "But off the Rock, they just can't wait to bring their money across. Staten Island's gonna be *the* place to live—there's never been a better time to develop. I'll get it done; you mark my words. We have the technology. We have the votes. That line will absolutely transform this borough."

"You got some serious opposition, Sean." George wasn't about to let it go. "The Historical Society isn't going to roll over while you bulldoze history. They've got some juice."

"They've got shit."

Davina was disgusted—it was Joy's funeral, for Christ's sake and Sean was turning it into a political rally.

As George finished up his meatloaf, Father Stephen seized his opportunity to speak, "How about you build us a new church?"

"I'll give you whatever the fuck you want. Anything for a man of God," Sean clapped the priest on the shoulder.

"The church isn't for me, it's for the congregation."

"Just promise to stay in Staten Island and I'll build you a *billion-dollar* megachurch," Sean said loudly to ensure everyone heard him. Then, as a quiet aside, "You've been traveling some lately, Father. Shopping for a new parish?"

Father Stephen shook his head. "Staten Island will always be my home, but I do like to see other parts of God's country."

Still scanning the crowd for Millie, Davina caught a glimpse of Kevin Monaghan. The guy was a retired cop turned home security expert—he was talking with Riley. Like Riley, Monaghan had always managed to find a reason to harass Davina back in the day, and she hated him for it.

Dr. Robert Fidanza approached Sean and his posse. Freakishly tall, he literally stood above the crowd. "I can hear you all the way from the buffet, Sean. Have a little decency."

"Look, Doc, I'm not interested in the dead. The dead don't vote."

Davina had heard enough.

She got to her feet—it was time to get the hell out of Dodge. There was a hell of a lot to process: Was the doctor to blame for Joy's rape and resulting suicide? Did Father Stephen know something about Joy's death? What other secrets had her friend taken to the grave?

She spotted Millie in a far corner and started to elbow her way through when someone grabbed her from behind, covered her eyes and mouth, and whispered in her ear, "Guess who?"

Acting purely on instinct, Davina whirled, grabbed the guy by the neck, hooked a foot behind his ankle, and dropped him hard on the floor.

The room went silent.

Everyone stared.

Davina's victim picked himself up from the floor. He laughed nervously—an obvious attempt to salvage *some* dignity. In her peripheral vision, Davina saw Riley heading her way, cutting through the crowd like a shark that had just smelled blood.

Just like old times.

"I'm so sorry I scared you," Nick Delafield said with a sheepish grin.

Davina mirrored his smile; she'd been hoping to bump into him, but not quite like that. "You caught me by surprise, is all. I—"

CHAPTER THREE

MONDAY, FRIENDS OF ITALY RECEPTION HALL

Riley was upon her, sunglasses covering his eyes like every other time he'd dealt with her. The cop spun Davina around, wrenching her right arm up her back, his left arm across her neck.

"Let's go, bitch," he growled in her ear.

"What the hell!" Nick put out a hand to stop him, but the detective simply motioned for people to move aside; he pushed through them if they didn't move quickly enough.

Davina went without struggle—she knew better than to resist—but nonetheless protested through gritted teeth. "I didn't do anything, Riley. It was a misunderstanding between friends."

"You're still leaving." Riley maneuvered Davina toward the vestibule; he was clearly enjoying the power and the spectacle.

As Riley shoved Davina through the hall's doors, the sudden flash of sunlight was blinding, and panic rose up inside her.

"What the fuck, Riley?"

Riley spun her around to face him, blocking the sun. "I want none of your fucking nonsense, Davina. Not today. You're leaving." Riley turned back to the hall and strode off.

"I didn't do *anything*." On the verge of tears, Davina brought a hand to her throat where Riley's arm had pinned her to his chest; terrible memories threatened to flood her mind.

Millie came out as Riley went in; the two almost collided. "What the fuck, D? I can't leave you alone for a minute. What the hell happened?"

"Let's just get outta here." Davina took off down the street at a brisk walk; she couldn't wait to fall into her air-conditioned car and breathe. Millie struggled to keep pace alongside her.

"Hey, Davina!" Nick jogged along the street after them, his face etched with concern.

Davina stopped, turned, and waited for him to catch up.

"I want to apologize for . . . all *that*." Nick held up his hands, as if in surrender. "I'm *so* sorry, Davina. I thought I was being funny. I thought you'd remember . . ." He smoothed back his dark hair and pressed down his gray tie. Nick's athletic build perfectly filled out his Armani suit. "And Riley—I swear to God, why does he have to be such a dick all the time?"

Davina couldn't help but notice how handsome Nick was. *More* handsome, really, than he'd been as a teenager. How could he be the son of such an ass-hat piece of work as Sean Delafield?

"It's not you, Nick. It's my fault. I overreacted and my kung fu kicked in."

Nick's mouth twitched and he rubbed at his butt. "Yeah, *literally*."

"Are you okay?"

"Yeah. Are you?"

"I'm used to Riley."

"It seemed like he was getting to you a little in there," Nick frowned. "Look, I'd love to catch up, but if I don't get back in there, the old man is going to turn Joy's memorial into a campaign rally." Reaching into his jacket, he pulled out his cell phone. "Give me your number—I'll call you, or you call me."

"Sure." Davina fished out her phone. In seconds, they'd exchanged numbers.

"Call me anytime. If you can't reach me on my cell, try the office number." Nick glanced back toward the hall. "Okay, I have to dive back in." And with that, he set off back toward the hall.

"I can't believe Nick remembers me."

"D," Millie lit a cigarette and blew out a long stream of smoke. "It's a lock. He ain't ever gonna forget you after that smooth kung fu move."

"I *knew* this would be a shit show," Davina said as she tucked a few strands of stray hair behind her ear. *But Nick Delafield remembers me.*

In Davina's aging Jetta, Millie adjusted her seat belt, and popped the question, "So? What was all the shit about Joy?"

"Stupid neighborhood gossip."

"So, why you were hell-bent on sticking around to listen to it?"

"Because it wasn't true. Saying Joy committed suicide. I knew Joy. No fucking way she'd kill herself. And if she did . . ."

"Even if you knew what was goin' on in her head, what could you have done? You had your own shit to deal with, D."

"She was my friend, Millie." Davina then cleared her throat to push down the impulse to cry.

They drove in silence for a few minutes, turning left onto Drake Avenue and then right onto Manor Road. She made a left onto Constant Avenue and another right onto Jewett and over to Forest.

"Two minutes to spare." Millie got out, pushed the door closed, and leaned in through the open window. She found her wallet and pulled out a ten-dollar bill. "You have a meeting tonight, right? You think after you finish you can pick me up a couple of soft tacos at Tommy's?"

Davina nodded.

"If you wanna talk later, y'know?"

Davina grimaced, "Do I look *that* messed up?"

Millie made a face, "Yeah. You do seem kinda messed up right now."

Davina took Millie's cash and replied, "Maybe later, Mil. Thanks."

Millie tapped the inside door panel and left to do her shift at DIY's gardening department.

During her short drive to Dobson's Gym for her own shift, Davina's thoughts turned to Nick Delafield. The guy had been like a big brother to her when he'd dated her older sister, Alessandra. That was over a decade ago, and Davina had been just a kid heading for a train wreck she couldn't see coming.

CHAPTER FOUR

MONDAY, DOBSON'S GYM

Located at the end of a strip mall next to a boarded-up Mexican restaurant, the gym was Davina's salvation. Its owner, Geraldine "Gerry" Dobson, had saved Davina's life three years before, when she was living on the streets and trying to get clean. Gerry gave her a job sweeping the floor and a cot in the office to sleep on. One day, she caught Davina ripping the shit out of a heavy bag and decided to train her one-on-one. After that, Gerry offered Davina a job as a kickboxing and martial arts instructor.

The place was packed. A row of advanced students worked the heavy bags suspended from the ceiling along the side windows while folks in warm-up or cooldown mode stretched in front of a floor-to-ceiling mirror along one wall. Dobson's always had a particular kind of chaos—the clash of iron and metal, fists hitting bags, and people grunting and pushing themselves to the limit on equipment for lifting, pushing, and pulling.

The ground floor was where the real combat went down—a red-and-blue mat for group classes. A smaller side room held a mat for private classes, and the basement housed the dank locker room, which Gerry had recently contracted to have renovated.

To the untrained eye, Dobson's appeared cluttered—free weights scattered here and there, errant towels hanging on treadmills and other apparatus, and the technicolor graffiti murals on the walls. But to Davina, it was the most perfect place on earth. Davina had first tasted blood, sweat, and the promise of a future at Dobson's.

A team of four instructors worked one-on-one with students on the floor mat; Davina spotted Carlo Donato in the mix—he was doing some version of Krav Maga that Davina had concocted especially for him. He seemed lost without his wife by his side, and Davina's memory flooded with the happenings at Joy's funeral. For all the sweat and body heat, the gym smelled cleaner than the Friends of Italy Reception Hall had for the wake. Davina credited Dobson's overworked A/C and twenty-four-hour dehumidifier for that.

Davina found Gerry in the office. Gerry hung up the phone when her employee walked in and got up from her chair, twisting the cap off a bottle of water. Just five-foot with curly hair, tan skin, and a little pointed nose, Gerry resembled a life-size Skipper doll.

"You look spent," Gerry began. "Should I ask how things went?"

"Not that great."

Gerry sat on the edge of her desk, "Spill."

"To start with, Riley was there. It wasn't pretty."

"Riley gets off on the power he thinks he has. Fuck him."

"Yeah, well, that wasn't the worst of it. The rumor mill was working overtime with shit about Joy. What the fuck is it with people? They can't even let the dead rest."

"And it messed you up?"

"No, Ger. It pissed me off. And don't even get me on with Sean Delafield spewing his campaign crap. It was a fucking circus."

"I'm sorry, Davina."

"The only good part about the whole thing was seeing Nick Delafield. He hasn't changed since he dated my sister—still sexy as fuck. I had such a crush on him back then." Davina's cell phone rang. Pulling it from her pocket, she saw it was Joe, her boyfriend of two years. She held up her index finger to Gerry. "Hey, what's up, Joe? I'm at the gym."

"You, okay?"

"Yeah, I'm fine, why?"

"Word has spread about the reception. Nick Delafield—"

"It was *so* embarrassing."

"Have dinner with me tonight. We'll talk."

"That sounds great. Love you, bye," Davina hung up.

Gerry sat back, arms crossed over her diminutive bosom, smiling at Davina. "When you talk to Joe, your face goes all . . . *mellow*. Joe is good for you."

"He is. But, am I good for him?"

"He obviously thinks so." Gerry got up. "Okay, I have a newbie for the tour in five. Sorry I couldn't make the wake with you—I'd have liked to have been there."

"You know the Sheridans?"

"Doris Sheridan is the real estate agent who got me this place." Gerry grabbed her fitness gloves off the desk. "Besides, Staten Island is a close-knit community. What affects one affects all." She pointed at Davina. "You should hit the bag or the mat, and hard. Work it off before your class. You know what I'm sayin'."

Davina descended to the locker room to change into leggings, throw a tank top on over her sports bra, and to tie back her hair. The walls were black and the lockers gray, giving the room a gloomy ambience. Overhead, the fluorescent lights flickered, showering Davina's tattoos and sinewy muscles with fitful light as she paused before a mirror to adjust her hair; she'd be glad when the place was finally remodeled.

Davina was proud of the reflection she saw and how far she'd come in the past three years. But, goddamn it, why had she gotten so many tattoos? Most of them, she couldn't remember getting. Maybe one day, if she had the money, she'd get them removed. All except for the chrysanthemum on her wrist.

She ran back upstairs. All the heavy bags were in use, so she stepped onto the mat and started her shadow boxing workout. She was so light on the balls of her feet and lightning fast, that her heels barely touched the mat. Thirty minutes of high-intensity, high-impact motion left her drenched in sweat and out of breath. To burn out the end of the workout, Davina dropped to the mat for a combined fifteen minutes of crunches, push-ups, and planks. Workout completed, she saw Gerry and a man who she guessed was in his forties standing at the edge of the mat.

"Feeling better?" Gerry asked.

Davina rolled her shoulders and stretched, "Absolutely."

"This is Don Anderson. He starts tomorrow and he wants you."

Davina judged Don to be a banker who loved the great outdoors if his deep tan was any indication. "I want to train with the best," he said. "And you're intense. I want intense."

"You got it." Davina glanced over Don's shoulder and spotted Joe as he stepped into the archway from the main gym. He looked sharp dressed in a light gray suit, crisp white shirt, and deep burgundy tie. The suit wasn't tailor-made, but it fit his long, lean wrestler's body well. Joe was taller than Nick Delafield and had deep blue eyes and a sexy, loose tumble of dark blond curls. His Irish great-great grandparents had immigrated to Staten Island in 1850, and no member of Joe Kelley's family had ever left.

Davina excused herself to go see Joe.

"What're you doing here?"

"I wanted to make sure you were all right. You sounded stressed on the phone."

Davina took his hands and squeezed them. "Gerry was right—you are good for me, Joe."

"Yeah, I am," Joe smiled. "So . . . did you *really* drop Nick Delafield?"

Davina nodded, "I'll tell you all about it over dinner."

"I was thinking that new Greek place."

"No, wait. Shit, it's Monday. I have my NA meeting. I can't miss it."

"You shouldn't. Dinner tomorrow?"

"Perfect."

Joe held Davina's hands a moment or two before giving her a kiss and leaving her with Gerry and Don.

CHAPTER FIVE

MONDAY, ST. MARGARET MARY'S ROMAN CATHOLIC CHURCH

DAVINA HAD HER FIRST HOLY COMMUNION AT ST. MARGARET Mary's when she was in second grade. She'd been confirmed four years later and had only been inside the church a few times since—not once after her fifteenth birthday. She had no logical reason to be there, considering she vacillated between not believing in God and being angry with him.

St. Margaret Mary, with its stately, imposing brick façade, ornate stained-glass windows, and fat bell tower was a pretty church. But, were it not for her Narcotics Anonymous meetings in its basement, there'd be no reason for Davina to go within a mile of the place. The meeting room also served as Sunday school class. Along one wall was a painting of Noah's ark with animals two-by-two and a massive rainbow, and on another, Christ returning for the faithful. Resplendent in flowing white robes and glowing halo, the Savior rode a blazing golden cloud accompanied by myriad smiling angels.

The grown-up chairs had all been rented out to a family birthday party, so Davina and her fellow NA members were forced to sit in kiddie seats. Davina stifled a chuckle as she glanced around the circle at her compadres with their dour faces and knees up to their chins. Although NA was a safe space for her, Davina was still rattled from Joy's reception, and the meeting had sparked something inside her that was uncomfortable and strange.

Davina was working the fourth step: the personal inventory. At first, she listed all the negatives in her life—her time in the streets, her work as a stripper, the drugs and arrests. Her sponsor, Charlene, a plump woman with a short blonde sixties flip 'do—made Davina promise every day she'd also repeat all the *good* things about herself.

That was hard as fuck.

The meeting was small—eleven people—and the topic for the night was gratitude.

"I'm grateful to have gotten through the memorial service for a high school friend without a drink," Davina shared.

David R, who'd just marked his sixth anniversary, chipped in, "Sounds rough."

"It was a lot of bullshit that had nothing to do with Joy. I just wanted to get out of there."

Jenny S, Davina's temporary sponsor when she'd first joined, said she'd been in NA two months when she'd gone to her high school reunion. "I was there twenty minutes before I had to leave. Came straight to a meeting. I'm grateful every day for being nine years clean and sober."

After the meeting, Davina hung back to help clean up and scrub out the coffee urn. Charlene stayed to put away the chairs.

Charlene, or "Charlie," was eleven years older than Davina. She was divorced, remarried, and had two kids with her second husband. She'd studied to be a doctor and began using drugs to stay awake and to fall asleep, and then to just feel good. It had taken her three years and four months to get clean. Unfortunately, she'd never made it through medical school.

Once they were done with the chores, Charlene and Davina walked out to the parking lot together.

"I should've said I'm grateful for *you*," Davina told her. "How long before this gets easier?"

"It doesn't. You have to *make* it easier. One day at a time. That's it."

Davina stopped midstride as a wave of nausea and dizziness hit her.

"Rough day?" Charlene put her hand on Davina's shoulder, taking care not to hug her. "Let's sit for a few minutes." She led the way to one of the stone benches in the neatly trimmed grassy area next to the parking lot.

Although not quite dark, the streetlights were on. Dusk had done nothing to alleviate the July heat, and the mosquitoes were quickly becoming an annoyance. Davina took a deep breath. She didn't want to burden anyone with the intimate details of her past, but she knew if she didn't talk, she'd implode.

"I've been having weird dreams."

"Weird how?"

"I'm being suffocated, hurt."

"What do you think it means?" Charlene asked.

"Nobody believes me, but I think . . . No. I *know* I was sexually assaulted."

"Recently?"

Davina shook her head, "I was twelve. It's hard to explain."

"Try me."

"I read about that poor kid in Fort Wadsworth last week. Losing her dad like that, almost losing her mom, and what that guy did to her..."

Charlene nodded, "It was horrible."

"I hadn't had a nightmare for a while, but after that . . . they came with a vengeance. Then the gossips saying Joy killed herself because she was raped in high school . . . and all of a sudden, I have these crazy thoughts in my head."

Davina glanced at the darkening sky. "I remember when Joy went silent on me and moved out of town. That's when I first started remembering . . . what happened to me."

"The assault?"

"*Rape.*" The word hung heavy between the two women. Davina held her head in her hands.

"Did you tell people?"

"I did. I told my parents there had been someone in my room. That's all I remembered—a man in my room I couldn't see—but I *knew* he was there. In my nightmares, he's lying on top of me and there's something around my neck." She pressed a hand to her collarbone. "I told my parents I thought something had happened, and the next thing I know, all the grown-ups were telling me I was making stuff up just to get attention; even my sister accused me of dreaming up imaginary monsters. They took me to Dr. Fidanza, and he blamed it on sleep paralysis. He recommended a therapist."

"And now you think it was real?"

Davina nodded, "I'm remembering . . . details. *Sensations.*"

Charlie frowned, "Ten years ago—that was around the time Son of Cropsey was—"

"About a week after Detective Riley arrested him."

Charlie's frown deepened, "And Joy? Do you remember when—"

"After. I remember I was depressed because Joy suddenly dropped off the face of the earth. Riley made a point of crowing Rob Cox's arrest every time he came to our house—which was a lot back then. God, I need a cigarette."

Charlene wagged a finger, "No, you don't."

Davina riffled through her purse anyway and found nothing. She gave up and took a deep breath of warm, donut-infused air instead.

"In every dream, I'm lying on my stomach. There's a heavy weight on top of me and the room is spinning. A disgusting *smell* fills my nose—it's a thick, sickly-sweet cologne that makes me want to puke." Davina paused. "I remember him touching me, Charlie. I *swear*. I remember he spread my legs and put something inside me. I had no idea what it was back then, of course. It was hard, yet soft, smooth, and he didn't stop even when I cried. And, in my nightmare, I see my own face in the mirror across from my bed."

"You never saw his face?"

"He was just a shadow. When Elena told me Joy had been raped, the floodgates opened and all this *stuff* just poured into my head. Then, I began connecting things I hadn't realized were connected." She touched a finger to her forehead. "The morning after, I woke up with a red mark on my forehead. It was the letter theta drawn in lipstick. I looked it up. At first, I thought Allie was playing a joke on me and I went to Mom. Allie blamed me and told Mom *I'd* put the mark there. She even yelled at me for fucking up her lipstick. I told them the man in my room must have drawn on my forehead."

"Theta?" Charlene asked. "As in the math symbol?"

"Yep." Davina drew a circle in the air with her finger. "It's a zero with a line through it." She made a sharp gesture left to right to splice the imaginary circle through its center. "It's Greek. I remembered it from high school physics—it's something to do with angles. When I googled it, I found out it also represents death and God in mythology, which kinda makes some sense, I guess. I washed it off after Allie accused me."

"Did the police ever—?"

"No one at home believed me, and Riley came around a lot asking his dumb questions. I think he was just trying to convince everyone he'd caught the right guy. Mom thought I was having nightmares because Dad had lost his job, and after a while, I started to believe everyone was right and I was just a silly, suggestible kid. It's classic gaslighting—I know that now—and I'm questioning everything that happened back then."

Charlene reached out to hold Davina's hand. "The nightmares stopped for a while?"

"I discovered if I was doped up enough, they weren't quite so vivid." Davina's tough façade finally began to fail. She cleared her throat. "It's been harder since I got clean. I get panic attacks, like I'm going to black out. Sometimes in my dreams I want to scream for help but can't because there's *something* around my neck."

Charlene scrutinized Davina with concern, "You should see someone."

"No police. They're . . . triggering. Same goes for therapists. I had a lot of trauma counseling with Dr. Donato. I guess she helped me in her own way, until the sessions cut into Mom's booze and sex life and she quit taking me."

"Not a cop or a therapist. I'm thinking about an old friend of mine—Geoff Wong. He's a crime reporter at the *Staten Island Advance.*"

"A reporter?"

"If there is any connection between what happened to you and Joy, he's the guy to get the answers. I'll tell him to expect you in the next day or so?" Reaching for her phone, Charlene gave Davina no choice but to agree.

CHAPTER SIX

MONDAY, TODT HILL

Jessica Balducci sat in the entertainment room of her palatial Todt Hill home while her mother, Sharon, flounced around, flipping on light switches in every room.

"What *are* you doing, Mom?" Jessica asked.

"Turning on all the lights. People will think the whole family is home."

"Calm down, Sharon. It's just an SBCA donor event. We'll be back home in a couple hours, three at the most." Jessica's father, Mark, straightened his bowtie in the oval mirror above the fake fireplace.

"I can't believe LaShawna is sick. I think it's just an excuse."

"We pay that girl a fortune to babysit a thirteen-year-old. I doubt she'd be making excuses."

Thanks to her pretentious parents, Jessica felt like she lived in a museum. Every room of the mansion was festooned with original paintings by contemporary artists no one had heard of, expensive rugs from far-flung corners of the world they'd never visited, sparkling antique trinkets locked in glass-fronted cabinets, and too many vases, statues, and objets d'art to be healthy. All the place needed, in Jessica's opinion, were red velvet ropes, Do Not Touch! signs, and a grumpy old security guard in an over-ironed uniform, and the place would give the Staten Island Historical Society a run for its money.

Groaning loudly for effect—why wouldn't they just leave already?—Jessica got up from the reclaimed-leather sectional to go grab a snack from the kitchen. Her body was still sore from swim practice. It had been the first one of the year, two weeks before school started, and it had kicked her vacation-softened butt. Even so, Jessica was *determined* to make the eighth-grade swim team, so she'd put her heart and soul into that practice.

Returning from the kitchen with a strawberry yogurt, Jessica sat herself back down and grabbed the TV remote from the West African Fair Trade coffee table.

"You sure you're going to be okay, Jess?" Sharon asked. She looked stunning in her floor-length, scoop-necked blue gown and double string of pearls. Jessica hoped she'd look as good as her mother did at forty.

"Yeah, Mom. I *have* done this before," said Jessica as she opened her yogurt. "Besides, I'm only gonna be watching TV."

"And no Snapchat after ten."

"Yes, *mother.*"

Mark put his wallet in his pocket and buttoned his black coat, "We'll be back by eleven at the latest."

Sharon kissed her daughter on the cheek, "Text us if you need us."

As Sharon and Mark made their way out the front door, Jessica heard the alarm system turn on. She sighed—it was as if the thing was there to keep her in, not anyone out. She hated that they still treated her like a little kid, even more than she hated being left alone in their ridiculously sized house. It wasn't so much the silence Jessica disliked. The place was just so big, and considering they'd only lived there for a year, the myriad rooms and long hallways made the house feel more like a movie set for some contemporary ghost story than a home.

Oh, brilliant, Jess. Let's think about ghosts.

Her father liked to joke that they'd bought the house because it was like a fortress. The gated community was impossible to enter if you didn't know the code, security guards were on patrol every night, and the alarm system was state-of-the-art. And, given his position as something high up in Housing and Development, Mark Balducci had considered it a prudent move.

With her parents finally gone, Jessica ran upstairs to put on her nightgown—the short, sleeveless one Mother absolutely *forbade* her to wear around the house—and then ate her yogurt. Next door, the neighbors were having a party; raucous music blared through speakers on their back patio, competing with the babble of conversation and laughter. Jessica attempted to drown out the noise with the TV. Prodding at the remote, she flipped through all the channels she wasn't supposed to watch and that her parents had forgotten to block. Settling on *Love Island*, a show she and her friends loved to watch on sleepover nights, Jessica lay back on the couch and feasted her eyes on the barely clad, impossibly handsome young men and wondered if what her best friend, Sarah Smithson, said they did to the hot girls in the bikinis when the lights were out was actually true.

Before long, the intensive swim practice finally got the best of her. As she drifted into a deep sleep, her face smashed against the pillow, Jessica smelled the chlorine in her hair.

I'm really gonna have to get some of that special swimmers' shampoo.

She awoke, disoriented from fatigue, with an overwhelming pressure on her back pressing her into the couch. Her panties were off, her nightgown hiked up around her waist, the smooth leather of the couch cool against her bare thighs. She felt something hard between her legs—probing, insistent, and was accompanied by a nauseating smell of rubber and cloying aftershave. Something squeezed her neck tight—something unrelenting and cruelly strong. She could barely breathe but Jessica felt herself floating away into the darkness.

Mommy.

Help me.

———

When Jessica regained consciousness, bright lights hurt her eyes and she was no longer on the couch. Strangers buzzed around her; some wore long white coats, and others pale blue dresses and cute little hats. For a few moments, Jessica thought she may have died and was in heaven.

Slowly, as the nebulous shapes grew clearer, Jessica realized she was in a hospital room, surrounded by doctors, nurses, a couple of people she didn't recognize, and . . .

"Mom, Dad." She tried to sit up, but the pain between her legs forced her back down. She hurt all over, but that was the part of her body where she felt the most bruised.

"My baby, my baby." Sharon leaned over the bed, sobbing; her tears soaked into Jessica's hair while Mark leaned quietly against the far wall, his expression blank.

"Jessica," a man's voice said—deep, gravelly. "Jessica, this is Detective Riley. I need to ask you some questions about what happened."

Sharon extricated herself from Jessica and stepped away from the bed —not *too* far. "Is this really necessary? Hasn't my daughter been through enough tonight?" she asked the guy in the dark suit.

"It's better to get as much information as possible while it's fresh in her mind," said another voice, a woman's—soft, filled with empathy— spoke up from beside the cop. "I'll be right here to make sure Detective Riley doesn't upset your daughter, Mrs. Balducci. If she feels uncomfortable or just doesn't feel like talking, all she has to do is say so."

Turning her head away from the cop, who didn't appear to be all that happy with the woman's intrusion, Jessica saw the owner of the voice perfectly matched her appearance.

"Hello, Jessica." The woman sat herself down on the edge of the bed and offered a comforting smile. The bed creaked a little. "I'm Dr. Donato. I'm a special kind of therapist who deals with the kind of thing that happened to you, Jessica. I'll be here all the way to help you through this. You can call me Angela."

Muttering something under his breath, Riley leaned in close. "Jessica, can you hear me?"

"I . . ." The words refused to come, her throat tight and sore.

"Jessica, do you remember anything about last night?"

"I . . ." Jessica searched her mind and found it to be fuzzy. "I don't know."

"Do you remember anything about the person who did this?"

She *wished* she could recall something, *anything*. All she could remember was she'd been home alone, watching TV, exhausted from swim practice, and had fallen asleep on the sofa. Next thing, she'd awoken in the hospital feeling like she'd been hit by a train.

"No."

What happened to me?

"Now, Jessica, I know that's not true." The cop sounded impatient, pissed even—like this was all Jessica's fault. "*Something* happened to you. I need you to try harder to—"

"I think that's enough for tonight," Angela cut the detective off. "Jessica needs her rest. I'm sure she'll be able to answer your questions in the morning."

Detective Riley paused a heartbeat or two, and Jessica saw defiance in his eyes. She hoped he wouldn't be demanding more answers from her, as she really didn't have it in her to talk about what had happened to her, especially since she had no idea other than whoever had hurt her had done so in the worst possible way.

Angela shot the cop a withering look and he stepped back from the bed. "Okay, Jessica. It's all good. We'll try again tomorrow."

Detective Riley straightened his already-straight tie and strode from the room without as much as a passing glance at anyone in the room.

CHAPTER SEVEN

MONDAY, DAVINA'S APARTMENT IN ROSEBANK

THE SKY WAS PITCH BLACK BY THE TIME DAVINA LEFT ST. Margaret Mary. A great weight had been lifted from her shoulders by unburdening to Charlie, who'd listened to everything with an open mind. Davina had no doubt that if someone had done the same when she was twelve, her life from that point would have been so very different.

She arrived home to find Nick Delafield sitting on the concrete steps outside her Rosebank apartment that nestled above Blue Star Grocery. He stood up, smiling, and the two faced each other for an awkward moment. He holding a bouquet of purple, red, and yellow flowers. She holding a plastic bag from Tommy's Tacos that reeked of fish and cilantro.

"Love me some Tommy's," Nick said.

"Millie's dinner. What are you doing here?"

"Waiting for you. I just finished up at Dad's campaign headquarters and I wanted to apologize for being so abrupt at the service this afternoon."

Davina's cheeks warmed; she was blushing. "I think I should be the one bearing flowers, considering I dumped your ass on the floor."

"No harm, no foul." Nick pointed behind him to the second-story window. "Are you going to invite me up or do I have to stand here looking like some idiot holding flowers?"

"Oh, uh . . . come up, please." Davina led the way, tripping over the bottom step. In one swift move, Nick had wrapped an arm around her waist and steadied her.

Davina tensed.

Nick's sudden, uninvited touch triggered memories deep inside Davina, and she fought hard not to put the guy on his ass again. "You saved Millie's dinner," she said with a forced laugh.

"My heroic deed for the day. C'mon, let's put these flowers in water."

Davina managed all the remaining steps without incident. Unlocking the apartment door, she called out to Millie and received no response.

"I guess she's not home yet."

"We could always eat her tacos and tell her you dropped them?"

"Tempting, but no. I've already eaten, and she went with me to Joy's service."

"I guess she earned her tacos, then," Nick said with flowers still in hand. "Vase?"

"Oh, I don't know if we have one. I mean, Millie and I don't get many bouquets." Davina rummaged through the kitchen cabinets. Eventually, Davina pulled out a mayonnaise jar filled with coins. "How's this?" Dumping out the coins on the counter, she filled the jar with water.

Nick took the plastic wrap off the flowers and stuck them in the jar. "Perfect."

"Coffee?" Davina asked, placing the jar on the square wooden dinette table. She became acutely aware of just how faded the pale green walls were and how her and Millie's furnishings were decidedly thrift shop. She also noticed for the first time their dining table had several bald spots where the finish and stain had been worn away by generations of elbows. It struck her that her place must have seemed all very poor white trash to the moneyed Nick Delafield.

"The furniture's a little old," Davina apologized. "It came with the place."

"It's homey," Nick smiled.

"Well, my home maybe, not yours," Davina retorted as she plugged in the kettle. She then measured the coffee; she had just enough to make two cups. After Davina set up the dripper, she turned back to face Nick, who was leaning on the kitchen counter.

Nick took off his cuff links, slipped them into his jacket pocket, and rolled up his shirt sleeves. "Life isn't always about money."

"Says the one who has it." *Shit, where did that come from?*

"No, seriously. Money really isn't everything."

"Try living without it." *Shut up, smart ass.*

Nick seemed not to take offense. "Remember the first time I came to your parents' house for dinner? I'd never had lasagna with peas and carrots before. Or since, come to think of it."

"I remember. That was a banner night. My mother was uncharacteristically sober."

"Were things that bad?"

"No. Worse. That's why it hurt me so much when you stopped coming over."

Now it was Nick's turn to blush. "D, I'm sorry. I didn't think you even noticed."

"Of course, I noticed. You were like a big brother. I looked up to you —you could always make me laugh *and* you listened to my stories. Everybody else treated me like I was wacko, but you never did."

"You weren't wacko. I liked all your scary stories. I thought you were a pretty cool kid," Nick replied with a warm smile. "Do you remember when I bought you that recorder?"

Davina covered her face in mock shame. "To document my lurid fascination with Slender Man?" She stared at the worn linoleum floor. "You know, I sort of had a crush on you."

"Seriously?" Nick winked. "I had no idea."

"I'd get totally jealous when you came to the house to pick up Alessandra. I'd watch you from my bedroom window opening the car door for her and wish it was me. Not that it was ever gonna happen—I was twelve and you were eighteen." She paused to savor the memory. "That recorder meant a lot to me. It was a friend I could talk to. I think I wore it out, I used it so much. It doesn't work anymore, but I still have it."

The kettle popped off, and Davina poured water over the grounds. She retrieved a mismatched pair of mugs from the cupboard and rinsed them out. "How do you take it?" she asked, pouring the coffee.

"Hot and black."

"Talking about me?" Millie appeared in the apartment's doorway.

"Coffee," Davina chuckled as she put the mugs on the table. "Tacos are on the counter. Change is in the bag."

"Cool. Thanks." Millie grabbed the bag, eyeing Nick suspiciously. She raised one brow. "I'll be in my room. Just pretend I'm not here." She headed down the short hallway on the opposite side of the tiny living room.

"So," Nick picked up the mug. "You were saying something about having a crush." He took a small sip.

"I can't believe I admitted to that."

"You know what I remember? I remember how beautiful both you and Alessandra were. Even at twelve years old, I knew you'd break hearts someday."

Davina almost did a spit-take. "Me? You're totally bullshitting me, Nick Delafield."

Earnestly, Nick put his right hand over his heart and raised his left as he replied, "Scout's honor."

Davina laughed, and it felt good, easy. She tucked her hair behind her ears and said, "Thanks."

Davina's phone dinged to notify her of a text. She picked it up and read the message. "It's Joe," she told Nick, as if he deserved some explanation.

Nick cocked his head. "Joe Kelley?"

"Yeah." *Shit. I forgot Nick doesn't know.*

"And how is my high school rival? He was the only guy to ever beat me on the wrestling mat *and* the dating field. We were first and second all through school—nearly lost Allie to him once."

"I'm dating Joe," Davina confessed as she studied Nick from the corner of her eye.

Nick's face fell. "No shit?" He pulled a hand through his dark hair. "You and Joe. How'd that happen?"

"Y'know, I'm not entirely sure."

"Well, I'll be damned. Little Davina and Joe." Nick leaned forward, his elbows on the table. "So, how is he?"

Davina blushed and wasn't sure if it was because of Nick's natural charm or from thinking of Joe. "Joe's good. He's a financial advisor with Evans-Claymore."

"He always was a smart guy. Even when he worked for my dad, I could see he had a good brain. Don't tell him I said this, but he was one of the good guys. They're hard to find, Davina."

"I know," Davina was forced to agree. "He makes me wish I wanted to be married."

"You enjoy single life too much?"

"Hardly. Marriage just isn't . . . in my immediate plan. Or my distant plan, for that matter."

"So, what *is* your plan?"

"To not have one."

"Okay, so aside from having no plan, what else have you been up to?"

"I'm a kickboxing instructor at Dobson's Gym."

"Awesome," Nick seemed genuinely impressed. "That explains the magnificent takedown at Joy's memorial. Oh, wow." He pointed at Davina's wrist. "I *love* the tat."

"Thanks. Chrysanthemums stand for truth."

"Telling it?"

"Searching for it."

"Look, if it's okay with you and it doesn't mess up things between you and Joe, I'd like to stay in touch." Nick drained his coffee. "The campaign takes up a lot of my time, but I promise to be better at staying close."

Davina smiled, "I'd like that, Nick."

"Good." Getting to his feet, Nick plucked his jacket off the back of the chair and hooked it over his shoulder. "I'll see you soon." Nick leaned down and kissed Davina's cheek before leaving.

Millie entered just as the door closed and tossed the cardboard taco container in the trash. "For what it's worth, I like Joe better. If he was a female, I'd date him myself. This one, he's slick, too much like his old man. Human-shaped bullshit walking around in a fancy suit. I remember his father bulldozing his way through Stapleton during his first campaign run. He talked real big about equality and opportunity. Build up the projects! A better life! More jobs! Just a big load o' crap." Millie put her hands on her hips. "Still waitin'."

"Nick's just an old friend, Mil. He used to date my sister."

"Just watch him. That's all I'm saying. He thinks he got it all goin' on."

"And he doesn't?"

Millie shook her head. "Not even close, sister."

What does she see in Nick that I can't?

CHAPTER EIGHT

TUESDAY MORNING, DAVINA'S APARTMENT

Davina awoke to a hand over her mouth. She was pressed hard into the bed by that familiar, unmovable weight. The sheets were damp from sweat and tears as she struggled for her life. A hand forced itself between her legs, prying them open despite her kicking and screaming and clamping her thighs tight shut. Helpless, Davina scanned the room in the dark, searching for something, *anything* she could use as a weapon. The mirror. She stared into it and saw the thick, faceless dark on top of her; it blotted out the glow-in-the-dark stars on her wall.

His face. Why can't I see his face?

The room spun, and Davina closed her eyes tight, willing herself to awaken from her terrible dream.

Mommy, where are you?

Davina sat up in bed, gasping. Her mouth was bone dry and her flesh crawled with goose bumps, despite the night's warmth. She flicked on the bedside lamp and set her feet firmly down on the worn hardwood floor, pressing down with her toes—it felt so good to be grounded.

There. It's real. Solid. I can stand on it.

"Hey?" Millie called out from behind the bedroom door. "You all good, D?"

"Yeah, I'm good. Just a bad dream—right up there with going to PE naked." Davina's voice was hoarse, but she tried her best to sound okay. She hadn't told Millie about the nightmares; she didn't have the heart to talk about her past again so soon after telling Charlie.

"I get those—'cept I'm pretty sure I did go to PE naked once." Millie padded off down the hall, heading for the kitchen. A moment later, "We ain't got no bread or nothing in here! And no damn coffee!"

"Shit. You got time?"

"Honey, I've got to work."

Davina sighed as she examined herself in the mirror over her desk. Even though she was a mess, it wasn't the hot mess she used to see reflected back at her. In the bad old days, Davina would wake to eyeliner running down her hungover face, and dead, soulless eyes. Absently, she traced the familiar circle and horizontal line between her brows with the tip of one finger. What had he meant when he drew that?

Naturally, she knew *what* the symbol meant. Aside from its significance in trig and Greek mythology, it was used in engineering to denote thermal resistance and transit angle, among other things—Davina had the ubiquitous Google to thank for that nugget of information. It truly was the symbol for all goddamn seasons. Even the Ghostbusters used a bastardized form of theta in their logo!

Davina's question still stood, though. What exactly had it *meant* to whoever had drawn it onto her forehead? Which one of its myriad connotations held significance to her rapist, and why?

Knowledge of such an esoteric symbol was clearly way above her education level. Maybe Charlie could shed some light on its significance to a psychopathic sex criminal?

"Groceries," she told the woman who in the mirror did not even resemble her. "That's an order."

Davina wasn't a big fan of grocery shopping. Too many people, way too close. Living above Blue Star Grocery made the ordeal a little easier, though. The store opened at 8:00 a.m., and when it was her turn to shop,

Davina was routinely in the first aisle by 8:10 and out of the store by 8:20. And she didn't have to circle for a parking spot.

The list was never long, with just the essentials: milk, bread, eggs, butter, coffee, peanut butter, spaghetti, tomato sauce, lettuce, Cheerios, and the occasional bag of Bugles Original and a jar of Smucker's, if there was a coupon. If Nick seriously thought money wasn't everything, he really ought to try grocery shopping without it.

In the bread aisle, two well-dressed older women were talking. Davina stood a few feet away, trying to figure out the difference between wheat, whole wheat, twelve-grain, and multigrain.

Oh fuck it, I'll just get white.

By the counter, the morning edition of the *Advance* caught Davina's eye. The headline read that a young girl had been attacked in her home in Todt Hill. Hands shaking, Davina picked up the top copy and scanned the page. Not too much detail, but the reporter—Geoff Wong, no less—was linking it with the Fort Wadsworth attack the previous week. It was all too close to home, too horribly familiar for Davina.

"You gonna buy that?" the clerk stocking shelves asked rudely.

"Oh, yeah." As Davina tried to mentally work out if she had enough change for the newspaper and the bread, someone walked behind her and left a waft of something sickeningly familiar in his wake.

Davina covered her face with her hands and, in a heartbeat, everything went black.

———

Davina felt the cold, hard linoleum of the shop floor against her back. Opening her eyes, she saw two women staring down at her in concern and blatant curiosity. Gino Romano, the Blue Star's and Davina's landlord, was there too; his cherubic face with black-olive eyes peering down at her was comforting.

"What the hell happened, Davina?" Gino knelt beside her; his crisp white apron bulged over his round belly.

"I'm fine." Davina put up a hand to back him away; his closeness was too much after her experience.

"Are you hurt?"

"No, no. Just embarrassed." Standing up, she noticed the jar of pasta sauce she'd had in her hand had shattered and spattered all over the floor.

Gino made shooing gestures at the two women, "Ladies, please, give her some room."

The two women sidestepped the pool of sauce and started back down the bread aisle. "What's wrong with her?" one asked the other.

They both gave Davina a backward glance. "Just look at her. Who knows what sorts of drugs she's on."

Gino grabbed a mop and dustpan. "You need me to call someone?"

"No, I'm fine now." Davina's grocery basket lay on the floor. She scooted the dislodged items back into it; everything was splattered with pasta sauce. The bread aisle resembled a grisly crime scene.

I could use a drink.

Davina's mind spun back to when she'd start drinking—or using—first thing in the morning. It seemed back then like a day was just too overwhelming to bear without her chemical crutch to lean on. Davina would find anything she could get her hands on to get her through the day. Or at least numb the anxiety and pain.

Channel it, she told herself. *Find something useful to do with this angst.*

She decided she'd seek out Charlie's friend at the *Advance* and get his take on the possible connections between her rape and Joy's—and the two new cases at Fort Wadsworth and Todt Hill.

She'd put the call in the moment she got upstairs.

CHAPTER NINE

TUESDAY, DAVINA'S APARTMENT

Back upstairs in her apartment, Davina called the *Staten Island Advance* and managed to land an appointment with Geoff Wong later in the day. That was the good news. The bad news was she'd have to squeeze in the meeting between lessons. With precisely nineteen minutes to get to Dobson's for her first lesson, Davina took a few minutes to throw back a cup of coffee and a bowl of Cheerios, and put the bowl, spoon, and cup in the sink before grabbing her car keys and rushing out the door.

Davina's regular clients, Skylar and Kayla Florczak, were waiting for her when she arrived flustered and with just minutes to spare. As usual, the sisters' appearance was fierce as hell, Kayla with her bleached-white marine buzz cut and pierced tongue, and Skylar dressed all in black with long sleeves that didn't quite cover up the self-inflicted razor scars on her wrists. The two were dark, edgy, and reminded Davina a little of herself.

Davina faced them on the center mat.

"Okay, let's do this. Show me what you got." She assumed the classic kung fu warrior stance—legs apart and bent, side-on to her opponents—and beckoned them with the fingers of one outstretched hand.

The sisters unleashed two-on-one with coordinated punches and intense roundhouse kicks that had Davina ducking and coming back at them with extended leg flexes. In one move, Skylar managed to get Davina down, but Davina hooked her ankles around Skylar's support leg and brought her crashing to the mat. That was just the beginning of a fast, furious bout—exactly what Davina needed to clear her head.

Finished, breathless and sweating, Davina smiled her approval. "Nice. *Very* nice. Skylar, you need to watch your leg extension. Remember to pull it fast. If you hold it too long, your opponent can get you down. And when you throw it, be sure you stay even with your opponent's torso." She demonstrated, "You always want to strike his center."

"Or his balls," Kayla added.

Davina nodded. "Those, too."

Skylar and Kayla marched off to the showers, and Davina made her way to Gerry's office.

"You look relaxed." Gerry was perched on the corner of her desk.

"Those two girls are fucking intense."

"So, you're the right teacher for them." Gerry gave a glance at the white memo board on the wall. "You have the newbie this afternoon."

Davina leaned up against Gerry's desk. "He's a bit of an oddity for Staten Island—a man happy to work with a female. Unless it's some weird sex thing."

Gerry laughed along. "Don Anderson wanted the best, and that's you. He saw that for himself."

"Most guys would prefer a man who's the second best. I mean, the testosterone on this island flows stronger than the current in the bay."

"I guess Don isn't like most guys, then."

Davina shrugged. "I have an errand to run in Grasmere. Shouldn't take much longer than forty. Are you cool if I run a few minutes late for Don's class?"

"First class—I'd rather you didn't. But I guess it's important. I can stall Don with filling out his waiver forms; just don't turn it into a lunch date."

Grasmere was less than twenty minutes from the gym if there was no traffic. Davina knew from experience that just one fender-bender would mean two miles of rubber-necking and she'd be horrifically late. As luck had it, Davina sailed effortlessly along the Martin Luther King Jr. Expressway in record time.

Like all professional buildings, the one containing the offices of the *Advance* was impressive in an understated way, with precisely the right mix of brick and glass. A covered walkway led up to the building, and all the appropriate flags were flying from the rooftop. In the lobby, a man smartly dressed in black trousers, a white button-down shirt, and black suspenders strolled by the grim-faced security guard with little more than a head nod.

"Are you here to see someone?" the security guard growled at Davina as she followed the smart guy.

"Yes. Geoff Wong—the *Advance*. I have an 11:30 appointment."

"If you could step over here a minute, please." The guard escorted her to the reception desk.

Great, no accident on MLK Jr. Expressway, but this guy's gonna jam me up.

The guard made a big production of phoning upstairs to verify Davina's appointment. "May I see your ID?" He held out a huge, meaty hand.

Davina took out her driver's license and placed it on the desk. She was then handed a clipboard. "If you would please sign in." Finally, the guard handed over a guest pass on a lanyard. "Be sure to wear this at all times in the building and return it on your way out."

"Right."

"Mr. Wong is on the third floor. You can take the elevator straight ahead. His is the second office on the left when you get out."

"The elevator?" Davina had a phobia about elevators; they aggravated her claustrophobia something terrible. "I'd rather take the stairs if that's okay."

"The stairs are emergency only," the guard grumped. He was about to say something else when a group of three men caught his attention. "Excuse me, gentlemen . . ."

With the surly guard's attention taken by the three businessmen, Davina surreptitiously flipped him the bird and ran over to the emergency exit door. Pushing it open, a rush of cool air from the stairwell caressed her face and she felt happy in her defiance. After what she'd been through, she'd be damned if some asshat in an ill-fitting uniform was going to make her take the elevator.

Jogging up the stairs, Davina checked her phone. Only a few minutes late. Had it not been for the security guard, Davina would've been bang on time. If she could get the meeting with Wong over with quickly, she'd make it back to Dobson's just in time for Don Anderson's appointment.

Finally, the third floor. Davina eased open the door, half expecting to see the security guard. She paused to scan the hallway ahead of her; there were four offices along the left side, all but one door open, and an open cubicle farm on the right. Davina straightened her workout apparel the best she could and wished she'd had time to change.

If wishes were wheels, we wouldn't have to take a ferry to Manhattan.

She lifted her head and strode down the hall to the third office on the left, feeling as conspicuous as a nun in a brothel.

CHAPTER TEN

TUESDAY, OFFICES OF THE STATEN ISLAND ADVANCE

GEOFF WONG WAS NOTORIOUSLY, OBSESSIVELY AWARE OF time; a Chinese mother and a military father had taught him that. For his entire thirty-five years, he'd worked to tight deadlines and had never missed one yet. Geoff *hated* it when people were late, and by his watch, Davina Speers was precisely four minutes overdue. Enough time to boil an egg, as his mother was so fond of saying.

At eight seconds before five minutes late, Geoff caught the fleeting image of an attractive young woman with stunning red hair hurrying past his office. A couple of seconds later, she backtracked and knocked on the open door.

"Come in."

"Mr. Wong? I'm so sorry. The guard downstairs—"

He held up his hand. More so than tardiness, Geoff hated excuses. "You must be Charlie's friend?"

"Davina Speers. I apologize for being late; this won't take long."

Admiring the view, Geoff walked around Davina and pulled out a chair. "Have a seat. You want coffee?"

"No, thanks. I'm good."

Davina sat down and rolled her shoulders. She was fit and tight and had a distinct edge to her Geoff wasn't entirely certain he liked. But the young girl was sexy in a Black Widow sort of way—the wavy, shoulder-length red hair, perfectly proportioned body, and eyes he was willing to bet changed color with her mood. The tight workout tank and near-painted-on leggings didn't hurt.

Stay focused. I've got a bad feeling about this one.

Returning to his seat behind the desk, he bridged his fingers and said, "So, talk to me."

Davina tucked a few strands of hair behind her ears. "You reported on the Fort Wadsworth and Todt Hill attacks."

Geoff leaned forward, his dark eyes studying Davina's face. "I'm writing about the Todt case as we speak. What's your interest?"

"Do you have any information other than what's being reported?"

"I'm afraid I can't offer much more than what everyone knows. The police are keeping a tight lid on it. Even if they weren't, anything I get from them would be confidential—until it's gone to press, of course."

"Oh."

Davina bristled visibly at the word *police*. Geoff read people for a living and was never wrong when instinct told him someone was holding back. "Do you know either of the victims?"

Davina stared hard at the top of his desk. "I had a friend who had the same sort of experience. Joy Sheridan. There are rumors—"

Geoff nodded his sympathy. "I was at the memorial as it was winding down. The rumors were still buzzing—tongues do love to wag on the Rock." He eased back in his chair. "I also heard you had a dust-up with Detective Riley after you floored Nick Delafield."

"Nice I added to the buzz."

"You certainly did, Miss Speers," Geoff said with a broad smile. "I heard Riley 'escorted' you out."

"Yeah, but it was an honest mistake—Nick startled me, I reacted, and Riley played to his audience. Nick was cool about it, though."

"You ever do drugs, Davina?"

Her head came up sharply; wariness crept into her eyes. "Why do you ask?"

"Reporter's instinct. I'm guessing it wasn't your first run-in with Riley—law enforcement."

"It wasn't." Davina hunched her shoulders and stared down at her knees. "It was a while ago. I'm in recovery, coming up on my one-year anniversary of being sober."

"Congratulations. And?"

"Yeah, I've had a couple of run-ins with the cops over the past ten years."

"And you're interested in young girls attacked on Staten Island because . . ."

"I was friends with Joy and I don't like what some people are saying about her. Maybe it's just a vicious rumor, maybe it's true. I owe it to her to find out which." Leaning forward, Davina's eyes met Geoff's. "Joy *changed* back in high school—like, *overnight*—and I'm thinking maybe it was because of something that happened to me."

"Explain."

Davina glanced around, as if wary of someone being within earshot. "I think I was attacked. In the same way Joy and the two recent girls were." Her jaw flexed, tightened as she continued, "I *know* I was attacked, but . . . Riley claimed he'd captured Son of Cropsey *before* it happened and nobody believed me. And now, there have been more attacks ten years later. Something is going on, Geoff." She put both fists on his desk and stood up to look Geoff dead in the eye. "I *didn't* make anything up. And neither did Joy or those other girls. I need to know what that means."

Whoa. "What are you suggesting?"

Davina shook her head and sat back in her chair. "Look, I didn't come here for therapy or absolution. All I want are some answers. If what happened to me back then also happened to Joy too . . . maybe Riley got the wrong guy. Or what if he got the right guy who did a couple more rapes while he was out on bail? And what if the cops put him away ten years ago, he did his time, and now he's out and back at it again? Or what if he didn't act alone? Or there's a copycat? Wadsworth, Todt Hill, Joy, me. All these crimes have to be related somehow."

Geoff rubbed at his smooth chin with both hands. "It was a pretty open-and-shut case. Rob Cox went away for all the attacks and he's still doing his time. He's gonna be an old man before he's even up for parole. As for attacking you on bail—they don't give serial rapists bail, Davina. But the idea of an accomplice or copycat—now that's something I can get my teeth into."

Geoff *wanted* to help the girl. There was something about her—a sincere vulnerability—that appealed to him more than the tight outfit and pretty face.

Davina consulted the clock on the wall. "Oh shit. I gotta be in Westerleigh in fifteen minutes."

"Give me your number and email address, and I'll let you know when I dig up something." Geoff tried not to stare at Davina's ass as she stood up and pushed her chair back to the side of the office.

Davina leaned over Geoff's desk to grab a pen and block of gaudy-colored Post-it notes.

"May I ask you a question?" Geoff requested .

"Of course." Davina stopped scribbling.

"Do you think Joy Sheridan killed herself?"

Despair flashed in Davina's eyes. "I do. I think she was raped ten years ago and she couldn't live with the pain anymore, so she ended it the only way she knew how."

"What makes you so sure?"

Davina stared blankly out the window then said, "Because after what happened to me, I've had the same thought a thousand times over."

Geoff furrowed his brow. He couldn't begin to imagine the mental pain it must take to decide it would be better to die. He watched Davina leave his office and couldn't help but think that had been one hell of an admission for her to make to a complete stranger.

CHAPTER ELEVEN

TUESDAY, DOBSON'S GYM

Davina was six minutes late to Dobson's Gym, but so was Don Anderson. Weaving her way between the equipment and crash mats, Davina absorbed the sights, sounds, and smells of the place—it was somewhere she felt truly at home.

"Looking good there!" she called across to Carlo Donato, who appeared particularly uncomfortable trapped in an expertly demonstrated chokehold by Santos, his personal trainer for the day.

Nonetheless, Carlo managed to raise a hand and grunt a reply to Davina before Santos twisted his body around and planted him hard on the green mat. Carlo really had to work on getting out of those holds.

The sounds of exertion always made Davina feel at home—grunts and growls of effort, the slap and thud of bodies hitting the mat. When Davina worked out on her own, she loved to hear her heart pounding in her ears and the swish of punches cutting through the air. She'd never figured out why most gyms played throwaway pop music to drown out those sounds.

"I'm *so* excited about this," Don said as he pumped his fists in the air.

Davina stifled a laugh. Don was wearing workout gear more suited for the beach than the gym, and she wondered if his red shorts weren't, in fact, swim shorts. He'd told Gerry he'd already had some training and just wanted to build on it, but Davina doubted it had been extensive. People who'd had any decent amount of martial arts training carried themselves differently—more balanced, more . . . ready.

"Show me your defensive stance."

Davina watched as Don settled into a half-crouch facing her—a sort of layman's horse stance. She could tell his weight was over his heels; she could knock him down with a hard sneeze.

"That," she told him. "Is a good way to get knocked on your ass. You need to face your opponent obliquely."

"This is how I learned it," Don argued.

Davina executed a roundhouse kick that whiffed by Don's head barely three inches from his nose. He jerked his head up and back and took a seat on the mat—hard.

"Like I said . . ."

Davina helped the guy back up and then showed him the stance he was *supposed* to take, placing him so that his left hip led. Once in place, Davina put her hands on Don's shoulders to tilt his upper body toward her. The guy didn't have much muscle tone there; he was definitely in need of some upper-body work.

"How does that feel?"

"Good."

Davina moved to offense position. "I'm going to come at you. Show me what you've got."

Don locked his back leg before replying, "Let's do it."

Ten seconds later, Davina had him down again. He was fast getting up and launched a punch that was just short of connecting with her chin.

Davina smiled, "You're not a complete newbie, I see."

"I might have boxed a little back in my youth."

"A little, huh? You wanna rev it up?"

Forty-five minutes later, they were both spent and still on their feet. Gerry approached the mat, applauding. She looked good in her tight green-and-black camo T-shirt that displayed Dobson's logo of a female warrior.

"She really is intense!" Don panted at Gerry; he rested his hands on his knees and fought to catch his breath.

"She's my protégé." The sincere expression of pride on Gerry's face made Davina feel damn good.

Davina, only a little out of breath but drenched with sweat, broke the moment, "I'd love to stay and hear more about how good I am, but I gotta hit the shower and get to school."

Don seemed surprised, "What are you studying?"

"Criminal justice," Davina said with a wry smile. Nobody ever believed she was as capable of hitting the books as she was being a sparring partner.

As she left, Davina heard Don asking, "Where does all that energy come from?"

"Existential angst," Gerry told him without missing a beat.

It was pretty close to the truth.

———

St. John's University was a clean, modern, sprawling campus. Its center point was a spectacular red brick and white stone building with arched windows and green-tiled pyramid roofing. The institution somehow managed to encapsulate old and contemporary in one fell swoop. It was a place of learning, a place that held so much promise for the future, and a place that provided Davina a grain of hope—all the bright young Staten Islanders it educated were the future of the borough—if they chose to stay, of course. Myriad students sat enjoying the sun on a lawn lined with tulips while others rushed to class. Even though Davina only studied at St. John's during the summertime, she felt like she belonged, and that was a feeling she only felt there and at the gym.

When Davina reached Spellman Hall, running late again, she was pleased to find the door of the lecture theater was still open. On the small stage, Professor Susan Blackman, a retired NYPD detective with a plump, sturdy frame and a perfect brunette pixie cut, had already begun. She threw a glance in Davina's direction as she slipped quietly into a seat on the aisle halfway down the sloping central ramp. Davina pulled out her cell phone to record the lecture, but the battery was too low. So, she pulled out her notebook and a pen instead.

Unruffled by the late arrival, Professor Blackman continued, "Perps select victims based on many criteria. Sometimes it's as simple as opportunity—they see a victim getting off a bus in a quiet location or walking down an empty street. In such instances, there are no identifying criteria for us to build a victim profile. It's nothing more than a crime of opportunity, and the perp may go years between attacks, which makes it even more difficult to catch them."

Davina put up her hand, "How are perps like that caught?"

"In most instances, it's down to sheer luck."

"The cops just catch a break?"

"By *luck*, I mean the perp slips up. Their actions are typically impulsive, and as such, not well planned. Repeat offenders who act on opportunity often become overconfident. They believe they can outsmart law enforcement. Their ongoing success emboldens them, and they take chances."

"What sort of chances?" The entire class was staring at Davina. She'd been there five seconds and was already peppering the prof with questions. "Sorry," she muttered.

"Don't apologize, Ms. Speers. That's why you're here." Blackman clasped her hands together and stepped away from the podium. "For some perps, the attack becomes boring. What gets them off is the chase, the thrill of getting caught—or not. They act boldly—they'll return to the scene of the crime, take trophies, and even insinuate themselves into the investigation. In some cases, they taunt law enforcement—anonymous phone calls, leaving notes or symbolic items—almost as if they are *signing* their work."

That stopped Davina's hasty scribbling and almost stopped her heart. "How about marking the victim?"

The professor nodded as she replied, "That's more common than you might think. Let's not forget rape is more about control and dominance than sex, so some kind of territory marking is inevitable. Sometimes, in cases where the victims would be able to identify their attacker, the perp may take to openly approaching the victim in some type of social setting to reinforce his dominance."

"Hiding in plain sight?" Davina's pulse quickened. Might *her* attacker still be keeping himself close?

Professor Blackman nodded again, "Exactly. They adopt a catch-me-if-you-can attitude. In many instances, the perp often is an otherwise productive member of society. He, or she, holds a respectable job, has a family, is well-liked, and behaves with complete normalcy. Neighbors and family members are almost always shocked to discover this dark alter-life."

Another student spoke up, "There are no clues? No telltale signs?"

"In hindsight, some people will say they knew something was off about the perpetrator, but often the reinterpreted behavior didn't amount to anything truly suspicious."It must be really sad having to live with that impulse."

Davina turned around to face the girl, "What's sad is victims having to live with the *results* of that impulse."

"You're right, Ms. Speers," Professor Blackman said as she returned to the podium and leaned against it. "The effect of rape, for example, is totally devastating to the victims. For children and adolescents, this may result in long-term psychological trauma such as depression, PTSD, anxiety, and repression of memories."

Davina's mind spiraled with Blackman's words: *repression of memories.*

A young, plain-faced young man across the aisle from Davina raised his hand, "Can you recover repressed memories?"

Blackman's smile was wry. "When I said repressed memories, I was referring to those we consciously repress, discard, or even reinterpret because they're too painful or frightening. The topic of unconsciously repressed and dissociated memories linked to sexual abuse is controversial and often argued. The 'memory wars,' we call it. Some say victims unwittingly dissociate and block out the memory to protect themselves from reliving the trauma. The cognitive dissonance—different class subject—then manifests as anger or anxiety."

Sounds fucking familiar.

"What if the memory of the event is recovered?" the girl asked next.

Professor Blackman sighed before she explained, "Maybe a better word is 'reconstructed.' Reconstructing a memory of abuse can help to resolve psychological issues, especially if the criminal is brought to justice. It gives the victim closure and a reason for their anger and depression. Just recognizing the source of the emotions can help alleviate them. But it can also cause great harm. I have also seen cases of so-called recovered memories that resulted in a family member being sent to jail for an alleged crime simply on the basis of a recovered memory, with literally no actual evidence presented—circumstantial or factual. I've seen families destroyed because a therapist insisted that the very fact that a child *didn't* remember being molested was proof that they had been."

Blackman paused to take a drink of water from a bottle on the podium then continued,

"Most of you are too young to remember this unless it's part of your coursework, but the Recovered Memory movement surged in the 1980s and '90s, possibly as a backlash against therapists who routinely dismissed accounts of incest and sexual abuse as fantasies. Unfortunately, one of the results of the movement was the implantation of false memories by therapists who interpreted a wide variety of symptoms as evidence of abuse. Uncovering repressed childhood sexual abuse became a cottage industry. Some people, especially children, are vulnerable to suggestion and can innocently construct false or pseudo memories of events that never actually occurred, especially if they are encouraged by a trusted authority figure, such as a therapist or doctor."

Davina spoke up, "So, any child's memories of sexual abuse should be assumed to be *false?*"

Blackman shot her a strange expression, "Absolutely not. I'm speaking specifically about therapists who were, shall we say, constructing narratives, and then pressing their patients to accept them as reality. In court, they were often cited for leading the witness. That's a far cry from simply believing a victim who comes to you on their own with an account of abuse. Now, the whole movement did cause a reevaluation of the types of symptoms that could be interpreted as signs of abuse. Take sleep paralysis, for example."

Davina's skin crawled at the phrase.

Blackman persisted, "You mentally awaken from sleep before your body, and you're unable to move. You see your room through an overlay of what's happening in your mind—the remnants of a dream, for example. Both seem equally real—or *sur*real. It happens to most of us at some point in our lives, and it can include tactile and visual hallucinations, often of shadowy or threatening intruders in the room. In fact, many alien visitation accounts are attributable to sleep paralysis. It's possible to interpret these hallucinations as bits of old memories—especially if you're looking for that sort of leakage, for lack of a better word.

Blackman further explained, "People who suffer from frequent sleep paralysis are also more likely to have emotional issues, including depression, because their REM sleep is so often interrupted. These symptoms can be misleading and, I think, many therapists were willing to be misled.

"But psychologists argue that actual victims can, and do recall some or all of a past event with different degrees of clarity. It's those explicit, consciously repressed memories that drive the trauma, the anger, the fear." Blackman paused to take another sip of water. She gazed thoughtfully at her audience.

"Now, let's not forget that eliciting fear is a big part of what a perpetrator gets out of their crime. Sexual abuse is, after all, an expression of personal power and control. The victim becomes a puppet for the perp to manipulate for their own gratification."

Davina was writing so feverishly she wondered how she was going to get it all down. *Sleep paralysis? False memories? This is all too close to home.*

Finally, Davina put down her pen and flexed her fingers. She wondered if her nightmares were simply bad dreams and memories of sleep paralysis. Would she be able to handle the shame if she was totally wrong about what had happened to her? If the symbol drawn on her forehead in lipstick had been a sibling prank, after all?

CHAPTER TWELVE

TUESDAY, LIQUID GAS PLANT, ARTHUR KILL ROAD

THE TWIN ROSSVILLE LIQUEFIED NATURAL GAS TANKS, AN
unsightly blemish on Staten Island's landscape, had stood abandoned for
decades, since being decommissioned following the explosion in '73 that
killed forty workers. Fat, bloated, and rusted, they stood in ongoing testi-
mony to the stagnation of the attempts to modernize the island.

Because of those decaying gas tanks, a group of business-suited men
and a woman had been invited to the location by real estate developer and
aspiring city councilman, Sean Delafield. They huddled in the shadow of
the looming, decrepit structures, which offered no relief from the swel-
tering late July heat and unbearable humidity.

Sean had gathered together Commissioner Vito Marino of the City
Planning Commission and a political appointee by the Staten Island
Borough President; Scott Kantor, lawyer and chairman of the Staten
Island Republican County Committee; Morris Moulton of the New York
City Industrial Development Agency; Jim Farmer of the NYC Neighbor-
hood Capital Corporation; Gino Romano, president of the Small Busi-
ness and Civic Association and owner of the Blue Star market chain; and

Darren Rivers, a Black banker. Nancy Briggs of the New York City Economic Development Corporation was the lone hen in the rooster shack. Sean's son, Nick, stood at the back, watching his father preach to his anxious choir.

"And with the NYCNCC in agreement for granting a low-interest loan, my plan for turning this vast wasteland into a thriving mixed-use site will be the first step in putting Staten Island on the map," Sean said as he lifted his arms in the direction of the tanks. "These monstrosities, these eight-hundred-foot eyesores, are going to be transformed into the most gorgeous high-rise condos you can imagine. For Christ's sake, they've got water views all around!"

"Condos?" Vito scoffed. "Who the hell's going to pay to live in an old gas tank?"

"Not the *tanks*, Vito. The *frames*. WilkinsonEyre transformed not one, not two, but three gas-holder frames into luxury apartments, and people are snapping them up."

Gino spoke up. "Where's WilkinsonEyre?"

"It's not a *where*, it's a what. They're an award-winning design firm out of London."

Vito rolled his eyes, "Jesus, Sean, this is Staten Island."

"Dad, *please* listen," Nick mumbled to himself.

Sean smiled his best political smile, "Let me help you all understand the concept. We'll clean this place up and put in a mall and a hospital center. That way, we can relieve the overcrowding at Staten Island U and the Richmond Medical Center. This sixty-six-acre wasteland will transform into one of the most lucrative pieces of prime real estate on our island."

"Impressive," said Scott Kantor, standing next to Gino Romano, and raising his hands as if to stop the flood of Sean's zeal. "But you're missing a major issue."

"And what's that, Scott?"

"The polls."

Sean shrugged, "Last I checked, they predict an easy win."

The banker, Darren, nodded, "It's only the primary, Sean. The numbers for November's general election are a lot less impressive. There's a likelihood of a Republican loss if you're the R on the ticket. Julia Ramirez is polling significantly higher."

Fucking millennial.

"If that happens," Gino said. "We can kiss our agenda, all this construction money, and the lofty contracts goodbye."

Sean's smile was condescending, "That's not gonna happen, Gino."

Scott pushed on, "Voters actually remember things, Sean. Your two-year prison stint for bribery, for example."

Darren palmed his smooth forehead, "It's the final two weeks to the primary. You love Staten Island, Sean. Do the right thing and bow out now. Just consider the fallout if you lose."

"First of all, I'm not bowing out. I *don't* bow, Darren," Sean growled. "Second, I *will* win the primary *and* the general." Catching Darren's eye roll and Nick's grimace, Sean snarled inwardly.

Gino stepped forward, "You're talking about developing sites that are the Rock's hallowed ground, Sean. Forty-three workers died here in the '73 explosion."

"So, we'll erect a nice monument."

"There's talk you're working to wrangle a deal through the federal government to convert Fort Wadsworth into a large upper-tier development," Nancy Briggs added.

Sean regarded the woman with some amusement. Privately, he opined the New York Economic Corporation should change its hiring practices; Nancy would make a sexy librarian, but a lady bean counter? Women and numbers were like oil and water to Sean.

Outwardly, though, Sean beamed at the woman. "Yes, I'm considering Fort Wadsworth. It's another eyesore that can be a gorgeous, income-producing asset."

Morris Moulton looked at him askance, "Have you no respect for the historical importance of the fort?"

"Forget history," Gino added. "How about common decency? For God's sake, even without the historical merit, these places are sites of horrific crimes. What's next on your list, Sean, the Farm Colony?"

That struck a bit close to the bone. *Why the hell are they pushing back like this? Hallowed ground, my ass. You wanna preserve history, Gino? How's about we open up a theme park and name one of the coasters after Son of Cropsey?*

Aloud, Sean declared, "There's crime because they are run-down trash heaps. All the more reason to tear down and gentrify."

Nancy spoke up again, "People are on edge enough without you blustering about bulldozing history. It's an easy target for the Dems to point out you're depriving the island of tourist revenue."

"It's time for people to move forward, Nance. Staten Islanders are so stuck in the past. Or am I the only one who sees that?" Sean pushed back.

Nancy Briggs and Morris Moulton exchanged glances, then moved into the shade of an outbuilding to engage in a dialogue with Vito Marino.

They could yak all they wanted. Sean had no intention of questioning his own objectives. There was only one way things were going to go, and he had laid it out plain and simple. He'd brought the group together in the scalding heat to show them the future, but clearly the bunch of pansy asses had no imagination.

Darren approached, "Sean, we need to talk."

Talk, yeah. Let's talk, you candy ass. What the fuck kind of tie is that? Your boyfriend sew that for you?

Sean, still smiling, put his hand on Darren's shoulder, "What's on your mind, Darren?"

CHAPTER THIRTEEN

TUESDAY, LIQUID GAS PLANT, ARTHUR KILL ROAD

A HAZY VAPOR AROSE OFF THE TWO LNG TANKS IN THE afternoon heat. Darren Rivers wished he wasn't wearing a suit. He felt Sean's large hand on his shoulder and saw the stink-eye he gave his lavender tie.

Asshole. At least I don't carry a loaded weapon shoved down my pants to feel like a big man.

Darren knew trying to reason with Sean was a fool's errand. He also knew the catastrophic reality of why Sean *had* to pull the plug on his political campaign—and fast. Sean was alienating his base more every day with his arrogance. And in a city like New York, professing any kind of conservative values made you automatically ripe for criticism, whether valid or not.

"You *really* don't see the damage you'll cause the party locally if you stay in the race?"

"No, I do not. Tell me again how *my* plan for revitalizing Staten Island is going to damage anything."

"You have an image problem, Sean." *This guy is as unpopular as Biden.*

Sean removed his hand from Darren's shoulder. "What image problem? Two years at Club Fed on a trumped-up bribery charge. Kiss my ass. You want to know who has an image problem? Staten Island has a goddamn image problem. We're more than the Forgotten Borough. We're the Beggars' Borough. We are New York City's unwanted stepchild, sniffing for crumbs under the table. When this plan goes through and that subway line comes in, this borough will be the jewel in the NYC crown. Revenue from the taxes alone will line the city's pockets so much they'll wonder why they'd not done any of this sooner."

Scott Kantor and Gino Romano approached, which put an end to Darren's attempted intervention. Sean was quick to shake hands with them.

"So great you guys came out."

Scott accepted Sean's hand, "We came out with the hope of convincing you to listen to reason."

"Scott, you're a great guy and a great Republican, but for a lawyer, you really gotta grow a pair and stop worrying about what other people think. People are sheep. They don't think for themselves. They go with the wave."

"What makes you think you're gonna make any waves?" Gino asked.

Sean narrowed his eyes, his Clint Eastwood squint, "Because everybody likes a winner, Gino, and I'm a winner. Delafield Development is a winner. I know how to run a business better than anyone; I know how to run a city. You think people want *more* Democratic bullshit? They don't. They want strong business and strong leadership, not some whiny little bitch with zero experience."

Darren couldn't hold his tongue, "This isn't the 1950s, Sean. Women are as strong and capable as any man, and they have a strong voice. People want to vote for real strength, not bluster, and not some future *hashtag #MeToo* roadkill."

Sean's jaw bunched, "Men are men. Men gape at women. Men like to touch women. That's life. End of sensitivity training." Sean nodded to

Nancy Briggs heading back to her car with her colleagues. "Prime example. Blouse is a little too open, skirt is a little high to show some thigh. Can't get it done *behind* the desk—get it done *on* the desk. Hell, they're probably headed back to town now for a little two on one at a Motel 6."

"Jesus, Sean." Gino made a sign of the cross.

Darren was well used to pricks like Sean Delafield. Locker room talk was the least of his worries. But if Sean was going down, Darren sure as hell wasn't going down with him.

"Gentlemen, you need to relax and trust the party vote. Republicans are tired of side-stepping and soft-shoeing. Our time has come, and I'm the man to get us there," Sean insisted.

"Frankly," Scott said. "I'm not entirely on board with your plans to revitalize Staten Island. To start with, I don't want a subway line here that connects us to the rest of New York."

"You prefer being the Forgotten Borough, do you, Scott?"

"I prefer being the *close-knit borough*. Nobody has the community-mindedness we have here. The Verrazzano from Brooklyn or the ferry from Manhattan have worked just fine since the first settlement."

"I don't know, Scott," Gino rubbed his chin. "I go back and forth to Manhattan a lot to the wholesalers. The ferry can be a bitch, and I think it'd be nice to be connected to the rest of the city and not feel so isolated."

"The ferry is free, Gino. And, as for being connected to the city. Connected to what? The grit, grime, and crime? Staten Island has whole-salers—local ones," Scott made his point loudly, his face reddening.

Gino huffed, "You think we don't have crime here?"

Scott shook his head. "Not like Manhattan."

"Scott, come on, do the per-capita math."

"Gino, you love Manhattan? Move. Me? I don't feel isolated. I feel lucky to have what we have, and I know the majority of Staten Islanders feel the same way."

Darren had heard enough; the truth needed to be said, "Look, before Scott starts waving the borough flag, forget the subway line—that isn't happening in any of our lifetimes. It comes down to this: The primary is less than two weeks away. We want, we *need* to be able to make the switch and give the nod to Julia Ramirez. With her, we have a strong chance. With you, Sean, the Democrats will destroy us."

"Wake up, Darren," Sean scoffed. "You think your best chance is with some fucking Latina bitch? You think she's got vision beyond pressing two for Spanish? I wonder whose desk she had to bend over to get on the ticket."

Gino threw his hands in the air, "Sean, you're just making the point for us. Your sexist and racist attitudes, your prison record, the new rumors surfacing—they're all stacking up to make you a very unattractive candidate."

Scott glanced from Gino to Sean, "What rumors?"

Sean's mouth pulled back to a smirk, "They're bullshit, Scott."

Gino turned to Scott, "Last week, a young woman came forward and accused Sean of sexual misconduct."

Darren fought to remain calm. He hoped to dear God the man hadn't grabbed the woman by the pussy. Frustrated, overheating, Darren slipped off his jacket, no longer bothered about showing the spreading pit stains on his shirt, and said, "She's filing suit. Claims the incident took place while she was under the age of seventeen . . . and working for Sean. She said there are others."

Scott turned on Sean, "When were you planning on telling us?"

"I don't have to tell you shit. Any of you. That stupid girl's accusation is totally without merit. I'm not sure I even met her. She was some summer intern who worked with Nick. She's probably got daddy fantasies."

Scott was about to blow a gasket, "You've got a big problem. You're toxic property, Sean."

"I'm beyond reproach, Scott. I work with Father Stephen's Opportunities for Today's Youth to give disadvantaged kids summer jobs. I see an application, I give some money-grabbing attention whore a break, and this is the thanks I get?"

Darren folded his jacket over his arm, "Whatever her motives, it's got the potential to explode. The backlash will screw us all. The girl claims she was fifteen at the time."

"It's totally unsubstantiated."

Darren kept on pushing, "Are you suggesting we wait until the claim *is* substantiated? Until others come forward? It'll be too fucking late then to do anything but kiss everything goodbye."

Sean raised his hands like some smarmy televangelist, "There is nothing to substantiate. I never touched *any* girls, underage, or otherwise."

"We're done," Gino waved off any further discussion. "I've stood out here long enough. You don't have the backing of the *Staten Island Advance*, and without that you don't have the muscle to win. Throw in the rumors and the prison term and we all go down in flames. And trust me, Sean, we are not about to let that happen."

Sean had no comeback. He simply stared at Gino as if he was crazy. Darren straightened his tie and cleared his throat. For his own sake, he desperately hoped they'd finally gotten through to the impenetrable Sean Delafield.

Breaking the pregnant pause, Sean checked his watch and declared, "I have a campaign meeting in fifteen. If you'll excuse me." And with that, he turned and headed off to the overgrown car park.

Darren stood in place and watched Scott and Gino leave in one direction and Sean in the other, which left himself and Nick alone in the shadow of the rusting gas tanks.

"We gotta talk," Nick said, a pained expression on his handsome face.

"Here?"

"I don't think either of us enjoys being in this position, Darren. I stand behind my father and you don't. That kinda throws a wrench into things."

Things.

"Is this because you think he's the best candidate or because he's your father?" Darren went straight for the jugular. "Listen, Nick, I can't tell you what to think or what to do. Just please don't judge me for what *I* have to do."

Reaching out, Nick touched Darren's shoulder, "I think we can get through this."

"What makes you so damn certain?"

"Because I love you."

Darren was stunned. "I love you, too." The words were bittersweet. He'd waited so long to hear them, but he wasn't so sure he and Nick would get through it. Not if they remained on opposing sides of Sean Delafield's political ambitions.

CHAPTER FOURTEEN

TUESDAY, GREEK ISLES RESTAURANT

DAVINA WAS RUNNING LATE AGAIN. SHE'D AGREED TO MEET Joe for dinner at Greek Isles at 6:30 . He waited patiently outside beneath the GRAND OPENING banner with its neatly drawn map of Greece. The blue awning over the front doors was threaded with twinkling white lights, creating a warm and inviting interior. Joe waited patiently with a smile on his handsome face, and not for the first time that day. Davina pushed away the thought that he was too good for her.

"I thought you'd stood me up," Joe said before he gave Davina a quick kiss on the lips.

"I would never." Davina executed a 360-degree turn to show off the lacy black top she'd scored at a local thrift shop.

A couple of people brushed by them; they excused themselves as they hurried into the restaurant. The smell of Greek lamb and tzatziki wafted out from the door.

Stepping inside, Davina and Joe were greeted by a stocky man with a ruddy olive complexion and dark bushy beard. He approached with open arms, "Ah, my friends. Welcome!" Stavros Scala embraced Joe in a tight hug and then pulled his head down to kiss him on both cheeks, "It is good to see you!"

"Good to see you, too, Stavros. The new place looks good."

Stavros turned to Davina and embraced her as he had with Joe; the Greek stank of cologne. Recoiling in horror, Davina tried to pull away, but Stavros wouldn't let her go. She felt his warm breath rasp in her ear.

"Stop!" She pushed hard against the man's chest and broke free. She bolted from the restaurant, almost knocking over an elderly couple on their way in.

"Well, pardon me!" the elderly man admonished as he checked to see if his wife was all right.

"Davina!" Joe ran to catch up. "Wait! What the hell happened back there?"

Davina was close to tears, gasping for air, desperate to get the cloying stink out of her head. "He grabbed me. Why did he do that?" Leaning against her car's hood for support, Davina fumbled in her pocket for the keys.

"Stavros is a hugger," was all Joe had to offer.

"I have to get out of here, Joe. I'm so sorry." Davina clambered into her car, gunned the engine, and burned rubber exiting the lot. In her rearview, she saw Joe dashing toward his silver Beemer.

She hoped he'd just give up on her and go home . . . and yet, she hoped he'd follow her.

By the time Davina got home, the feeling of utter panic had dissipated, but she was still agitated and anxious. She propped herself against the kitchen counter, clutching a bottle of water, trembling, trying hard to talk herself down.

Hurried footsteps on the stairs belonged to Joe. She'd left the door unlocked, expecting him, *hoping* for him.

"Are you all right?" Joe approached her slowly, as if confronting a cornered wild animal.

Davina nodded, "I nearly ran you down. Sorry."

"I'm fine—worried about you, though."

"When Stavros hugged me, I had a panic attack. I think his cologne triggered it. Ever since Joy's memorial, I feel like I'm losing my mind, Joe."

Joe took hold of her hand, a sweet, gentle gesture. "Sit. Please?"

Davina nodded and seated herself. Joe pulled a chair around and sat facing her, their knees nearly touching.

"Talk to me," his voice was soft, soothing.

"I'm scared, Joe. I'm freaking out at stupid things and I don't know why. Stavros made me feel trapped, *suffocated*."

"You don't like being held, Davina, but Stavros didn't know that. He's just a friendly guy."

"This isn't about him, it's about me. Even feeling his breath on me freaked me out." She gripped Joe's hand tightly. "There was a guy in Blue Star who walked past me wearing the same cologne and I fainted. Gino had to help me up."

Joe's face paled visibly. "Why are you only just telling me this now?"

"I dunno. I didn't want to freak you out."

Joe squeezed her hand for reassurance. "I'm worried about you, Davina. I care about you—about what happens to you."

"I know, I know. I . . ." She looked deep into his eyes. "Have you ever tried to remember something—something you saw or experienced—but you can't remember *all* of it? Just tiny bits and pieces?"

"Sure, of course."

"That's what I've felt like for years, Joe. Like there's something right there at the front of my brain, but I just can't reach it." Davina choked back tears. However much she wanted Joe to understand, it was impossible to put all she was feeling into words. She was going to have to tell him things she wasn't comfortable sharing.

"Why are you with me?" she deflected. "You have so much going on. Your life is all planned out nicely. Why me?"

"I guess I can't resist a challenge," Joe said with a fond smile. "Especially a beautiful challenge who can kick my butt."

Davina took her hand from his. "I'm serious, Joe. You deserve to be with someone who has her shit together, not this train wreck."

"I love trains." Joe reached across to caress Davina's cheek. "I love *you*."

"And I love you, but . . ."

Joe's smile dropped at the word *but*.

"I do love you, Joe. You know that. But I've got things about me I need to fix. I'm so frustrated with Staten Island. I can't stand living here. I feel like I'm *suffocating*."

That word again.

"You want to leave? How could you? I love the Rock."

"I know." Davina glanced down at her hands.

"I can't even imagine living anyplace else. Where would you want to live if not here?"

Jesus, he thinks this is Valhalla or something. "Manhattan. It's my dream to live in Manhattan. Even a studio the size of a closet would do."

Joe grimaced, "Manhattan? Seriously? That's the last place I'd want to live. I want my house to have a front yard with grass I gotta mow and shrubs I gotta trim. My kids should be able to ride their bikes safely in the street. Manhattan is no place to raise a family, Davina. Besides, my family is from Staten Island. My work—my career—is here, and I have strong ties to the community and local businesses."

Davina stared at the bottle of water on the table. "I could never have a family. I don't know the first thing about families. Not good ones, anyway."

It was a painful truth Davina always reminded him of, but Joe had a one-track mind and ignored her.

He just shook his head and gave her an I-don't-get-it smile. "I'm sorry. I've got an early morning meeting." He stood up, his chair scraping on the linoleum. "Are you going to be okay if I go?"

Davina gave him a reassuring nod.

Joe leaned down to kiss her, lingered when she didn't pull back, and then was on his way out.

Alone in the kitchen, Davina held her head in her hands. *How much longer? How much fucking longer before I get a grip on myself?*

CHAPTER FIFTEEN

TUESDAY, DAVINA'S APARTMENT

Davina's stomach growled. Woefully empty, it reminded her that she and Joe hadn't gotten a chance to eat. There was a little coffee left from the morning. Maybe she'd just have that with some milk in it—and a cigarette. That sounded good.

Coffee and a cigarette.

Millie came out of her room, coffee cup in hand like she'd read her roommate's mind. "That boy is one helluva catch, D."

"I didn't know you were home."

"So, what's the deal? You gonna marry his ass?"

Davina sat down. "The best thing I can do for Joe is *not* marry him."

"He's smart enough to decide for himself what's best for him, and he's decided that's you."

"I love him, Mil. But it's better for us both if we're not together for the long haul."

"Right. Handsome, kind, successful, patience of a damn saint, undemanding. Yep, you don't want that for too long." Millie drained the last of the coffee and put the cup in the sink.

Davina smiled with some reluctance, "Yeah, he'd make a great husband."

"So? What's the problem?"

"Sex. Or absence thereof."

Millie sat down beside Davina. "You two haven't done it?"

Davina fingered scratch marks on the table. "Yeah, we have. I mean, we *sort of* have . . ." *Why is this so fucking hard to say? You're not a child. Just say it.*

"Sort of?"

Davina squirmed in her seat. "That's the problem, Mil. I . . . *can't.*"

Millie pursed her lips. "What do you mean you can't? You're saying you never came with Joe?"

Davina shook her head. "No. It feels good and I like the connection, you know, but . . . it's weird because he can't be on top of me, he can't put his arms around me."

Millie's dark eyes widened, "You've *never* come? Ever?" Millie leaned against the wooden chair. "Not even once? With anybody?"

Davina lowered her head. "Despite my reputation, Joe's the only guy I've ever been with."

"What's the problem? His technique needs refining?"

Davina shrugged. "I can't let myself get that . . . *naked.* Inside, I mean. In here." She pressed a hand to her heart. "I mean, I want to, but then I can't stand being held or touched like that. I hate when people put their hands on me, and the idea of somebody lying on top of me is just..." Davina squeezed her eyes shut and shuddered.

"So, how do you cope at work?"

"That's different. The touching is quick and it's pushing away, not pulling in. Plus, I'm in control. I'm not at the mercy of—" Breaking off, Davina shook her head.

"I never heard anything like this, Davina. Might you be one of those asexuals?"

"Nope. I'm definitely attracted to men—to Joe in particular—but when it comes to actually *having* sex . . . I flat-out panic." Davina got up and went over to the sink. She ran the cold water and splashed her face.

She patted her face dry with a handful of paper towels from the roll on the counter. "Even *thinking* about it scares me."

Davina had never gotten into the details of her past memories with Millie, though she knew her roommate would listen and not judge; she was just so exhausted even thinking about it.

But the time felt right.

A deep breath.

"I think I was raped when I was twelve, Mil. Nobody believed me so I pushed it all down and got it out in kicks and punches. Since the rape last week at Wadsworth, and now this thing with Joy, I just can't stop the feelings coming back to the surface. If I wake up with Joe's arm around me, I want to run. I know how fucked up that sounds because he's the guy I love."

"It's not as fucked up as you think, D," Millie told her. "You went through something terrible, but you're working on yourself 'cause that's what needs to be done. That's why you work at the gym, right? 'Cause without it, you'd be weak. It's why you go to NA. You are the strongest person I know, D."

Davina sat back down. "Thanks for that, Mil."

"You know, when I was growing up and started to eye up the girls, I thought I was fucked. A Black woman who likes girls—ain't nobody gonna accept me now. But I'm a fighter, too, D. So, I say I'm gonna work to accept myself every day. I'm gonna fight the hate and I'm going to live my life."

Davina smiled warmly, "I admire you for that."

"You got your own mountain to climb. You can't escape your past. Sooner or later, you've gotta face it and face it down." Millie lit up a cigarette, took a puff, and pointed the burning tip at Davina. "What you need is *answers*. Did you meet with Geoff?"

"I did, thank you," Davina said. "And I'm gonna get my answers, Mil. Then maybe people will believe me."

"Well, if it helps any, I believe you." Millie stood up. "Sorry to do this, but I got a hot date. You gonna be okay?"

"Yeah." Davina didn't much relish being left alone. "Good luck."

"Don't need luck—I got *charisma*."

After Millie left the apartment, Davina stayed put. Her stomach complained anew, so she decided to make a peanut butter sandwich. The air from the AC unit in the living room window was pleasantly cool; Davina focused upon the feel of it on her skin as she sipped cold coffee and ate her sandwich.

Joe texted her.

> Thinking about U, babe. Hope you're better.

> Thx. Feeling a little better. Made a 〜. Sorry abt tonite.

> We'll reschedule. Love you.

> Ditto. Talk soon.

Davina set her phone on the table, facedown. How was it possible to be in love and still feel a dark, empty void inside?

CHAPTER SIXTEEN

GEOFF WONG SAT AT HIS DESK. THE DAY HAD BEEN productive since his brief talk with Davina Speers. He'd made a bunch of phone calls and spent a good deal of time online and in the paper's database in the name of research. He had one last call to make that he knew would be fruitful.

"Frank?"

Geoff could almost see Frankie Armitage grimacing as he said, "Wong."

"I have a question."

"Go on."

"Those recent attacks on young girls."

Frank's voice was a growl, "Dreadful business. What about them?"

"Are there cases the media and public aren't seeing? Or aspects being withheld?"

Frank's hesitant silence was as good as an admission. "Come on, Wong. I'm nearly retired. A law enforcement pension is a good thing— don't make me lose it."

"Totally off the record, Frank. I'm not looking to write an exposé. I get why the cops have to keep some stuff quiet. But this is important."

Frank grumbled, "There are always rapes, Wong. But these two are... *different*."

Well, that was one question answered. Geoff deeply inhaled. "That's it? You can't tell me what makes them different? What's the NYPD not saying?"

"They're not saying. So, I'm not saying."

"Fine," Geoff hid his frustration well. "What about the similar attacks ten years ago—the Son of Cropsey cases? Ancient history, right? Is there some telltale sign the rapist left—?"

Frank grunted then said, "He signed his work."

That revelation sent an unpleasant tingle up Geoff's spine. "*Signed* his work? How?"

"I really can't say. I mean it, Wong."

"Are the new cases signed too?"

Geoff's answer was a resounding *click* as Frank hung up.

Geoff immediately fired up his computer to search the article database to find out who'd worked on which stories—maybe they were still around. The system was down. Geoff leaned back in his chair, hands cradling his neck. He was going to have to go old school.

The stark concrete basement of the *Advance* was a treasure trove of information for anyone with the time and patience to look. it felt like strolling through a tomb, which was probably why it was often referred to as such. Geoff would have to rummage through the old print editions carefully packed away in boxes and stored on shelves. All were marked by month, year, and neighborhood. Here were dusty, wall-to-wall references to Staten Island's history of murders, rapes, and drug busts. It was laborious, tedious work, and not for the faint of heart . . . or arachnophobic.

"I didn't think you ventured down here." Justin Cooke, one of the sports reporters, glanced up at Geoff from a microfiche reader over in the corner. "What brings you to the Land of the Dead?"

"The network is on the fritz again." Geoff walked by and waved a hand in greeting. "I have a little fact-checking to do."

Geoff didn't bother with microfiche. The images were always grainy, scanned at some weird angle, or sections were redacted on somebody's orders. He much preferred the paper files, as they included cross references to boxes containing the reporter's original notes.

That Frank hadn't been forthcoming wasn't a total surprise, considering Riley was spearheading the investigation into the new attacks and didn't like his actions questioned. Geoff had asked Riley during the most recent police presser about possible connections between the Todt Hill and Fort Wadsworth attacks and Son of Cropsey, and Riley had shot him down so fast. Geoff *knew* the cop was hiding something.

But just because Riley showed no interest in revisiting the past didn't mean it was going to go away quietly.

Geoff spent twenty minutes of searching to find the shelves for the right year; the *Advance*'s archives were in constant flux as each year's editions were brought down for boxing and shelving. In a perfect world, since everything was—theoretically—digitized and stored on the newspaper's massive RAID array, the physical editions should have been warehoused off-site. But the paper's hierarchy was tight-fisted, which meant every edition since the inception of the paper was kept onsite, which made for an overcrowded storage site.

After finally locating the year he was looking for, Geoff used his phone to brush away a fat, hairy spider and pulled two boxes from the shelf, setting them on a nearby table. He rolled over a chair and began fishing out the papers. Since Son of Cropsey dominated the front pages, he was spared the chore of riffling through each edition. As a result, in less than two hours, he'd pulled half a dozen boxes of newspapers and journalists' notes from the shelves and managed to piece together an alarming puzzle.

Cross-referencing the archived records with what meager information he could glean from his off-the-record police sources on the current attacks, Geoff picked out a number of striking similarities: the type of chokehold the guy used, and the old, abandoned locations he typically chose—although the Todt attack had been at the victim's home. Geoff wondered about what Frank had told him about Son of Cropsey signing his work. Since Frank clearly had no intention of spilling, it occurred to Geoff that Davina Speers might be a good person to ask.

One article in particular caught Geoff's attention: a girl—name withheld, of course—aged fourteen, sexually assaulted and left for dead at the Great Kills train station. The attacker had used a choke hold to render the girl unconscious, so her memory was vague. She'd definitely been sexually manhandled.

Geoff pulled off a sticky note attached beneath the headline and snapped a photo of the article with his phone. Only when he returned the sticky note did he realize what it said: *JS, 14.*

Joy Sheridan?

The age would be right. But the date of the attack was *after* Rob Cox —Son of Cropsey—had been arrested. If Davina's story was solid, she'd been raped after the fact as well, and now there were two more chokehold rape victims with only piecemeal memories of the actual assault.

Geoff scratched his head and glanced around the room. How was it no one had put those pieces together before? Davina Speers might just be onto something after all. The cops were calling the current attacks random, but that strained credulity. There were too many similarities. Either they were dealing with a copycat or they'd gotten the wrong guy ten years ago and the actual Son of Cropsey was back. If so, where had he been, and why start up again?

And, had he signed his work?

Davina Speers had propelled him into a bigger story than she realized, and Geoff wasn't inclined to let it go. He still had time to get the story in before the paper went to press. He could lead with it in the morning edition.

Returning to his office with a wealth of new information and an earth-shattering exposé to write, there was one more thing Geoff needed to do. He picked up his phone and called the police department.

A loud, exaggerated sigh, "I've got no new information for you, Wong."

"It's an easy one this time, Frank. A criminal record."

"Go on."

"Davina Speers. S-P-E-E-R-S."

"Gimme a minute."

Geoff leaned back in his chair, still holding the phone to his ear. The hold music was some homogenized smooth jazz.

"Wong?" Frank came back a few minutes later. "So . . . Davina Speers." The sound of pages being flipped.

"It's a long one, huh?"

"She's been picked up for a lot of stuff—shoplifting a pack of smokes, buying pot . . ."

"That ain't so bad."

"That's just the juvenile rap." Frank cleared his throat, and Geoff leaned forward in his chair. "She spent a lot of time on the streets—a junkie. Brought in more than once for solicitation, culminating in a bust at the XXX-TASY Gentleman's Club."

"I remember the place fondly." It was Geoff's attempt at humor; in reality, it wasn't the kind of place he'd choose to frequent.

"She was an underage stripper—nice."

"Damn." No wonder Davina was leery about crying rape. "And lately?"

"Let me see." Frank flipped through more pages. "It's like a goddamn novel, Wong. Multiple stints in rehab, but it seems like this last time *might* have taken. No arrests in over a year—although she came pretty fucking close at Joy Sheridan's funeral."

"I heard."

"Caused a scene, and Riley dragged her sorry ass out of there. She was probably high on something—you know how her sort are."

"Thanks, Frank. You're the best."

Hanging up the phone, Geoff considered Davina's background. She was far too young to have been through so much, and her checkered past was coming back to bite her in the ass.

But, could he trust her? Davina Speers was the most puzzling combination of tough and vulnerable that Geoff had ever encountered. There was an element of danger to her he found both appealing and unnerving; just being in the same room with her was exhilarating.

Davina could be onto something about Joy. If the Son of Cropsey was back, Davina was the only one making the connection.

She could be the key that busts the case wide open.

Awakening his MacBook from its slumber, Geoff typed up the article with painstaking detail. Once done, he looked up at the clock and saw it was eleven minutes past 10:00 p.m. After reaching over to the information Davina left on his desk, Geoff picked up his cell phone.

CHAPTER SEVENTEEN

TUESDAY, DAVINA'S APARTMENT

IT WAS LATE.

Davina had cleaned up after her Spartan dinner and was just about ready to call it a day when her cell phone rang. Assuming it was Joe checking in, she didn't bother checking the screen and answered sweetly, "You love me and wish me sweet dreams?"

"Hey, we only just met."

"Who is this?"

"Geoff Wong."

"Oh." Davina was glad the reporter couldn't see her bright red face.

"You were right about your friend having been attacked ten years ago."

Wow. The guy really did cut to the chase. "I was?"

"You sound surprised."

"I wasn't expecting you to find something so fast."

"She was attacked at the Great Kills train station." He paused, as if for effect. "Listen, I wanted to let you know I've written the story up for the morning edition. The headline's going to be 'Is Son of Cropsey Back?'"

"Are you asking my permission?"

"No. It's a question the public deserves to have answered. Rob Cox is still in prison for the Son of Cropsey attacks. I guess you've already figured out what that means. There's no way the recent attacks are random. There'll be a way to tie the two together."

Davina rubbed at her forehead with her thumb—around and around in a circle. She was about to tell Geoff she might have something when he interrupted her thoughts.

"Meet me at the Boro 5 Diner at 10:00 a.m. tomorrow?" Geoff asked.

"I have a boxing class. How's 11:00?"

"No can do. Mandatory staff meeting."

"Okay—12:30?"

"Yeah, that should work."

"I think I'll head to the station before we meet. Take a look around."

"Why?"

"I want to see for myself where Joy was attacked. I can take a few pictures if you want."

Geoff laughed, "You sound like a budding investigative reporter."

"Nah," Davina replied. "I'm just morbidly curious."

Hanging up on the reporter, Davina wondered what kind of pure hell Joy had lived through since her assault. Perhaps one so filled with despair that she was driven to take her own life. Davina knew from bitter experience that even when the memory of something so terrible was hazy and uncertain, it still had the power to haunt.

Maybe if I'd known back then, we could have helped each other.

For the first time in over twelve months, Davina had the craving for the soft, pleasantly dazed feeling that went along with drugging memories into oblivion. Surely, given the circumstances, one hit wouldn't be too bad?

Quickly, Davina tried to thrust the craving down. She forced herself to remember beyond the sweet, obliterating buzz and to how she'd awake the next morning feeling like shit, thoughts dominated by her next hit.

She called her sponsor, "Sorry it's late, Charlie. You got a sec?" Davina clamped the phone tight to her ear as she walked into her bedroom and lay on her bed.

"Of course," Charlene's voice was calm, soothing, and made the craving go away.

"Something doesn't feel right."

"You want to use?"

Davina examined the chrysanthemum tattoo on her wrist. How fucked up had she been when she got it? Enough to not remember getting it, that's how much. "Yeah. I was thinking about it. It's been a rough coupla days."

"You're stronger than your cravings, Davina. Trace it back. What do you *really* need?"

Davina thought for a moment or two. "I guess... truth, reality. I need to know what happened to me. I want the people I care about to know. To *believe* me."

"I know. Millie knows. Think about who else needs to know and just tell them. Remember, though, sometimes things happen that are never fully explained, and we're left with unanswered questions. It makes us all a little crazy."

I feel that.

"Crazy—thanks for that, Charlie."

"You use sarcasm to defend yourself. Does it work, Davina?"

"Most of the time. I'm in step four, Charlie. I'm supposed to be taking inventory, and people think I'm taking inventory of something that didn't happen."

"We've talked about gaslighting, Davina. Remember the exercise we did a week ago? Reframing the past? Did you do it?"

"I . . . started."

"You didn't finish?"

"You can't rewrite the past. The past is its own thing."

"Not rewrite it. *Reframe* it. The past is in your mind. Your imagination."

So, I'm gaslighting myself? Is that even a thing?

Charlie was silent for a moment and then said, "Finish the project, Davina—*tonight*. Take out your notebook and reframe the past. Take ownership of it. It'll make the cravings go away—I promise. Call me tomorrow and read to me what you wrote."

"I will. Thanks, Charlie."

"It's what I'm here for."

Davina hung up. She was grateful for Charlie, even if she didn't always appreciate the guidance and wisdom the woman dished out.

Davina got up from her bed and flipped on the desk lamp. Sitting at her little secondhand desk, she took out the notebook she brought to every NA meeting. It contained mostly scribbles, doodles, and fragments of thoughts she'd seen fit to jot down. While she was determined to not be a failure at NA, Davina came up against a shit ton of internal resistance; it didn't help that the meetings were held in a fucking church.

She opened the notebook to a blank page, picked up a pen, and wrote at the top, *Reframing the Past*.

She stared at that page for a good fifteen minutes before finally writing:

Something terrible happened to me when I was twelve. I was raped. In my own room, where I should have been safe. I know this, but everyone tries to make me think I'm imagining it—or worse, that I have a disorder, or I'm trying to punish someone, or get attention any way I can. Okay, not everyone, *but the people who were close to me at the time. The ones I counted on to keep me safe—my family. One minute I'm so sure of what happened, the next, I'm second-guessing myself. And when that happens, I freak out. Every damn day. I feel like I'm losing my mind. I wish I was numb. How in God's name do I reframe* that?

Davina bit into the cap of her pen.

I reframe it by claiming it was for a reason. I was attacked for a reason. Joy was attacked for a reason.

Davina put the pen down, leaned over, and pressed her forehead on the page, as if she might impart her thoughts and emotions directly onto it. She closed her eyes.

What possible reason could require anything that fucked up?

So, the real attacker might face justice?

CHAPTER EIGHTEEN

WEDNESDAY, STATEN ISLAND FARM COLONY

Manor Heights was silent, but the ghosts of the Staten Island Farm Colony were screaming. They were such delicious screams, but they'd soon be silenced if that monster, Sean Delafield, had anything to say about it. The crooked politician had purchased the entire forty-six-acre site, including the abandoned Seaview Children's Hospital, Willowbrook State School, and a few other decrepit buildings. He had ambitious plans for it all.

The Colony had existed since the 1800s, a sort of bucolic debtor's prison designed to provide housing for indigent populations in exchange for their labor—mostly growing crops to feed dependents of city institutions. It had long been the home of infamy; the screams rumored to come from the Colony had spawned legends.

And now the institution was a literal ruin of its former self, a ghost comprised of decaying brick buildings smothered by encroaching woodland and littered with discarded metal bed frames, crumbling stone, and wind-blown litter.

A killer, given the moniker "Cropsey," had prowled the wooded landscape way back in the 1920s. He'd murdered a seven-year-old boy and snatched other children to sate his nefarious tastes. Then, suddenly, he'd stopped. Whoever he was, he wasn't the first Cropsey and wouldn't be the last.

Like everyone else on the Rock, Delafield knew all about the rash of disappearances back in the 1970s and at least one rape, for which Andre Rand was growing old and frail behind bars. Then, there came the spate of sexual assaults and rapes of young girls a decade or so ago. They'd been attributed to Rob Cox, once an orderly at Willowbrook, then a hardened drug dealer, and subsequently a resident of Monroe County Penitentiary, which was to be his home until 2037.

The media, ever hungry for a sensationalist spin on a big story, had been quick to christen Cox, "Son of Cropsey." But the man had not helped his cause in the least. He'd appeared every inch the serial rapist and killer at his trial; he had those wild, crazy eyes and sprayed spittle when he spoke. In the end, he'd taken a plea bargain that saved his sorry ass from the needle.

It was bizarre that the Farm Colony still existed, even in an abandoned, decaying form. Vacant for well over forty years, it was a sorry shell of its former self, its abandoned buildings crumbling and haunted. Perhaps it was the ghosts of the tortured souls themselves that caused every redevelopment plan to fall through, and maybe they'd do the same to Sean Delafield's scheme to turn the site into some disgusting, park-like, multi-use complex.

The police, the parents, everyone spoke of the ghosts as if they were victims. They were not. They had called to Andre Rand and the prior bearers of the name Cropsey just as they called out now. They were as much perpetrators as those who committed such barbaric acts on their behalf.

Just like fourteen-year-old Seraphina Bellano.

She was curled in a ball in the corner of one of the crumbling rooms of the abandoned children's hospital; her balled-up denim jacket serving as a makeshift pillow. Blood was smeared across her forehead. In the cold light, the wet outline of Seraphina's blood resembled a smiley face. It was her own fault—she shouldn't have struggled when she was snatched from her family barbecue.

The walls that framed her tiny form were gaudy with graffiti, vivid in the silver moonlight filtering through the broken roof and shattered windows; smiley faces and elaborate tags overlooked the nest made especially for her.

Shadows skittered and danced around them both, waiting and watching, an ethereal audience. The rustling of summer leaves outside the broken windows sounded like faint applause, and the sharp tang of cologne hung heavy in the night air, overpowering enough to mask the dank reek of mold and decay.

Seraphina's leggings were pulled down just enough to show off the top of her pale buttocks; the neckline of her cheerful yellow shirt was torn down to her navel to reveal a lacy bra and flawless, porcelain skin.

She was absolute perfection.

Perfection stirred. She moaned slightly as she awoke from the drug that would, sadly, shred her memories of their time together.

"Seraphina?"

A sharp intake of breath, then Seraphina asked, "Where am I?"

"You're in the hospital." Low and calm, Son of Cropsey's voice was soft—no need to panic the girl.

Her eyes glistened beautifully in the moonlight as she fought to focus. "What hospital?"

"I'm going to take good care of you, Seraphina." A tug at the waist band of the girl's leggings and they slid with ease from her limp legs.

She tried to wriggle away, but the drug rendered her too uncoordinated to do much more than quiver. "No. No, please . . ."

"*Please?* My, you are eager, aren't you?"

"No, please *don't.*

It took little effort to flip the tiny girl onto her stomach and lay atop her—leaving just enough space to gently run a hand up the inside of her thighs. "Are you *begging?*"

"No!" Seraphina's voice echoed throughout the cavernous room. It was quickly silenced by an arm wrapped around her neck to form a V, her chin resting upon the elbow.

Seraphina wriggled and squealed, trying to get away. She let out a muffled scream, and the V had to be tightened.

"You can't escape. You really don't *want* to."

"I—I do! I want to go home!"

"No, Seraphina. We both know that's not true. You shouldn't lie. If you want to enjoy yourself with Cropsey, you must stop pretending. Quit screaming. If you don't, I'll have to put you to sleep again, and neither of us wants that." The arm tightened again to cut off more blood to her brain. "Do you want to sleep, Seraphina?"

Silence.

"Good girl." The grip relaxed on Seraphina's neck—just enough to allow her to stay conscious. That way, it would be so much more satisfying for both of them.

Seraphina's legs parted at the gentle insistence of one hand—she had slipped into compliance mode, just as they all did. Only, the others had all put up at least some resistance before the inevitable; Seraphina really did want it to happen.

The girl's moans were quite intoxicating as it eased inside her a fraction of an inch at a time—she was obviously pure, and pain was not the required response. Arching her back a little, she raised her hips as if to welcome the intrusion, the beginning of her womanhood, as it worked its way inside her.

Without warning, the moon's silver gleam was stained with the hot red and blue of flickering lights, followed by the cacophonous wail of sirens, hurried footsteps, voices chattering, and shouting.

"Police! Exit the building with your hands up!"

The footsteps were close—dangerously so.

"Shit!" It was a wrench to have to leave Seraphina's warm, accommodating body, especially as she was so obviously enjoying their special time together, but the only options were to run or be caught.

"Seraphina Bellano?" Fists pounding on the door accompanied the shouting; the door was old wood, its hinges all but rusted through. It didn't take too much effort for the cops to break it down, despite being nailed to its frame.

As the door crashed inward, Son of Cropsey slipped out through a broken window and ran off into the night.

And with that, Seraphina Bellano was all alone.

Some yards from the ruin, behind a screen of shrubs, Son of Cropsey sat in an abandoned, rusted wheelchair that had long ago lost its wheels and was concealed by the inky shadows cast by the old hospital. It was possible from that vantage point to surreptitiously watch the police go about the business of saving Seraphina and searching the darkness for her assailant.

"Search the grounds," the cop in charge was saying to a pair of uniformed officers who looked barely out of grad school. "And bring in the K9s—he can't have gotten far. Goddamn it! This is why we didn't come racing in with sirens."

"Detective Riley." Another uniform appeared from the gloom of the hospital building. "The girl—we've got something."

Of course, they'd found it. In the panic the cops had caused, there hadn't been enough time to retrieve it from the girl, and so it had remained inside her for the NYPD to discover and bag as evidence.

Still, it was even more frustrating to have been denied Seraphina's sweet flesh at such a crucial moment, but gratifying to have evaded capture yet again. Had the police arrived even a moment later, there would have been much less chance of escape.

And yet, the notion of capture, of being held to account, of being *stopped*, didn't induce the feeling of dread one might expect.

It was . . .

Exhilarating.

CHAPTER NINETEEN

WEDNESDAY, DAVINA'S APARTMENT

Davina awoke to a good-morning text from Joe. The time on the cellphone's screen told her it was 10:30 —she'd overslept.

Davina sprang out of bed and hurried to the kitchen. Millie stood by the coffeemaker as it steamed and gurgled; she assessed Davina disapprovingly.

"Sleep in your clothes again?"

"Yeah, I just sort of fell into bed."

"Coffee's almost ready. Looks like you need it, babe."

"Thank God."

"No, thank *Millie*. God had nothing to do with this. Though I suppose he did arrange for there to be coffee plants."

Davina poured herself a cup. "How was the date?"

"Promising. I took her dancing." Millie danced her way to the kitchen table where she sat down with a copy of *Baseball Digest*.

"I was having crazy cravings last night," Davina said.

Millie studied her with concern. "You call Charlene?"

"Yeah."

"I'm sorry I wasn't here for you."

"Shit, Mil. I didn't mean to make you feel guilty. You're fine. I'm glad you had a good time."

Millie snapped her fingers in the air. "Sho' did."

Davina smiled. Millie's good moods always seemed to make Davina feel better as if she drank them in through her skin. She got herself a bowl of Cheerios and settled at the table, munching loudly as she checked the news on her phone.

"Shit," Davina exclaimed.

Millie looked up. "Shit, what?"

"A fourteen-year-old girl was snatched from her backyard yesterday. She was taken out to the Farm Colony and sexually assaulted."

"It's on the news already?"

Davina shook her head. "Looks like somebody at Precinct 121 leaked it—there's just no integrity in the police force these days." She chuckled at her own joke and scrolled down the article. "It says here they found her in the old hospital. Her folks had sewn one of those mini-GPS trackers into her jacket, which was just as well because the guy threw her phone in the river."

"Sounds like something my parents would have done back in the day, if mini trackers had been around. They never trusted me—thought I'd turn out to be a dyke or something," she winked.

"The guy ran off when the cops turned up. Apparently, he told the girl he was Cropsey."

"Didn't they put that guy away years ago?"

"Supposedly. So, it's either a copycat—"

"Or your detective friend got the wrong guy."

"Yeah. Riley's gonna shit his pants when fingers start pointing. I always thought there was something off when they said they'd caught the guy. It all seemed too quick, too . . . *neat*."

"That hospital always gives me the creeps."

Davina wasn't about to argue that point. The Farm Colony hospital was the place of countless terrifying stories of ghosts, grisly murders, and even satanic worship. And now, the resurgence of Son of Cropsey? Scrolling down the leaked article still further, she came upon a stock picture of the hospital—it really was the place of nightmares.

A jab of the finger and the screen went black. "I gotta go, Mil." Davina jumped up and dumped her unfinished bowl of cereal into the sink.

She drove to Dobson's Gym in a daze.

New victims were piling up atop the old—three to date, and counting. And the sick bastard was still out there.

Another Son of Cropsey, a twisted copycat.

Or maybe the same one who had fucked up her life a decade ago because Riley put away the wrong man?

Entering the gym, Davina saw Gerry holding court at the center of the floor with her martial arts class. Don Anderson, Davina's morning student, was there, trying his best to keep up. She had to give the guy props; even she wouldn't put herself through one of Gerry's classes before her own.

Gerry waved, and Davina pointed to the stairs to let her know she was going to go change.

As she reached the bottom of the short staircase, Davina heard Gerry instruct her class to do their cooldowns before they took to the showers; the clock was ticking. Davina made a beeline for the women's locker room, knowing Don would head straight to the solo class space. It'd be good for him to wait a few minutes, to have time to catch his breath before his class with Davina.

The locker room was empty. Davina opened up her locker, took out her black workout outfit, and pulled off her top. She had it halfway over her head when the lights went out, leaving her in complete darkness.

Davina yelped, ripped off the top, and thrust her bare back against the cold metal of the lockers, her hands raised defensively. She held her breath and listened; all she heard was the unsteady drip of water coming from the showers. The remaining silence made its own sound inside her head: a high, quivering *hiss*.

Hearing footsteps on the stairs, Davina tensed, fists clenched so hard, fingernails dug into her palms.

A blinding flash of white light started Davina as the fluorescent strips stuttered back on. Gerry stood at the end of the row of lockers closest to the door, staring at her.

"D, you okay?"

"The lights went out."

"I heard you scream."

"Knee-jerk reaction." Davina forced herself away from the lockers, still trembling. "My imagination . . ." Davina scanned what she could see of the room—the entrance to the showers and toilets, two of the sinks along the inside wall, lockers.

"Hun, the lights flicked off, that's all. You know the switches are fucked—it's one of the reasons I'm having this whole room redone. Work starts Thursday—they're putting in LEDs, which are far more reliable and will cut down our electricity bill."

Though women from her class were trickling into the locker room, Gerry waited for Davina to finish dressing and walked up the stairs behind her, which made Davina thankful all over again for her older, more level-headed friend. Calmer for having left the locker room behind, Davina made her way to the sparring room, where Don Anderson waited at the center of the blue-and-red mat.

"I'm ready for you." His hands were on his hips, and he had a twinkle in his eye.

"I'll be the judge of that." Davina launched herself straight at him.

After forty-five minutes of pure, unadulterated torture, Don was a crumpled heap on the floor, very much out of breath and sweating profusely. Propping himself up on his elbows, he gave Davina a wonky grin. "Another round?"

"I think you've had enough for today," she said, turning to go. She had an appointment with Geoff Wong to keep.

Don's grin slipped farther sideways. "I hate to see you leave, but I love to watch you go."

"Oh, please," Davina groaned as she headed back to the locker room. Don was an okay guy, but she hoped his flirtatious behavior wasn't going to become a habit.

There was nothing all that special about the station in the Great Kills neighborhood of Staten Island. It sat at the end of Nelson Avenue, where Giffords Glen ended and Brower Court began. The building was red brick, with a gray roof that made the station appear more like a provincial library than a train station. Through the square archway, the platforms were chipped concrete with steel trim painted a utilitarian sea-foam green.

First opened in 1860 as Giffords Station, it had been rebuilt in the '30s. There had been some upgrades since, but the place was badly in need of another do-over. The Rock's movers and shakers had bigger things to occupy their money-grabbing minds than some old, rundown muggers' paradise. The train tracks sat below the level of the surrounding ground because they'd had to dig a thirty-foot-deep trench for the tracks to avoid underground springs and quicksand, which meant Great Kills had been pretty much unstable from the ground up. Perhaps that's what contributed to its dark history of violence, drugs, muggings, and much worse? Davina had spent a lot of time in Great Kills' gloomy, forgotten corners during her time as an addict, and the train station had been a frequent haunt, a perfect place to score.

Stone-cold sober, the idea of venturing into the station on her own made Davina uneasy. She wished for a moment she'd taken Geoff Wong up on his offer to go along with her after lunch. *Nonsense.* Common sense dictated the sight of Davina's Dobson's Gym T-shirt and well-muscled, tattooed arms would ward off any potential muggers.

The long gravel passage leading from the station building to the platforms was sandwiched between a chain-link fence on the left and an overgrown four-foot-tall stone retaining wall on the right. Davina walked it swiftly, taking the stairs up to the northbound St. George platform two at a time; the platform would afford the best view of the tracks and south-bound platform.

Even in broad daylight, she noted a group of teenagers smoking weed. Passing by them, Davina held her breath to keep from catching a craving. A little farther along was a pile of dirty laundry that may or may not have belonged to the vagrant passed out beside it on a bench. The air was filled with a rancid odor emanating from either the guy or the overflowing trash bin that sat baking in the hot afternoon sun. Davina noted that both security cameras atop their poles overlooking the platform were busted. From the looks of it, they'd been that way for a good long while.

For a Staten Island crime hotspot that generated nasty headlines and citizen petitions on a weekly basis, it amazed Davina there was no priority to repair the security system. Although, she realized that repairs might have been futile, as the vandals would undo them as quickly as they were made. Even the emergency call box had been trashed.

How the fuck do Riley and his crew keep their jobs?

Davina imagined Joy at the station ten years ago. Why had she been there alone? Was she going somewhere? Meeting someone? A boyfriend, maybe? Who might that have been? Who might know? Elena? Someone else from the old gang?

Behind Davina, the potheads with their baggy, low-hanging jeans and ass-backward baseball caps were getting rowdy, pushing and shoving one another. One of them performed wheelies on a skateboard—he toppled and landed at the very edge of the platform, one arm dangling over its side. His buddies laughed like they'd crapped themselves.

Yeah, it's all shits and giggles until somebody lands on the tracks.

Where might Joy have been attacked? Geoff Wong hadn't specified; maybe the reporter's notes would say? She glanced up and down the platforms and decided that because so many people were here and the location was visible to the surrounding homes and businesses, this would not have been the spot.

Thinking about how eager she'd been to escape the passage to the platforms, Davina thought maybe Joy had felt the same way. Turning in her heels, Davina made her way down to the graveled walkway. It was empty. She glanced back at the platform. No one in sight there, either.

This was the place.

A noise: behind her, among the shrubs and beyond the chain-link fence. It moved to her right.

Relax, Davina. Five breaths. It'll be a cat or a raccoon. It's broad daylight, you're not twelve anymore, and you know how to defend yourself.

Rolling her head and shoulders to shake off the fear, Davina turned to continue back to the station.

Without warning, someone grabbed her from behind so ferociously that she had no time to defend herself. An arm clamped tight across Davina's neck, a strong arm clad in a dark, coarse sweatshirt, and the acrid stink of cheap cologne flooded her mind with terrible memories. Even as her survival instincts kicked in, the assailant's other arm wrapped around Davina's waist and a booted foot kicked her feet from under her. Rendered helpless, no purchase on the loose ground, Davina was dragged through a gap in the chain-link fence and into the thicket of cedars that nestled behind it.

Choking and unable to cry out, Davina reached up to pull the arm away, only to find she couldn't. She was strong, but without leverage, she was powerless. Instinct screamed to find her footing or hook an ankle behind her attacker's, but the dried, slippery tree debris beneath her made that difficult. Struggling, Davina managed to wiggle two fingers into the crook of the arm about her throat, just enough to keep breathing. But, as she got purchase, the arm shifted, giving her air but cutting off the blood to her brain.

A classic blood choke—focus, Davina!

On the verge of blacking out completely, Davina wrapped a leg behind her assailant's, only to have him anticipate the move. He rammed her face-first against a tree trunk, knocking the breath from her lungs and pinning her to the rough bark. His knee pressed against her thigh, rock hard, jabbing into the muscle. Desperate, Davina reached up behind her head and tried to claw at his face. She only managed to scrape his hand. Gloved, damn it. In a burst of frantic purpose, she sunk her nails into the wrist exposed between glove and sleeve and stomped down hard on her attacker's instep with the heel of her Nikes.

Following a loud grunt of pain, the arm tightened around her neck. Davina's world began to fade into darkness.

Stay on your feet.

Fight, Davina.

Fight for your fucking life.

CHAPTER TWENTY

WEDNESDAY, GREAT KILLS TRAIN STATION

I knew you would be contrary. Even back then, I knew it. And yet, as you struggle in my arms, I am more fond of you than ever.

Mind spinning back to when Davina was so much smaller and weaker, Son of Cropsey tightened the grip on Davina's neck. This close, her shampoo smelled wonderful—something spicy with hints of strawberries—well worth taking a second or two to inhale a deep breath and enjoy. She had such beautiful red hair, so much nicer than when it was dyed black—that was disappointing, but just a phase most girls go through in their search for identity.

She was a strong girl. She'd been strong ten years ago, but nothing like this. Little Davina Speers had grown up to be a mean, lean fighting machine, as the saying went.

I've seen you in that gym, kicking and punching to beat all that pent-up anger out of yourself. Were you angry with me, my perfect girl? Or angry at yourself for not understanding? I never wanted to make you angry. I wanted to liberate you. Don't be angry at me for what I'm forced to do. It comes from love.

Davina was putting up a good fight, but fear clogged her mind and turned her reflexes to chaotic impulses. It was important to keep her off balance. If Davina got both feet on the ground, the struggle would switch to her favor in a heartbeat.

Back then, in Davina's bedroom, she'd struggled against the inevitable at first, before finally realizing there was no escape and it would be easier to simply give in. Son of Cropsey liked to think she *wanted* to surrender herself in that way.

Just like she did now. The frisson of expectation that Davina would relent was delicious, so sweet to feel her fight hard against what she so desperately wanted. It increased the longing, made the anticipation of the inevitable so much sweeter.

I saw you at Joy's service. I had a feeling you might be a threat, and now, here we are. You should have never gone to the Advance. *I have to shut you down before you get completely out of control. We can't have you getting out of control, can we, Davina?*

Fighting the urge to press a hand between Davina's legs, to attempt to penetrate her through the thin, stretchy fiber of her leggings, Son of Cropsey recalled how wonderful that contact was before. But now she was dangerous, fighting for her life, and such pleasures would have to wait until she was subdued.

Nine seconds: All the time it took for a blood choke to work its magic.

Davina Speers was nine seconds from unconsciousness, from the inevitability of death, and she obviously realized it. Unable to resist the urge, the predator shoved a hand between Davina's thighs and ground her hard against a tree trunk, but that instinctive grab for an instant of pleasure caused a shift in the choke hold.

A train pulled into the station with a *whoosh* and a blast on its horn, and a group of late arrivals—chattering like monkeys—jogged up the passage on the other side of the fence. Taking advantage of the fleeting distraction, Davina jackknifed, using the shift in position against her assailant.

Davina's knee connected with Son of Cropsey's groin, causing an explosion of white-hot pain and a total loss of balance; in that instant, the balance of power between assailant and victim flipped. Davina screamed like a banshee; her cry lost in the siren of the arriving train. He grabbed at her once more and with murderous intent. Davina had crossed a hard line, and there'd be no regret silencing her once and for all.

With an audible grunt, Davina lashed out with a foot, catching the rapist square in the jaw. And, as her would-be killer rolled down the slope and deeper into the trees, Davina ran.

Son of Cropsey skidded down to the bottom of the hill, cursing Davina, cursing the uncontrollable urge to touch her.

We are not done with each other, Davina.

CHAPTER TWENTY-ONE

WEDNESDAY, GREAT KILLS TRAIN STATION

DAVINA, LYING FACEDOWN ON THE GRAVEL PATHWAY, FELT her heart thumping hard in her chest. Opening her eyes, she saw pea gravel stretching away from her in a trail, the bottom of a stone wall, and in the distance, fat strips of sea-foam green metal tilted sideways.

It isn't tilted. I'm on the ground. I tripped over my own damn feet.

Davina's body was on fire. Something trickled into her eyes, stinging them, clouding her vision.

He'd been there, waiting. Son of Cropsey. He'd choked her yet not choked her. She'd been able to breathe, but her brain had been closing down.

Davina attempted to move her feet, but they were held fast and refused to move. Feeling trapped and helpless, she used all the reserves she had to not panic. Craning her neck, Davina saw her feet were caught in the twisted remains of a rusty section of chain-link fence. It had been cut or wrenched from its neighboring section to create a loose flap.

Shuddering and cold with shock, Davina rolled over onto her back and quickly brushed her hands along her arms, across her body, and down her legs to check that she was still in one piece. She hoped to dear God she was, and knew she had to be on her feet and gone as quickly as possible as the rapist was highly likely to still be around and might come back to finish the job he'd started.

Satisfied nothing was broken, Davina disengaged her gym shoes from the fence and, using the wall for support, rose to her feet. She walked briskly back through the station to the parking lot and climbed into the sanctuary of her car, heart still racing.

Was he nearby? Watching her?

Why had she not smelled the cologne she connected with her attacker? Had he sent someone else to do his dirty work? No, Davina *knew* it was the same person who'd lain on top of her and forced her legs apart when she was a child. Had the attack been an opportunistic one, a purely chance meeting? Or, had he forgone the cologne, knowing it would have likely alerted her to his presence in the bushes?

Yes!

As terrified as Davina was, she felt a surge of validation: If she wasn't on to something, Son of Cropsey wouldn't have risked everything to silence her in broad daylight.

Only one other person knew I was coming here.

Grabbing her cell from her bra top, Davina checked the time: 12:07. She then pulled up Geoff Wong's number in her contacts and called. "Where are you right now, Geoff?" she demanded.

"At the office. What's wrong, Davina?"

She combed pieces of gravel, twigs, and cedar needles from her hair with her fingers. "You're still at the paper?"

"Of course. What's wrong?"

"Prove it." Davina was painfully aware she sounded like a crazy person, but she *had* to be sure.

"Okay, okay." Wong hung up.

"I fucking *knew* it," Davina growled just as her phone lit up with a Facetime request. She thumbed the OK button, and there was Geoff

Wong's concerned face. Behind him, sure enough, was the office she'd sat down in only the day before.

"Happy now?" Wong asked. "I'll see you at Boro 5, and you can tell me what all that was about. Get yourself something to eat—you sound like you have low blood sugar. I may be a few minutes late, but I'll definitely be there. Okay?"

Davina felt stupid; how the hell could she have suspected Wong? "Okay," she mumbled, then hung up and stared blankly at her phone. She believed Wong, of course she did... But that didn't mean he couldn't have told someone—possibly *intentionally*—where she would be right before lunch. On the other hand, her attacker might just as easily have followed her from the gym. That thought was gut-wrenching: Dobson's was Davina's safe haven.

Davina wiped blood from her lip where she'd scuffed it on the tree as she'd fought for her life—literally. Davina had no doubt whatsoever that Son of Cropsey had more nefarious intentions than copping a quick feel through her leggings. Checking herself in the rearview mirror, she discovered she had no blood on her face after all. She only had a film of sweat. All things considered she didn't look so bad. Davina Speers, cat with nine lives.

Plugging her keys into the ignition was a struggle; her hand was shaking so much, her whole system high on adrenaline. Nevertheless, Davina threw the Jetta into reverse, backed out of the parking space, and aimed the car down Nelson. Just as she crossed Giffords Glen, a trio of cop cars rolled into the station lot, lights flashing, sirens wailing.

Was Detective Riley in one of the black-and-whites? A fleeting thought crossed her mind: maybe she ought to report her attack to him? Dumb idea. The asshole would only find some way to turn the assault back on her, demand to know why she was hanging out at the station, and maybe even suggest she was trying to score or turn a trick. The latter thought pushed any ideas of talking to Riley far from her mind. Even the notion of hearing him imply that she might be selling her body made her nauseous.

How much would she tell Geoff Wong about what had just

happened? She wanted to call Joe and tell him everything, but he'd only worry. She wished Millie were there. A big part of Davina was too afraid to tell any of them; they might think she was making up her old stories again —or was batshit crazy.

I'm not crazy yet, but I sure as hell am getting there fast.

CHAPTER TWENTY-TWO

WEDNESDAY, BORO 5 DINER

THE BORO 5 WAS PACKED AND NOISY. THE CLATTER OF utensils and plates competed loudly with the chatter of the lunchtime patrons. Geoff had managed to snag a booth in the back; its yellow vinyl bench seat sported a long tear covered with dark gray duct tape. The booth was as private as he could get with only one other behind it. He was slurping at his hot coffee and contemplating the laminated menu when Davina arrived.

Davina flagged down a passing waitress before taking a seat. "Could I get a cup of coffee?"

"I'm not your waitress," the slim young blonde grumped. She glanced at Geoff and smiled, "I'll send someone over."

Davina sat down opposite the reporter. "That information you gave me about the station? Who else knows Joy was attacked there?"

"Only Leroy Myrow—my predecessor," Geoff told her; he appeared startled by her directness, as if he was expecting a little pleasant chitchat.

"Did you tell *anyone* I was going there today?"

"Of course not. Why?"

Davina glared at the tabletop, silently flexing her jaw . . . and her hands.

God, she's shaking, thought Geoff. A chill like an icy finger traced along Geoff's spine. He put down his mug. "What happened, Davina?"

A waitress—this one older, rounder, with graying hair—brought Davina a glass of ice water and a cup of coffee. "Are you ready to order?"

After the long meeting, Geoff was starving. "Gimme the burger platter deluxe with onion rings."

Davina hesitated, then said, "Tuna melt, coleslaw, and fries." She waited for the waitress to be well out of earshot, then said, "I was attacked."

Geoff exhaled, like he'd been punched in the gut. "Seriously?"

Davina nodded. "Grabbed from behind and dragged into the trees. The guy caught me off balance—shoved me up against a tree and put me in a chokehold. I'm lucky he got ahead of himself and I got away. I don't believe for one fucking minute it was a coincidence or a crime of opportunity."

"Jesus, Davina. Did you recognize him?"

She shook her head. "He was wearing a balaclava and a hoodie, but I know it was him."

"Who?"

"The guy who raped me when I was twelve, only without the disgusting aftershave. I just *know*, Geoff."

"Did you report it to—"

Davina raised both hands in that universal gesture of *really?* "Riley or one of his law enforcement buddies? I'm not quite *that* stupid."

Suddenly, Geoff felt like he was on trial. "Wait. You thought I might've leaked your whereabouts to someone who wants to hurt you?" The expression on Davina's face had changed in a way he didn't much care for. "You actually think I told someone *on purpose*."

Her green eyes were wary. "The thought did cross my mind."

Geoff leaned toward Davina across the table and lowered his voice. "Let's get one thing straight here. I'm a journalist. If Jeff fucking Bezos himself offered me all his goddamn money to give him information that would put another human being in danger. I. Would. Not. Do. It. Clear?"

After regarding him a moment or two, the corners of Davina's mouth lifted and she shrugged. "Clear."

That still doesn't explain how he *knew where you were, Davina.*

Davina poured two small cartons of cream in her coffee and took a sip. "Did you find anything new since yesterday?"

Geoff sat back in the lumpy vinyl seat. "About ten years ago there were four girls, all aged fourteen to sixteen, all attacked with the same MO— two of them *after* Cox was in police custody. I just emailed you their names and addresses."

"Joy was one of the four?"

"Yes. There was Joy Sheridan, Elizabeth Pine, Brianna Fisher, and Amber Winters. And please don't ask how I got the information. My sources are—"

"Confidential. I get it."

"Given they were all underage, and the sexual nature of the assaults, the paper never ran their names. As for the addresses, a lot can change in ten years, so don't count on them still being around."

"What can I do with names and addresses that might not be current?" Davina scrolled through the emails on her phone, as if Geoff may have been lying to her. She visibly relaxed when she came upon the email he'd sent minutes before.

"Whatever you want." Geoff hid his impatience—was the girl *never* grateful? "I'm only sharing this because you asked, and I agree with you that something is fucked up. The cases all got buried when Riley had Cox put away, but I think you're right that there's more to it than meets the eye."

Were you signed, Davina? Geoff was dying to ask.

"How much more?" Davina asked.

The dowdy waitress brought their lunches and left a handful of fresh napkins.

"In Leroy's archived case notes, he mentions there was a Detective Packer. Apparently, he never fully bought into Rob Cox being guilty. Cox had a record as long as his fucking arm, but there was nothing more than circumstantial crap to tie him to the attacks."

"Packer?"

Geoff bit into his pickle spear; it was cold and bitter—just how he liked them. "Ron Packer, lead detective on the Son of Cropsey case."

"No, that was Riley."

Geoff shook his head, swallowed, and said, "No. Riley was the one publicly credited with catching the guy and closing the case. It was originally Packer's, though."

Davina dug into her coleslaw. "Why would Riley get all the credit?"

"No clue. Packer retired to Tampa shortly after the case broke, and Riley was hailed as the hero of the hour. All I found in the archives was some obscure reference to the investigation not moving fast enough, and within two weeks of Riley taking over the case, there's a perp in custody." He finished the pickle spear, took the top bun off the burger, and tapped out two dollops of ketchup from the Heinz bottle on the table. "I've reached out to Packer, but he's not returning my calls."

"So, what does that mean for the current attacks?"

"Hard to say." Geoff dragged a rough paper napkin across his mouth. "But, if I was a betting man, yeah, I'd say he's back. The four new cases are all in different police jurisdictions, and the cops aren't sharing intel."

Davina scoffed, "Do they ever?"

"In big cases, sure. Cops tie into the general databases, like the NLETS, for information. Sorry, NLETS is—"

"National Law Enforcement Telecommunications System," Davina cut in. "I'm studying criminal law."

"There's some inherent resentment toward Riley, which doesn't help."

"Completely understandable." Davina nibbled on her tuna melt and checked her surroundings, half expecting the cop to be standing over her shoulder.

"The details are sketchy, but from what I gather, Riley arrived on the Rock under a cloud of suspicion. Seems he was over at Manhattan South but was involved in a friendly fire incident—his partner died in a drug bust."

Davina stopped midbite and stared at him. "Are you saying what I think you're saying?"

"What do you *think* I'm saying?"

"Riley was involved in the death of his last partner? If that's true, what else is he capable of?" Davina put down her sandwich and brought a napkin to her lips. Blood. She fished an ice cube from her water glass. "Bit my fucking lip."

"This is getting to you."

"Riley and I've got history. Was he reprimanded?"

"Only if you count being reassigned here." Geoff shrugged. "The only other person involved was dead so Riley gave his account and was cleared. But the money and drugs went missing, and he landed himself here."

Davina smiled, "Cleared because he killed the witness?"

"Maybe he did, maybe he didn't. Riley's an opportunist; could be his story is legit—his partner got between him and the dealers he was trying to shoot and they got away with the goods. Some cops swear by him, others want nothing to do with him. Either way, Riley hit it big when he closed the Son of Cropsey case, and he's been pretty much untouchable as a result."

Davina shook her head. Light from the fixture over the table gleamed in her coppery hair. "We live in a fucked-up world."

"A *deranged* one. Staten Island is the perfect home for Riley; the majority of our cops will never pull their gun in a twenty-year career. Riley pulls his like the island is Tombstone and he's Wyatt Earp. Cops here are among the most corrupt anywhere, with a library of civilian complaints that read like crime novels. And they're promoted in spite of it."

"More likely *because* of it," Davina corrected. "So, what if the guy who attacked the two girls and me is the same Son of Cropsey and he's back? Riley is never going to admit he made a mistake."

"His admitting anything is irrelevant. The story broke this morning." Geoff brought it up on his phone and spun it around to show Davina. "The question is already being asked."

Davina read the headline: "Is Son of Cropsey Back?"

"You mean *you* broke the story this morning. You've really poked the hornet's nest."

"That's what I'm counting on. You don't get hard answers asking soft questions, Davina," Geoff sounded sage. "I contacted the family of the Todt Hill victim. She's with an aunt and uncle until her mother is out of the hospital for nervous exhaustion. I was hoping to talk with the girl, but her aunt shot me down. The family has formally asked the media to respect their privacy. I have to honor that request." He hesitated again, then put on his reporter hat and asked the question he was dying to ask. "My source at the NYPD told me Son of Cropsey liked to sign his work. Do you know anything about that?"

Of course she did.

Davina's reaction was immediate, electric. Her face blanched and her mouth dropped open in an audible gasp that was almost a cry. She blinked rapidly, and Geoff was afraid for a second or two she was going to break down in tears.

Geoff broke the silence, "I'd say it means something to you."

"He . . . left a mark on my forehead. Drew it with my sister's red lipstick."

"What mark?"

Davina snagged a napkin, pulled a ballpoint pen out of her fanny pack, and drew a circle with a line slashed horizontally across the middle, then pushed the napkin across the table to Geoff.

"Theta," Geoff stated the obvious. "What does it mean to Son of Cropsey, though?"

"It could be 'no' or 'not,' as in his victims are worth nothing. It could mean he's playing Death or God. The guy's a psycho. Who the fuck knows what it means to him?"

"He must have signed *all* the girls he assaulted," Geoff added.

"But it was never reported."

"In cases like that, the cops keep something back—helps weed out the time wasters. They're obviously not going to make it public now—*especially* now—and I'm pretty sure my source isn't going to give me anything more. I also doubt the victims and their families are going to tell a reporter squat if the cops have instructed them not to leak important details."

Davina got a burst of energy and was ready to leap out of her seat. "But they might tell *me*. I'm not the media. I'm a victim. A survivor like them. I reckon I could approach them in a way their families would be okay with. I can at least try."

Geoff tucked his phone back in his pocket and eyed his sandwich. "Okay, Davina," he said. "Try."

CHAPTER TWENTY-THREE

THE WAITRESS TOPPED OFF THEIR COFFEES AND LEFT THE check.

"You done?" Geoff asked Davina and reached for his wallet.

"What's my share?" Davina asked.

"I said I'd buy you lunch," he said with a smile.

Davina turned her head at the sound of a hubbub at the diner's door. Sean Delafield had just walked in like he owned the place. He was grinning his best shit-eating grin and making queen waves with both hands—all part of the campaign swing. Davina made a face and watched as Sean made his way through the diner, delivering hearty claps on the back.

Sean spotted Davina and Geoff and marched over, breezing by tables with a distracted nod of his head. He loomed over Geoff, an obvious attempt to intimidate. "I'm glad I caught you here, Wong. It saves me a trip to your office."

"Is there something I can do for you?" Geoff slipped his wallet back in his pocket.

"You can explain why the *Advance* is refusing to support my reelection bid."

"I don't speak for my bosses or the paper."

Sean's voice quietened, "Don't give me that PC bullshit, Wong."

Geoff cocked his head and retorted, "Okay, how about I give you a chance to tell your side of the story in an exclusive interview? I have some time right now, as it happens."

"And have you twist my words out of context?"

"I give you my word everything you say will go to print entirely as you say it. No twisting."

"I'll have my people call you," Sean sneered before he affixed a counterfeit smile and moved on to continue his rounds through the diner.

Davina shot Geoff a curious glance. "What was that about?"

"The paper's not endorsing him in his bid for the council seat. I'm not sure why he's surprised. Our managing editor was the one who helped put him in jail for two years for bribery. It cost Sean his council seat, and now he wants it back."

Geoff Wong, Davina realized, saw more than his share of corruption. It was, after all, his job to ferret out and expose it. "Is that a big deal? A council seat?"

"It has a lot of weight locally and can be a springboard to higher places. It's doubtful Sean will regain the seat without the *Advance* backing him. The position does hold a lot of power, and it's clear Sean wants it badly. In my humble opinion, it would be a huge blow to Staten Island if he got the seat back. But things don't always work out the way they should."

"No shit."

"He'd be able to—" Geoff's attention was drawn toward the diner's small foyer, his face blank. Davina followed his gaze. Detective Riley had just walked in with a couple of his cop cronies.

"Perfect," Geoff murmured.

Riley's eyes shot directly to Davina. An expression then slithered across the cop's face she couldn't read. Turning, trailing his buddies, Riley approached their booth. Dressed in a dark gray suit with burgundy tie and spit-shined shoes, Riley presented as sleek and sinister; the cop's swarthy good looks made him incredibly handsome to those who didn't know what a snake he was.

Riley and his men stood on either side of the booth, deliberately preventing Davina and Geoff from escaping. Riley leaned in, palms flat on the table's edge, and looked Geoff straight in the eye.

For once, I'm not the focus of Riley's attention, Davina thought.

"I saw your article this morning, Mr. Wong." Sean leaned in a little closer. "Son of Cropsey is *not* back."

Geoff took the bait, "So, how come the Fort Wadsworth and Todt victims have the same MO?"

"You ever heard of copycats, Wong?" Riley snarled. "I know for sure it ain't Son of Cropsey because I put the bastard away ten years ago." He turned to Davina, then back to Geoff. "You *both* understand?"

"I understand you put *somebody* away ten years ago," Geoff countered. "But I also know there were similar attacks *after* Rob Cox, including the recent ones."

"I don't give a shit about any alleged *similar* attacks. We live with crime every goddamn day. Get it?" The cop swept his hands outward with an exaggerated motion, purposely knocking Geoff and Davina's coffee cups into their laps.

Davina jumped but had nowhere to go to escape the splash of coffee. She took the mug off her lap and put it back on the table. Luckily, there hadn't been much left, and what had been there had grown cold. She wasn't the least bit surprised by the cop's dick move.

Riley looked at the other cops and laughed. "Oops. My bad." Turning back to Geoff, he said, "Let me be clear. If anything happens to any more kids, I'll publicly blame you and the *Advance* for inciting it. The recent attacks are unrelated to anything, even each other until I say otherwise." He pointed at Geoff, then Davina, then said, "And make no mistake, I'm keeping a close eye on the both of you. So, watch your fucking asses."

Riley was about to say something else when his gaze fell on the napkin she'd used to draw the theta for Geoff. The cop's face turned an ugly shade of deep red that was pretty damn close to the color of his tie. Standing bolt upright from the table, Riley turned tail and bustled over to where Sean was chatting with some folks at the counter. His pair of deputies followed Riley like puppy dogs after a belly rub. At the counter, Sean and Riley shook hands and embraced like two old friends.

"He's bluffing," Geoff said, mopping at the spilled coffee with bunched-up napkins.

Davina's smile and response contained no humor, "Trust me, I know *Detective* Riley. He doesn't bluff."

Geoff's phone rang, its tone shrill, grating. Pulling it out of his pocket, he scanned the screen with raised brows.

"What is it?"

"Late-breaking story on SI Live."

"Saying what?" Davina leaned into the table.

"They're linking the recent attacks to Sean Delafield's properties."

"Are you thinking Sean Delafield might be involved in the attacks?"

Geoff frowned. "I'm not thinking anything other than the attacks took place on property he either owns or has expressed interest in acquiring for development. Fort Wadsworth and the Farm Colony, for example. Probably just circumstantial, but worth a dig around."

"I hate to go, but I do have places to be." Davina tapped a finger on her phone; Geoff's email was still open. "I also need to wrap my head around all this." Davina slid out of the booth.

"Where are you going, Davina?"

"To follow up with Son of Cropsey's old victims." She paused, her lips twisting. "Starting with the class of 2010."

Geoff stood, joining Davina in the aisle. He reached back, picked up the theta-adorned napkin, folded it, and tucked it into his shirt pocket. "I'm going to dig a little deeper into another case from about nine years ago—the mom was killed. I don't think it was investigated closely enough."

"Why not?"

"African American single mom and daughter from the projects. It barely got a mention in the *Advance*. Anyway, I'm gonna see if anything connects." He patted the pocket into which he'd stuffed the rapist's autograph.

As Davina and Geoff exited the diner, Sean Delafield and Detective Riley followed Davina with their eyes, leering. Davina wasn't bothered one iota—she was used to it. She saw Sean's eyes flick to her chrysanthemum tattoo and imagined she saw a glimmer of something . . . recognition? Fear? She tucked her wrist behind her back and stepped quickly outside and onto the sidewalk, almost bumping into Father Stephen, who was on his way in.

"So sorry, Father. I wasn't watching where I was going."

Father Stephen smiled amiably. "No worries. Davina, isn't it?"

"You remember my name?"

"Yes," he warmly replied . "What sort of priest would I be if I didn't know the people I served? At your friend's memorial, we couldn't decide how we knew each other. Afterward, I realized I'd taught you in Sunday school when you were a little girl. I spent a summer at Saint Margaret Mary, oh, many, many years ago now."

Pushing her uneasy feeling about the priest aside—it was likely paranoia following her encounter at the station—Davina tried her hardest to remember the man. Nothing. "You must've been very young," she said.

The priest tilted his head to one side and said matter of factly, "Fresh out of seminary. You were quite young yourself. I'm not really surprised you don't remember me."

Davina felt unaccountably ashamed but confessed, "I didn't go to church much past middle school. Sorry. My family got a little messed up and I wasn't really feeling the whole Jesus thing."

Shit. That was rude.

The priest remained unflappable. "He'll always be waiting if you ever wish to return. God doesn't note the passage of time. He literally has all the time in the universe."

"Thank you, Father." After the confrontation with Sean and Riley, Father Stephen's gentle presence, like his philosophy, was a breath of fresh air for Davina.

Father Stephen bowed his head. "If you'll excuse me, I have a lunch date."

"I highly recommend the tuna melt," Davina told him.

Father Stephen laughed as he made his way inside the diner. "That actually does sound quite appetizing."

CHAPTER TWENTY-FOUR

WEDNESDAY, BORO 5 DINER

Davina sat in her car and plotted the addresses Geoff had given her on her Waze app. The three surviving victims were all less than fifteen minutes from Rosebank. Two of the ten-year-old addresses were in Silver Lake, and one was in Grymes Hill; the neighborhoods were adjacent and thoroughly upper-middle class.

Davina stared out the window, thinking. She had a class at Dobson's in forty minutes. She could take it and make her visits later, or. . .

She texted Gerry.

> Need to cancel class. Something I have to do.

> U OK? Wassup?

> I'm fine. Xplain later.

Propping her phone on the center console, Davina gunned the Jetta's engine and set off to the first address on her list.

Brianna Fisher had lived at one of the Silver Lake addresses; Davina could only hope she still did. The neighborhood was beautiful, with tree-lined streets and stately homes with what seemed to be acres upon acres of neatly mowed grass. Situated close to Silver Lake Park, it was a quiet community, shockingly different from where Davina had grown up merely two neighborhoods to the southeast. The exterior of Brianna's home, if it was *still* Brianna's home, was red brick, white siding, with an immaculately landscaped front yard and a glistening white front door.

Davina knocked on the door and waited. When, finally, the door opened, a woman peered through the thin opening.

"Yes?"

Davina put on a hopeful, wide-eyed expression. "Is Brianna Fisher here?"

"Who's asking?"

"I'm a friend of hers from back in the day. My name is Davina Speers."

The door opened up all the way to reveal a ruddy-faced, middle-aged woman. She wore a floral print blouse with navy pants and matching ballet flats. "I'm Helen Fisher. I didn't know Brianna had any friends left on Staten Island."

"Is she here?"

"No." Helen pursed her lips. "Would you like to come in anyway?"

The interior of the Fisher home was no less stately than the exterior, albeit a bit fussy for Davina's tastes. The place smelled of furniture polish, and clear plastic coverings lay over the Georgian furniture—it looked more like a show house than a home. Davina was willing to bet the house had a more casual room at the back of the house, and that was where the Fishers did their *living*.

"Would you like a butter cookie?" Helen Fisher held up a Royal Dansk tin.

"No, thank you. I just had lunch."

"Make yourself comfortable. I have to go out soon, but I have a little time right now. How do you know Brianna?"

"We were friends in junior high. She's not here anymore?"

"Brianna moved to Montana straight after graduating high school."

Davina took a deep breath. She'd thought long and hard about how to handle the delicate question of each victim's attack; there was a definite risk of going at it too hard or too soft. But Davina had decided the stakes were too high not to take a risk.

"After what happened to her, you mean?"

Helen blinked but did not appear offended or surprised. "Yes." The syllable was clipped, hurried. Helen grabbed two cookies and put the lid back on the tin. "My daughter left Staten Island behind. She has a good life in Montana, far away from the past. She said she couldn't breathe here anymore."

"Like she was being suffocated?"

Helen set the cookies on the saucer next to her half-drunk coffee and picked up the cup. She gave Davina a long, quizzical stare over the rim. "You talk as if you've experienced something . . . similar."

Davina tucked a strand of red hair behind her ear. "I . . . yes, I have. I was hoping . . . I thought maybe our stories could help others. Other victims."

Helen's expression softened. "I'm very sorry to hear that, Miss Speers. Rob Cox ruined so many innocent young girls. But I think sometimes it's best to forget such terrible things. I must admit I agreed with Brianna's decision to leave. What happened to her in Mariner's Marsh was nothing short of a nightmare—one she lived and relived night after night. Brianna was never a strong girl growing up. I honestly don't know how she survived it." Helen's mouth tugged down at one corner and her eyes misted.

"I don't think you can ever really forget, Mrs. Fisher."

"Helen, please."

"Helen. Can I ask a difficult question?"

Helen's smile was weak, false. "When it comes to my Brianna, all questions are difficult."

"How did Brianna's father deal with what happened to her? And her leaving?"

Helen sighed. "William walked out not long after Brianna's assault. He and I just couldn't stop arguing about it. He wanted to stop her from going out at night. I tried to explain that Brianna snuck out the window. He . . . blamed me. To be honest, Davina, I blamed myself."

"She went to Mariner's Marsh to hang out with friends?"

"No. Her friends were going to Silver Lake Park, just up the street from here. But, at some point in the night, she . . . lost track of them and herself and her surroundings. Brianna doesn't remember much except darkness and pain and . . . fear."

I remember the fear like it was yesterday.

"Did your husband happen to work for the real estate developer Sean Delafield?"

"William was a carpenter—fine cabinetry—but I don't remember him ever working for Sean Delafield. It's always possible, though. He's a politician now, isn't he? Sean Delafield, I mean. I don't really pay much attention to that sort of thing."

Davina was willing to bet Sean had once had plans for Mariner's Marsh. The wetland, sandwiched between the Bayonne Bridge and the Arthur Kill, was dotted with the decaying docks of a long-dead shipyard, a defunct ruin of an iron foundry, and the watery graves of a handful of nineteenth-century sailing ships. Legend had it there was a network of tunnels running beneath the area, too—likely a throwback to the Prohibition days. The marsh had won out over man's best efforts to conquer it and was now home only to marine wildlife and myriad birds. The *Advance* had once carried some talk of making it a nature preserve—the furthest thing from Sean Delafield's mind, of course.

"You said she lost track of her friends. Do they have any idea what happened to her?"

"They said she was with them for a while, then she just . . . *wasn't*. One of the girls said she thought Brianna had gone to the public restrooms, which at that time of night might have been closed. When Brianna didn't come back, they thought maybe she'd just walked home. He must have taken her . . ." Helen Fisher looked down at her hands and fell silent.

Mariner's Marsh was a good twenty-minute drive from Silver Lake, which suggested either Brianna had gotten into a car with her rapist willingly—either because he pulled a weapon on her or she knew him—or she was incapacitated and then manhandled into the car.

"Did you know the man who attacked you?" Helen found her voice.

The woman's readiness to believe a complete stranger was not lost on Davina. "I couldn't see him clearly and . . . my memory of what happened to me is *really* foggy."

Helen's face lost some of its color. "Brianna was always frightened of the marshes," she said quietly, shaking her head. "It's difficult to imagine she'd have gone there with *anyone* of her own accord. Kids think they're immortal, you know? Invincible." She eyed Davina. "Were you like that as a teenager?"

Davina grimaced, "I didn't feel invincible, that's for sure. I felt... *cursed*." She shook herself; this wasn't about her. "Is it possible Brianna might've gone to the marshes on a dare?"

"Her memories were so vague—terrifyingly vague. She remembers being with friends at Silver Lake Park, though even that's hazy. And she remembers waking up in a pool of mud. And blood. My little Brianna thought she was dead and had gone to hell for disobeying her parents." Helen sniffled; her eyes glistened with tears.

"Mrs. Fisher—Helen—after the assault, did Brianna have any strange markings on her face? On her forehead?"

Helen squinted. "When I first saw Brianna at the hospital, her entire face was bloody—I could barely recognize her. She'd had to claw her way out of the mud and brush, and she'd fallen a few times before she made it to the Yacht Club and got help."

Davina tried not to let her disappointment show.

"Did you have . . . markings?"

Davina nodded. "I wondered if I was the only one—I thought maybe it meant something. I thought maybe there were more of us than got reported."

A flash of anger lit Helen Fisher's eyes. "I read that article in the *Advance* saying he's back. I can't . . . *won't* believe it. When that horrible man was sent to prison, I felt relief for the first time since Brianna was attacked. I don't want anyone taking that away from me."

"I understand. I'm sorry if I've caused you any pain."

Helen reached a hand toward Davina. "No. It was good to talk to someone who understands what Brianna went through." She checked her watch and got up from her chair. She smiled fleetingly. "I'm meeting my fiancé for an afternoon matinee." Lifting her left hand, Helen showed off her fat solitaire diamond.

Davina rose too. "Thank you for your time, Helen. And congratulations on your engagement."

"When Brianna left for Montana, I almost went with her. It was hard without her at first, especially with her father gone. But I'm glad I stayed. I have a second chance to be happy." With that, Helen Fisher ushered Davina to the door and back out into the magnificently maintained neighborhood.

Although there were some similarities in Brianna's case—the sexual assault, blurred memory, sense of suffocation—Davina had learned nothing concrete. It struck Davina that of the cases she now knew about, only two had taken place in the victim's home; the others were at isolated locations, all of which, so far, had some connection to Sean Delafield. Even Great Kills Station was the center of the Staten Island train route that figured in his well-publicized plans to connect the island to Brooklyn via rail crossing alongside the Verrazzano Narrows Bridge. But Mariner's Marsh had no public connection to Sean Delafield. Was there something he'd yet to reveal? That was something Geoff Wong or his many sources might know.

No one but Brianna would be able to divulge if she'd had theta drawn on her forehead. Davina refused to be disappointed by this—there were others to interview—but she felt sorrow for poor Brianna. She may have left Staten Island, but she'd never be able to leave behind what Son of Cropsey did to her.

Back in her car, Davina checked the next address. It was only a few blocks away from the Fisher house. As Davina drove by Silver Lake Park, she imagined Brianna there with her friends, young, carefree, and before her whole life imploded.

CHAPTER TWENTY-FIVE

WEDNESDAY, ADULT TOYZ EMPORIUM, GULF ST.

"Hello, Tom." Stacy Frazier greeted him with a warm, welcoming smile. "What brings you here on a Wednesday afternoon? Needing a little ooh-la-la in the boudoir?"

The store was not large, the front fitted with shelves stocked with lubricants and massage oils. Toward the back right were the erotic costumes and accessories. Opposite were the dildos, ticklers, balls, vibrators. In the long display case were the specialty items. Stacy stood behind the display, hands resting on the counter.

Riley knew Stacy from the business association and other affiliations. He eyed her disapprovingly. Stacy was fighting a losing battle against age, and it showed. She was starting to thicken but still wore tight leggings and blouses that only exaggerated her weight gain. Her makeup was now applied, not to enhance, but rather to hide the wrinkles. Her blood-red nails were too long, drawing attention to her veiny, spotted hands, and though her blouse was modestly unbuttoned to hint at her cleavage, the overall effect made her appear a parody of what she once was. Still, she remained a perfect host and owner for that kind of a store:

part shrink, part Whore of Babylon. Wasn't that in Revelation, he wondered? Mother of prostitutes and abominations of the Earth? Something like that.

"I'm on duty," Riley grumbled. He didn't understand the point of sex shops; he couldn't figure how they stayed in business. How much time could a decent human being spend in the sack? After a while, wasn't it all too much trouble? And dressing up? Halloween in the bedroom? Seriously? Hell, given the way his marriage went south, he should know.

"I do apologize," Stacy replied with a theatrical flourish. "Hello, *Detective* Riley. Are *you* needing a little ooh-la-la—"

"Do you recognize this?" Riley pulled out his cell phone from his inside jacket pocket. He scrolled through the image file and then held it up so Stacy could get a good, close look at the picture of the small black, fist-shaped dildo that had fallen out of Seraphina Bellano at the derelict hospital.

"Yeah." Stacy squinted at the picture of the toy in the evidence bag; it resembled a small Black baby's arm with a tiny clenched fist. "I used to stock them."

"Used to?"

"They just didn't sell, Tom. You know how it is."

Riley shook his head. No, he didn't know how it was. "Staten Islanders are a funny bunch," Stacy said with a wry smile. "They like what they like, and resist what they don't. I took in a whole range of these things—different sizes, colors, some with stretched-out fingers and others balled up . . . like your starter fist there."

It grated on Riley that she referred to the vile thing as *his*, and he reckoned Stacy knew it, too. She was playing with him, and he was in no mood for games. "You sell any recently?"

"I haven't sold one—ever," Stacy told him with a shrug.

"You ever had anyone asking for one?"

Stacy gave him a hard stare. "Nobody asked me," she told him. "But I'm not here all the time. Even if I was, I couldn't give out that kind of information—you know that. This kind of business is built on privacy and discretion. Word ever got out I gave information to every damn cop who asked for it, I'd be out of business in a week. You want that kind of info—you'd better have a warrant, Detective Riley."

Riley scanned the racks of sex toys that covered every wall of the store. There were latex dicks of all sizes, alongside a multitude of vibrators, fake breasts, edible underwear, and—alarmingly—a display of limbless torsos sporting eerily lifelike genitalia. But nothing even remotely fist shaped.

"I hope you had them on consignment." It was Riley's turn to play. Stacy was forever running her mouth at the SBCA; thought she was some big shot businesswoman because she owned a couple of the island's smut stores. It felt gratifying to put her back in her place.

"Hindsight's a wonderful thing in business, Detective," Stacy said with a wry smile. "Had I known how uptight and picky Islanders were, I'd have insisted on sale-or-return. As it turned out, I was lucky the Brooklyn population isn't so prudish."

"Brooklyn?"

"Yeah, I sold the job lot for cost to Stephanie Abelman. Seems her particular niche of clientele are connoisseurs of the fist."

Riley grimaced; Stacy was actually getting off making him squirm. "You mean the fags?"

"I mean the *gay* community, Tom." Stacy let out a long, exaggerated sigh. "It's time you brought yourself up to date. You're not *that* fucking old."

"I'm old enough to remember when gay meant happy," Riley growled. "You gonna give me Abelman's address, or do I need a fucking warrant for that, too?"

As he watched Stacy scribble down the Brooklyn address on a neon orange Post-it, he tucked his phone back into his pocket. He'd have one of the uniforms follow up on the lead—they'd take their time, most likely not get the right information, and he needed time to think. It was a long shot for certain, but Riley knew it was best he kept as much of the Son of Cropsey case under wraps until he could figure out how exposed he was likely to be over Rob Cox.

Stacy handed over the Post-it. Riley mumbled a thank you and made his way back out onto the street. He hoped to hell nobody he knew had seen him.

Retrieving his phone once more, Riley stabbed at the screen and held it to his ear. "Judge Wilkerson, I need a warrant signing." No time for small talk, and besides, he couldn't stand the decrepit old man, no matter how useful he was. "Within the next half hour. I'll send an officer over to pick it up."

Riley stood by his car and listened intently as the old judge complained at him.

"You don't have to tell me I need probable cause, Your Honor," Riley all but spat out the last two words. "But this is no way to make your granddaughter's DUI go away now, is it?"

A moment or two of silence followed.

"Thank you, Your Honor. Now, if you could put me on to your assistant, I'll give her all the details."

Then, Detective Riley climbed into his car and drove away from the store.

....

CHAPTER TWENTY-SIX

....

WEDNESDAY, SILVER LAKE

Amber Winters's home was modest in comparison to Brianna Fisher's but equally loved and well-cared for. The two-story house was painted a cheery yellow, which matched the tall sunflowers growing out front. White curtains hung in the windows, and pink, yellow, and white flowers had been planted in the multitude of flower boxes. A long-haired golden retriever sat out front in the shade of a willow tree, connected to the porch by a long, nylon leash; as Davina walked by, the retriever wagged its tail. She smiled back. Not a guard dog, then.

Davina walked up the wooden steps of the porch to the front door and rang the doorbell. It played the first four notes of Big Ben's chime.

A female voice called out, "Coming!"

Davina turned toward the street: children were playing, making happy sounds, birds twittered, a jet flew high overhead. Ahh, the pleasures of suburbia.

The door opened. A screen door between them rendered the woman inside into a smoky shadow. She appeared to be around Davina's age and wore a pale-yellow sundress and white sandals with daisies on them. Her earrings were large yellow hoops that perfectly matched the dress. Davina's eyes flicked immediately to the woman's forehead, but it was covered with a fringe of thick, wavy blonde hair cut into a neat, choppy, collar-length bob.

"Are you Amber Winters?"

"I'm Amber *Prescott*. Who are you?"

"Davina Speers." Of course. She got married!

"Are you selling something?" She eyed Davina up and down with suspicion.

"I'm not selling anything." Davina offered a smile and glanced down at the No Solicitors plaque by the doorframe. "Something happened at Staten Island Castle about ten years ago. It's something that happened to . . . several people, and Amber Winters was one of them."

Amber's Stepford Wife smile faded. "Why don't you come in?" She pushed open the screen door, and Davina walked inside.

The interior of the house was cool but not refrigerated like so many American homes. It smelled pleasantly of potpourri—orange and cinnamon. Amber led the way to the living room, which looked like an HGTV makeover. Family photos lined the butter-yellow walls, ivory-colored trim made everything seem crisp and fresh and . . . *cheery.*

On the mantel, Davina spotted a black-and-white photograph of Amber with a distinctly fifties hairdo, dark lipstick, and a large straw hat with a brim that covered her forehead.

"Can I get you some iced tea?"

"That would be nice, thank you."

Davina heard a squeal and then noticed a baby in a bouncy seat next to the pale stone fireplace. No more than six or seven months old, the kid could have been the Gerber baby, he or she was that picture perfect. The baby smiled up at Davina; and to think she'd always been told dogs and kids were good judges of character.

Davina seated herself in an overstuffed chair while Amber poured her a glass of iced tea from an etched glass pitcher on the coffee table.

"I'm afraid you may have me confused with someone else," she said as she poured.

"Oh?"

"That whole Staten Island Castle thing." Amber laughed. "That was Amber *Winters*, not me."

"Amber Prescott is your married name?"

"It's . . . yes, my married name."

"Sweet baby."

Amber's eyes lit up. "Arabella, yes. Isn't she adorable? She's six months old—such a good baby. We just came in from shopping. She *loves* being in the car. My husband's at work all day, so it's just us two girls."

Amber handed Davina the iced tea before taking Arabella out of the bouncy seat to cuddle her.

"You said your name was Davina?"

"Yes." Davina sipped her tea; it was remarkably sweet. Her eyes returned to Amber's fringe. What was beneath it?

"I heard about the Amber Winters case on the news, back when it happened. So very sad. So *horrible*." She made a face.

Amber Winters, whom Davina *knew* was the woman standing in front of her, had been brutally raped at the Staten Island Castle, which had once been a hospital—Staten Island's first, as it happened. The place had been closed and abandoned for decades before it was finally demolished in 2012. The infirmary had been famous for its cornerless rooms, which were thought to mitigate the spread of disease.

The things people used to believe.

"And what's your interest in the story?" Amber held Arabella close to her bosom.

"I had a friend who was assaulted by Son of Cropsey around that same time. A *close* friend. I wanted to understand what happened to her."

"So why don't you ask her?"

"She died," Davina said bluntly. "Her funeral was this past Monday."

Amber's sweet, homely face fell blank for a heartbeat, then she frowned. "I'm *so* sorry to hear that."

"If Amber Winters did live here, I'd want to ask her about her experience." Davina figured playing along with the woman's charade to be the best ploy—no point calling her a liar to her face.

"How very morbid of you."

Awkward silence followed, and Davina glanced around at the bright, airy room. Amber Prescott, nee Winters, was hiding her pain behind a hell of a lot of fake cheer.

"Where does your husband work, Amber?"

"In the office of St. Joseph's Church."

"Father Stephen's parish?"

Amber nodded, smiling. "Father Stephen Chapelle. Did you know his surname is actually *Chapelle*? I find it fascinating so many people whose names match their vocation—like the Olympic runner Usain Bolt, or the father and son baseball players named Fielding, or the pitcher named Outman. Did you know there were two female meteorologists whose names were Blizzard and Freeze?"

"I did not." Davina smiled the best she could; the poor woman's avoidance techniques were well-polished.

"I wish I could help you, Davina. I do, but . . ." Amber flapped a hand—Davina's cue to leave.

Davina made ready to make one last-ditch attempt at getting through to Amber Winters, when the baby spat up, covering the front of her romper and her mother's dress with stinking white milk.

"Bella! Oh, Lord!"

Amber leapt up from the couch, holding the child at arm's length, and for a moment, the golden curls over her forehead parted just enough for Davina to make out the suggestion of a faint curve of white scar tissue. Otherwise, the woman's forehead was as flawless as the rest of her. Could it be part of a larger scar? There was no way to tell. No way to ask.

Davina rose and pointed at the mewling, puke-covered baby, who looked about ready for round two. "I'll leave you to it."

"Thank you, Davina." Amber carried Bella into the kitchen and sat her down in the sink. "You can show yourself out."

Davina hesitated. "If you ever feel like talking, I can give you my number."

Amber threw her a puzzled frown. "And why would I want to talk to you about something that didn't happen to me?"

Oh, what the hell.

"Actually, I didn't tell you the whole truth, Amber," Davina blurted out. "My friend, Joy, *was* attacked by the same serial rapist who assaulted Amber Winters. But the real truth is that I'm asking for me. I was raped too, by the same monster, when I was twelve. I'm trying to work my way through it and, with Joy gone, I was hoping to find other victims—*allies*." She paused there, half-expecting Amber to throw her out then and there. "He left a mark on my forehead."

Amber froze.

In the silence, broken only by baby Bella's ominous gurgling, Davina searched her fanny pack for something to write on. Pulling out a Dobson's Gym business card, she scribbled her name and cell phone number on the back and set it down on the coffee table.

Then she left.

Back on the sunlit street, Davina took a last look at the Prescott home. She could understand someone going to great lengths to forget such a traumatic past. It made sense for Amber Winters-Prescott to create a new persona and deny the old one, but why the hell would she want to stay in her childhood home?

Davina checked the next address Wong had emailed her. The last victim was Elizabeth Pine, her address less than five minutes away in Grymes Hill. Davina wondered if it was even worth it to try; the deeper she went, the more frustrating the trail became.

Why did you have to kill yourself, Joy?

CHAPTER TWENTY-SEVEN

WEDNESDAY, GRYMES HILL

Grymes Hill was another nice neighborhood. That so many of Son of Cropsey's victims came from upper-middle-class homes was not lost on Davina.

I sure as hell didn't. Joy didn't. Does that mean anything?

Elizabeth Pine's house was on a corner. The blue shingles were faded and the roof appeared tired, but it might just have been in keeping with New England Colonial style. The well-worn doormat read: Did You Bring Wine?

Davina knocked on the door. She heard shuffling sounds and, finally, the door was flung open. Davina was confronted by an overweight, middle-aged woman. She scrutinized Davina from the doorstep with suspicion etched in every one of the myriad lines on her face.

"Who are you?"

"Davina Speers."

"Go figure. I'm Rita Pine."

Rita Pine had curlers in her hair and a martini glass in one hand. From her tipsy walk, ever-so-slightly slurred speech, and distant gaze, Davina guessed happy hour had started sometime earlier in the day.

"Is Elizabeth in?"

Rita's face fell. "Elizabeth hasn't lived here in a very long time. She's at Harvest House."

Davina's stomach flipped. Harvest House was a nursing home.

The hand holding the martini shook as Rita added, "She *lives* there. As a patient. If you can call that any kind of living."

Davina took the plunge. "Is it because of what happened to her ten years ago?"

"What's it to you?" Rita took an aggressive stance, seeming like she'd fight Davina, martini glass in hand, if she had to.

"Because the same thing happened to me. I'm trying to understand *why*."

Rita Pine turned on her slippered heels and shuffled back inside the house, practically *daring* Davina to follow. Davina accepted the dare.

The living room was a cluttered mess of magazines, newspapers, and dozens of cat tchotchkes that didn't look to have been dusted in a long while; a real orange-and-white tabby was curled up asleep under the stained coffee table. Above the fireplace, a shelf held a series of trophies and, from the gold-painted statuettes atop each one, Davina knew they were martial arts awards.

Unlikely to be Rita's.

Rita moved a pile of magazines off a rocking chair: *Better Homes & Gardens, Creative Knitting, Bon Appétit, Condé Nast Traveler.*

"Sit. Can I get you something? I have a pitcher made. Martinis."

"Thank you, no."

Rita sat down with a winded grunt in the armchair opposite Davina. "What do you imagine I can do for you?"

"Tell me about Elizabeth."

"Ten years ago, my daughter was raped and left for dead. She has limited capacity." Her voice trembled. "Her brain isn't right anymore. It was too much to handle by myself, so I had to stick her in Harvest House. It's the best I could afford."

"I'm so sorry to hear that, Mrs. Pine. Can I ask what exactly happened to Elizabeth?"

"Why do you want to know? You some sicko?"

Davina cleared her throat. "My friend may have taken her own life because of what happened to her, me, and Elizabeth. I've been trying to reach out to other victims—I hoped maybe we could help each other."

"There's no helping Elizabeth—heaven knows they tried. She had brain doctors, shrinks, even the best trauma counselor on Staten Island, but not one of 'em could fix what Son of Cropsey did to my baby."

For a moment, Davina was afraid Rita Pine would send her packing, but then she took a hearty sip of liquid courage and began talking.

"My daughter was out selling Girl Scout cookies door-to-door with Ellen Nielsen's girl, Lisa. They decided to split up so they could cover more houses, and when they were done it was dark. Elizabeth decided to take the train home instead of walking—figured it was safer that way." Rita let out a half-laugh, half-grunt. "She was grabbed off the platform at Great Kills so fast she couldn't even scream." Rita refilled her martini glass from the pitcher on the side table; her hand shook, and a drop or two spilled onto her lap. "She was found two days later in the woods near the station. The bastard left her for dead. Dr. Fidanza said it was a miracle she survived."

Davina brushed away a tear making its way down her cheek. This monster, this abhorrent creature didn't only destroy the lives of his victims —he destroyed entire families. He decimated futures and hopes and dreams. He ravaged them physically, emotionally, and spiritually, and left them to suffer, imprisoned inside themselves for a lifetime. Davina desperately wanted to ask if Elizabeth had been marked in any way, but Rita spoke again.

"Some days, I think it would be better if she'd died, but then there are days where I can see little pieces of my Elizabeth inside the stranger she's become. The Elizabeth who was happy, who loved me and her dad to the ends of the earth. That Elizabeth, my *baby*, is still in there somewhere." Rita made eye contact with Davina. "I just don't know how to get her to come out and stay."

Davina pressed her fingers to her lips; certain she was going to start sobbing. The pain in Rita Pine's face was too much for her to deal with. Elizabeth's mother didn't drink to drink, she drank to *escape*—except there was no escaping. Davina knew that kind of pain intimately and also knew nothing could dull it; she'd tried everything during her fucked-up days.

A few minutes passed before Davina managed to find her voice and her nerve. "Mrs. Pine, I need to ask you another question. This is important. After the attack, did Elizabeth have any odd markings on her forehead?"

Rita frowned. "Markings?"

"Like a circle with a line across the middle." She mimed it on her own forehead.

"I don't know that I'd call it a *marking*. Elizabeth had a curved scar on her forehead. Not a whole circle—maybe half of one. It was just a red welt by the time they found her. The police thought she might have hit a tree branch, or her attacker may have slashed at her with a blunt knife."

Well, that was something, at least. "Someone told me Son of Cropsey liked to sign his . . . his victims."

Rita shook her head, her expression dark. "The police said it wasn't him—they'd arrested him hours before Elizabeth was attacked, you see. They told me someone else had attacked Elizabeth."

Davina's chest felt tight. Here was another poor soul banished to purgatory in order to stoke Detective Riley's overinflated ego. "Would it be okay if I visited Elizabeth? Maybe even today?"

Rita placed her drink carefully on the coffee table. "I guess so. But Elizabeth gets confused easily. Sometimes she gets very upset. You can't do anything to upset her."

Davina shook her head. "No. Never. But maybe I could reach her— the Elizabeth that's locked up inside."

Davina saw the faint glimmer of hope in Rita Pine's eyes. It was agonizing to witness because she didn't really believe she was offering much hope. Davina stood up and approached Rita, crouched down in front of her chair, and gently placed a hand over hers. "I don't want to cause either of you any more pain, Rita. I'll understand if you'd rather I don't see Elizabeth."

"Elizabeth doesn't have visitors except for me. It'll be nice for her to see a new face." She gazed deeply into Davina's eyes. "I'll call Harvest House and tell them you have my permission to visit."

Davina blinked back her tears. "Thank you."

"I want you to come back and tell me about your visit. I want to know what my daughter says."

"Okay." Davina nodded. "I can do that."

Rita's eyes seemed to come into sharper focus as she spoke, "Elizabeth's nurse is Jane Edelson. I'll make the call and tell her to expect you this afternoon?"

Davina nodded. "Is there anything I can bring to Elizabeth? Something special she might like?"

A genuine smile crossed Rita's lips. "M&M's. Elizabeth always liked M&M's."

CHAPTER TWENTY-EIGHT

WEDNESDAY, STAPLETON HEIGHTS

Leaving the Jetta in the parking lot, Davina walked into the little market, savoring the caress of the air-conditioned breeze on her hot cheeks. She picked up a sharing bag of M&M's for Elizabeth and a Red Bull for herself; she needed to stay alert.

At the checkout, Davina surprised herself. "I'll take a pack of Marlboros."

She hadn't bought cigarettes in six months. She preferred instead to bum them off Millie to avoid taking up the habit again. Staring at the pack in her hand, it dawned on Davina she was more of a mess than she thought she was.

"On second thought," she told the clerk with an embarrassed grin. "That's probably the last thing I need."

Davina got to Harvest House at quarter to four, a little later than she wanted. Rita had told her as they parted ways that the home served dinner at four thirty, but if Elizabeth was having a good day, they could take their time. How utterly fucked up was it for a young woman, a girl only a little older than Davina, to be served bingo meals for the rest of her life?

She circled the parking lot twice before a white SUV vacated a spot and she snagged it. Davina crossed the blacktop to the nondescript white-and-gray three-story building. The structure was like a big concrete box with windows—a prison minus the bars.

Elizabeth was raped, so they throw her in fucking jail.

The cement walkway was tucked neatly between two expansive sections of lawn so perfectly manicured, they appeared painted. No flowers were anywhere to be seen, and despite the long row of arborvitae trees cushioning the edge of the property, not one bird sang; life was suffocated here. The humid heat added to the heavy, morbid stillness.

Davina pulled open the glass front doors and went inside. Like the little bodega where she'd bought the M&M's, the air was cool to the point of chill. But unlike the market, it carried an unpleasantly clinical, antiseptic smell.

Like they're trying to cover up the smell of death and decay.

The deserted lobby was carpeted in green and white. The dark green leather couches were in pristine condition, unworn as if nobody ever sat on them. On the glass-topped coffee table, assorted magazines were fanned out perfectly beside a Keurig coffee setup.

Davina proceeded through the lobby to the reception area. A sturdy woman in her mid to late fifties glanced up at Davina over wire-rimmed bifocal glasses. The woman's braid was so tight it made Davina's forehead hurt just looking at it. At least her smile was pleasant.

"How can I help you?"

"I'm here to see Elizabeth Pine. My name is Davina Speers."

The receptionist adjusted her spectacles and scanned her computer screen. "Yes. Mrs. Pine called." She wrote Davina's name on an adhesive badge with a blue bar declaring VISITOR and handed it to her. "You'll need to wear this until you leave the building."

Davina peeled away the adhesive backing and stuck it above her heart. "Thanks."

"Elizabeth is on the second floor. The elevator is there to your left. Check in with the ward nurse, Jane Edelson, at the reception desk and she'll direct you to Eliza's room."

Eliza.

"Thank you."

On the way down the hallway, Davina passed by the solarium. A handful of residents quietly watched a baseball game on a huge flatscreen. They lounged in comfy-looking chairs, a few with Styrofoam coffee cups by their sides. In one corner, a caregiver read a book to a small group; one nodded off, and the others hung on her every word. Everyone looked comfortable, but the aura of the place was something terribly sad.

Luckily, the door to the stairs was adjacent to the elevator. Eschewing the receptionist's direction, Davina pushed open the door and made her way up the stairs, taking two at a time. She realized the stairwell smelled of disinfectant too and tried to imagine having to live in such a place. The effort brought her to the rock-solid conviction that Elizabeth Pine didn't belong there—she didn't deserve to have her life stolen and her family destroyed. Elizabeth needed to be where life still existed.

Behind the second-floor reception desk, a young woman with chin-length black hair and pink scrubs was waiting for Davina. Glancing at the visitor's pass, she double-checked, "Davina?"

"Yes."

"I'm Jane Edelson. Can we talk for a few minutes? I need to prepare you for Elizabeth's condition."

She ushered Davina into the nurse's lounge and closed the door. They sat comfortably, side-by-side, on a black-and-gray striped couch.

"You are aware Elizabeth suffered a brutal attack. The physical damage was beyond horrific." Jane hesitated, swallowing hard. "The attacker used a metal pipe to penetrate her."

"Oh, dear God." Davina closed her eyes to fight back the nausea. "Elizabeth's mom told me she was attacked, but—"

Jane nodded. "Rita blames herself for letting Elizabeth go out without her. Between you and me, whoever did this acted with such violence, I doubt Rita would have been able to do much. Sadly, beyond the severe internal injuries, Elizabeth suffered hypoxia—her brain was starved of oxygen, which resulted in a level of brain damage we call acquired brain injury that rendered her unable to perform basic daily tasks for herself and has left her with severe memory loss. In some ways, it's a blessing, as she doesn't remember what happened to her."

"Will she ever recover?" Davina fought the sinking feeling in her stomach; she knew the answer before Jane spoke.

"We really don't think so," the nurse replied. "There has been some improvement over the years, but Elizabeth's brain is too badly damaged for any neuron rerouting to allow her a recovery beyond where she is now."

"Rerouting?"

Jane nodded. "When brain cells die, as in the case of strangulation that restricts their oxygen, or through alcohol and drug abuse, they can't grow back. Instead, the brain reroutes the connections around the damaged areas to get things working again—that's how stroke victims can learn to walk all over again."

"So, Elizabeth is stuck here forever?"

"It's not so bad, Miss Speers," Jane reassured . "We make all our guests comfortable and as at home as we possibly can. We also give them daily physiotherapy and life-skills training. When she first came to us, she couldn't feed or dress herself, or use the toilet on her own. She can do those things now, but mentally, she's at around the level of a bright four-year-old. On her good days."

"Can she speak? Is she able to understand what's said to her?"

"Yes. Most days she's relatively coherent, although you have to go very slowly or risk confusing her and she'll shut down. Elizabeth will check out occasionally as if she gets lost between thoughts, and it's sometimes difficult for her to find the right words, so she doesn't always make sense. She'll get frustrated when that happens. It's a lot like dealing with someone with dementia. I wanted to let you know so it might help you approach her."

"Do you have any advice on how I should speak to her? I mean, do I ask questions directly, drop hints, or . . . ?"

"The only advice I can give is to take your cue from Elizabeth. If you see her getting frustrated, don't pursue it. Let her go at her own speed. Sometimes she's a dripping faucet and other times she's a fire hose."

Davina nodded. "I brought her a bag of M&M's. Her mother said she's fond of them. Am I okay to give them to her?"

"She'll love them." Jane smiled and stood up. "I'll take you to her."

"The receptionist downstairs called her Eliza."

Jane nodded. "Sometimes that's what Elizabeth calls herself. Her mother says she went by that name when she was a little girl but stopped using it in sixth grade because it wasn't grown-up enough. Now she wants to be Eliza again."

Davina felt a strong urge to turn and run. Was seeing Elizabeth going to be too much for her to deal with? Merely the thought of the metal pipe was beyond disgusting. Why was Elizabeth's attack so much more brutal than the other girls? Professor Blackman had covered the use of objects in sexual assaults in a recent lecture: rather than pure, unadulterated hate toward women, it typically had to do either with erection problems or a perverted mother complex. The first one was self-explanatory, the latter had to do with the perp seeing women as bearers of children rather than sexual beings and so had no desire to have sex with them—so they used a proxy instead.

A metal pipe, for instance.

None of Son of Cropsey's other victims had suffered hypoxia; something was different about Elizabeth Pine's case.

Elizabeth had a private room with blue carpeting and too much furniture for such a small space. The bedspread, pink with embroidered flowers, had been made for a child's room. Inside the room, the antiseptic smell of the hallway was overlaid with the tangy scent of lavender.

Elizabeth sat on the bed, watching a rerun of *Three's Company* on a wall-mounted TV. Her blonde hair was pulled into a long braid and draped over her shoulder.

"Elizabeth?" Jane Edelson said. "You have a visitor."

"Mom?"

"No, she's a friend of your mom's. This is Davina."

Davina stepped forward. "Hi, Elizabeth."

"Hello."

Davina wasn't sure if it was a good sign or bad one that the young woman didn't insist on being called *Eliza*.

"May I visit with you?"

Elizabeth nodded, and Jane left the room. Davina reached into her fanny pack for the M&M's and held the brown packet out to Elizabeth. "I brought these for you. Your mom said you like them."

Elizabeth took them, smiling, and tore open the bag with childlike eagerness. "Thanks. You can sit if you want."

"Okay." Davina reached for a desk chair.

Elizabeth patted the edge of the bed. "Sit here."

Davina smiled and seated herself facing Elizabeth. Being so close, Davina saw the faint scar on Elizabeth's forehead. Rita Pine had been right; it was semicircular and little more than a fine white curve. It reminded Davina of the glimpse she'd caught of Amber's scar.

Elizabeth's mark was so faded, Davina might have easily missed it if she hadn't been looking for it. Had there once been a line through it? Davina was itching to ask.

"How are you feeling today?" she asked.

Elizabeth shook a few M&M's out of the bag and into her hand, popping them into her mouth. She didn't chew them right away but, instead, savored them as the candy shell melted in her mouth.

"Fine," Elizabeth said once she'd eaten her candy. She held the bag out to Davina and shook it "M's," Elizabeth said. "My favorite."

"They're so good, right?" Davina took a few and ate them one by one, melting them on her tongue just as Elizabeth had. "Did you ever try the pretzel ones? They're *really* good."

Elizabeth tilted her head. "Pretzel?"

"You've never heard of pretzel M's?"

"There's no such thing." Elizabeth knitted her brow and hugged herself.

Davina remembered what Jane told her about Elizabeth's mood swings. Was it possible that Elizabeth would lose it over M&M's she'd never eaten? The expression on the girl's face made Davina cautious about pressing on.

"Do you like living here, Elizabeth?" Davina took a strategic change of tack.

"I like it. Nurse Jane is nice." Elizabeth unwrapped her arms and poured out a few more M&M's. "Night nurse is okay, too. Her name is Anya. She's older."

"Yeah, Jane seems really great."

"Sometimes, I have Nurse Lisa. But she's not here every day." Elizabeth dished out a few more M&M's. "I used to have other nurses, but I forget them." Elizabeth glanced from Davina to the TV and back again. "I get stuff confused."

Davina smiled sweetly. "Is that why you live here?"

Elizabeth stared at the television. Another episode had come on.

Davina watched the show with her. "I sometimes get stuff confused too," she admitted.

"And scared? I get scared."

"And scared, yes."

"Is that why you're here? It's safe here."

"Oh . . . no. I'm just visiting with you, Elizabeth."

How the hell do I ask what I need to ask?

"So, you don't ever have to live here? I *have* to live here. I had an accident."

They sat quietly. At the next commercial break, Davina broke the silence, "I had an accident, too. When I was twelve."

Elizabeth turned to look at her. "You did?"

Davina nodded. "Yes. There was a scary man—he hurt me."

Elizabeth shook M&M pieces out of the bag one at a time; she watched each piece fall into her open palm with great deliberation. When she spoke again, her voice was higher, childlike, "My mom says, 'Eliza, don't talk to strangers.'" She looked at Davina. "I didn't."

Davina nodded. "I believe you. Me neither."

"My Girl Scout uniform got ripped and messed up. I couldn't wear it anymore. Did you have a uniform?"

"No. I was in my pajamas."

"What kind of pajamas?" Eliza wanted to know. "Mine had penguins."

"Mine had little spaceships."

"Did he rip them? He ripped my uniform when he grabbed me and when he . . . it was very, very dark." Eliza stared down at her lap. "I couldn't see. I get afraid in the dark now. It's hard to—" Elizabeth made circular motions with her hands around her throat, and then pointed at her chest. "Breathe. There was something heavy on me. I don't want to say."

"Elizabeth—you can trust me, okay? You can tell me what happened. Because I *know*."

Silence. A blank face.

"Talk to me, Eliza . . . Beth." The combined names seemed safest.

When she spoke, Elizabeth's voice was deeper, more adult. "The bad man smelled bad. Sweet and bitter at the same time—like perfume. I remember him being behind me—*on top* of me. He pushed something inside me, and I wanted him to stop."

"It hurt."

"It hurt *so bad*." There was so much anguish on Elizabeth's face. "He was choking me."

The rank smell. Insistent probing to gain penetration. The chokehold applied from behind— the same hold wrestlers, cops, and martial artists used. It was the same hold the guy at Great Kills had used.

Davina swallowed hard, fighting against the panic of the remembered asphyxia. "I bet you fought hard, didn't you?"

Elizabeth nodded. "I did tae kwon do. I tried to use what my sensei taught me, but it didn't work . . . *it didn't work*."

"What else do you remember, Elizabeth?"

"His hands were made of plastic." Elizabeth massaged her own hands, her expression still blank.

Latex gloves. Yes, that too. Medical grade. Thin enough to offer dexterity. Strong enough to prevent tearing.

Elizabeth went on. "And he hid his face with a hood."

"The perfume," said Davina. "I remember that too. He was wearing a strong cologne that made me feel sick. D'you remember—?"

"Yes. When I smelled it, I got scared and couldn't breathe. People tell me my memory's bad—it's got lots of holes in it."

Davina bit back a curse. "Your memory's fine, Elizabeth. Don't let anyone tell you it's not."

Elizabeth's eyes searched Davina's face as if looking for answers. "Why did he do that to me?"

Davina opened her mouth, but no words came out.

Jane bustled back into the room. "Is everything okay in here?"

"Elizabeth and I were talking about scary things that have happened to us." Davina rubbed Elizabeth's back as she rocked back and forth.

"Are you all right, Elizabeth?"

"Yes," Elizabeth replied but continued to rock.

Jane turned to Davina, "I think that's enough for today."

Davina got up from the bed, wondering if she'd perhaps pushed Elizabeth too far. Then she met Jane's eyes and saw the warmth there.

Saying her goodbye to Elizabeth, Davina swallowed the lump in her throat. *It could easily have been me sitting there.*

Outside in the hall, Davina turned to Jane, "That mark on her forehead. Do you know anything about it?"

"It happened during the attack. Why do you ask?"

"I wondered if there was more of it when she was admitted here. Was it a complete circle? A circle with a line through its middle?"

"I don't know," Jane said, then met her eyes. "I caught what you said about 'scary things that happened to *us*.'"

Davina nodded.

Jane's mouth twisted in a rueful grimace, "I wish I could help you find out about the scar, but I don't have access to Elizabeth's admittance records. Maybe you can ask her next time you're here."

"Yeah, I'll do that," Davina said as she made her way back to the stairwell.

CHAPTER TWENTY-NINE

WEDNESDAY, HARVEST HOUSE EXTENDED CARE HOME

DAVINA SAT IN HER CAR FOR SEVERAL MINUTES AFTER LEAVING Harvest House. It felt bittersweet to know she was not alone, that she was part of a tragic sisterhood of women—of *young girls*—who'd been terrorized and violated. Riley and the NYPD might well scream copycat to save their own bacon, but if the scar on Elizabeth's forehead had once been the same shape as the lipstick tracing on her own and what she suspected Amber Prescott-not-Winters was hiding under her trendy haircut, it spoke volumes. Especially if the latest victims also carried the same signature. She understood why the cops hadn't released details of the theta symbol during the investigation, but why not after Riley caught Son of Cropsey?

The only plausible reason she could think of was they didn't truly believe they had the right man.

Adding that to her mental list of details to dig into, Davina started the Jetta and pulled out of the Harvest House parking lot.

Davina realized she was getting close to the Empire Outlet Mall in St. George, where her sister worked. Allie had never once stood up for her, had never believed her about the attack. All she'd cared about was a damned wrecked lipstick she'd replaced a day later.

Alessandra was six years older than Davina, and she'd had her future all nicely mapped out with Nick Delafield. He was her ticket out of their dysfunctional home. She was going to have the white picket fence and the golden retriever—just like Amber Winters-Prescott. The whole fairy tale had fallen to shit for reasons Alessandra had never fully disclosed, and now she worked as a shift manager at Modern Girl.

By the time Davina got to the mall and wrangled a parking spot, she was ready to spit bullets.

The swanky, modern outdoor mall comprised a series of carefully arranged glass and steel cubes with stunning views of the Upper Bay and trimmed with rectangular stone pavers in varying shades of gray. The place was crowded for a weekday; shoppers carried luxury shopping bags crammed with bargains and stuff they likely didn't need. This was bougie Staten Island, not like the strip malls Davina frequented as a kid.

Making her way to Modern Girl, just past Annie's Pretzels, Davina spotted Alessandra in the store's front window display. Her sister, as always, was hard to miss with her maroon hair, four-inch heels, and bountiful boobs that threatened to pop the straining buttons on her blouse. Alessandra had some teenage employee schlepping a pair of nude mannequins from one side of the window to the other.

Davina knocked on the glass. "Hey, Allie, I need to talk to you."

Alessandra barely glanced at her. "I'm working, Davina."

"I'm not leaving."

Alessandra turned and gave her sister a cold glare, caught something in Davina's expression, and frowned. "What is it?"

Davina entered the store and approached her sister at the window platform. "I *know* what happened to me, Allie."

"Oh. My. God. Not this again." Alessandra returned to the display; she ordered the teenager to position the mannequins' arms in a more welcoming manner. "I don't have time for this, Davina."

"Make time."

Alessandra let out an exasperated sigh and pointed toward the dressing rooms at the back of the store. She turned to the teenager, "I'll be right back."

Alessandra took Davina by her elbow, hustling her along. Davina shook off the hold as the two barreled their way through stacks of denim jeans and overpriced designer T-shirts. All five of the dressing room cubicles were empty; the returns table was piled high with clothes. Alessandra steered Davina into the employees-only section.

"Okay." Alessandra folded her arms across her ample chest. "For the *hundredth time.* They caught Son of Cropsey almost a week before you concocted your story—he was some Black guy, Bobby something or other."

"It wasn't a fucking story, Allie. And it was *Rob* Cox."

"Whatever. The guy confessed. You weren't attacked, Davina—you made it all up the same way you always used to make stories. It was a fixation with you."

"What if there were *two* guys, Allie? Or what if the cops got the wrong guy and made him confess?"

Alessandra picked a belt off the floor and threw it onto the returns table. "You mean like they beat him with a rubber hose? Stop it, Davina. You're being ridiculous. You had a nightmare and spun it into a crime thriller."

"He was on top of me. Behind me. I almost puked from his cologne. He had his fucking fingers *inside* me. Is that vivid enough for you?"

"I seriously don't have time for this. You need to stop trying to make something out of nothing, Davina."

"The Todt Hill girl was in her own bedroom when she was attacked— just like I was—*two fucking days ago!*"

Alessandra's eyes bugged out. "Two days? Davina, it's been *ten* years. Even if the guy was out and still alive—"

"*Only* ten years, Allie. *I'm* still alive. So are his other victims—Brianna Fisher, Amber Winters, Elizabeth Pine. He likes young girls."

"I'm *so* done with this." Alessandra hurried out of the dressing area.

Davina grabbed her by the arm and spun her around. "Was Mom screwing Riley? She was, wasn't she? I remember him being around the house a lot back then, especially after my attack—he used it as an excuse to see her."

"What's that got to do with anything? Yeah, they had their thing, until he moved on to something fresher. Riley's just another piece-of-shit, sex-crazed Y chromosome. So what? Are you going to somehow twist him into the story, too? Ooooh, maybe the cop did it."

"Maybe he did," Davina snarled.

"For Christ's sake, will you listen to yourself?" Alessandra pulled her arm free and rubbed where her sister's fingers had dug into the soft flesh.

"I don't know why it's so hard for you to believe me," Davina lowered her voice; the teen employee was staring in their direction.

"Probably because your story was always changing and you can never remember the important bits—a bit too convenient, don't you think?"

Davina swallowed down her anger. "He strangled me and gave me brain damage, Allie. It's called ABI—look it up! I struggle with remembering stuff and connecting things because the guy who raped me in my own bed fucked my brain up!"

"Now you're just being melodramatic," Alessandra scoffed. "There's nothing wrong with you, and nothing happened to you back then. You're still trying to hog the limelight after all this time."

"I *know* what happened to me, and I'm going to find out why it happened."

"You do what you want, Davina. You always do. You've always been selfish. You ruined my life and don't give a shit."

Davina spoke softly, "*I* ruined your life? How? And, damn it, I *do* care. You never even tried to explain what happened with Nick . . . or Dad."

"What was the point? You only care about yourself, Davina." Alessandra brought her hands to her face; tears were rolling down her flushed cheeks. "Dad was a project manager for Sean Delafield. He lost his job for some stupid shit he did, and he was so ashamed, he split."

"What stupid shit?"

"A fire broke out. There were hundreds of thousands in damages, but the insurance wouldn't pay out because of purposeful negligence based on what the fire chief claimed he'd found. There was even some talk about arson. Dad insisted he'd warned Sean of a potential fire hazard, but no one believed him. So, Dad dropped our family and picked up the bottle. End of story."

"Why didn't I know any of this?"

"You were too busy wrapped up in your own stupid world. At least Mom stayed, even if she was fucked up. Instead of college, I had to go to work. And then there was Nick. He was always Daddy's boy. Within weeks of the fire, he ghosted me." Alessandra shook her head; her wine-colored curls swished around her face like so many thick snakes. "Maybe that was for the best—I know how big brotherly he was with you, but he could be very rough with me."

Davina took a step forward, getting in her sister's face. "I'm sorry about what happened, I truly am. But, Allie, I went to hell. Did you ever bother to come after me? No. You wrote me off—you and Mom. I had to fight my way back on my own, and I'm still fighting every single day."

"Whatever, Davina. You don't even come by the house anymore. Mom asks about you all the time."

"I'm sure she does—when she needs somebody to blame for her life turning to shit." Davina stormed out of the employee area.

"Sure. Walk out, Davina. Just turn your back, right?" Alessandra called after her. "It's always about you. *It's all about you!*"

Davina cut a furious path out of the store, almost plowing down two young girls deciding between tank tops. By the time she got to her car, Davina just wanted to cry. It was then she saw the ticket on her windshield and, from the corner of her eye, the squad car parked over by the mall's exit. She snatched the ticket from beneath her wiper and read it.

Broken taillight? I don't have a broken taillight.

Davina walked around to the rear of her car and found shards of plastic from her tail light littered on the ground. Davina glanced over at the cop. He smiled and gave her a salute.

You can't scare me off. Nobody can. Not anymore.

Making a big show of screwing up the ticket, Davina climbed into her car, pulled out of the parking spot, and drove past the cop car. Rolling down her window, she smiled and waved.

"Have a nice rest of your day, Officer."

Tell Riley to go fuck himself.

CHAPTER THIRTY

WEDNESDAY, OFFICES OF THE STATEN ISLAND ADVANCE

Assistant DAs weren't all that different from cops. In some jurisdictions they were actually embedded with the police department as expert consultants. Gayle Ceine hadn't been one of those, but she'd worked on the prosecution in the Son of Cropsey case.

No one in the DA's office liked closed cases revisited, especially old ones as neatly buttoned down as Son of Cropsey's. Geoff's headline about the possible resurgence of the rapist didn't take long to ruffle feathers, so he wasn't surprised when Gayle got in touch.

"Wong, we need to talk. Now." Blunt as ever, no time for niceties or bullshit.

Geoff told her he knew just the place.

———

Off-limits to the public, shuttered for over twenty-five years, the old Paramount Theater was the site of a nine-year-old cold case Geoff was convinced was connected to Son of Cropsey—based on the MO. The case had been swept under the rug because the rapist, thanks to Detective Tom Riley, was incarcerated. He thought the theater still looked incredibly grand, despite its decades of neglect, with its art deco style, towering facade of weathered red brick, and stone-built entryway. The theater's name was still displayed above the doors, picked out in stone, a sad echo of the glory days when people would travel from all over Staten Island and beyond to catch the latest movies. A far cry from the modern soulless multiplexes that sucked so much of the joy out of experiencing Hollywood on the big screen.

Geoff watched Gayle slide out of her cab and dart across the street; she didn't appear happy.

This is gonna be a tough job . . . and I wouldn't have it any other way.

Gayle Ceine was mid forties, medium height and build, with curly dark brown hair cut to collar length. She wore black pants with a white blouse and had diamond studs in her ears. Furrowing her brows, she opened with, "I thought this place was shut down."

"It is."

"So, we're breaking in?"

"I did a piece on it a few years back—I've got some sway with the nice folks who run the ghost tours after I gave them some love in the article. They let me have a spare key anytime I want to impress someone." Geoff grinned and pulled open the glass door. "After you."

"Jesus Christ. What a dump. *This* impresses people?" Gayle stared up at the lobby ceiling, which had once been a glorious vault full of art deco glory but was now damp-stained and broken through in places.

"You'd be surprised. This *dump* was one of the most prestigious movie houses in Staten Island," Geoff said. "Folks from all over the island flocked to the Stapleton district for it. Seated 2,300 people."

"Looks like it should be haunted."

"Rumor is that it is. You'd be haunted, too, if you'd been around since 1930." Geoff dug his hands in his pockets and tilted his head toward the double doors at the entrance to the theater proper. "The house had a Wurlitzer theater organ with two consoles—one of only ten in the whole country. The theater's been empty for twenty-five years now after they tried to convert it into a nightclub. Alas, that only lasted a couple of years. It gets used as a set for TV and movies now and again."

Gayle darted Geoff a glance and stepped ahead of him. "So, what's your bullcrap about the Son of Cropsey case? My time is precious."

Yeah, it's especially precious when there's something you don't want to see.

"I'm looking into a rape and murder that took place here—about nine years ago. A thirteen-year-old Black girl was attacked and her mother killed."

"I don't remember that at all." Gayle sounded defensive. "It was probably never prosecuted. We don't catch *all* the bad guys, you know."

"I think it was Son of Cropsey."

Scoffing, Gayle shook her head. "Rob Cox was put behind bars *ten years* ago—you know that."

"I'm not so sure Cox is the right guy, though." He motioned for Gayle to follow him into the theater house. "The attack took place in here."

Gayle's gaze pulled upward; the ceiling, painted a vibrant purple and gold with a flock of birds flying in a circle, was cavernous and majestic. "I've never seen anything like that."

Stop gawking at the architecture and face the facts.

The stage was dark except for one light in the center. A ghost light. The effect was appropriately haunting.

Geoff pointed to the proscenium. "The mother's body was found center stage. The daughter was found in the stairwell of the stage left emergency exit. She'd been attacked just like the others—chokehold from behind, lost consciousness, memory in tatters. She kept rambling on about stinky cologne, too—another common thread, along with the graffiti on her forehead."

Gayle shot him a narrow side-eye but didn't respond directly to the graffiti comment. "Is that why you ran your story? You're resurrecting a closed case based on an unrelated cold case?"

"It's more than just a cold case. This is an unsolved murder nobody is showing any interest in. The young girl was brutally raped, her mother is gone, and nothing's been done about it."

"Wasn't my case, Geoff."

"Maybe not, but you read the headlines like everybody else when it happened. Didn't it dawn on you it might be connected to the earlier cases?"

Gayle looked him in the eyes. "No, it didn't. You're going to embarrass yourself, Geoff. And worse, you're going to embarrass the *Advance*."

"It's called journalism."

"It's called *fear-mongering*. Just how far are you willing to go to ruin your reputation?"

"I'll go as far as it takes to get to the truth."

"What's in it for you, Geoff?"

"Answers. There's a whole new crop of young rape victims whose attacks are disturbingly similar to Son of Cropsey's. Look, you asked for this meeting, Gayle. If you came all the way out here to clamp a lid on my story, that's not happening. So, I gotta ask: What's in it for *you?*"

Gayle pointed a perfectly manicured finger at him. "You can quote me on this, Geoff—this is not connected at all to Son of Cropsey. End quote. And make sure you spell my fucking name right."

Losing her cool. That tells me everything I need to know.

"Detective Riley and his team investigated every angle to get Rob Cox off the streets. They questioned whether Son of Cropsey or his victims had anything to do with attack locations: the tanks, the Greenbelt hiking trail, the old hospitals. They examined possible connections to the Girl Scouts and church youth groups. They checked out other kids' organizations, the families' religious backgrounds, ethnicities, hobbies, school routes. They even examined the subway line that runs through Staten Island for the rapist's means of moving about, but nothing popped. There wasn't a camera, not a single witness, no DNA, nothing to link the girls to each other or the rapist to the girls."

"Being attacked linked the girls to each other," Geoff threw in. "The police kept some evidence to themselves—like how Son of Cropsey marked his victims."

Gayle fixed him with a gimlet-eyed frown. "Where did you get that from?"

"A confidential source," he told her with a smug grin.

The ADA shook her head. "The accused didn't kill anyone, Geoff—you know that. The attacks were targeted specifically to young girls on their own." She hesitated, then added, "Police thought they were asphyxiated with plastic bags. Hence the memory loss."

Geoff felt a chill along his spine. "There's no mention of plastic bags in our archived records."

She shrugged. "You know how it works, Geoff. The cops don't reveal all the evidence they find—even to the press."

"No, they don't. And now, we've had three more girls raped in recent days—all with the same MO—strangleholds, no clear memories, two of them at historic sites. Add in a murder, and we've got a big problem. He's upping the stakes. C'mon, Gayle, you know the pathology. This behavior isn't about sex. It's about control, risk-taking, thrills, poking the ant hill."

"Look, I can't recall everything that went on nine or ten years ago, and I wasn't privy to all of it anyway. But I do remember there wasn't a stone left unturned. Everybody worked their asses off to see Son of Cropsey caught."

"Okay, so why Rob Cox? What made him pop?"

"All the girls remembered a strong, bittersweet smell, like cologne. Then, a forensic shrink was able to coax from one of the girls that she thought the perp was Black because she swore his hands were black. It was through dumb luck one of the cops from the 120th Narco Squad pinched this guy."

"He wore gloves."

Gayle shrugged. "The cops placed Cox in the general vicinity at the time of the attacks, and he had prior sexual assault charges that hadn't stuck. Oh, and he liked to douse himself in that awful cologne that was all the rage back then . . . Hatchet, Axe, whatever the fuck it was."

"Did you ask the victims if it was the same cologne?"

"No need. The attacks stopped the minute Cox was in custody." The ADA turned and headed back out into the lobby.

Geoff followed. "No, Gayle, they didn't. I know of at least one cop who was on the case that has doubts about the collar. I found cases in our archives that fit the MO, which happened *after* Cox's arrest, including Mariah Washington's."

"Who?"

"The Black thirteen-year-old—the one attacked *here*." He pointed over at the stage.

"So, what—Son of Cropsey took a nine-year vacation?"

"Maybe he took advantage of Cox's arrest and hit other areas, then came home. The recent attacks are no coincidence, Gayle."

"Look, off the record, I'll admit we were all under a lot of pressure to close the Son of Cropsey case. But, bottom line, there was enough evidence for the grand jury to indict, and Cox confessed. What more do you need?"

"Something more solid than convenient circumstantial evidence. Shit, the case is closed, everybody washes their hands, life goes on, and now the attacks have started again and nobody has questions? Ask yourself, if your perp is the right one and he's still behind bars, then who the hell raped Mary Lamont, Jessica Balducci, and Seraphina Bellano?"

Gayle didn't appear too surprised that Geoff knew the victims' names —the guy knew everybody worth knowing who could feed him information, and the 120th Precinct cops weren't known for their discretion. "Listen, this wasn't some innocent, dumbass coerced into a confession—if that's where you're going with this. Cox was a hardcore career criminal with a record a mile long who needed to be off the streets. Leather gloves and bondage paraphernalia were found in his apartment."

"*Leather?* Not latex?"

Ignoring the question, Gayle went on, "He was big, strong, and scary. He was the type of Black guy who'd look at you and you'd be handing over your wallet. Okay?" She grabbed the door handle. "We're done here, Geoff."

Ah, the unsubtle fragrance of racism. Nice, Gayle, real nice.

Geoff held the door shut. "The Son of Cropsey attacks a decade ago were among the worst Staten Island has ever seen. The guy didn't just assault those girls, he *brutalized* them—physically, emotionally, mentally. If I am right and he's back, this little haven of ours is going to hell."

"Son of Cropsey is *not* back, Geoff. At worst, it's some copycat playing the part, and we'll put him away just the same as we did Rob Cox. Linking the recent attacks to the ones ten years ago might make for dramatic headlines, but where's your proof?"

"I'll find it."

"Just let the cops do their jobs, Wong." Gayle pulled open the door. "And thanks for the tour. I always wanted to see the inside of this place."

CHAPTER THIRTY-ONE

WEDNESDAY, PARAMOUNT THEATRE

Gayle Ceine knew her stuff. Geoff had to admit that much. There was no cracking her facade. But he was left with the growing suspicion that she knew a lot more about what had gone on inside the Son of Cropsey investigation than she was letting on. The red herring about the plastic bags was an especially cunning dodge. His next stop, he decided, would be Dobson's Gym, where he hoped to catch Davina during her last class of the day, which he knew started at 6:30 .

Of course, he could just call, but Geoff was an old-fashioned reporter; he preferred face-to-face. And he did harbor an intense curiosity to see Davina at work. The petite, muscular body intrigued him as much as he found it alluring. As Gayle Ceine put up a wall of icy intelligence, Davina put up a wall of physical strength and sensual electricity around her very real vulnerability.

Dobson's parking lot was full; the gym was popular with hardcore workout addicts. Any chauvinistic idea that a woman—especially a tiny woman like Geraldine Dobson—couldn't run a hardcore gym could be put to rest watching her work her clients to death. Normally, Geoff wouldn't be caught dead in there; the last thing he wanted was to be the only Asian in the room who sucked at mixed martial arts.

Inside, the gym smelled of the sweat of bodies that lived off juice and protein shakes. Sounds of exertion, grunting, and the fierce clanking of metal fittings filled the air. Dobson's was an equitable mix of men and women, white and brown. In fact, the only thing missing was a diversity of body type—*everyone* was ripped.

Davina stood at the center of a blue-and-red mat in the main room. A group of a half dozen or so people sat around her in a circle, cross-legged. They watched Davina pirouette, savaging the air with graceful kicks and powerful jabs. Her taut muscles were incredibly well-defined; she had agility, speed, and precision. Geoff was pretty sure she could kick the living shit out of anyone she chose to.

Geoff loosened his tie, feeling horribly out of place. Davina spotted him and waved, before returning her laser focus to the students.

"Can I help you?" A voice startled him. Turning, Geoff recognized Gerry Dobson from a small article a junior reporter had written about the gym some months before. The gym owner was even more ripped than Davina.

"I'm here to meet with Davina."

"She's pretty popular." Gerry turned to face the mat.

"Oh, it's not that," Geoff felt he had to explain. "My name is Geoff Wong. I'm a reporter for the *Advance*."

Gerry grinned. "Ahh. She told me about you."

"She did?"

"Davina tells me everything. I'm her den mother."

I'd choose you as a den mother.

Davina's group applauded and got to their feet. Some dispersed—places to be—while others gathered around Davina to chat; each smiling, glowing face was relaxed and calm.

Davina approached, unwrapping tape from her hands. "What are you doing here?"

"I needed to talk to you. You have some free time?"

Davina glanced past Gerry toward the staircase that led down to the locker rooms. "That was my last class, and I'd invite you downstairs, but—"

Gerry interjected, "You guys can use my office. I've got a class in ten."

Davina led the way. Geoff followed, visually checking out the place—not exactly state-of-the-art, but it did look incredibly professional and well-tended.

"Nice place." Geoff followed Davina into the office.

She closed the door. "It's my salvation. Don't know what I'd do without it."

"You ever think of working at one of those fancy gyms like Equinox Fitness?"

Davina's reply was quick and certain, "No. Not interested." She made herself comfortable in Gerry's chair behind the desk. "Are you here for a report? Because I have one."

Geoff caught the tension in her voice and turned away from perusing the multitude of photos of fitness champions and ripped, barely clad models on the walls. "Me too. I just came from a meeting with one of the ADAs on the Son of Cropsey case—Gayle Ceine—she's one hell of a tough cookie."

"I would imagine she has to be."

"I tried to convince her the recent attacks proved the newest Son of Cropsey wasn't behind bars. But she was adamant they've got the real perp in jail. She says the investigation was thorough and we have a copycat."

Davina's cheeks pinked. "What—now *you're* convinced?"

"No, because saying it was thorough and it *being* thorough aren't the same thing. Plus, she tried to throw me a false trail and reacted when I mentioned I knew the rapist signed his victims."

Davina leaned forward and clasped her hands on the desk. "I talked to two of the Son of Cropsey victims today—and the mother of a third."

Geoff perched his butt on the corner of the desk and quicky said, "And?"

"I asked them about the theta marking. Brianna Fisher's mom said her daughter's face was covered with mud and blood after the attack and she never noticed a mark. But Amber Prescott had a faint scar on her forehead—I only saw part of it, but enough to be confident it was theta. Poor girl reckons she wasn't the victim of an attack . . . that Amber *Winters* was."

"She's dissociating?"

Davina shrugged. "That's her way of dealing with it. She has a husband and a baby—a fresh start. I had drugs, remember."

"Okay. What's behind door number three?"

Davina took a deep breath and let out a loud, weary sigh. Her green eyes appeared to darken a shade or two. They met his and stopped his breath for just a second. They were filled with pain and sorrow.

"Elizabeth Pine. She's institutionalized, Geoff. Harvest House long-term care home. She was attacked more savagely than any of the rest of us and sustained brain damage from asphyxiation. *And* she has a semicircular scar on her forehead. Her mom said it was swollen and red when they found her. Now it's just a tiny white sliver. I know what it was—the bastard *carved* theta into her head."

Geoff nodded slowly, his mind working through the ramifications. "We need to know if other victims have that mark—then and now."

"Mine was drawn on with lipstick, so it wasn't permanent. If he did that to others, then it's going to be harder to make a solid connection—at least not one that would stand up in court."

"Yeah, but Gayle mentioned the cologne, which is something that also wasn't in the press package. She said a number of the victims ten years ago talked about the smell—strong, bittersweet."

He saw Davina shiver.

"Yeah. You think she knows about theta?"

"Going by her reaction, I'd say it wasn't the first time she'd heard about it. She made a big point of telling me she wasn't completely on the inside of the case ten years ago, but she's all over the new ones. If the pervert is using these girls as canvasses, then the odds of this being a copycat go way down."

"Have you heard anything from Packer yet?"

Geoff shook his head; it was negative. "Plus, I tried reaching out to the aunt and uncle of the Fort Wadsworth victim, but no dice. The mom's still in the hospital."

Davina kicked her legs up onto the desk and massaged her muscular calves. Geoff forced himself not to stare and made a business out of settling into the side chair across from the desk.

"Maybe I should take that one," Davina suggested. "I was going to talk to the Balduccis next, but I can add Mary Lamont to my list." She shook her head. "This may sound crazy, but what if everybody is in on the cover-up? I mean *everybody*. The cops, the DA's office . . ."

"A lot of folks would have to be involved for them to get away with keeping the connections under wraps all this time. You and Joy were both outside the time frame, attacked after Cox was apprehended."

"And Elizabeth."

"Of course. I've learned from experience that for something that big to get swept under the rug, there has to be a whole network of crooked people holding the broom."

"You think?"

"My inside source at the 120th is scared shitless of being found out talking to me. It's possible this goes deep, and he's not sure who he can trust. I don't know if you know this, but Staten Island is a dumping ground for bad cops. We're kinda like Australia back when Britain needed a place to ship all its criminals."

Her lip curled wryly. "I wish I could say I was surprised."

"We've got the highest number of NYPD officers who've been sued by private citizens. Most of them work, or have worked, narcotics in the 120th Precinct. The 120th also has the highest number of misconduct allegations of any precinct in New York. One narcotics sergeant was sued *sixteen times* and still promoted to lieutenant."

"Oh, but that's just because they perform aggressive, proactive polic-ing," Davina snarked, pumping a fist in the air.

Geoff laughed along. "Yeah, that. Or it's because we're so isolated from the other boroughs, the bad cops are off the radar. And it's those men of such sterling character who were part of the team that unearthed Son of Cropsey."

Davina dropped her feet to the floor and fixed the reporter with an intense gaze. "Riley was in the 120th?"

"Yes. So were Packer and Monaghan. It makes me think. What if . . . God, I hate to say it. What if it's more than they just got the wrong guy and realized, after the fact, they'd gotten it all wrong? What if they knew *when* they arrested Rob Cox that he wasn't their guy?"

"Jesus. But why would they protect . . . ? *Jesus*," Davina repeated, massaging her temples. "That's all kinds of sick, Geoff. I *need* to talk to the latest victims because I have to know for certain if the real Son of Cropsey is behind bars."

Davina stood up, circled the desk, and snagged a hoodie from a hook by the office door.

Geoff smiled. "You'd make one hell of a good investigator."

"That's why I'm going to college."

"Trust me—a degree won't make you a good investigator, Davina. Balls of steel will."

"Ovaries," she corrected him with a wink. "And they're *titanium*."

CHAPTER THIRTY-TWO

WEDNESDAY, TODT HILL

Davina parked in front of Lenny and Anne Gibsons' house. Theirs was a simple two-story brick home with a packed flower garden and a statue of the Blessed Mother out front. If Geoff Wong was right, the home was where the victim of the Fort Wadsworth attack, Mary Lamont, was staying until her mother recovered from her own injuries. Neither of them would ever completely recover from the loss of a husband and father.

Few other cars were parked on the street, which made Davina's Jetta, idling as the air-conditioning cooled the interior, stand out. She glanced at the dash clock.

Maybe they're having dinner. Maybe I should respect their privacy. Maybe that's the best thing I can do for Mary. For them all.

She was just thinking about leaving when a man holding a pizza box tapped on the driver's side window, startling her. He motioned for her to roll down the window.

Davina cracked it. "Yes?"

"Do you mind if I ask what you're doing here?"

Jesus, there's neighborhood watch with pizza now?

"I was just leaving." She glanced over at the house and back to the delivery guy; he was late thirties, with a full head of sandy blond hair and a close-cropped beard. She judged him to be too old to be delivering fast food. She pointed to the house. "Do you know the family? I heard about Mary's attack. I was wondering how she was doing."

The man balanced the pizza box in one hand to scratch at the corner of his eye with his free hand. "She's my niece. This is *my* house."

Davina's stomach flipped. "Oh, I'm *so* sorry," she stammered.

"How do you know Mary, Miss . . . ?"

"Speers. Davina Speers. I don't know your niece, but I do know what she's going through."

His brow furrowed. "How could you possibly?"

"I was the victim of the same crime—I think the same criminal—about ten years ago."

Gibson studied her for a moment, and then his stiff posture relaxed a little. "You were assaulted, too?"

Davina nodded. "Honestly, I meant no harm coming here. I thought there might be something I could do to help Mary. I know what it's like to go through trauma like that."

"She doesn't talk about it." Lenny Gibson glanced at his house. "Not at all. I don't know if that's . . . normal. Hell, what's normal about any of this?"

"I didn't talk much about it, either. Not for a long while. But I might have if there'd been somebody back then who could understand."

"Mary has a therapist, Miss Speers. Even Dr. Donato can't get her to talk."

Davina smiled at the memory of Angela, the one person who hadn't accused her of making up stories. The one person who *listened*. "With all due respect, Mr. Gibson, having a therapist is not really the same as having someone who understands because they've been through the same thing and survived."

Lenny said nothing for several seconds, just stood there holding his pizza in one hand, like some bizarre modern art statue. Davina wasn't sure the man believed her, but at least he hadn't called the cops—yet.

He subtly inclined his head. "Would you like to come inside?"

"Yes. Thank you, Mr. Gibson."

He opened the Jetta's door. "Please, call me Lenny."

Lenny ushered Davina across the street and into the house. "Anne?" he announced his return.

A woman's voice called out over running water, "I'll be right there, Len. Just put the pizza on the dining room table."

The vertical blinds in the dining room were pulled tight and, as Davina glanced around, she noticed *all* the blinds in the house were closed. She knew it wasn't so much to keep out the strong late-afternoon sun; it was more about keeping looky-loos from peering in, a ploy to make Mary feel safe.

The Gibsons' abode was a nice middle-class home. The furnishings weren't fancy but appeared comfortably worn—lived in, as her father would have said—and there were more family pictures in the dining room china cabinet than china. It matched Davina's idea of what a happy home looked like.

Lenny put the pizza box in the center of the dining room table, where three places had been set. "This has been terrible for Anne. Mary's mom, Samantha, is her sister. She was badly injured trying to fight off Mary's attacker. She's in ICU in an induced coma until the swelling on her brain goes down. Mary's dad, Hal—"

Anne entered the dining room, her dark auburn hair coiled into a tight, neat bun. Wiping her hands on a clean white towel, she immediately zeroed in on Davina. "Who is this?" she asked her husband.

"Davina Speers."

Davina stepped forward and offered a hand for the shaking.

"She's a victim, like Mary," Lenny explained.

Anne spoke softly but with a tinge of sternness, "I'm very sorry for you, Miss Speers, but we asked for privacy."

Lenny grasped the back of a chair. "She might be able to help Mary."

"Time and doctors will help Mary. Not strangers. Strangers we don't need. What we do need is some peace and quiet. We all need time to heal."

Davina looked back and forth between the couple as they spoke. It was as if she'd disappeared.

"Anne, it's not about what *we* need, it's about what Mary needs."

"Mary needs privacy."

"She doesn't even talk to us."

"What do you want her to say? She's in shock. I'm in shock. Everybody in the neighborhood is in shock. For God's sake, Lenny, this is Staten Island. This kind of thing just doesn't happen here. Staten Island was always safe, and now—"

"Staten Island was never safe." The words tumbled from Davina's lips before she could hold them back.

Anne stared Davina square in the eyes. "Were you sent by the paper? A reporter called asking for an interview earlier today. I deleted his message."

Davina shuffled and glanced down at her Nike-clad feet. "No, ma'am, and I don't want to intrude. I just felt drawn to reach out to Mary. I thought maybe I could help."

Lenny scratched his cheek. "What could it hurt, Anne? Maybe Mary will open up to someone who's experienced the same trauma."

It was several seconds before Anne addressed Davina with a pointed finger. "I don't want to see one word of this in the *Advance*—or anywhere else, for that matter. Do you understand me?"

"You have my word."

"You either help Mary or you're out the door."

"Understood."

Anne peered up to the heavens and shrugged her shoulders. "I don't mean to be rude, but the whole thing has just been so damn hard." Davina could see she was on the verge of tears.

"I do understand, Mrs. Gibson. Trust me."

"That pizza is probably cold. Put it in the oven for a few minutes, Len. I'll tell Mary dinner is ready." She shot Davina a warning expression and left the room.

Lenny turned to Davina, apologetic. "Anne's tough. So's Mary." An awkward silence followed. The greasy smell of cooling pizza filled the dining room and had Davina's stomach growling.

"Oven."

Lenny picked up the box and walked to the kitchen. "I'll be right back."

Thinking it rude to sit at the table before the family, Davina wandered over to the china hutch to take a look at the family photos. One showed Lenny and Anne in a verdant park with their arms around each other; standing beside them were the Lamonts—a smiling Samantha, Hal, and Mary. Mary couldn't have been more than seven or eight; her little curls were caught in a gust of wind.

I was once that age. I once smiled like that. It only took one person to blow it all up.

Davina had to admit that even though she was once younger and less tainted, she had never truly been innocent. Her mother's drinking problems predated Raymond Speers's absence, and quite possibly—mostly likely—they were the reason for it. Nothing had ever been perfect in the Speers home, but with Davina's rape and the sudden evaporation of her dad's job, things had quickly deteriorated from slightly dysfunctional to completely fucked up.

"Do you want a beer or soda or something?" Lenny asked as he walked into the dining room, beer in hand.

"No, but thanks." Davina turned from the hutch, not wanting to give away that she was staring at their family photographs.

"We get the pizza from Vinnie's down the street," Lenny made with the small talk. "Local guy. Family's been making those pies for generations." He took a swig of his beer and stared at the walls, considering his words. "You gotta understand Anne. Mary is like a daughter to us—we have no children of our own."

Their heads turned at the sound of an upstairs door opening and footsteps on the stairs. A second later, Mary appeared. She wore baggy sweatpants and a long-sleeved pink sweatshirt with a black cat on the front. Her brown hair was pulled into a loose ponytail, her pretty blue eyes a void. A large bandage dominated the center of the young girl's forehead, secured by medical tape.

The breath caught in Davina's throat.

Davina saw deep-rooted pain in Mary's eyes. As if sensing the scrutiny, Mary turned away from Davina's gaze.

Anne set another place at the table. "Did you offer Davina a drink, Len?"

"Of course." Lenny took another sip of his beer. "I'll check on the pie."

Anne sat silently at the head of the table; Mary sat to her right. Without being invited, Davina took the place across from Mary. It was awkward not being introduced to the girl. Davina assumed Anne had explained who she was and why she was there upstairs.

Lenny returned with half the pizza on a large dish. He placed it in the middle of the table and sat at the head of the table opposite Anne. Nobody spoke.

Davina broke the silence, "I'm Davina." She looked into Mary's eyes again. "I know."

"Cool sweatshirt." Davina smiled.

"It's my favorite." Mary looked down at it.

Mary's eyes darted between her aunt and her uncle. She didn't answer. Everyone reached across to grab a slice of the pizza, and Anne put one on Mary's plate.

Davina spoke, "I had a cat when I was growing up. I called him Nougat, like the candy."

Still, no one said anything.

Davina continued, "He was white and kind of fat, liked to sleep on my bed."

Mary pulled some cheese off her slice. "My cat's name is Dixie." She spoke slowly and didn't meet Davina's gaze. "She's gray."

"That's a nice name, Dixie. Did you name her?"

Mary nodded. "Do you still have your cat?"

"Oh, no. He lived to be very old, though."

Mary's eyes met Davina's for the first time. "Did you get another one?"

"No. Maybe someday."

"Do you miss him?"

"Yes."

Mary spoke softly, "I miss my dad." Tears welled in her eyes.

"I miss mine too," Davina said softly. "We have a lot in common."

I remember how he used to hold me and smile . . . before he left us. How could he do that?

Anne and Lenny turned to Davina. Mary stared at her pizza slice with her hands clasped in her lap.

"Why don't we give them a minute, Anne?" Lenny said.

Anne sighed. "I don't see why not. I don't have much of an appetite." In unison, they got up from the table and left the room.

"My dad died." Mary brought her napkin up to dry her eyes.

"I'm so sorry."

Mary met Davina's eyes. "Was your dad killed?"

"No, he ran away."

"Are you a doctor?" Mary inquired, a glimmer of life appearing in her baby blues.

"No." Davina leaned in a little closer and spoke softly. "I'm a survivor, like you."

"A *survivor?*"

Davina nodded. "What happened to you last week happened to me ten years ago. I was twelve."

Mary tilted her head, puppy-like. "You were younger than I am."

Davina nodded again. "Yeah. So, I do *understand*, Mary."

"I want it to all go away." Mary placed her hands on her belly. "The memories, the pain. I want *everything* to go away. I want people to stop staring at me. I want to disappear. I want my mom to get better." A solitary tear trailed down her cheek. "I want my dad."

Davina couldn't help herself; she felt tears on her own cheeks. "I promise it will get better. *You* will get better."

Mary lifted her eyes to Davina. "Like you?"

"*Better* than me."

"What did you do to get better?"

"That's a good question. To be honest, meeting people like you helps me a lot."

I can't lie to this kid and tell her I'm healed. I'm fucking not. But I'm sure as hell trying.

"Why?"

"Because I know I'm not alone."

Mary almost smiled. She looked down at her pizza and shook her head. "I feel sick." Mary pushed back the chair as she stood up, sprinted from the dining room, and raced up the stairs.

Coming back into the room, Anne watched her niece flee. "She was choked unconscious. The rape was horrifying. Merciless. The only consolation is Mary and Samantha are still alive and Mary's memory has gaps about the details of what that monster did to her." Anne's focus was suddenly on Davina, sharp and hot. "Do you remember what happened to you?"

"For a long time, I didn't. I didn't *want* to remember, and my family, the police, and the therapists convinced me the memories weren't real. So, I believed that for a long time. But . . . the memories came back."

Anne's face was pale. "That's horrible."

"Actually, I think I can handle them better as an adult. But back then, it would have been much easier if I'd had people like you and Lenny to help me work through it: people who understood what I'd been through, people who believed in me. Mary needs you to believe in her, Mrs. Gibson."

Anne held Davina's gaze for a moment, then nodded and walked over to the stairs. "I need to check on her."

Lenny stood in the doorway. "That's the most Mary's talked, the most *emotion* she's shown since . . ." He glanced toward the staircase and back to Davina. "I guess she needed somebody who could relate."

"I should go." Davina got up from the table. "I'll leave you my number. If Mary wants to talk or there's something I can do for her, call me."

"Thank you, Davina." Lenny took off into the kitchen, returning with two pens and two business cards. Lenny handed over a pen and one of the cards. He then scribbled his number on the back of the other card and handed it to her. "If you'd like to visit again, just call."

"Thank you." Davina glanced at the front of the card: Leonard Gibson, Building Inspector, Richmond County.

"Why does Mary have the bandage on her head?"

"There's a . . . cut on her forehead."

Davina all but held her breath. "Does it look something like this?" She sketched theta on a paper napkin.

Lenny stared open-mouthed at the drawing; his gaze drawn to Davina's forehead. "Theta—yes. Did he do that to you too?"

"In lipstick—I washed it off."

Cold rage roiled in Davina's chest. Son of Cropsey was not only back, but he was picking up where he'd left off with Elizabeth Pine. Worse, he was taking greater risks, assaulting victims in daylight, in the presence of an audience . . . then murdering the audience. Mary's mother had survived, and Davina couldn't help but wonder if that was deliberate, just another way of ramping up the risk.

As Professor Blackman would put it, Son of Cropsey was *escalating*.

CHAPTER THIRTY-THREE

WEDNESDAY, NEW SPRINGVILLE, THE SHAOLIN CLAN BAR & GRILL

DAVINA HAD JUST WALKED THROUGH THE DOOR OF HER apartment when she got a text from Joe, asking her to meet him at the new Shaolin Clan Bar & Grill for dinner. It crossed her mind to beg off—the day had been long and emotionally exhausting, but she really wanted to see him.

The Shaolin was less than a mile from the Empire Outlets Mall, and as she drove by, Davina replayed, with some regret, her fight with Alessandra.

Davina's rift with her sister was one of the hardest things to accept about the whole sorry mess. When Dad lost his job at Delafield's, for reasons Davina was just beginning to understand, Allie had blamed him for Nick's sudden absence. When Dad abandoned them, it was inevitable Alessandra had to transfer that anger and pain *somewhere*. Unfortunately, she'd picked on the person least able to weather it.

On the corner of a dead-end street, the two-story restaurant would be hard to miss, even without the opulent gold lettering plastered over the entry. The establishment was an old brick building, refurbished for a modern Chinese kung-fu feel—the brick continued inside. The cylinder-shaped pendant lights cast a warm, casual glow about the place, illuminating the dark wood bar, which ran the entire length of one wall. Booth tables spanned the opposite side; small, square tables that seated four were arranged along the middle of the room; and a large flat-screen television took up much of the back wall.

The bar was crowded with people out to watch the Mets game. Loud with excited chatter, the atmosphere was punctuated by raucous cheers at almost every move the Mets made.

Standing in the foyer at the top of a short flight of brick stairs, Joe held Davina's hand and asked, "Do you want to go someplace else? I didn't think it would be so noisy."

"No, it's okay. It's . . . drowning out the noise in my head."

One of the hostesses led Davina and Joe to a booth at the back of the room in the corner farthest from the bar. Once settled, Joe held Davina's hand as they perused the leather-bound menus.

"You look beautiful today," Joe told her.

"Thanks." She'd showered and changed into a black sleeveless shift dress with a square neckline. She'd matched it with low-heeled black sandals and had curried her hair to a burnished curtain. Davina smiled and tucked a few strands behind her ear.

"I love it when you do that." Joe leaned over the table to kiss her.

Their waitress approached; she wore all black—slim-fitting pants and utilitarian shirt. Her hair was tied back in a neat braid. "Good evening. Welcome to the Shaolin." She gave a little bow.

"Thanks." Joe pointed to an entry on his menu. "We'll take two sparkling waters. Zucchini bites and spicy wings to start." He put the menu down as the waitress walked away. "I'm starving."

"Thanks for ordering for me." Davina raised an eyebrow.

How did I end up with such a traditional guy?

"I know what you like." Joe released Davina's hand and fiddled with his chopsticks.

"I like this place." Davina glanced around. "It's much better than P.F. Chang's."

Joe loosened his tie. "So . . . how's your day been?"

"It was . . . *full*."

Joe quirked an eyebrow at her, but she didn't expand further. How could she begin to explain what a roller coaster her day had been—and why? Davina wanted only to unwind and clear her head; if that meant lying by omission to Joe, then so be it.

And so, they talked about the minutiae of Joe's day at work, the weather, the Mets, until the conversation inevitably switched to Davina's NA meetings.

"I'm making progress. Charlie says she can see it."

"I'm proud of you, babe."

"Thanks. I'm doing my best, but . . ." Davina's attention wandered toward the TV. She understood why people sat before it, zoned out. Zoning out seemed like heaven to Davina's overactive mind. Fighting hard, she brought her focus back to Joe. "Some days I just don't know."

Joe gazed intently into her eyes. "You've got this, D."

The waitress returned with the water and appetizers. It all smelled amazing, and Davina was surprised to discover she was hungry. She hadn't eaten since Boro 5, and a lot had happened since then. She dipped her zucchini into the creamy sauce and took a bite. A drop of sauce landed on her chin, and Joe reached over to wipe it away, laughing.

"Hey!" A drunk guy staggered toward the booth, pointing at Davina. "D' I know you, missy?"

Davina shook her head. "I doubt it. I sure don't know you."

"Yeah, I *do* know you," the guy insisted; the stink of booze emanating from him had Davina's eyes watering.

Joe gave the guy a fierce look. "Why don't you just keep moving, buddy?"

"Why don't you mind your own fuckin' business?" The drunk turned to Davina. "You're a stripper. How about a little lap dance for Papa Harvey—for old time's sake?" Struggling, he fished out a few crumpled twenties from his front pocket.

Joe stood up.

At six-foot four, he towered over Papa Harvey. "Look, buddy—you're drunk. Why don't you just move on before we call the manager?"

"Look at you, big shot. So, call the fucking manager. Here, I'll call him for you. Hey, *manager!*" He made an exaggerated look around. "Must be busy." He turned his attention back to Davina. "You could work what your momma gave ya *real* good, as I recall."

"Come on." Joe motioned to Davina. "Let's get outta here before I have to lay this guy out."

Davina got up. "Joe, it's fine. He's drunk. Let it go."

"Hey, what's the matter?" Harvey did a little dance, twerking his plump butt and shaking imaginary titties. "You only do private shows now?" He reached for Davina. "Is that it? No more lap dances for poor ol' Harvey?"

In an instant, Joe had Harvey pushed up against the wall, the drunk's shirt bunched in his fists. "I told you it was time to leave."

Harvey laughed in Joe's face. "Is that all you got, junior?" Then, surprisingly fast for one so inebriated, he landed a hard punch squarely in Joe's gut. Joe doubled over, and Davina screamed and coiled to step into the fight. Joe quickly recovered—his years as a varsity wrestler kicked in— and he grappled with Papa Harvey. The drunk let out a loud roar and tried to dig in. Patrons fled as the two knocked over tables, sending food and drinks crashing to the floor. With the two locked so tight in combat, there was no way for Davina to intervene.

Harvey had Joe by forty pounds, but Joe managed to get the older man in a headlock, refusing to turn him loose even as he gasped for air, clutching wildly at his throat. Joe's jaw clenched, his broad shoulder muscles straining as he applied his considerable strength to the drunkard's neck.

Within seconds, Papa Harvey was out cold and on the floor.

Davina stared at Joe in shock; she was breathing heavily, each breath a short gasp. "What the fuck did you do?" She pointed to Harvey's lifeless form on the floor.

"What did I do?" Joe repeated, shaking his head. "The guy was—"

"I know what the guy *was*, Joe. But, what the fuck? A *chokehold?*" Davina felt tears come to her eyes as panic raced through her.

"D, he *punched* me."

"You choked him out in seconds, Joe."

"I didn't choke him, Davina. I cut off the blood to his drunken brain and knocked him out. He'll come to with a bad headache."

Seemingly out of nowhere, Detective Riley and a trio of uniformed cops raced through the restaurant's foyer and down into the dining area, pushing patrons and serving staff out of the way as they went. Catching sight of Davina, Riley strode right up to her.

"*You* again? You just can't stay out of trouble, can you?" He pointed to Harvey, who was still out cold on the floor. "What'd you do to him?"

Joe stepped in. "I did it—he had it coming. He was harassing Davina, I asked him to stop, and he punched me."

Riley took handcuffs off his belt. "Turn around."

The bartender approached. "Officer?"

"*Detective.*"

The bartender gestured at Harvey. "He started it. They were just sitting there and this guy harassed them. He's drunk."

"Is that so?" Riley still held his cuffs. He turned to Davina and smiled maliciously. She turned away; the mere sight of the cop terrified her. Riley sidled up close, leaning into her ear. "You keep pushing it, Davina, and your luck is gonna run out." She felt his warm breath on her cheek, smelled his aftershave.

Please, God, don't let me faint.

After what felt like an age, Riley pulled away and clipped his cuffs back onto his belt. He cracked a smug smile. "Now, get out of here you two."

Joe stared Riley down a second or two before grabbing Davina's hand and leading her out of the Shaolin.

Davina felt Riley's eyes on her, hot and dangerous. Breaking free of Joe, she ran for the car.

Joe put that drunk guy in a chokehold.
Like it was nothing.

CHAPTER THIRTY-FOUR

WEDNESDAY, NEW SPRINGVILLE, THE SHAOLIN CLAN BAR & GRILL

As banker Darren Rivers approached the restaurant, he saw Davina Speers charging out into the parking lot. She was dressed for a date and appeared extremely distressed. Darren considered calling after her to see if she needed help, but just then, a tall young man ran from the restaurant and caught up to her. Darren thought he recognized the guy but couldn't put name to the shadowy face.

Not my problem.

Straightening his tie, Darren made his way into the restaurant, which appeared to be in the ebbing stages of some chaotic event. Patrons stood around in little knots, murmuring; some nervously returning to half-eaten meals; and a large man lay on the floor—he appeared to be either unconscious or dead. Detective Riley stood over him, having a heated conversation with the restaurant's manager.

Darren seated himself at a stool at the far end of the bar, around the corner from the other patrons. From there he could see the entire room, along with the front door and foyer, while still enjoying a measure of privacy. He scanned the room for Nick; he hadn't arrived yet.

He waved down the bartender. "Can I get a drink?"

The bartender, a young guy not much older than eighteen or nineteen, appeared shaken. "Yeah." He nodded over to the big guy on the tiled floor. "My second damn day on the job and a fight breaks out. What can I get you?"

"House red." Darren offered the guy a smile; he was cute. "You might want to grab a glass yourself."

"I wish. House red it is."

Darren was just thanking the bartender for the wine when Nick walked through the door. He spotted Darren and shot him a boyish grin.

Why does that motherfucker have to be so handsome?

Nick took the empty stool to Darren's left, combing a hand through his hair. "Sorry I'm late. There was traffic."

"Welcome to Staten Island."

"What'd you order?"

Darren lifted his glass and brought it to his nose. "A smoky red for a romantic evening."

After a quick glance around, Nick reached over and placed a hand on Darren's knee. Darren momentarily bristled, though he knew no one in the bar or the restaurant would be able to see the gesture. It was dangerous to show affection in public—for both of them—but sometimes, Nick didn't seem to have any reservations about it. That struck Darren as odd, because Nick had the most to lose. It was as if he just shut down his social filters and guardrails situationally . . . or simply ignored them. Darren admired that about Nick Delafield . . . and feared it— the guy was a mass of contradictions.

Nick gestured at the bartender. "I'll have what he's having."

Darren smiled. "Great minds think alike."

Nick squeezed Darren's knee. "Except that we don't think alike at all."

That was true enough. Maybe that was part of the attraction. Darren sipped his wine and heaved a sigh. It was pleasurable being in Nick's company, regardless of the strange, jarring static that always seemed present whenever they were together. Darren liked to tell himself it was sexual electricity.

"Your hair is growing out." Darren wanted to reach across and touch Nick's luscious hair, burying his fingers in it. But he couldn't, of course.

Nick combed a hand through his hair again, and one of the dark curls fell over his forehead. "I think it's more laziness than anything else."

"Then laziness looks good on you."

Nick laughed and glanced down the bar at their fellow patrons. Some were glued to the game on the TV screens high on the back wall, and others were watching the EMTs tending to the guy on the floor, who had come around and was sitting up, rubbing his head.

The bartender then arrived with more wine. Nick and Darren clinked glasses and stared into each other's eyes . . . but not for long.

"The campaign meeting went great," Nick broke the moment.

Darren shook his head. "No, Nick. We're not going to talk about political campaigns—not tonight."

"So, you're the *avoidant* Darren tonight?"

"I'm not being avoidant. We just haven't had a civilized evening in a while."

Nick leaned over and murmured, "And what would you consider *un*civilized?"

Darren recognized a Nick Delafield dodge when he saw it. "Us getting into another fight."

Nick removed his hand from Darren's knee and leaned against the bar, putting distance between them. "Are we supposed to not be ourselves? We have differing opinions, Darren. That doesn't mean we shouldn't talk."

Darren lowered his voice, "Don't be so manipulative, Nick. Are you interested in the health of this relationship or not?"

"So, it's a *relationship* now?"

Darren frowned. "What do you mean?"

"I mean . . . sometimes I feel like I'm just your fuck buddy."

Darren had absolutely no comeback for that—it hurt. It was as if Nick *wanted* to make him explode. Well, he wanted to explode, damn it. He felt like strangling Nick and leaving Riley a good-looking corpse. He'd thought they were long past the stupid courting dance.

Words finally came. "You're more than that to me, Nick, and you damn well know it. I shouldn't need to explain it all to you . . . again."

Nick turned his head and made a face at the mirrored wall behind the bar. "You're a different person behind closed doors."

"I have a professional image to maintain. It's very important to me."

Facing Darren once more, his eyes wide, Nick replied, "And you don't think *I* have an image to maintain? I've got a lot on the line too."

"Of course. Do you ever suppose you'll tell your father about us?"

Nick fell silent and studied his drink. "Right. Ten seconds ago, you said you didn't want to get into a fight—and here we are."

And whose fault is that?

On the far side of the dining area, Darren saw the EMTs had gotten the big guy upright and were guiding him toward the door. The guy started yelling, his speech terribly slurred: he was drunk off his butt.

The bartender approached Nick and Darren and leaned on the bar. His eyes followed the drama of the drunkard, the EMTs, and the cops. "That nut job has done nothing but shout and threaten all night."

Darren was reminded of the cute girl in black running out the door. "Was he bothering someone in particular?"

"Yeah, some chick. Her boyfriend didn't take kindly to the harassment and took him out." The bartender smiled and put a menu card on the counter. He tapped it with a finger. "I recommend the chicken skewers. Potstickers are good, too."

"Brilliant." Darren sipped at his wine. "We'll take an order of each."

"Are we done fighting now?" Nick asked once the bartender had gone.

"*I* never started."

Nick turned to face Darren. "Can I ask you an important question?"

"Try me."

"What's going to happen to us when my father wins?"

Darren could hardly dignify that question with an answer. Nick was so damn blind to the truth that there was no way Sean Delafield would win back the council seat.

"I think the question must be—what's going to happen when your father *loses*."

Nick's face spasmed as if rejecting the very idea that Sean Delafield could ultimately fail at anything he did. Then, the two sat silently, waiting for their food in a static fog of tension.

Finally, Nick got up from his stool. "I think I best go."

"Hold on." Darren grabbed his sleeve. "I know we've got differences, but—"

"No, I think you're right, Darren. It's impossible to do this without fighting." Nick made no effort to pull away.

"That's not what I said," Darren replied. "I said I didn't want to talk about your dad and his political aspirations *because* it always leads to us fighting. I get it, okay? We need to compartmentalize things." He let go of Nick's arm and gestured at the empty barstool. "Now will you sit back down . . . please?"

Nick slid back onto his seat. He glanced at the bartender, who was at the far end of the bar, before murmuring, "Sex and politics make strange bedfellows."

Darren snorted. "Who're you calling *strange?*"

They both laughed, and Nick said, "I'd say we're both pretty strange, but that makes the sex even better."

Darren studied his lover's handsome face for a moment, and more than anything, he wanted to lean in and kiss those welcoming, smiling lips. For all that Nick indulged in quick touches, clandestine squeezes, and subtle wordplay, Darren knew a blatant show of attraction or affection would undo him . . . and probably kill their budding relationship. Nick liked to play at being the risk-taker, but Darren doubted he was up to *real* risk.

Like Nick had said, he had a lot on the line, too.

CHAPTER THIRTY-FIVE

WEDNESDAY, DAVINA'S APARTMENT

By the time Davina and Joe climbed the stairs to the apartment, they were arguing, neither one listening to the other. Davina was still out of breath.

"You act like you've never seen a chokehold," Joe said, rubbing at the stubble on his chin.

"Yeah, I've seen one, Joe. I've *felt* one. It's how Son of Cropsey puts his victims out."

Joe seemed confused. "Son of Cropsey?"

"Do you not follow the news? There've been three girls attacked and raped in the last two weeks."

"Are you accusing me—?"

"*No!*"

"Then what *are* you saying, Davina?"

"Nothing. I was just surprised how quick you put that drunk guy down."

And with such fucking skill.

"You'd have been happier if he'd beat the shit outta me first?"

Davina ignored the petulant outburst and opened the apartment door. Millie was there, standing in the kitchen with her evening's date. They both glanced over when the door opened and then went back to their own conversation in low voices. Davina went into the living room and tossed her purse onto the sofa.

Joe followed, lowering his voice, "What the hell was that guy saying, anyway?"

"He said I was a stripper. Happens he was right, Joe. I *was* a stripper. Okay?" Even as Davina whispered the confession, she felt as if her life was spiraling down the drain with every word. "I lived on the streets and did whatever it took to survive. It's not like there were a lot of job opportunities out there for messed-up head cases like me."

Joe raised his hands to bracket his head. "I'm not sure I can even process that, Davina. Yeah, I knew you lived on the streets but a *stripper?* You were a stripper, and you never thought to tell me?"

Davina saw anguish in Joe's eyes. It hurt and it made her angry. How messed up was *that?* "How could I tell you? I just explained it to you—it was a living. But that was then, and this is now. What does it matter?"

"That guy remembered you."

She narrowed her eyes at Joe. "Wow. I guess I was either so good or so bad—"

"Oh, right."

"You know what *I* can't process? I can't process how you're so fucking good at chokeholds. You wanna tell me about how you did that?" She snapped her fingers in front of his face. "Just like that. Reflex."

Joe face-palmed. "You teach kickboxing and martial arts. You know how to put an attacker down with one kick, one punch. You even *teach* chokeholds. I was a wrestler in high school and college, and every wrestler knows that move. Heck, every *cop* knows that move. Schoolkids have to be told in special assemblies to quit choking each other out for fun because they copied it off the TV. You can look chokeholds up on YouTube, for Christ's sake."

From the corner of her eye, Davina saw Millie turn to her date—a pretty, petite Asian girl with ass-length, iridescent black hair—and say, loudly enough to be heard, "I think I gotta get this, hon. They look like they're about to kill each other."

Millie's date lifted her brow and nodded. "Yeah, love hurts." She kissed Millie good night on the lips and made haste to the door. "Good luck, you two," she called over and gave Joe and Davina a finger wave.

Marching into the living room, Millie turned on Davina and Joe, crossing her arms over her chest like some vexed schoolmarm. "What the hell's going on here?"

Davina sighed. "Some drunk just outed me for being a stripper back in the day, and Joe is having a hard time wrapping his head around the fact that I'm not Snow White."

Millie sucked in her breath. "Ouch."

Joe shook his head again, emphatically this time. "That's not what I'm having trouble wrapping my head around, Davina. I just can't believe you've not said a word in all the time we've been together. I know about the drugs, about what you went through at home—"

"I didn't tell you I stripped because it has nothing to do with anything. It was long before I even knew you."

"I'm not judging. I'd have understood."

"Really? Because you don't look so understanding at this moment."

Joe flapped his arms at her, his frustration clear. "That's because some drunk in a bar blurted it out. I would have understood if *you* had told me."

"Lordy, lordy." Millie threw her hands in the air. "I had me a nice date and now you two come up in here arguing about chokeholds and stripping."

"I'm so sorry, Millie," said Davina. "We can take this to my room."

"Don't you dare! This is entertaining. Think I'll get me some popcorn." Millie turned to Joe. "Look, now you know. What's it matter how you found out? You *know*. She's still Davina. Nothing's changed. She made some hard choices and survived them."

Joe's temper visibly deflated. "Yeah. Yeah, you're right." He turned to Davina. "I was just . . . thrown off balance, that's all."

"Maybe I should have told you, Joe. I'm sorry." Davina dropped onto the shabby sofa and massaged her temples. "God, what a day."

Millie put her hands on her hips and lolled her head. "There's more?"

Davina looked up at her and Joe. "I've been warned off by the cops."

"Warned off about what?" Joe perched on the arm of the sofa. "Who warned you off?"

"Yeah." Millie settled herself into the even shabbier chair opposite. "What he said."

"Riley. I was having lunch at Boro Diner. He showed up and threatened me."

"What the fuck?"

"He had one of his cops bust my taillight, too. Then ticket me for it." Davina rocked her head against the overstuffed sofa back; it felt comforting. "I guess the word is out about me. That's probably why Riley showed up so fast to the Shaolin."

"So, now what?" Millie asked.

Davina shrugged her shoulders. "Nothing. Nothing I can do. I can't exactly go to the police over it, can I?" She managed a wry chuckle.

"Why?" Joe asked. "Why are they after you? Because you took Nick Delafield down at Joy's memorial?"

Davina shook her head. "It's all tied into the Son of Cropsey case. Suggesting he collared the wrong guy hit Riley's ego hard, and now he thinks he's gonna scare me off."

Millie snorted. "Except you don't scare *that* easily."

"Wait," said Joe. "What does this have to do with—"

"Joy Sheridan, Joe. She was raped ten years ago—*after* Riley caught Son of Cropsey. I've been trying to find more evidence that he arrested the wrong man, and he's losing his shit over it."

Joe shook his head. "I don't get it. How does Joy being raped—"

"It's not just Joy. There are others."

Like me—the words jumped into her mind, but she held them at bay.

"I met two of the victims today. One of them, Elizabeth Pine, is in a convalescent home because of what that fiend did to her. Put her in a chokehold and raped her with a metal pipe."

Millie winced and covered her mouth with both hands. "Shit," she murmured against her fingertips. "*Shit.*"

Joe looked away.

Davina stood up and started to pace, rubbing at her bare arms as if she were cold. Her words came out in a rush, "My panic attacks are starting to make sense. The-the weird clues I've been seeing in the other cases—they're all pieces of the rapist's MO the cops didn't make public. I spoke to my sister, Alessandra, who still completely refuses to accept what happened to me. She knows for certain Riley was having an affair with our mom back then. Geoff Wong suspects the cops got the wrong guy too, and these recent cases—"

Joe stared at her like she was some crazy person. "Davina. Slow down. I don't—"

She raised a hand to silence him. "I'm thinking it was him at the train station—unfinished business and all that."

Millie asked the obvious question, "Train station?"

"Great Kills. It's where Joy and Elizabeth were attacked." As Davina described her assault at Great Kills, Joe and Millie listened in stunned silence. She ended the recitation with her hands at her own throat.

"What the fuck?" Millie whipped out her phone. "It's probably on the news. Is that where you got that bruise on your cheek, D?"

"It won't be on the news," Davina told her. "I got outta there before the cops showed up and never reported it. Mil, it was just like before. The-the chokehold, everything. I thought Geoff Wong had tipped him off."

Joe stood and turned her to face him. "What do you mean, 'like before'? What happened to you that Alessandra won't believe? What are you not telling me?"

Davina stared into his eyes, his beautiful blue eyes, dark with unease, and knew she had to come clean—it had become a night of revelations. "I was one of the others raped after Son of Cropsey was supposed to be behind bars."

"*You?*" Joe's voice was strangled with emotion. "He . . . attacked you? When?"

"I was twelve. No one believed me because Riley said he had the guy.

They said I was just being dramatic, trying to get attention, dreaming, lying, whatever."

Joe closed his eyes. "And Riley and your mom—"

"Yeah. Riley and my mom."

"And this thing at the train station?"

"This morning, just before noon."

"Jesus, Davina. When were you going to tell me?" He didn't wait for an answer. "You should've called me. You could have been killed. This isn't a game, D. Somebody wants you dead."

"Yeah, I'd say at least one person wants me dead, or at least too scared to keep digging. But I can't back down, Joe. I can't."

"Why?" Desperation laced Joe's voice. "It's not your job to solve this case."

Davina met his gaze so he could see the desperation in her face. "I'm not out to solve a case, Joe. I'm looking for *answers*. I want to know what happened to me, what happened to Joy—and Elizabeth and Mary and Jessica and Seraphina and any other girls he's savaged. If the cops don't give a shit, then it *is* up to me, because I'm the only one who *does* give a shit."

"This has gone too far, D," Joe told her. "If you've got evidence the guy who . . . attacked you is still out there, we have to go to the cops."

"Joe, the cops are all in on it. I only know of one who's not, for sure, and he intends to retire with his full pension, so he's keeping schtum."

"Then what, Davina? What can you do?"

"There was another detective working the Son of Cropsey case ten years ago. He was the lead on it and didn't believe Riley arrested the right guy. When he got into it with Riley, the crooked bastard won. That detective—Packer—retired to Tampa, and Riley got all the honor and glory. I need to go see him, go to Tampa, to find out what he knows." Davina dug her phone from her purse. "If I catch a red-eye—"

"What the fuck? Just call the guy, Davina," Joe said.

"Geoff Wong tried that—Packer doesn't pick up. Now it's my turn to try. I've got more skin in the game here." Davina studied her phone.

"There's a flight at 2:00 a.m. that gets me to Tampa by 5:30. I'll be home by lunch tomorrow."

Joe took out his wallet, pulled out a VISA card, and held it out to Davina. "Book two seats."

"I'm just going to fly down, talk to Packer, and fly straight back. You don't need to come with me, Joe. You've got work. I'll be fine."

"Yeah, because I'm going with you. You're a hell of a lot more important to me than work." Joe popped the card on her phone's screen. "Two seats. See if you can get a window."

I can't believe I'm doing this. Then his words truly hit her: *more important to me than work.*

She swallowed hard and booked the flight for the both of them.

CHAPTER THIRTY-SIX

THE 737 CAUGHT TURBULENCE BUT STILL MANAGED TO ARRIVE in Tampa eighteen minutes earlier than expected. After a quick breakfast at a local Denny's, Joe and Davina Ubered to Coral Winds Estates. Being Florida, it wasn't yet 10:00 am and the heat was up to 82 degrees and 82 percent humidity. Davina swore she'd never complain about Staten Island temperatures again.

A few hundred yards to their right was the golf course dotted with little groups of golfers making their way from green to green. To the left and straight ahead were rigid rows of two-story blue-and-white townhomes. Except for the occasional floral wreath or welcome sign, all the units appeared identical. The homes were new, designed to look like Mediterranean villas, and were well-tended with a little patch of colorful flowers out front.

"I guess Florida considers these estates." Davina pushed her sunglasses up onto her head.

"It is all very Floridian," Joe agreed. He wiped perspiration from his forehead and brushed his hair back with a flat hand.

"How the hell do people live here?"

Joe laughed. "That's what people say about New York."

"I'll take New York over Florida any day. It feels like I'm walking through a sauna."

They meandered along a limestone walkway that curved around to join a sidewalk running the entire length of the row of townhomes; retired Detective Ronald Packer occupied the end unit.

"Watch where you walk. Alligators could be hiding in the grass here," Davina warned, smiling.

Joe took her hand. "Don't worry. If I see one, I'll put him in a chokehold."

"Very funny." Davina was surprised she was able to laugh about it. But in taking the time to fly to Florida with her, and pay for it, Joe had regained her trust.

Not that he should've lost it.

Finally, sweaty and over-hot, Davina and Joe arrived at Ron Packer's place. Davina rang the doorbell. After a minute, when nobody answered, she knocked.

Still, no answer.

"Maybe he's not home." Joe tried to peer through the sidelights that bracketed the door.

"He *has* to be." Davina knocked harder, desperation growing in her chest.

Then a voice from behind startled her, "Who are you?"

Davina and Joe turned around. The speaker was unmistakably Ron Packer; he wore a camo bucket hat, cargo shorts, and a white T-shirt under a safari vest. He had on a pair of Teva sandals and carried a tackle box and fishing pole.

"Detective Packer?" Davina asked.

"I said, who are you?" Ron stood his ground.

"I'm Davina Speers. This is Joe. I've been working with Geoff Wong."

"You need to go home." The ex-cop brushed by on his way to the front door. He didn't invite them in but left the door wide open.

Davina met eyes with Joe. "Should we go in?"

"Ladies first."

"I don't know. This is a stand-your-ground state."

Packer yelled from inside the house. "Are you two coming in or not?" Two beats. "I'm not gonna shoot you." Another beat. "And close the door behind you—it's hot as balls out there."

Davina went in first, followed by Joe. The door led directly into the living room, which resembled an IKEA showroom. The walls were white; the couches, chairs, and tables in various shades of grays and blacks; and a seventy-five-inch OLED LG-TV dominated one wall. A glass-top coffee table stood in front of the couch, where the previous day's edition of the *Staten Island Advance* lay next to copies of the *Tampa Bay Times* and *Field & Stream* magazine.

Davina relished the cool rush of the A/C. "If I could have a few minutes of your time, Detective Packer. I'd like to talk to you about—"

"I know what you're here to talk about, and I can't help you." Ron dumped his tackle box on the floor in front of the television. "You wasted your time and money coming down here. What happened back then is done and over. Go home."

"Detective Packer—"

"I'm retired."

"Mr. Packer—it's not done and over for me. I was one of Son of Cropsey's victims."

That stopped Ron cold. He eyed Davina but remained silent.

Davina reminded herself to breathe. "Detective Riley didn't pay any attention to me, and others like me, because he'd already decided he'd gotten his guy. You said you didn't believe that to be true."

"It doesn't matter what I thought then, and it doesn't matter what I think now. The case is closed."

Packer went into the kitchen. An uncomfortable silence followed as he nuked a cup of coffee before returning to the living room. "Miss Speers, I'm sorry for what happened to you, but what's done is done." He slurped his drink loudly.

Fucking asshole. What's done is done?

Davina straightened her back and squared her shoulders. "Joy

Sheridan—remember her? She killed herself because she couldn't live with the memories anymore." Davina pointed to her temple. "Another girl, Elizabeth Pine, is trapped inside her own mind because Son of Cropsey left her brain damaged. She's twenty-four and stuck in a nursing home for the rest of her life."

"I'm well aware of the victim histories."

Davina stepped forward. "Mr. Packer, can you at least tell me why you didn't think Rob Cox was the right man?"

Packer hesitated for a moment, grimaced, and motioned for them to sit in the Scandinavian-style armchairs across from the couch. "You want water or something?"

Davina and Joe both shook their heads.

"I know, deep down, you *do* give a shit." Davina leaned forward, elbows resting on her knees. "Please. Help. Me." She paused. "Did Tom Riley get the right guy?"

Packer's jaw bunched. "No comment," he said. "Cox had a molestation charge, and they found kinky bondage stuff at his place. But that single charge of sexual molestation, he managed to shake as a drunken one-off. Cox was far worse than people knew."

Davina almost choked. "What could be worse than raping minors?"

"A double homicide of drug dealers that was never resolved. Their bodies were found in Mariner's Marsh Park. Rob Cox was known for his drug-related activities in the area."

"Meaning?"

"Meaning—there's no hard proof of anything other than Cox being your rapist, just . . ." Ron shook his head. "Here's what I can tell you for sure: Riley's guy was already in custody and going down for the double murder. He admitted to dealing, but not to the murders. The cops had enough on him to send him away for life—and he knew they'd pin the murders on him. That's life in prison."

Joe nodded. "So, the lesser charge was a windfall, then."

"Riley was able to dredge up enough circumstantial evidence to make a case implicating him in the attacks—times and places he'd allegedly been seen, security footage of him near the homes of one of the victims." Packer shrugged. "He agreed to a deal that got him fifteen years instead of life. He confessed to the rapes, not murder."

Davina's face felt numb. "But he's *not* Son of Cropsey." She met Packer's gaze. "You still read the *Advance*. You follow the new cases?"

A nod.

"Geoff Wong's article?"

"Yeah."

"So, you know this isn't a copycat. We're dealing with Son of Cropsey."

"I don't know that, Miss Speers. Copycat criminals pop up all the time—it's one of the downsides of sticking everything out in the media and glorifying them on TV shows."

"Retired or not, you've still got instincts," Joe said. "What's your gut telling you?"

"To let the cops do their jobs. I'll admit I didn't like Cox's confession —I said as much to assistant DA Ceine. There was too much pressure to close the case. Pressure from Riley, pressure from that scumbag Delafield who told anyone who'd listen that the rapes looked bad for Staten Island." Packer paused, gulping down some more coffee. "There was civic pressure from the Small Business Association and even the goddamned Historical Society. There was no sense in me trying to fight all that."

Davina sat back; a puff of dust rose up from the chair. "Who did you investigate when you were leading the investigation?"

"Anybody and everybody. If you lived on Staten Island, I investigated you. If you were involved with kids, I investigated you. If you were breathing, I investigated you," Packer snorted. "We had profilers in from the Fed's BSU and we tried a bunch of psychics. Both avenues were as useless as each other until Cox was caught by good, old-fashioned police work."

"Did you originally think victims were asphyxiated with plastic bags?" Davina asked.

"Early on. We found plastic bags at a couple of the crime scenes, but the doctors didn't see evidence the victims were suffocated that way. Plus, none of them remembered having a bag over their heads—not that they remembered much. That was part of the MO—he slipped them something that messed with their memories. And he didn't cut off their air—he cut off the blood to the brain."

"Yeah," said Davina. "He uses a blood choke."

"Can't refute that."

She pointed at the *Advance* on the table. "You read Wong's piece on the attacks that were unaccounted for. Do you remember the one at the Paramount Theater?"

Ron nodded.

"Geoff said the cops never followed up. My roommate knew more about that case than the cops did."

Ron snorted. "Or at least more than they *admit* knowing." He got up and adjusted the vertical blinds on his back slider to block out the creeping sunlight. "I was on my way out of the department when that one came in. The police didn't follow up because real cops aren't like TV cops. Real cops are overworked and underpaid and don't have the resources to work a closed case. Besides, there wasn't much to follow up on. The lead detective on the case had one witness who put a White guy at the scene, but the witness turned out to be less than credible. Changed his story three times, and his description of the perp was in doubt. The guy was tall, he was short, he was medium build, he was stocky. Maybe he wasn't White—maybe he was Hispanic or a light-skinned Black." Ron shrugged. "No cop was going to waste time following up that bullcrap."

"Who was the lead on that case? Riley?"

Packer inclined his head. "Could have been."

"So, if this was still an active case and you *were* investigating," Joe ventured. "Who would you look at?"

"The butcher, the baker," the ex-cop replied before pausing. "The banker."

Was that a clue? "Darren Rivers?" Davina eyed him suspiciously. "He's Black."

The retired detective eyed her with some mirth. "It's an expression. And I didn't say I thought he did the crimes, but he was working in the mortgage department at Richmond County S & L back then, and I heard through the grapevine Riley was braying about a sweet mortgage deal Rivers got him right after Cox was put away."

Joe sat back in his chair. "You think it was in exchange for . . . what?"

"I already told you I don't *think* anything." Ron tapped the bottom of his coffee cup with a splintered fingernail. "I just want to sit at the end of the pier with my line in the water." The guy's dark brown eyes were suddenly alight with wry humor.

Davina wished she could read them—*him*—more clearly. He obviously knew far more than he was prepared to divulge. "Thanks for all that," she told him. "It's not proof, but it's a small piece of the puzzle."

Ron got up to set his coffee cup down on the kitchen's granite peninsula. "I'm guessing you two have a plane to catch."

They took the hint.

On the way out, Davina stopped and turned around. "One last question, Mr. Packer."

The cousin of a smile. "Why am I not surprised?"

"My attacker left a mark on my forehead in lipstick. Theta—a circle with a line through it. According to the Wadsworth victim's uncle, Mary Lamont had that same mark carved into her forehead. Amber Winters has a circular scar she keeps covered with a lot of hair, and there's a faint mark on Elizabeth Pine's forehead."

Ron searched her eyes. "Yes, our victims had thetas incised or drawn on them with something. We thought it was a 'no' sign at first, which kind of made sense—like the girls were nothing to Son of Cropsey. But it also means death or divine, depending . . . or both."

"How can it be both?" asked Joe.

"*Theta* is the first letter of both death—Thanatos—and God—Theos, in Greek." His mouth twitched. "Rob Cox didn't know theta from the hole in his ass. Good day, Miss Speers, boyfriend Joe."

He shut the door on Davina and Joe, leaving them to the mercy of the wet Florida heat.

Davina stood on the doorstep for a moment. "He wants me to look into Darren Rivers, but not Riley?"

"Maybe it's because, good or bad, Riley is a cop. You know how cops stick together—no matter what."

"That is so fucked up."

Joe sighed and peered out across the pristine, rolling green of Coral Winds Estates. "That it is."

As they walked away from Packer's picture-perfect retirement home, Davina caught a glimpse of the cop jabbing away at the keys on his cordless house phone with a thunderous look on his reddened face, and she marveled at how old people still used those things.

————

Sean Delafield waited with growing impatience for his call to be picked up. He had not been in the best of moods before Ron Packer's call, and hearing from the ex-cop after so many years had just made his day a shit-load worse.

"Kev, where the hell were you?" Sean barked the moment Kevin Monaghan answered.

"I was taking a dump, Sean, calm down."

"I don't care *what* you were doing," Sean said. "*I've* just had Ron fucking Packer chewing my goddamned ear off."

"About what?" the retired cop asked.

"What the hell do you think?" Sean's grip on his temper was wafer thin. "He spent the last ten minutes telling me how he is sick of covering for us and how he's just had a visit from Davina Speers and her tall escort."

"Why?"

"They were asking him about the old Riley case and my supposed involvement in it. They'd flown to Florida specially to talk to him."

"Well, isn't that nice? What did he tell them?" Kevin was sounding a little concerned.

"He said he told them nothing and kicked them out—but I think he *wanted* to say something. Sounded to me like retirement's getting to the old bastard and he wants to get all that shit off his chest before it's too late."

"Oh."

"Yeah, oh," Sean growled. "You need to sort it out, Kev. Make sure Packer keeps his fucking mouth shut before he lands us all in prison."

Kevin remained silent for what felt like an eternity to Sean; he wanted action, and he needed it done yesterday. Packer might have been a has-been, washed-up old cop, but there would still be people who would listen to what he had to say—especially those who wanted to see one Sean Delafield's return to politics crash and burn before it even got started.

"Kevin?" Sean prompted.

A sigh. "Yeah, I'll deal with it, Sean. But you and Riley are gonna owe me big time."

Sean hung up on Kevin, confident the job would be done, and done well. The guy might have been one almighty douchebag, but he sure as all hell knew how to get things fixed.

CHAPTER THIRTY-SEVEN

THURSDAY, DOBSON'S GYM

Walking into Dobson's Gym, Davina's throat tickled and she let out a loud cough. A hell of a lot of dust hung in the air, which she found odd because Dobson's ventilation was usually pristine. Having just arrived back from Florida that morning, Davina thought she might just be tired and oversensitive.

The gym was quiet for a Thursday morning; only a handful of people were working out on the equipment upstairs.

Making her way to Gerry's office, Davina opened the door and all but fell over Gerry doing push-ups on the floor. "Well, this *is* new."

Gerry kept pumping as she talked. "Gotta get away from the dust— the construction workers have started on the locker rooms."

"Oh, right. I forgot."

"How was Florida?" Gerry finished and got up. She walked over to the desk to snag her water bottle.

"Ex-Detective Packer was never convinced Riley got the right Son of Cropsey."

Gerry pursed her lips, as if deep in thought. "You must be exhausted."

"I am, and I have Kayla and Skylar at 3:30 today."

"Shit, D, I forgot to tell you. They canceled." Gerry dropped into her desk chair. "You can take the afternoon off and rest up."

It was divine providence; Davina felt like she needed to sleep for a week. "I'll give them a call."

"Maybe let it be." Gerry took a stress ball from the desk drawer and began to squeeze it.

"How long are they going to be working downstairs?"

"The rest of this week. I got the guys at a discount, and they promised me they can work fast. I hope so, because I'll lose clientele. No one wants to work out with all that racket going on." She sneezed. "Not to mention the dust. Oh yeah, your sister called."

"Huh?" Davina cocked her head. "Alessandra? Called here?"

"She said she was trying to get ahold of you but you weren't picking up. She was concerned."

"I don't believe that. She could have called Joe."

"Maybe it was just a gesture?"

"Alessandra is not one for gestures. Or subtlety. Honestly, I don't really want to talk to her again."

"Still gaslighting?"

"That's only the start of it. She blames me for running away and leaving her to be the adult in the room. My childhood home was a death-trap. The streets were far safer."

Gerry smiled warmly. "And led you here."

"Exactly. You know I can never repay you for that."

"You don't have to. Having you here helped me as much as it helped you. I was going through some shit of my own when I got you off the streets."

"You were?"

Gerry sighed and looked sadly down at her desk. "I lost a child."

Davina was taken aback. "Why didn't you tell me?"

"I was having a fling with a hot gym shark. Thought I was in love, but he disappeared the minute he knocked me up. I was surprised how much I wanted that baby though. But the pregnancy failed at six months." Gerry stared vacantly out the window. "I guess it was never meant to be."

"I'm so sorry, Gerry." Davina couldn't help but feel a little hurt Gerry had never told her about the miscarriage before. Then again, Davina was a fine one to talk about keeping things to herself.

"That's when you came along. I had someone to take care of."

Davina smiled. "Then I guess we both lucked out."

The phone rang on the desk. Gerry picked up. "Hello? Oh, shit." She shot a glance at the wall clock. "I totally forgot. I can't be there in half an hour. I've got guys working downstairs."

Davina gave her boss a quizzical face.

Gerry put a hand over the receiver. "I gotta go to the bank. I keep forgetting to drop off the checks, and my bookkeeper wants my neck." She spoke into the phone again. "I understand, Drew, but you'll just need to wait."

"I'll go."

"Hold on." Gerry covered the receiver. "To the bank?"

"Which one?"

"Richmond Savings & Loan."

That's exactly where I need to go. "Let me do it."

Gerry spoke into the phone. "Done. They'll be there in half an hour. Now take some Xanax." Gerry hung up.

"Detective Packer hinted about looking into Darren Rivers. This is the perfect field trip. I'm thinking there's a link between the Staten Island police and the SBCA."

"Don't get me started on the SBCA and what they're trying to do to the Rock," Gerry growled. "I'm just waiting for them to decide the gym is a landmark that needs to be torn down. You wouldn't believe what those monsters are capable of." Gerry pulled out a stack of checks from her desk drawer and handed them over.

Davina took them. "It shouldn't take too long."

"Take your time. Nothing going on around here."

Davina walked to the door and turned. "Gerry?"

"Yeah?"

"Thanks for telling me what you did. It couldn't have been easy—I'm glad I know."

Gerry nodded her head. "You share your secrets, Davina, I'll share mine."

CHAPTER THIRTY-EIGHT

THURSDAY, RICHMOND COUNTY SAVINGS & LOAN

SEATED AT THE POLISHED BLACK-LACQUER CONFERENCE TABLE in the main conference room of Richmond County Savings & Loan, Darren played nervously with his pen. The dire expressions on the faces around the table perfectly mirrored his own.

We gotta do this now if I'm going to keep my goddamn career.

Darren Rivers straightened his tie and took a sip of water. "You know why I've called this meeting. Sean is—"

Gino Romano snorted, "Sean is off his rocker."

"I can't argue that. I was convinced we could persuade him his criminal record was a drag on the ticket, that he couldn't possibly win the general election. I thought—we *all* thought—he'd be happy to work behind the scenes, gobble up property, and get even richer."

Gino pinched the bridge of his nose and screwed up his eyes. Kevin Monaghan ground his teeth.

"He's not willing to be persuaded," Darren continued. "Or *threatened* into dropping out. I showed him the poll numbers, I reminded him how much scrutiny he'd be under as a council member, and none of it had an iota of impact."

"That's because he's got too many yes-men around him in his campaign HQ," Gino threw in. "They're all telling him how great he is—especially that daddy's boy he's got running the show."

"Whatever the reason, we can't just carry on with business as usual," said Darren. "Sean's past threatens the party—threatens *us*." He studied each face.

Kevin cleared his throat. "You think Sean running for office is going to expose . . . *other things?*"

"Yes." Darren put down his pen.

Scott Kantor glanced at his watch. "Look, I don't have all afternoon. Darren's right—Sean isn't going to bow out and he'll end up screwing us all."

"How about we cut his brakes?" Gino Romano wasn't entirely joking.

Scott gave him a side-eye. "A little drastic, Gino, don't you think?"

"Desperate times, Scott. We can't all behave like lawyers."

Darren tapped the table with his fingers. "Let's be serious here. We have a problem and need to come up with a viable solution." He glanced at Gino. "Not the *Sopranos* Solution."

"Maybe we should try talking with him one more time—all of us?" Stavros suggested.

"We've talked ourselves blue in the face. He's just not listening," Darren said to the restaurateur.

Scott agreed. "Maybe we need to scare him out of the race."

"You know, that's not a bad idea." Kevin Monaghan pointed his finger at Scott. "I may have just the thing."

"What *thing?*" Gino asked.

"The video from Scott's bachelor party. Remember?" Kevin met the eyes one by one of the men gathered around the table. "Oh, come on. We were all there."

Darren's heart sped up. *That was a fucked-up night.* "What about it?"

"Underage strippers, underage hookers, more coke than booze. I doubt Sean wants that night to go public. I still got the video. I can send him a copy with a warning. You know how I operate—don't get mad, get even."

Scott flapped his hands, panic on his face. "No way. We'll all be implicated."

"You honestly think I want that shit to blow back on me?" Kevin snarled. "Where the fuck do you think the coke and teenage girls came from? Don't worry, Scott, I'll edit the video so only Sean and the girls and the drugs can be seen. I'll create an anonymous, untraceable email account so it looks like it's come from one of the hookers."

"I don't like it," Gino mumbled.

"So, you'd rather cut his brakes? That ain't getting even, Gino, it's a murder rap."

Scott leaned into the table. "Okay, so we send him an anonymous email without any video. It can still look like it's from one of the hookers —warning him to drop out of the race or she'll send the video to the *Advance*."

That had Kevin smiling. "That'll give me more time to edit us all out."

Stavros nodded his head. "We can give him a deadline of noon tomorrow, or—"

"Soft pedal the theatrics," Gino raised his hands. "Let's avoid nuclear options unless Sean gives us no choice."

Darren considered the plan. It could work. Sean was full of bluster, but if he thought his shenanigans at the party were going to be exposed, it might just do the trick. Still, there was a risk Sean would suspect what was really going on and call their bluff. He might also decide to ensure the destruction would be mutual.

"We done here?" Gino got up from the table. "I've got a refrigerator repairman coming at 4:00."

"I do too." Stavros shrugged. "I wonder if it's the same guy."

"It's fucking Staten Island." Gino laughed. "Of course, it's the same fucking guy."

"I've got to get back to the office." Kevin stood.

Darren met Kevin's eyes. The two had a rocky relationship, but having Kevin on his side was crucial. Knowing Kevin used to be Ron Packer's partner made things even more complicated. Riley had scratched Darren's back, and Darren had scratched his. Kevin had been involved in the Son of Cropsey fiasco ten years ago, and that was lethal information.

"We need a contingency plan," Darren spoke up. "There's a chance this will work, but we all know Sean's ego. He might not bite."

"What d' you suggest?" Stavros asked.

"Send a second anonymous email directly to the *Advance*—ostensibly from one of the hookers. 'Sean Delafield hired me for a drug-fueled party and I have a video to prove it' kind of thing. 'The man shouldn't be back in office. He should be back in jail. He's a liar, a phony, and a crook. Signed, An Anonymous Voter.' Let the *Advance* run with it. It's do-or-die time, guys."

Nods of agreement went around the conference room.

"Then we're decided," said Darren. "An email to Sean with a noon deadline and an email to the *Advance*. Consider it done. And one last thing. When we're with Sean, we act like he's going to run and that we hope he wins."

The door to the conference room opened and Father Stephen stepped in. He glanced up at the clock. "I hope I'm not late. I was told 2:30 ."

"You're right on time, Father." Darren got up and outstretched his arms. "Please, sit down."

Father Stephen took a chair and straightened his clerical collar. "Darren tells me that you gentlemen feel Sean Delafield's return to office would pose a moral threat to the community. Is that correct?" He scanned the table with a concerned expression. "Is there anything I can do to help?"

CHAPTER THIRTY-NINE

Driving to the bank, Davina tried to assemble the jumble in her head. Maybe Riley's only incentive to get the case closed was to receive accolades and sweet deals from Darren Rivers? Maybe he was eager to reinvent himself after the death of his partner? And maybe, just maybe, there was much more to it than that.

Davina mentally mapped out the scenario: Fort Wadsworth, Todt Hill, Great Kills Station, the Paramount. Did the locations have anything in common? Did the strangler-rapist, now murderer, just take opportunities where he found them, or was the location part of a larger pattern? Other than the victims he attacked in their own homes, the dominant feature was attacking in public—sometimes in broad daylight. "Risk-taking," as Professor Blackman had said. Did the two girls she knew of—herself and Jessica Balducci—represent an aberration from the pattern, or merely a different type of risk-taking?

Davina didn't know if it was better or worse that her attack happened behind closed doors. For years after, she'd lived in the same hellish room, until it became a twisted relief to be using and out on the streets. She no longer had to be confined within the walls that caused her nightmares. She didn't have to deal with Alessandra's gaslighting and a drunken mother who didn't care . . . and Riley telling her she was just acting out.

The streets were hell, but I felt safer there than in my own bedroom. In the streets you expect *danger and are ready for it.*

No matter how much Davina tallied the similar details of the attacks, the jarring differences stood out. The girls were twelve to sixteen years old, and the places Son of Cropsey attacked were mostly, possibly all, linked in some way to Sean Delafield; some of the families were linked to the politician, too.

Pulling up to the bank, Davina snapped open a Red Bull and considered Son of Cropsey's apparent love of aftershave. Was the strong scent designed to overwhelm his victims' senses, to distract them from anything else they could identify later? It seemed a bit out there, but who knew with such a psychopath? She consigned the Red Bull to the cupholder and made her way into the bank.

The lines were ridiculous. Seven windows. Two tellers. It was worse than the post office. Davina chose the line that seemed to be moving the quickest and glanced around the bank's lobby. She took note of the high ceilings, wood paneling, granite floors, and brass fittings; the setting was all very old-school. In a polished glass case, she espied a display boasting a local award given to the bank for its commitment to community service and the support of local youth groups. Each of the four shiny brass awards was mounted on a wood plaque and had small gold lettering declaring each of the consecutive years they had been won. Next to them was a picture of Darren Rivers standing proudly at the center of a girls' swim team that had been sponsored by the Savings & Loan and a handful of the island's Catholic charities.

Little girls in swimsuits.

She was almost to the front of the line when Darren, Stavros, her landlord Gino, Kevin Monaghan, Scott Kantor, and Father Stephen walked out of a door marked STAFF ONLY. They were smiling and joking among themselves, as if in the midst of some private joke.

As they walked by, Davina said, "Hi" and waved.

Gino threw her a genuine smile. "Davina!"

Darren straightened his tie. "Have you been waiting long?" he asked.

"Yeah, looks like I came on your busiest day." Davina pointed to the line, which was mostly behind her now. "I'm here to deposit Dobson's takings."

She turned to Stavros, who stood to Darren's left. "I'm so sorry for the other night—"

Stavros put up his hand. "Joe explained you were having some . . . health issues. Stay well, okay?"

"Say, Davina," Darren said, "there's a meeting of the Small Business and Civic Association tonight at the Historical Society's Colony Hall." He handed her a business card. "This'll get you in. It's at 8:00 p.m.. We'd *love* to see Miss Dobson there."

Davina took the card. "Thanks. She can bring a plus one?"

"Good idea." Darren smiled.

"I'm catering the buffet," Stavros chipped in with pride.

Davina's mind tormented her with a flashback to the embarrassing incident with Stavros. Garlic. Tzatziki. Cologne. She swallowed audibly.

The men walked away, leaving Davina two people from the front of the line. She glanced down at Darren's business card; she'd get Gerry to the meeting if she had to drag her there. Davina didn't give a rat's ass for the SBCA, but she was keen on taking Ron Packer's hint to check into Darren Rivers.

CHAPTER FORTY

THURSDAY, ST. JOHN'S UNIVERSITY

At 6:00 p.m., the guest speaker for Davina's Criminal Psych class wrapped up her talk on profiling prolific sex offenders to a long round of enthusiastic applause. Detective Louise Sheffield was attached to the Brooklyn 66th Precinct but had started out in the 120th; the irony of the woman's chosen topic was not lost on Davina.

Detective Sheffield was kind of a celebrity among those studying crime and criminal law. She was the very first trans woman to head up a profiling department anywhere and also happened to be damned good at her job. Sheffield had three best-selling books on high-profile cases and the psychology of violent criminals. She was just the person Davina wanted to speak to.

Class over, Professor Blackman gave out a reading assignment, dismissed the students, and shook hands with Detective Sheffield. While most of the class hurried away toward the upper exits, Davina made her way down to the stage where the detective collected her papers and slotted them carefully into her chic Chanel briefcase. Close up, the cop was stunningly beautiful; incredibly feminine and tall; she had stylish, short-cut hair that was bleached platinum white; her body was lean yet curvy; and her dazzling blue eyes looked like they'd seen plenty.

"Detective Sheffield? Davina Speers." She put out her hand. "Great lecture—I learned a lot."

"Thanks." The detective locked her briefcase. "I happen to be a fan of your professor."

"Do you mind if I ask you a few questions about profiling?"

Louise consulted her watch. "Sure. Walk me out to my car? I'm meeting some of my old crew from the 120th at Richmond Republic, a cop bar."

As Davina and the detective left the auditorium, she asked, "Did you ever work on the Son of Cropsey case?"

The detective shook her head. "I didn't catch that one, but I made a point of reviewing the case notes."

Davina shifted her backpack. "What drove that guy? Any ideas?"

Walking slowly out into the tiled hallway, a janitor passed by, pushing his cleaning cart toward the lavatories. Half the lights were already off.

"I like to think of this more as brain wiring, the way the mind works, rather than motivation. For rapists, it often boils down to two things: personalization and objectification. It's all about them; and to them their victim is not even human." Sheffield spoke like she lectured—with authority and dispassion. "You're familiar with the Kevin Coe case."

"Yeah, I just looked him up for your lecture—he was on Blackman's suggested reading list. The South Hill Rapist from Spokane, Washington, right? Dozens of rapes attributed to him, and there was something about a dominating, abusive mother. Someone wrote a book and made a movie about the case."

"That's right. Coe was diagnosed as a narcissist, compounded with histrionic and antisocial disorders. People like Coe see other people as objects put on this planet to do with as they please. A woman walking down the street wearing certain clothing, revealing or not; a woman casting a glance in the perp's direction—almost anything can be twisted in a rapist's mind to trigger that predation response: She or he wants me. I'm entitled to possess her/him/it. There are cases of abusive fathers—and mothers—believing because they made a child, they have the ownership right to exploit them for their own sexual gratification. In some especially disturbing cases, parents believe it's their duty, their *obligation* to introduce their kids to sex or 'break them in.'"

"I just don't understand how anybody can possibly ever cross that line," Davina said.

The detective nodded. "There are theories that the part of the abuser's brain that prevents them from doing such a thing to any child, let alone their own, is somehow defective or impaired—in much the same way frontal lobe damage has been identified in many serial killers. It's also the same part of the brain associated with impulse control."

"So, biologically, there's just no stopping themselves," said Davina. "They can't help it."

"Correct. But there's also what's called the vampire syndrome."

"Where the abused become abusers?" Davina recalled the nature versus nurture argument in a previous class: Are people born with certain proclivities, or are they molded that way by their parents?

"And, for a majority of these earlier victims of abuse, their later abuse of others can seem almost normal, even justified to them. Call it a twisted version of cultural transmission, where one generation passes down its freakish values and deviant behaviors to the next generation."

"And those who abuse or rape for pleasure?" Davina asked, her mind on Son of Cropsey.

"Ahh, the good old sadists," Detective Sheffield replied. "Those rapists derive sexual gratification from their victim's fear, torture, suffering, and helplessness. Their own anger and sense of power are eroticized. Inflicting pain induces sexual arousal. More often than not, they strangle their victims just to render them unconscious and provide an ultimate power between life and death. Between that and the trauma of such an attack, it explains why so many get away with their crimes—the victims' memories are simply wiped clean."

"Would that be classed as power tripping?" Davina asked; the detective's mention of strangulation was a tad too close to home for comfort.

"That's a quaintly colloquial way of putting it, Miss Speers. Sadistic rapists rarely reach climax without escalating their victim's terror. This can lead to ritualistic, bizarre behavior, which is actually helpful to the police. It allows us to discern patterns of behavior and build a profile of the environment he prefers, as well as his victim type, of course."

"So, is it logical to conclude that someone who craves power and control might have lived a life in which they were denied both?"

Sheffield nodded. "Good assessment. Such people externalize their own victimization, their own self-loathing, and suppressed rage in an explosive act of violent rebellion."

"But why target young girls?"

"Ah, good question. Did you know there are studies now that suggest pedophilia is a hardwired behavior? Like some people have fetishes relating to feet, latex clothing, spanking—it was thought such responses had their roots in childhood experiences. Now, some MRI research has shown there's a region in the brain that triggers a sexual response whenever people see something *sexy*. Except in the case of pedophiles, whose brain triggers a sexual response only when they see images of children. But remember, feeling sexually excited doesn't always mean acting on it. It turns out pedophiles are also typically shorter than average and are three times more likely to be left-handed. That doesn't mean we're locking up every short southpaw."

"You keep saying *people*," Davina chipped in.

"It's not just men who are pedophiles and rapists, Davina." A fleeting expression on Detective Sheffield's face told Davina she was perhaps speaking from experience. "Although it's rare, there are cases of women sex offenders too, and even couples who enjoy abusing together—including some parents who assault their own children."

They reached the exit of the John J. DaSilva Academic Center; Detective Sheffield opened the door for Davina, and they stepped out into the parking lot. The area was nearly empty; the air, warm and humid, smelled of cut grass, overhead lights casting eerie shadows in the otherwise serene setting.

Detective Sheffield thumbed her key fob, and the lights of a Ford Ranger flashed not far from Davina's Jetta. "Sadistic rapists can start as early as junior high, likely crossing a line with someone they know—a friend, a neighbor."

"A sister." Davina shivered involuntarily.

The detective looked at her quizzically. "And, strangely, this particular kind of rapist almost always blames the victim," the cop continued as they walked across the lot. "In their mind, the victim *wanted* the rape. She was literally asking for it, teasing, seducing him. He may even see the rape as payback—punishment or reward—for sexually arousing him."

"Narcissism again."

"The rapist builds a mental construct in which his actions are not rape, because in his aberrant mind he's giving the victim what they want. Strangely, by the way, some of these men can be remarkably attractive. Appearances can be very deceiving." Detective Sheffield pulled open the Ranger's back door and threw in her briefcase.

Davina furrowed her brow. "So, outward appearance aside, they're actually passing along their own inner trauma."

She nodded. "Trauma, depression, PTSD, anxiety, self-loathing—you name it. I've seen it all, Miss Speers."

"Son of Cropsey's victims certainly experienced every bit of that," Davina said quietly. She glanced up at the detective. "I've met with several of them."

Detective Sheffield cocked her head and crossed her arms over her chest. "Really? You're taking this class seriously."

"I have personal reasons."

"Ah."

"Last question, I promise. Do rapists ever go dormant?"

"It has been known. If the police get too close, or they feel they've made a mistake or lost control during an assault, they'll go to ground. How long they're out of commission depends on when the compulsion becomes so overwhelming that they're forced to act."

So, it's possible. It's possible Son of Cropsey disappeared around the time they caught Cox only to come back all these years later.

"May I ask why this is so personal for you, Miss Speers?"

"I was raped by . . . someone like Son of Cropsey."

Detective Sheffield straightened. "I am so sorry. I figured that's what you meant by personal. It's why you're studying criminal psych? To figure things out?"

"Like every other student who takes psych classes, right? I think we're all a bit screwed up. But I can't get the one question out of my head—*why me?*"

The detective appeared uncomfortable. "All I can say is most rapists don't choose their victims haphazardly. Some have agendas. Others may be opportunistic, spotting weaknesses they can exploit—like someone whose walk suggests they are less athletic and fit and therefore less likely to run or fight. Just the same as predators in the wild."

Davina nodded wryly. "Yeah, I watch Animal Planet. Predators always attack the weakest and slowest in the herd."

"Exactly. People who drag their feet, shuffle along, or exhibit timidity or unease are targeted more often than people who walk fast and fluidly."

"That's probably why I hit the gym—survival instinct." Davina took a deep breath and let it out. "I have to admit I was pretty damned vulnerable for a lot of reasons when I was a kid." She met the detective's eyes and was pleased to see compassion there.

Detective Sheffield's expression changed. "But Son of Cropsey was different. I'm one of those cops who believe that there was something more to that perp's motivation and choice of victims. Something didn't look right, but I'm not sure what."

That sent a shudder down Davina's spine.

"But on that cheery note, I really must run or my wife will kill me." Sheffield reached for the door latch.

"Do you think the cops caught the right guy?" Davina couldn't help herself.

The detective paused. "It certainly appears they caught the right guy. But then again, you know what they say about appearances. Good night, Miss Speers. I hope you find your answers."

CHAPTER FORTY-ONE

THURSDAY, OFFICES OF THE STATEN ISLAND ADVANCE

Geoff was in a writing haze on his follow-up piece to the Son of Cropsey story; he'd alluded to the attack and murder at the Paramount and gone big on the theory that it was largely ignored by Staten Island's law enforcement because the victims were Black.

His phone dinged: an email.

Mr. Wong,

I know Sean Delafield wants to run for office again. I can't sit back and let this happen without reaching out to you. Six years ago, Sean Delafield hired me and two other girls for a private party, which turned out to be a drug-fueled night of crazy sex. I was an underage sex worker at the time. I'm not proud of what I did, but Staten Island needs to know just what kind of man he is.

I have a cell phone video from that night. It proves Sean Delafield is a pedophile, a liar, a phony, and a crook. He shouldn't be back in office. He should be in jail. I know you're one of the top reporters at the Advance, and

that's why I'm telling you all this. Please do what you can to make sure that this horrible man is never in a position of power.
Sincerely,
A Concerned Voter

Geoff frowned. Was this for real? He knew Sean Delafield was a scumbag, and such an anonymous tip could blow up the guy's political aspirations. It was a perfect rerun of the Jeffrey Archer case back in England in '01. He'd lied about his association with a prostitute in a libel case against a newspaper—and won—twelve years previously, and then all went quiet. Until he decided to run for mayor of London. Then one of his cronies had an attack of conscience and spilled the beans. Archer resigned his candidacy, did four years in jail, and still became a Lord.

Just goes to prove, Geoff thought, *shit really does float.*

He typed out a quick response.

Dear Concerned Voter,
I appreciate you sharing this with me. Are you willing to send me the video? Unfortunately, I can't go to press on an anonymous tip alone.
Geoff Wong

He pressed *send*, and within seconds his email bounced back. Strange: If Concerned Voter wanted him to actually do something, surely, she'd realize he was going to need more solid information. Otherwise, what was the point of contacting him?

Geoff turned to his office window. The sun drifted down toward the horizon, and the sky was an orange-pink haze. The paper had a looming deadline to get the late edition out, which meant Stan Clemmons, Geoff's editor-in-chief, was still in his office across the hall. Geoff printed out the anonymous email and headed across to Stan's office. As it was, he bumped into Stan just as he stepped out of the elevator. He clutched a white plastic bag with a Styrofoam container inside. From the deliciously greasy smell, Geoff guessed burger and fries.

"Wong." Stan pushed his bifocals up onto his long, pointy nose.

"You got a sec?"

"Sure."

Geoff followed Stan into his office and waited for him to get comfy behind the expansive wooden desk. Placing the bag to one side, Stan cleared a space amid the stacks of files. "You want some fries?"

"No, thanks."

"I won't stand on ceremony." Stan picked up his burger and took a bite. "Okay, what you got?" Stan spoke around a mouthful of burger.

Geoff leaned in. "I got this email a few minutes ago." He pushed the paper across the desk. "Anonymous, of course."

A smile came to Stan's lips and he put down his burger, wiping his hands on a crumpled napkin. "I guess it's a start. No actual video?"

"No attachment, and my reply bounced."

"Could be a hoax."

"Could be legit."

Stan leaned his elbows on his desk. "There's a hell of lot of people who don't want to see Delafield back in office."

"Yeah, two of them are sitting in your office."

Stan tore open a ketchup packet and squirted it over his fries. "We could go to the police."

"There's not enough information for them to even file a report. Besides, I need to establish merit. Remember I told you about Davina Speers?"

"The Son of Cropsey woman?"

Geoff imagined Davina cringing if she knew she'd been saddled with that moniker. "She has a past that includes the sort of, um, *activities* described in the email. Shady stuff for a teenage girl—she might be able to shed some light."

Stan laughed. "You're gonna get a lot of journalism awards because of that girl. Maybe you should marry her."

That face wouldn't be a bad one to wake up to in the morning. "Not my type."

"You think she sent the email?"

"Not her style. She's more in your face—she wouldn't hide behind emails and burner addresses."

Stan smiled again. "Then she *is* your type."

"I'm gonna follow this," Geoff went on. "I think it's going to lead to something big. If I can persuade whomever it is to put their money where their mouth is and send even a few stills of the video, we've got the story of the decade."

Stan sighed and chomped on a soggy french fry. "Okay, follow it to where it goes. But don't forget the deadlines—especially on that funding story."

"I'll tell you one thing," Geoff said. "If this email *is* legit, it'd be good to find out who arranged the drugs and underage sex party. Sean wouldn't dare dirty his hands. He might have had a good time, but someone else made it happen for him."

"Why would some random hooker care?"

"Maybe she's an ex-prostitute with a crisis of conscience." Geoff walked to the office door. "Either she has an axe to grind and wants to take Sean Delafield down, or she loves Staten Island so much she can't bear to see him back in power." His mind spun to Monica Coghlan, the prostitute who'd ruined Jeffrey Archer's chances of mayordom. She'd been killed in a horrific car wreck before she got to see the man convicted.

CHAPTER FORTY-TWO

THURSDAY, STATEN ISLAND HISTORICAL COLONY HALL

By the time Davina met Gerry outside the hall's spacious Grand Ballroom, the place was packed and the drinking was already in full swing. The ambient noise was high, everyone raising their voices to be heard over everyone else. Caterers in white jackets ran a constantly shifting obstacle course across the polished wooden floor refilling glasses and snack trays. Around the room, high, arched windows looked out into the night, and overhead, sparkling period chandeliers shone down on the predominantly male gathering.

So many organizations on Staten Island depended on the white-collar money the business association soirees attracted—including female sports teams. Davina reckoned if someone like Gerry Dobson was in charge, they'd be sending Olympic-level athletes into the national programs, historic buildings would be preserved, and Staten Island wouldn't be turned into Vegas-lite, courtesy of Sean Delafield's plans to turn the Farm Colony into a casino-cum-retirement village.

"I'm gonna mingle." Gerry surveyed the room. "See if I can't scare up some new business." She held a green bottle of chilled Pellegrino water she'd picked up at a kiosk by the door. In her skin-tight green gym catsuit, Ms. Dobson was drawing quite some attention.

"I'm going to scrounge up whatever I can from the buffet," Davina told her. "Do you want anything?"

"Protein, if they still have it. I'm watching the carbs." Gerry placed a hand over her rippling six-pack abs.

Davina laughed and set off for the buffet.

Gerry was rock solid—inside as well as out. She was the very essence of a strong, powerful, intelligent woman. Fresh off the streets, Davina had thought there was no way she could ever become that kind of woman, but she was sure as hell going to try.

I wanna be Gerry Dobson when I grow up.

Reaching the buffet, Davina cast a glance over her shoulder and saw Gerry was fiercely working the room. Despite her short stature, the woman's fiery red hair made her stand out, and her undoubted charisma radiated out in waves.

As for Davina, she couldn't help but feel more than a touch out of place. The room was filled with the island's business elite—the movers and shakers, the politicians and incredibly well-connected. It really was no place for a lowly gymnasium worker with no ambition other than to stay clean; she had absolutely nothing in common with any of them.

Meandering along the buffet, Davina scooped up some Greek salad and a piece of pita bread. For Gerry, she got meatballs. The overpowering reek of garlic was potent. Clearly, a Stavros signature. Her two plates full, Davina headed across to Gerry, who was in conversation with the group Davina had grown to think of as the Staten Island Mafia. All the usual suspects were there: Darren Rivers, Sean and Nick Delafield, George Modica, Gino Romano, Dr. Bob Fidanza, and Kevin Monaghan. Hovering on the periphery was Father Stephen and, next to him, Davina recognized Carlo Donato from Dobson's. Carlo appeared desperate to be included in the inner circle, listening intently to Sean Delafield's pontifications, mirroring the others' laughter, and inching closer with each sip of his drink.

It was odd to see Carlo alone; other than his time at the gym, he was never without his adoring wife by his side. Davina wondered where she was.

"Hello, Davina." Angela Donato startled Davina.

Davina spun around. "Angela," she said through a mouthful of pita bread. "It's lovely to see you again." Her erstwhile therapist hadn't changed one bit in the ten years since their weekly sessions: same hair, same trim figure, same homely taste in clothes, same sympathetic smile.

"You were at Joy's funeral," Angela said with a sad smile. "You should have come over and said hello."

Davina shrugged and nibbled absently at her bread; it was cold, tasteless, and had the consistency of cardboard. "I was going to, but I kinda got caught up in something."

"I saw," Angela replied with a sardonic grin. "Detective Riley is a bully who likes to abuse his position. It wasn't fair for him to throw you out like that. Joy would have been disgusted." A flicker of sadness settled upon Angela's face. "How have *you* been, Davina?"

And just like that, Davina was back in Angela's warm, cozy office, settled back on the overstuffed armchair with her eyes closed as she struggled to put words to the ordeal everyone refused to believe her about. Everyone apart from her trauma counselor.

"Oh, you know—same old, same old." Davina managed a smile she hoped was reassuring.

"I think you've done really well," Angela said. "Considering what you went through back then. I heard you'd been through a couple of rough patches, but I knew you were strong enough to pull yourself through them—"

"You guys still doing the ghost bus rides?" Davina jumped in; she had no desire to rehash her old therapy sessions with Angela. Those days were long gone, buried in the past, and Davina fully intended for them to stay that way.

Angela peered across the room at her husband, who had managed to squeeze himself into the Delafield group across the room, between George and the skinny priest. "They're more popular than ever since we included both Cropsey and Son of Cropsey's old haunts—pun *totally* intended. Of course, you'd see for yourself if you ever accepted my open invitation for a complimentary tour," Angela chastised, giving Davina a friendly wink. "The Historical Society is talking about adding another bus, maybe even more if the subway scheme ever takes off—more tourists, you see."

"And more New Yorkers moving to the Rock—I guess they're all going to want to see where the ghosts are."

"I guess they will." Angela's tone flattened. Her eyes fixed upon Carlo across the room and she took a step away from Davina. "If you'll excuse me, I need to visit the restroom. It's been lovely seeing you again."

"Lovely to see you too," Davina replied as Angela walked away. For a therapist, Angela could sometimes be a tad blunt. Davina had gotten used to it back in the day. But she'd also forgotten how much Carlo disliked the idea of New Yorkers invading the Rock. It was an attitude shared by the majority of Staten Island's residents, and one Angela appeared to have picked up from her husband.

Checking around to see where Gerry had found them a table, Davina saw to her horror that her boss had gravitated toward Sean Delafield and his band of sycophants. Her heart sank as she realized she had no other option than to join Gerry. Weaving through the throng of expensive suits and forced laughter, Davina headed for the group; for once, Sean was allowing someone else to speak.

"What I'd like to do," Father Stephen was saying, "is resurrect the Staten Island Film Festival."

Kevin Monaghan, a glass of Guinness in hand, chimed in with a chortle, "That's what you people do best, Father—resurrect the dead!"

The group laughed but fell into silence when they saw Davina inch by, plates in hand. They eyed her with suspicion, and once more, she felt so terribly out of place.

Then, Davina caught Nick's eye. He gave her his 1000-watt smile. Blushing a little, she inched toward the group of stony-faced men as Sean Delafield broke the awkward silence. "You want to bring things back?" he said loudly. "You want to make for a greater Staten Island?" There was a low rumble of "here we go" groans. "Bring back the plan for the

NASCAR racetrack. Even better, we lay out a Monte Carlo Formula One Grand Prix through town."

Gerry jumped right on in. "That would destroy Old Richmond Town and other historical sites—just for a racetrack? Local businesses will not be happy for keeping their customers away for the duration of the race."

Sean scoffed. "You kidding me? They'll do more business than they can handle on race day."

Gerry shook her head. "Except that it never actually works that way. Ask anyone whose business has been in the path of a marathon or a bike race."

Davina was surprised to hear her boss so vehemently standing up against progress—as if what Staten Island really did need was a bunch more Luddites to prevent the place from venturing into the twenty-first century.

Davina handed Gerry the plate of meatballs.

"Thanks, D." Gerry was too much on a roll to eat. "Besides, history is who we are. History is our roots, and I, for one, would not agree to have you rip those roots out for another one of your asinine money making schemes."

"I have to agree," said Davina; she felt all eyes on her. "I've volunteered a few times at preservation events, and I think it's very important for Staten Island. I mean, the broader tourism potential is great and wouldn't close any streets."

Silence again. Why was it that when Davina opened her mouth it felt like she'd stepped out of line? Why did she make these men so uncomfortable? She glanced at Nick, but his expression was neutral and told her nothing. As the conversation resumed, she turned and found George Modica, the fire chief, staring at her. He looked away the instant their eyes met.

Sean gave a dismissive laugh. "You need to get yourself a sense of vision, Gerry. You have no idea what this plan will do for Staten Island."

"You mean what it will do *to* Staten Island."

Kevin threw back the rest of his beer. "Don't you own part of that route, Sean? Kinda cozy arrangement. Reminds me of what your father did to that Girl Scout Camp."

Darren made a business of loosening his tie. "Let's change the subject, shall we?"

"I agree." Nick darted a glare at his father.

Sean threw a smirk in Nick's general direction, then turned to Gerry. "You want to preserve history for history's sake? Fine. We can move the old houses."

"You mean like your father promised to do?"

Sean's smile was obviously fake. "Exactly."

"He moved one and leveled the rest." Gerry looked around at the group. "I wasn't too sure about joining the business association tonight, but now. . ." She let that sit there for a moment, and Davina was sure her boss would flip them all off and leave. But she didn't. Instead, she met Sean's eyes, "Now, I'm *in*. Just to be certain none of this shit goes down."

Darren raised his glass as Sean and Gerry continued to stare each other down. "That's great news. I, for one, am glad you accepted our invitation tonight."

"I need another drink." Bob Fidanza glanced around for a waiter.

Turning her head to hide her amusement, Davina saw George staring at her yet again. She gave the man a half-smile but he turned away and lowered his eyes.

"Gerry, how's that gym of yours?" Gino popped a meatball into his mouth.

"Still teaching Staten Island how to kick ass and take names. Well, let me rephrase that, *Davina* is."

Davina smiled. "I'm just doing my part."

"*Women* fight there?" Father Stephen seemed genuinely surprised.

"Of course," Davina replied. "They need self-defense training nowadays more than ever."

"Until they end up in my office with twisted this, bruised that." Dr. Fidanza laughed.

"Or in my confessional," Father Stephen added.

Gerry touched Davina on the shoulder, a sparkle in her eye. "I'm so proud of this girl. You ask me, *she* should be running Staten Island, not a bunch of stuffed shirts and money-grabbers."

Davina scoffed, feeling awkward under the spotlight. "I really don't think so."

"Me neither," Kevin Monaghan murmured under his breath.

Davina bristled. Monaghan had been Ron Packer's partner ten years ago, and he *had* to know that they'd let Son of Cropsey get away. The recent assaults were as much on the retired cop as they were on Riley.

"Who runs the world? Girls!" Sean slurred the last word in a high-pitched whine. Red-faced, he lifted his glass in a mock toast and splashed half his group with whiskey.

Nick was mortified. "Dad, maybe you should slow down."

"Maybe you should speed up." Sean tilted his glass to his son. "That's what your problem is, my boy. You're slow on the uptake—always have been."

Darren cleared his throat and made an exaggerated show of checking his watch. "Why don't we all freshen our drinks? Make the most of the open bar before they close it at nine."

Needing no further encouragement, the men dispersed, leaving Davina standing next to Gerry.

"Thanks for the meatballs," Gerry said, stabbing one from the plate. "I need 'em after swallowing Sean Delafield's bullshit."

Davina took a bite of her bread. "I hear that."

"They act tough, but *we're t*ougher." Gerry flexed her bicep and punched Davina gently on the shoulder.

Davina then realized George was again staring at her from the opposite side of the room. When she met his gaze, he turned to join Darren at the bar. George placed a hand on Darren's shoulder and whispered something into his ear.

Oh, to be a fly on the wall, Davina thought.

CHAPTER FORTY-THREE

THURSDAY, STATEN ISLAND HISTORICAL COLONY HALL

As Darren sipped at his fresh vodka tonic, he felt a hand on his shoulder. Turning around, he saw Fire Chief George Modica peering at him. He appeared concerned, and agitated—there were fat beads of sweat on his broad face.

"We have to talk."

"About?"

"It's her."

Darren stirred his drink and tossed the plastic swizzle stick into the trash. "What are you talking about, George?"

"The girl with Gerry Dobson. She was one of the strippers at Scott's party."

"You're drunk, George."

"I've had *two* fucking beers. I'm telling you, Darren, it's *her*."

"George, that was six years ago. How could you possibly recognize her . . . with her clothes on?" Darren chuckled and took another sip of his drink.

"I still have a copy of the video Kevin sent to all of us. Sometimes I watch it for ol' time's sake—if you catch my meaning—and I swear I'd know that stripper in a heartbeat."

Darren eyeballed Davina; she was deep in conversation with Gerry Dobson. He knitted his brow. He knew Davina had a shady past, but she didn't look anything like *any* of the young girls there that night—even a half dozen years on.

He pulled George away from the bar and out of earshot. "Now you listen to me. Davina Speers is not one of those girls, all right?"

"If she is, we could be fucked, Darren. She'll know *everything*. I know we wanna bring Sean down, but this fucking video could bring *all* of us down." George's eyes were wide, filled with panic, and Darren was beginning to wish he'd never briefed the idiot about their plans to threaten Sean with the party video.

Why do I always have to be the adult in the room? Darren put his drink down on a nearby table. "You're going to give yourself another heart attack, George. Davina definitely wasn't there that night. And, even if she was, what's she going to do now that she couldn't have done a thousand times over in the past six years?"

"Who knows why women do the crazy shit they do?" The fire chief loosened his collar, which was covered in grimy sweat. "Thirty-five years married, and I can't figure out my own wife."

"Maybe you married the wrong woman."

"They're all the same."

Well, there's your problem. "The way all us Blacks are the same?"

George had an expression like a startled fish for a half second. "No, man. I didn't . . . I'm sorry. I'm a little buzzed is all."

Darren placed a friendly hand on the older man's shoulder. "None of those girls are ever going to talk."

"So, why is she here?"

"Davina's here because I invited her boss and she tagged along."

"Who tagged along?" Stavros sidled up to Darren and insinuated himself into the conversation.

"Stavros, Darren won't listen to me," George whined.

"I don't blame him." Stavros smiled. "Cheers." He lifted his glass to toast the banker.

"Great job with the food," Darren said.

"I didn't make enough—I never do. Only cater a Staten Island event if you know how to feed an army."

"What do you know about Davina Speers?" George interjected.

"George," said Darren, "for fuck's sake, give it a rest."

Stavros was confused. "What about Davina Speers?"

"Doesn't she look familiar to you?"

Darren grimaced, wondering if he ought to get him to sit down in a quiet corner where no one could hear his crazy rambling.

"George, she lives on the Rock—everybody looks familiar." Stavros laughed.

"I'm *serious*, guys. Davina was at Scott's party. She had dark hair back then, and black nails and smoky eyes—how the hell do you not remember a fucking Goth stripper?"

"Davina *wasn't* there." Darren eyed George. "You're drunk and mistaken, George."

"You fuckers laugh all you want. If she's the one that takes us down, you just remember who saw it coming." George grunted. "If you'll excuse me, I need more beer—see if that calms me down."

As George bellied up to the bar, Stavros shook his shaggy head. "He's really worked up?"

"He's an idiot who can't hold his free beer." Darren studied Davina again. Fiddling to tuck strands of red hair behind her ears, Davina smiled affably as she conversed with Gerry Dobson. Sure, she had tattoos and a hard past, but all Darren saw was a decent girl who wanted to stay out of trouble and maybe do some good in the world. He couldn't believe she was ever a stripper or hooker, and no way had she been at Scott's party.

He'd have remembered that, surely.

Wouldn't he?

As Darren scrutinized her, Davina gestured with her arms spread to her sides, which flashed a tattoo on her left wrist he'd not noticed before— a chrysanthemum. A tickle of cold ran up the back of his neck. He glanced toward the bar where Father Stephen was saying something to George, his voice lost in the general hubbub.

Stavros tilted his glass. "Maybe the Padre can calm old George down."

"Unlikely."

Father Stephen put a gentle hand on the other man's forearm. He shook his head.

George said something, his lips barely moving.

Darren knit his brow. Were they discussing the Speers girl?

The priest's grasp on George's arm tightened, and concern troubled his usually placid brow.

"I've had enough, Father! I'm at the end of my rope!" That part of the conversation, everyone in the vicinity of the bar heard. George, like a man with the devil on his tail, slammed his drink down hard on the bar and stormed off.

Stavros spoke for both himself and Darren Rivers. "What the hell was all that about?"

CHAPTER FORTY-FOUR

THURSDAY, STATEN ISLAND HISTORICAL COLONY HALL

STANDING NEAR ONE OF THE ARCHED WINDOWS THAT PEERED out onto the meticulously landscaped gardens, Nick couldn't help but catch the tense exchanges between Darren and George, and then between George and Father Stephen. Something was definitely wrong. If the tension involved his father—and Nick suspected it did—he'd have to get to the bottom of it to protect him. With that in mind, Nick approached Darren and Stavros, who stared after George Modica in silence.

"I see you're still drinking beer." Darren tilted his glass toward Nick.

Nick grinned. "I like the classics."

Darren took a sip of his vodka tonic. "I prefer the hard stuff."

"Rough night?"

"It is what it is." He loosened his tie.

Yeah, yeah, I know. My dad is a dick. Tell me something I don't know. But his interests are my *interests.*

"I gotta go talk to Gino." Stavros threw back his drink and placed the empty glass on the table. "That tahini he sent to the restaurant was crap."

He walked over to join Gino Romano and Kevin Monaghan, who were deep in conversation. Stavros no sooner got there when all three men turned to stare at Davina. That made Nick uneasy. If he were a good-looking woman like Davina, three old skeezes were the last men he'd want looking at him like that. *Speculatively*—that was the word. Nick wondered why.

Darren spoke softly, "Where were you all day?"

Which is my fault? "Helping Dad with the campaign. Trying to keep him in line."

Darren sighed and stared down at his shoes. "He needs to play his cards closer to his vest."

"Like you?"

Their eyes met briefly, before Darren looked away. "Not here, okay? Or are you suddenly good with your father seeing us together?"

Nick made a dismissive gesture and switched subjects. "What happened just now?"

"Just now?"

"You, George. The guy was sweating through his damn shirt."

Again, with the shrug. "Maybe he is doing blow tonight."

"The fire chief—seriously?"

"There's a lot of shit you don't know, Nick."

"Fuck you, Darren. Don't talk to me like I'm a child."

Darren glanced across the room at George. "Did you happen to hear any of our conversation?"

"I heard something about the girls in Scott's bachelor party video." Darren's surprise made Nick laugh. "I saw it years ago. It was kinda boring—the girls looked robotic and fake. I didn't even get to the end."

"How'd you get to see it?"

"Scrolling through porn on my dad's computer. He's got tons of that shit, and most of it is a helluva lot better than that dumb bachelor party video. It was so dark you couldn't see the girls' faces . . . plenty of T and A, though." He laughed.

Darren lifted his brow. "I didn't know you had a predilection for pornography."

"It was a phase."

"Cozying up to Davina Speers—that also a phase?"

Nick smirked. His feelings for Davina were confusing the hell out of him, to say the least. "It bothers you I like women? Kind of judgy of you, isn't it, Darren?"

"You're actually attracted to women? It's not just a cover—you're bi?"

Attracted. Yeah. You could say that.

"Why does it make a difference who I'm attracted to in general as long as I'm attracted to you in particular?" Nick took the last sip of his beer. "I'd rather talk shop, okay?"

"You wouldn't be Nick Delafield if you didn't." There was resignation in Darren's voice.

"It's two weeks to the primary. I saw what went down at the tanks—you all want my father to bow out gracefully." Nick laughed. "You know my father doesn't do anything gracefully—and he *never* bows out of anything."

Darren met Nick's eyes. "Your father's a liability."

"My father is a *visionary* . . . and a total prick. But he'll get things done."

"Not if—Nick, you want me to be honest?"

"Yes."

"Sean has a lot to learn. We both know about his arrogance and what that's going to do to the Republican ticket."

Fucking asshole. "The voters will overlook that minor indiscretion."

Darren's dark eyes widened. "Are you serious?"

"Of course. Just think about all the other shit people are prepared to overlook when their best interests are being taken care of. Staten Island is a broke dump, and my dad is going to change all that. His developments will breathe new life into this borough."

Darren peered into Nick's eyes. "Jesus Christ. You really believe that. Look around, Nick. This place is a destination. It makes millions every year in tourism, business conferences, and weddings alone. There are businesses sprouting up all over the island—businesses your dad has nothing to do with." He sighed. "You really are just like your father."

Nick stood tall. "There's nothing wrong with that."

"Meaning, you don't see anything you don't want to see—either of you. Be careful, Nick." Darren's eyes twitched sideways a split second before Sean Delafield clapped his son hard on the back.

"There's my boy!" His drunken voice boomed above the room's chatter.

Nick jumped and smiled at his father. "Dad. Hey. Hey, Scott," he greeted the lawyer Scott Kantor, who was hot on Sean's heels.

"Darren." Sean raised his glass. "Scott was just telling me how we've all moved past the nonsense at the tanks." He gave Darren his trademark shit-eating grin. "The Small Business and Civic Association and the bank are throwing their support behind me. Go ahead, Scott, tell 'em."

"The entire party just *loves* Sean Delafield. The union rank and file are one hundred percent behind him," Scott gushed.

"What can I say, Sean? Everybody loves a winner." Darren's voice was flat.

"We're going to put Staten Island on the map," said Nick, clapping a hand to his dad's shoulder. "You'll see. Delafields get things done."

Sean turned to his son. "Don't be such a blow-hard, Nick. I don't need you to be my number one. This is *my* campaign, not yours."

Nick felt like he'd been gut punched. "What the hell . . . ?"

Sean dismissed Nick with a flap of his hand. "I'm gonna start celebrating my win tonight. If you'll excuse me." Sean turned and made his way through the crowd, back toward the bar.

Darren watched him go. "He's got some real chutzpah after two years behind bars for felony bribery." He turned to Scott. "None of what you said was true."

Scott sighed. "I'm not really sure. Sean has done me a lot of favors, though—he's sent a hell of a lot of referrals my way."

"If I'm not mistaken, Darren," Nick said with a wry smile, "the paper-work for my father's real estate deals has your signature on it. I really don't think you can afford to shut my father out. You've all benefited, and will continue to benefit, from his influence. He's a one-man Angie's List, and you know it."

Darren adjusted his collar. "Whatever you say, Nick."

That's right. Whatever the fuck I say. My dad owns *you. Stop fighting it and stop fighting me.*

CHAPTER FORTY-FIVE

THURSDAY, STATEN ISLAND HISTORICAL COLONY HALL

"He's been staring at me all night. What the fuck is his problem?" Davina grunted. The attention George Modica was giving her was creeping her out.

Gerry glanced over at the man. "Maybe he has a crush on you."

Davina grimaced. "That's gross, Gerry. This whole thing is gross." She hated the crowd, the inane chatter and false bonhomie, and the all-pervading stink of alcohol that made her miss drinking.

I'm gonna have to call Charlie.

Despite the craving, Davina knew she wasn't going to pick up again. The drunken conversations and immature behavior going on around her served as a stark reminder why she'd given up the stuff in the first place. There were a bunch of years in her past Davina could barely remember—morning 'til night, she'd be in a warm daze and wake up to the same problems coupled with a punishing hangover. Drinking was never much more than a temporary escape.

"You should confront him." Gerry nodded toward George.

"That would be too weird."

Gerry leaned in closer. "Him staring at you like that is weird, Davina. Don't rent him space in your head—go take up some of *his* space."

Davina marveled at the simplicity of her boss's philosophy. "I've got a lot to learn from you."

"You've learned most of it. Get yourself over there. If you need reinforcements, just raise a hand and I'll be right there."

Gerry had a point. The old Davina would have just stood there and taken it, no matter how uncomfortable the old man made her feel. Or she would have left. The new Davina took action: She sauntered over to George and Scott Kantor.

"Hello." Davina stood in front of them. *This is gonna be awkward.*

George's eyes widened. "H-hello."

"Pretty loud and chaotic in here, isn't it?"

Scott grinned and brought a hand up to his ear. "What did you say?"

Davina laughed at the little joke.

George didn't. "I gotta get a drink." He made to leave.

"You have one in your hand." Davina's words stopped the guy in his tracks.

George glanced at the beer in his shaking hand. "I mean . . . some food. Gotta get some food."

"I'm pretty sure all the best stuff is gone." Davina nodded toward the buffet.

"I'm sorry."

Davina frowned. "What are you sorry for, Chief Modica?" She caught a sudden whiff of cloying cologne and at once felt light-headed and nauseous.

"Do you need this?" George held his beer out to her.

Davina waved him off. The smell made her knees weak; she considered calling Gerry over.

"Your cologne." She coughed. "What is it?"

George seemed self-conscious, puzzled. "That good, huh?"

Davina regained her composure—damned if the disturbingly familiar fragrance was going to take her down. She suppressed a gag. "I couldn't help but notice it."

"It's Dolce & Gabbana by Man."

"It's nice," Davina lied; she wanted to pull her shirt up over her nose and mouth.

"My wife hated it so much she almost left me." George laughed. "Joke!"

Davina faked a smile.

"If you like it, you'll have to talk to Scott—he's got some secret way of getting discontinued products. "For a lawyer, he does a lot of side wheeling and . . . you know." George turned to where Scott had been standing, but the guy had disappeared. "He probably went to get a drink."

"I see." Davina noticed sweat stains on George's shirt. His forehead was shiny and his cheeks were flushed. Davina suddenly realized the sandy blond hair was a toupee. "I have a question for you."

"Another one?"

"Yeah. It's just that, you've been looking at me all night and I wonder if I have something on my face or I've done something to upset you. Have I? Done something to upset you?"

George was silent; his face wasn't. It spoke volumes about some deep negative emotion. Fear? Anger? Davina couldn't read it.

George cleared his throat and wiped his brow. He took a long chug of beer. "I'm sorry. I didn't realize I was."

Seriously?

Davina's phone pinged. She pulled it from her purse—it was a text from Geoff Wong.

> Meet up?

> At SBCA meeting. Colony Hall. Just wrapping. Meet me here?

> Learn anything?

> Yeah. How shady local bizmen are.

> Welcome to my world. Be there in 20.

When Davina was done, George was gone. Across the room, Gerry was deep in conversation with Father Stephen.

Nick Delafield appeared out of the crowd. "Hi, Davina."

"Hey."

"Having fun?"

"Nope."

"Drinking and politics not your thing?" Nick smiled.

"Not so much."

"Can't say I blame you." Nick's relaxed presence was comforting. "I'm going to bag this meeting. You want to get a drink?"

"I don't—"

"Club soda?"

Davina tucked her hair behind her ear and glanced down at her phone. "I'm meeting a friend in a few."

"Joe?"

She felt Nick's intensity kick up a notch—was he *jealous?* "No. Geoff Wong. From the *Advance.*"

Nick pulled a stink face. "I know who he is."

"You don't like him."

"I take issue with how he characterizes my dad."

Honestly, you mean? "We all have different political views," Davina said.

"The *Advance* blows hot and cold with Dad's campaign. They haven't thrown their support behind him this time around."

"How about we avoid talking politics, then?" Davina offered Nick a friendly smile. "Listen, we can do the club soda another time."

"Nah, D." Nick wrapped a brotherly arm around Davina's shoulders and guided her toward the bar. "Let's do it now."

No doubt Geoff Wong wanted to discuss rape, murder, and cover-ups. Not exactly the kind of conversation Davina wished to have around Nick Delafield. She realized she'd much rather talk about why he'd worked his way back into her life.

THURSDAY, STATEN ISLAND HISTORICAL COLONY HALL

DAVINA SAT AT THE END OF THE BAR NEXT TO NICK. SHE checked her phone for the time—9:00. Geoff was due in ten minutes or so. She'd texted that he could find her at the main bar.

"Vodka tonic for me, and she'll take a club soda with lime," Nick instructed the barman.

What is it with guys ordering for me?

"Actually, I'd like a Beck's non-alcoholic, thanks."

She caught Nick's quiet snort; she'd surprised him by pushing back. Good.

"So, you come here often?" Davina asked Nick with a playful tap on the arm.

"Didn't you know the Staten Island Historical Colony Hall is where all the cool kids hang?" Nick took off his jacket and draped it over the back of his chair. "And the beautiful, sassy women, of course." He winked.

Davina groaned.

"You look tense, Davina." Nick seemed genuinely concerned.

"I sometimes get weird about those kinds of things. Men in close proximity." *With cruel intentions.*

Nick grinned. "Men like me?"

The question surprised Davina . . . and disturbed her a little. Was Nick becoming like the other men in the room?

The bartender returned with the drinks; Nick and Davina held their glasses up in a silent toast.

"It does good to be away from the bullshit for a while." Nick unbuttoned the top two buttons of his shirt. "It can go on forever. Especially if somebody gets my father going."

"You mean, like Gerry did?"

"Listen, I get where Gerry is coming from, but she's got to realize Staten Island is changing. People have to change with the times. That's progress."

"I don't think Gerry has anything against progress. She does have a problem with your father wanting to erase the island's history. She's dedicated to preserving it."

"The old-timers are dying off," Nick said after a moment of companionable silence. "Their kids aren't interested in preserving old Staten Island. They're interested in getting cold, hard cash—and thanks to how prices have skyrocketed in Manhattan, people are eyeing Staten Island. Chinese, Russians, Mexicans. They can't live in Queens or Brooklyn anymore, which is a good thing for Staten Islanders who want to sell. Supply and demand will always drive value upward."

"Gerry is never going to see it like that, and neither will I," Davina countered. "Not that I'm a Staten Island fan, but the way some of the old neighborhoods are overcrowded by developers cramming three and four houses to a single lot is just *hideous.*"

"Progress isn't always pretty," Nick said, as if the cliché explained and excused anything. He set his empty glass down on the bar. "Besides, those old houses Gerry wants to preserve weren't always there. Something else was torn down to make way for them. A hundred years from now, those three or four houses on a single lot will be razed for something else. That's growth. You stay mired in the past and you die."

"You can honor the past without being mired in it, Nick."

He leaned toward her, earnest. "Gerry might not like my father's ideas, but even she has to admit they're for the betterment of Staten Island. Isn't that what we all want? That's why my father is so hot for the council seat. He'll be in a position to do a lot of favors for everybody—Darren, Scott, Gino, Stavros. All of them." He motioned in the general direction of the banquet room. "People aren't seeing much beyond their noses. They'll understand his vision once he's in."

If he gets in. "You're a mess of contradictions, Nick."

"I am?" Nick combed a hand through his hair and gave Davina a crooked grin.

"I remember how sweet you used to be with Allie. All these years later, you're still a sweet guy."

"But?"

"There's an edge to you I didn't see before."

The grin turned to a grimace. "Does it bother you?"

"No—but it makes me curious to find out who Nick Delafield really is."

"You've got the same guarded look Alessandra used to have. Although," he added, "you do it way cuter."

"Thanks . . . I guess."

"You know, for sisters, you and Alessandra are complete opposites. If she was more like you, I might not have ended things."

"Allie says you bolted. After the thing with Dad."

"Things fell apart, and I didn't make any attempt to fix it. Alessandra lived in her own mental box—nothing was open for discussion. You might not like what I'm saying, but at least you *listen*. That's a big thing in a relationship. Alessandra would get something in her head, and there was no changing it. Controlling, opinionated, insistent . . ."

Tell me about it. "My sister is kind of a sore subject with me right now." Davina cleared her throat and took a sip of her drink; it was cold, the bubbles tickled the back of her throat, and it invoked memories of a life long, long ago. "Um, can I ask you a question?"

"You can ask me anything." Nick leaned in, his eyes—slightly blood-shot, she noticed—lazy and warm.

Davina's heart rate went up. Jesus, she was twenty-two and crushing like a twelve-year-old. "What's up with George?"

"George Modica?"

"He's weird. The way he talks, the way he *smells*. He's been staring at me from the moment I walked in tonight."

Nick chuckled. "I wouldn't sweat it. George is one of those guys who likes sitting on the beach to watch the girls—if you catch my meaning."

"There's other women here, but he was staring at *me*."

"You're worth staring at. I do it, too, but I'm a little more discreet."

For a moment, Davina thought Nick was about to kiss her. She leaned back in her stool. This was not a fond older brother; this was Nick coming on to her. Davina felt guilty. Being so close to Nick, feeling the sexual tension between them, made her feel like she was cheating on Joe.

"I don't mind if *you* stare at me." *Holy shit, Davina. What are you doing?*

"Good. You know, you're a mess of contradictions too." Nick motioned to the bartender. "The whole Joe thing doesn't make sense to me."

"Why not?"

"Because the guy's got no edge to him. No *bite*. He was good competition when we were growing up. Maybe he still is." Nick peered into Davina's eyes. "But I always thought there was something distinctly *pedestrian* about him."

Davina found Nick's words offensive. And funny. If there was one thing Joe wasn't, it was pedestrian. She snorted. "Maybe it's the blond hair and angelic blue eyes? Trust me, the guy's got an edge—and a real solid core to balance it out."

"Well, you know him far better than I do." A lascivious wink. "Just always thought you'd go for someone . . . darker. *Rougher*."

Davina's heart clenched, but she laughed it off. "Not just no, but *hell* no. I can safely say dark and rough are nowhere in my list of things I go for in a man."

"Right." Nick placed a hand on the back of Davina's chair. "Now I'm going to ask *you* a question."

"Okay."

"Do you love Joe?"

Davina gulped. "I . . . yes, I love him. I mean . . . I never *expected* to love him. I never imagined myself to be the relationship type. But, yeah."

"I'll give you a little insight." Nick leaned in even closer, his breath warm on her cheek; Davina felt goosebumps crawl over her skin. "Men don't care if you're the relationship type or not. They see something they want—they take it."

There was a time when that would have sounded romantic to Davina. Not anymore. "Tell me something I don't know, Nick."

"Okay. You don't know Joe worked for Delafield at the same time as your dad. On the same construction project, as it happens."

Davina fell silent, remembering what Alessandra had said about the fire ending their dad's career—the thing that had caused him to fall into a bottle and run away. She knew Joe had once worked for Sean Delafield, but he had never once mentioned that he had worked with her father.

CHAPTER FORTY-SEVEN

THURSDAY, STATEN ISLAND HISTORICAL COLONY HALL

GEOFF SPOTTED DAVINA AND NICK AT THE END OF THE counter and walked over. They were deep in conversation, their body language screaming their mutual attraction. It made him invisible until he spoke.

"Is this a bad time?" Geoff ventured.

Startled, Davina and Nick turned to face the journalist.

"Oh, hi, Geoff." Davina put down her glass. "Please, have a seat."

Geoff sat himself down on the opposite side of Nick so he could see Davina. Not good enough; it was awkward. Geoff considered ways he could get Nick to leave—the guy would be a spare part to the conversation he'd come to have. "I came across something I wanted to run by you, Davina. I could use your input—it's kind of confidential." He shot a quick glance at Nick.

"I should get going." Nick took the hint and slid from his stool.

Geoff smiled flatly. "No offense."

"None taken." Nick snatched up his jacket from the barstool. "I need to prep for a campaign meeting anyway. See ya soon." He kissed Davina's cheek, nodded at Geoff, and departed.

As Geoff moved to the stool Nick had vacated, he noticed how close Delafield had pulled it to Davina; their knees must have been touching. "I didn't mean to interrupt."

"You didn't. What's up?"

"This." Geoff took out the email he'd printed out from his pocket. He unfolded it and handed it to Davina.

Davina read through it a couple of times and brought a hand to her mouth. "I don't know what to make of this, Geoff."

The journalist's voice was scarcely above a whisper. "I'm going to put this as gently as I can, Davina. I know you were a stripper and you were arrested at a club that was later busted for employing underage girls. I was thinking you might know something about this."

"Wait a minute." Davina's eyes narrowed. "Do you think I sent this email?"

"No. Not for a moment. I'm just asking if you have any ideas. You know more about this sort of thing than I do."

Davina laughed. "You think ex-strippers have some secret sorority and we all meet once a month to discuss political matters?" She swirled the dregs of near-beer in her glass. "It isn't like that at all, Geoff. I don't even remember all that much from those days—I was high or drunk off my face most of the time. Sometimes even both." *That's probably a good thing, all things considered.*

"I'm not judging you, Davina," Geoff sounded defensive, "and I don't mean to insult you. I just have a feeling you can help me with this. It's from an untraceable server, and if it's legit, I want to follow through."

"I'm not lying to you, Geoff. It was another lifetime and it's filled with blanks. I barely have memories of it. I was a party girl paying for her next fix. I admit that I could have been there at the party or just as easily not. My mind's a complete blank—I couldn't swear one way or the other."

"You once had a relationship with Nick Delafield?"

Davina jumped straight on that one. "My *sister* did. I was just the annoying little sibling."

"Right, your sister was in a relationship. So, you would have recognized Sean Delafield if you had been at that party?"

Davina leaned in. "Geoff, you're not listening to me. I don't think you understand what drinking and drugs do to someone's head."

"I do. They mess with it. That's the point."

"Yeah," Davina said. "So, what's the point of the email? Blackmail? Assuming there *is* a video, of course. I'm guessing if they'd attached a clip or couple of stills, you'd have shown them to me."

"The point is somebody wants Sean Delafield out of the council race —in a big way. And they're willing to make this kind of threat. It is possible there is no video and this is a hoax, but I have a feeling there's more to this." Geoff fell silent as the bartender approached. "I'll take a Bacardi, dark."

That tickled Davina. "Funny. I pegged you for a rum and Coke guy."

"You have good instincts. That's my drink of choice, but tonight deserves straight rum. Dark."

The bartender brought over the drink. Geoff lifted the glass to his nose, inhaled deeply, and closed his eyes. "I'd say you were missing out, but I know how inappropriate that would be."

"Yes, it is. And I'm not missing out. I remember *that much* of those days." Davina held up her thumb and pointer finger an inch apart.

Davina's eyes were suddenly distant. Had he offended her? Or was she remembering something that could be of use to him? "What is it?"

"I was just thinking . . . in the conference room, George Modica kept staring at me—almost like he *recognized* me. It could be he saw me dancing at the club, but if there is some party video with me in it, he might have recognized me from that."

Holy crap. "There's a chance. He certainly moves in Sean Delafield's inner circle."

She smiled wryly and shook her head. Golden radiance from the indirect lighting over the bar gleamed softly in her hair and set it ablaze. "I could barely recognize myself back then. I looked totally different. Wore a ton of makeup."

"Did you have the tattoos?"

"Just the chrysanthemum." Davina glimpsed down at her wrist. "But I could've been wearing something that night that covered it."

"I doubt that, given the circumstances . . . I'm sorry." Geoff regretted the flippant remark the second it left his mouth.

"Good point." Davina scratched her chin and smiled to let the reporter know she was cool with the faux pas. "A lot of the girls had tattoos."

"Did George say anything to you, or did he just stare?"

"Just stared. Like he'd seen a ghost. I confronted him, but he disappeared when I got your text."

Bold move. "Davina, can I ask you a sensitive question?"

"Sure." She picked up her glass and sipped.

"Did you ever turn tricks?"

Davina shook her head. "No. No, and *nope.* I just . . ." She shivered, as if a bad memory had awakened. "I do know a lot of other girls went down that particular road."

"The email suggests there was sex—underage sex."

"I wouldn't be surprised," Davina said. "Private parties were never just about girls taking their clothes off. It was kind of *expected*, you know."

"Do you think it's possible you ever had sex without your knowledge?" Geoff felt terrible even asking Davina that. Why? He'd never been so squeamish before.

The distant expression returned to Davina's eyes. "I don't know. I feel like, if I did, I would have a memory of it. Like I remember what happened to me ten years ago."

"I'm sorry; I know these are awful questions."

"It's fine. My life these days is mostly about answering awful questions."

Funny, so is mine.

CHAPTER FORTY-EIGHT

FRIDAY, GEORGE MODICA'S HOME, RURAL NEW SPRINGVILLE

George hadn't slept all night; Davina Speers filled his mind and kept him staring at the ceiling 'til the sun came up. He didn't care what Darren or anyone else said—Davina was *definitely* the girl in the video. He was certain of it.

I'll lose everything over this.

His sleeping wife, Karen, lay on her side with her back facing him, snoring. She wasn't the most loving or understanding woman in the world, but George didn't want to lose her. He didn't want to lose *anything*. He'd worked his ass off his entire life, and one stupid fucking video could take him down. It was bullshit. It was just drugs and sex—that shouldn't ruin anyone's future.

It was too early to be getting up, but George was hungry. So, he wrapped his blue robe around himself and padded into the kitchen. He made coffee, grabbed the carton of eggs from the fridge, and scrambled a couple. Then he put two pieces of bread in the toaster.

He'd just sat down with his plate and a cup of coffee when the doorbell rang, followed by several light taps.

"George!" The voice was muted but emphatic.

"What the fuck?" George put down his fork and considered not answering. Who the fuck would be knocking on his door at such an ungodly hour?

"*George!*"

"Jesus." He got up from his chair and walked over to the front door. *6-fucking-30!* Whoever it was better have a fucking good reason.

George opened the door, beyond irritated.

"Morning, George."

"What do you want?"

"May I come in?"

"I'm not dressed." George glanced down at himself and was suddenly painfully aware just how short the robe was.

"Just for a minute. It's important."

George stepped aside to allow the visitor in. "Want some coffee?"

George turned and walked back to the kitchen. As he reached into the cupboard for a coffee mug, an arm clenched around his neck from behind and he couldn't breathe. George saw stars and struggled, but he was too weak against his assailant's strength.

George Modica's mouth dropped open to scream, but nothing came out.

"Nine seconds, George, and this will be over."

CHAPTER FORTY-NINE

IN THE WAKE OF THE SBCA MEETING AND HER CONVERSATIONS with Nick and Geoff, Davina's mind was reeling. All night, she'd been turning things over, creating mental lists, analyzing sentences, words, glances. As soon as she climbed out of bed, she'd taken out her NA journal and flipped to the back. There, Davina made four columns: Evidence, Modus Operandi, Connections, Effects on Victims.

Evidence:

- Sean Delafield (alleged) video
- Theta drawn on victim's forehead: lipstick, knife or sharp blade, mud (whatever is available at the scene?)

Modus Operandi:

- Uses blood choke or chokehold
- Marking the victim (see above)

- Murder a new/recent trend—kills the protector, not the victim

Connections:

- Most rapes at historic, supposedly haunted Staten Island locations
- Sean eager to erase those sites—has purchased, is purchasing, or may be planning to purchase. Coincidence?
- Riley and the 120th Precinct investigated and closed the case
- SBCA not backing Sean

Effects on Victims:

- Panic attacks from smells, embraces, sharp visual memories
- Unable to tolerate intimacy
- Trauma—hiding the scar

There were just too many things that didn't fit together. Or least, Davina was unable to see the dotted line. Other details seemed too vivid. Was it possible that Sean Delafield had not realized all the crime scenes (with only the two exceptions that she knew of) were properties he had interest in?

Finally, discouraged at her lack of progress, Davina had given up and headed to the gym to find serenity and comfort.

"Hey, D!" Don Anderson, who'd swiftly become a fixture at Dobson's, put up his hand to high-five Davina.

"Hey, Don. How's it going?"

"You look ready for some action." Don punched the palm of his hand with his fist.

"You could say that." Davina relished the prospect of releasing some of her pent-up frustration. "I've got a few things I need to purge."

"Tell me about it." Don dropped to the floor and started on push-ups.

Although so many things about the SBCA meeting troubled her, the conversation with Geoff fucked with Davina's head the most.

What if I was at that party? What if things happened that I don't remember? What if I . . . ?

That was what really got her: not having control. Davina felt like her rape and the subsequent negative reaction of the people she cared about—and who were *supposed* to care about her—had stripped all control over her mind, her body, and life. It didn't get much more fucked up than that, and the more she hunted down answers, the more questions popped up to confound her.

In the locker room, which was still a mess thanks to the ongoing work there, Davina changed into her new workout apparel: tight purple tank top with matching purple leggings. Standing in front of the mirror, Davina chuckled and stared at herself—she resembled a long, muscular grape with red hair; the two colors clashed wonderfully. Still, it was a sign of progress—all the black clothing she'd worn until recently had to go, even though she still kept them in a large trash bag. Ostensibly, she was waiting to find the time to donate them all to the Red Cross, but in reality, Davina wasn't quite ready to completely let go.

Once dressed, she found Gerry upstairs behind her desk drinking some green concoction that smelled like dirty feet.

"We gotta talk about your choice in beverages, Gerry."

Gerry took a sip through her environmentally friendly paper straw. "Just because I don't live off cornflakes, doesn't mean you get to judge me."

"It's Cheerios, thanks. And that's out of fiscal necessity."

Gerry put down the glass and leaned back in her chair. "You saying I don't pay you enough?"

"No, I just don't work enough." Davina sat on the corner of Gerry's desk.

"You don't show up to work enough. The work's here if you want it. I've got a half-dozen clients who want on your roster."

I've got important shit to do, and you know it.

"I gotta talk to you about something." Gerry's tone was serious.

"What?"

Following a moment of silence, Gerry sighed loudly before saying, "George Modica is dead."

Davina brought her hand to her chest. "*What?*"

"This morning. I just got the text from the SBCA. I'm already on the damned mailing list."

"How?" Davina shook her head in disbelief. "We . . . we just saw him last night. How did he die?"

"Heart attack, apparently."

"I can't say I'm too surprised. All that sweating last night, the red face."

Gerry took another sip of green juice. "The way he stared at you was odd—like he'd seen a ghost or something. Maybe you whipped him up into such a horny state his old ticker gave in? Or, maybe he is—*was*—just one of those kinds of guys who had a thing for hot young chicks."

"Dirty old man, you mean?" Davina suppressed a shudder at having been mentally undressed by a dead man walking.

"Just goes to show how much we don't know about those we think we know." Gerry sounded uncharacteristically cryptic. "Take your friend last night, for example."

"Nick?"

"No, the old lady you were speaking with at the buffet."

"Angela?" Davina couldn't help but smile. "Angela's not *old*—and she used to be my therapist, not a friend. She can't be much older than forty, Gerry."

"I overheard a gaggle of women trash-talking. They do love their gossip at the SBCA, that and sordid little affairs, apparently—I'm *definitely* joining now! They reckon your therapist's marriage is nothing but a sham, and her and hubs only stay together for the good of their ghost tour thing." Gerry eased back in her chair. "I heard he can't get it up. Must be why he's at the gym three times a week—getting rid of all that frustration."

"Jesus, Gerry," Davina mumbled. "You're as bad as they are—spreading rumors about someone you don't even know. I know Angela and Carlo have had nothing but bad luck trying to have a family, but that's just plain mean."

"Yeah," Gerry said. "I heard all that, too. A bunch of miscarriages and a coupla SIDs—maybe that's why poor Carlo got ED? It's so bad, they say, there's some speculation about whose baby Mrs. Donato just lost."

Davina could barely believe her ears. One night in the presence of Staten Island's upper echelons and she was spouting conjecture and downright unpleasantness.

"The lady who runs the adult store here heard from her friend in Brooklyn, who owns Stephanie's Love Supplies over there, that Carlo has been spending a hell of a lot of money with her. Do all sex shop people know each other?"

"It's a small world, Gerry," Davina said. "What's he been buying? Porn?" She hated herself for asking, for allowing herself to be sucked into tittle-tattle that meant she'd not look at Carlo Donato quite the same again.

Gerry shook her head. "*Nobody* buys porn these days, Davina." She laughed. "Nah, he's been stocking up on dildos and vibrators like the sex toy apocalypse was coming. Stacy thinks it must all be to keep Angela satisfied enough to not leave him."

"Stacy?"

"Runs the Adult Toyz Emporium here on the island—keep up, D." Gerry huffed. "Anyhoo, it turns out the funniest thing about the whole story is that Stacy is more pissed at Carlo taking his money over the bridge than she is shocked at what he's buying."

Even Davina couldn't help but raise a smile at that; it was just so typical of the hard-boiled Staten Islanders and their sad little isolationist attitudes.

Keen to divert the conversation from the Donatos and their—supposed—marital problems, Davina cut in. "I talked with Geoff last night."

"How did that go?" Gerry appeared a little put out by the shift from her juicy gossip.

I can't. I can't tell Gerry all this. Some things I just have to keep to myself. "We just discussed his Delafield article."

Gerry grimaced. "Don't get me started on that asshole again."

Davina stared at the desk in confusion. George's death had shaken her more than she thought it should. Something didn't seem quite right; the timing was too much of a coincidence.

"You okay, D?" Gerry asked, concerned. "I didn't think you'd take it this hard—you only just met the guy."

"I don't know, Ger. A bunch of strange things have happened since Joy's service. It's like some crazy puzzle, and I can't put the pieces together."

"It's not your job to put the pieces together."

Yes, it is.

"I don't know if it's good or bad that Geoff Wong now knows my past. Maybe I've been too open with him."

"You were on the streets. You did what you needed to do to survive. You must *never* be ashamed of that, Davina."

Davina stood, too antsy to sit any longer. She walked over to the window and peered out into the gym with her arms folded across her chest. "I just wish it wasn't all so fucked up."

"The world is getting more and more fucked up by the day—you're not unique, D."

Davina turned to Gerry and smiled. "Thanks, Ger."

"I'm doing my best, too." Gerry got up from her seat to join Davina at the window. "You know I joined the SBCA last night."

Davina gave a sharp, sarcastic laugh. "I'm sure Sean Delafield is thrilled."

"That narcissistic loon needs to be stopped."

"I talked with Nick after the party."

"I saw you in the bar when I went to the ladies' room. You guys seemed pretty cozy."

Wait, what the fuck are you implying, Gerry? Did it look like there was something romantic between us last night? Shit—what if Joe finds out?

Davina shrugged it off. "He's just a nice guy. We have history. Or rather, he and my sister had history. She was his girlfriend, I was the infuriating little sister—he was always nice to me, though."

"No child of Sean Delafield could be *that* nice a guy," Gerry growled. "I'm sure he wants all the same things his dear ol' pops wants."

Davina was about to argue the point but then recalled her conversation with Nick in the bar. "I guess there's a grain of truth in that. Nick just puts it in a prettier, more subtle package."

"I wouldn't get too impressed with that package if I were you. Corruption dressed up with a pretty smile is still corruption. You're smarter than that, D."

Davina touched the cheek Nick had kissed. Gerry made a good point: Nick did believe in greed masquerading as progress.

You're smarter than that.

"I gotta go clear my head." Davina made her way to the door. "I really wish George Modica hadn't died."

Gerry tiled her head. "Really?"

"Yeah. I had a shit-ton of questions to ask him." *Like why the sight of me threw him into a sweat-soaked panic and whether or not there was someone on Staten Island prepared to kill to keep him quiet.*

CHAPTER FIFTY

FRIDAY, RICHMOND COUNTY SAVINGS & LOAN

Darren's office was pure bedlam: the phone rang, Darren's cell buzzed, and the intercom blared. Darren picked up the office phone just as Stavros burst through his door. Darren held his finger to his lips, signaling Stavros to say nothing.

"This is urgent," the Greek protested.

Annoyed, Darren put his hand over the mouth of the phone. "Give me a minute."

"He's dead. George is dead," Stavros blurted out.

"You think I don't fucking know that?" Darren snarled. "We all got the fucking text, Stavros."

"We were supposed to meet for breakfast, but he didn't show. I drove over, and his house was crawling with EMTs and cops. Karen was standing on the lawn with the police—crying her poor eyes out. What the hell is going on, Darren?"

Darren threw up his hands in exasperation; it was clear he wasn't going to get to finish his call. The guy on the phone was still talking, but Darren hung up without a reply. "Why is everybody in a panic over this?"

"You don't get it. If the cops go through George's stuff and find that video, we're all screwed."

Darren didn't even attempt to hide his frustration with Stavros. "Nobody is going to find it. There's no reason for his place to be searched. George had a heart attack. End of story. Karen and their kids will keep a few mementos and toss the rest. Even if they found it on his computer, they're not going to want to keep a low-res video of Poppa George with a bunch of strippers and coke—that's the kind of secret a family keeps to itself."

The phones were still ringing, shrill, insistent. Darren picked up his office line again. "Yeah, sorry about that—I'll call you back." He then answered his cell. "I can't talk. I'll call you back." He then watched Stavros again, who was pacing back and forth in front of the desk. "Go home, Stavros, and quit worrying or you'll wind up like George."

Did that sound like a threat?

"You need to take this more seriously." If Stavros interpreted the comment as something sinister, he didn't let on. "We don't know who George talked to about the video. I saw him talking with Davina Speers last night just before he left. What if he said something? Or what if she recognized him and said something? We can't afford to have that video found. None of us can."

"Stavros, go home. It's not going to be found."

"For God's sake, why would he even keep it—the fucking idiot?"

"Probably to jerk off to," Darren said without humor. "Sean and Kevin have copies too. And most likely Scott, since it was his bachelor party."

"Yeah, except they're all smart enough to keep quiet about it. George never had a steady hand. That fucking video is probably on his desktop for anyone to see, and everyone knows his password is *Karen*."

Darren sighed; the day was already shaping up to be long and trying. He had to change his approach. "Stavros, sit down—*please*. You're making me nervous, and with this shit blowing up, the last thing I need is to be nervous."

Stavros did as requested. Darren had never seen the guy so upset. He seemed almost as agitated as George at the business association meeting. It was time for some babysitting.

"Let me get you a drink," Darren said.

"It's 9:30 in the morning."

"Exactly."

Darren reached down to the drawer on the right side of his desk and took out the bottle of bourbon. He put two glasses on the desk and poured.

"I suppose it's not such a bad idea, given the occasion." Stavros reached over and grabbed one of the glasses. "I'm still hungover from last night—a little hair of the dog is just what I need."

"If George never had a steady hand, we have to make sure that we do." Darren took a hearty swig of his bourbon; it felt good burning its way down to his stomach. "Good stuff, huh?"

Stavros nodded absently. "I can't wrap my head around it—George is dead. I mean, death doesn't drive home 'til it's one of your own."

Pussy. "You just keep running your restaurant and let me put out the fires."

Darren topped off his glass and fought the panic rising up inside. The plan was going to shit. Exposing the video was only ever intended to get Sean to relinquish his plan to get back on the council. There had never been any real intention to share it with the *Advance*—George knew that. Even if, by some freakish happenstance, one of the strippers in the video had been Davina Speers, no one would ever know. Now, because George couldn't tell a feint from reality, he was dead, and Darren faced dealing with one man after the other losing his shit. If only they'd allowed him to take care of everything in the first place.

That confident assertion was followed by swift doubt. Had they shot themselves in the foot with the video plan? Was there even the slightest possibility of George's fears about the Speers woman being real? He hadn't thought so, but the chrysanthemum tattoo gave him pause. One of the girls that night had definitely had a flower tattooed on her wrist. He'd noticed it only in passing: naked or not, women just didn't interest him in that way.

"He wasn't a healthy man," Stavros said, staring into his bourbon. "George was overweight and always stressed out." He paused to take a sip. "He was convinced Davina Speers was at Scott's shindig—I sure as hell don't remember her."

"Even if she was," Darren replied, "it's not going to leak. And if it did, the 120th Precinct would invite us to their boys' club for a showing."

Stavros laughed along with Darren. "That's funny."

"Glad I could make you laugh. Now, if you don't mind, I have a hundred phone calls to make."

Stavros threw back the remainder of the bourbon and slammed the glass onto the desk. "I gotta get back to the restaurant. Looks like I'll be catering another funeral."

"If Staten Island keeps going in this direction, you'll see a lot of work coming your way."

Stavros stopped dead and eyed Darren with suspicion. "What's that supposed to mean?"

"Don't get your Greek panties in a bunch, Stavros," Darren scoffed. "All I mean is folks are dropping like flies. Now, go home."

After Stavros was gone, Darren saw his cell phone had received twenty-two text messages in the short time Stavros had been in his office. Darren poured himself another glass of bourbon—he was tense and definitely needed it. It was unlike him to feel such anxiety; being cucumber-cool was his superpower, the key to his survival and his prosperity. It wasn't easy being a gay Black man in a predominately straight, White borough.

Sure, he was upset about George's death, but it was hardly surprising. The guy was a coronary or a stroke just waiting to happen—and it might well have been the best thing to happen. With one of the circle's greatest liabilities out of the way, there was one less nervous prick coming to Darren for help.

An idea sprung to mind. Darren reached down for his cell and dialed.

"Yeah?" The voice seemed tinny, distant.

"We need to talk." Darren rocked his office chair back and forth.

"Later, Darren."

"No, not later. *Now.*"

"Okay. Talk."

"In person. I can't have this conversation over the phone."

"Getting paranoid on me, buddy?"

"I'm not paranoid." Darren's voice was measured. He swallowed the lump in his throat. "There's a correct way to do things. Meet me at my place in two hours."

"I'm busy."

"Yeah, we're all busy, but you'll want to make time for this. Promise." Darren hung up the phone before the reply and swigged his bourbon.

I've got to believe I'll come out on the other side of this.

CHAPTER FIFTY-ONE

FRIDAY, DARREN'S APARTMENT IN ST. GEORGE

Darren unknotted and removed his tie, took off his jacket, and laid them both over the arm of the overstuffed leather couch. He put on some Etta James and retrieved a chilled bottle of Pinot Grigio from the refrigerator. Two glasses sat on the chrome coffee table in front of the sofa.

The lush apartment always gave him a sense of warm satisfaction. There were Andy Warhol prints and black-and-white concert photos on the walls: the Rolling Stones, Radiohead, Gaga. Darren had worked damned hard for everything he had in life, and he wasn't about to allow it all to slip through the cracks of Staten Island's foundation. Darren Rivers was going to reach heady new heights.

Pouring himself a glass of cool wine, Darren slid open the door to the patio overlooking the water and New York City skyline. One day, Darren would live on the other side of the water, and he'd no longer have to deal with Staten Island bullshit.

I'm gonna clean up this mess and cut my ties to this place, starting today.

It was a drinking day. That much was certain. Darren didn't mind too much because the alcohol never seemed to go to his head. If anything, it made him more focused and steadied his nerves.

The doorbell chimed.

Darren walked back inside. Glass in hand, he opened the door for Nick.

"Hi." Nick's voice was soft, alluring.

Darren smiled. "Come in."

Nicked turned to face Darren as he closed the door. Reaching out, he gently touched his arm. "Listen, I know we've been fighting, and I'm sorry, I—"

"I didn't ask you here for that." *Gotta rip the Band-Aid off right now.*

Nick took his hand away. "You okay?"

"Hard to say. In some ways—*hell no*. In others, better than I've been."

Darren was keen to get straight down to business: He had to get some shit off his chest. He ushered Nick into the living room and poured him a glass of wine. They sat half facing each other on the couch.

"Starting early?" Nick leaned over and picked up his glass.

Darren ignored the comment. "The news about George has spread like wildfire. My phone has been popping all morning."

"I'll admit, it's shocking as far as the timing goes, but not all that much of a surprise, given the guy's health. Didn't he have a fourth heart stent put in last year?" Nick sipped delicately at his wine.

"Fifth."

Nick nodded and set his glass down. "I gotta ask something—straight up, Darren. Are you behind my father or not?"

Seriously? "You know the answer to that, Nick."

Nick bristled. "Yeah, I know the answer to that, but I'm here to persuade you otherwise." He placed his hand on Darren's knee.

Darren brushed Nick's hand away. "No, Nick. I'm not on board with him. And neither is the bank, the SBCA, or the unions."

"You're not serious. Scott said—"

"Scott was lying."

"Why would he—"

"He was sucking up, Nick—can you not see that?"

Nick leaned back, putting more distance between them. "You can all go screw yourselves, Darren. Dad doesn't need any of you to get the nomination. People love him. He's a lock."

"Are you really that blind to your father's very public weaknesses? If he gets the nomination, the only thing that is a lock is his loss in November. We can't allow that to happen."

Nick laughed at him. "There's nothing you can do to stop him, Darren. You'll see. And also keep in mind that whatever you take away from my dad, you take away from your greedy selves."

"My God, how brainwashed are you? He's a drag on the ticket, Nick. Either Sean Delafield bows out gracefully or the *Advance* receives the video from Scott's bachelor party."

"Not that fucking video again. You're joking, Darren."

"The video of your father snorting coke with a trio of young—*very young*—strippers is no joke." Darren got up and walked over to the window; the view soothed him. "We have our hands tied. We're not about to have him bring down the party through his stupid ego. I respect the fact he's your father, Nick. But Sean Delafield is an arrogant prick, and you know it."

"You're angry with *me* over this," Nick spat.

"Frustrated, yes. Angry, no." Darren chose not to meet his lover's eyes.

"No, you're angry because I can't choose between my father and you."

Darren sighed deeply and stared out the window. "That's some fucked-up Freudian shit, Nick. I'm *not* a father figure. I also keep our relationship separate from business *and* politics. Apparently, you have trouble doing that."

Nick got up and strode to the front door. "Fuck this, I'm leaving."

Darren laughed at him. "Go on, prove my point, Nick."

"Fuck you." Nick left, slamming the door behind him.

Darren took a long glug of wine and wondered how long it would take Nick to calm down. Once he did, could he be trusted?

How the hell did I get myself into this situation?

Darren had never expected to find himself in a relationship with Sean Delafield's publicly heterosexual son. Nick was a good fifteen years younger and had put up a convincing pretense of being straight for his entire life. Darren had been floored when Nick admitted to being attracted to him, and it had taken some time to come to terms with the facet of Nick Delafield no one else knew about. But, once he had, the attraction had been completely mutual. Too late to admit the liaison was unwise for a whole host of reasons, or that it had come with a spider's web of complications. Too late for Darren to regret his involvement with the enigmatic younger man.

Darren knew the relationship would have to go on the back burner. The political situation was dire, and it was time to take action. He and the others had been on their heels for too long; Sean Delafield hadn't responded to the email, which indicated he wasn't about to back down. They had to push things further. Edited right, the video couldn't hurt any of them, as long as Kevin kept the original under wraps and any copies were destroyed.

Darren sat down heavily on the couch, poured himself another glass of wine, picked up his phone, and called Kevin Monaghan. "I just spoke with Nick Delafield."

"My condolences."

"Thanks. Listen, his old man isn't responding. Send the video to the *Advance.*"

"The edited version."

"Naturally."

"Are you sure about this, Darren?" Kevin sounded more than a little apprehensive. "I mean, I'm 100 percent with our plan, but there's no turning back once the video is out there. If the cops or the press get their hands on the original, we're all fucked."

"Destroy it, Kevin. And we'll make sure the others all destroy their copies."

Kevin hesitated. Then, "I've already edited the video down to show only Sean, the girls, and blow. It's ready to go."

"So, send it."

Darren ended the phone call and leaned back on the couch; he was finally relaxing. With Etta James serenading him, Darren flipped on the news. Soon, Sean Delafield would be the top headline, and not for virtuous reasons.

A feverish knocking sounded at his door, followed by the rapid *ding-ding-ding* of the doorbell. With a smug grin, Darren got up from the couch; it was most likely Nick with that cute, boyish grin of his and some half-assed apology.

Darren picked Nick's glass up from the coffee table and made his way to the front door, which he held and gave a dramatic sweep of the arm toward the living room. He'd taken two steps when he was shoved hard from behind. Darren let out a surprised squawk as he dropped the glass and fell; his forehead hit the hard tiles with a resounding *crack*.

CHAPTER FIFTY-TWO

FRIDAY, DOBSON'S GYM

DAVINA'S SESSION WITH DON ANDERSON HELPED CLEAR HER mind. George Modica's death had rattled her. The timing made her insides squirm and saddled her with a lingering fear that maybe—just *maybe*—she had been at Scott Kantor's party that night.

She walked into Gerry's office; hair still damp from the shower. "I'm heading out."

"You okay?"

Not sure. "Yeah. Gonna go do a little detective work."

Gerry gave her a squinty appraisal. "Why not give it a break today?"

"I can't quit. I made someone a promise."

That someone was Rita Pine. Davina had promised she'd follow up after seeing Elizabeth again at Harvest House. As she drove up to the Pines' Grymes Hill home, her phone dinged with a text from Joe.

Hey, U OK?

Davina realized with a pang of guilt she hadn't so much as texted Joe since he'd dropped her off at the gym the previous afternoon. She also had the distinct feeling she hadn't thanked him enough for paying for the Tampa trip.

> Dead tired. Just got to the Pines'. Call you tonight. Thank U properly.

> It's a date.

Davina pocketed her phone and glanced over at Rita Pine's house. A huge red, white, and blue sign declaring support for Sean Delafield's opponent sat defiantly in the center of the lawn.

☆☆JULIA RAMIREZ FOR CITY COUNCIL!☆☆

Davina smiled. "You go, girl."

When Rita answered the door, she looked a hell of a lot better than she had mere days earlier. And, she didn't have a drink in her hand. "It's good to see you again, Davina." Her smile was genuine.

Davina stepped inside the house and saw that, instead of a cocktail pitcher, a steaming cup of tea sat on the coffee table. Definitely a good sign.

"Can I get you anything?" Rita smiled warmly; her eyes were clear and sparkled with what Davina thought resembled *hope*.

"I'm good, thanks." Davina seated herself. "I'm sorry I didn't get back to you right away. I was out of town until late yesterday afternoon."

Rita sat on the couch. "I thought you forgot, but that's all right. I saw Elizabeth, and she said she liked meeting you. She looks forward to seeing you again."

"Rita, around the time of Elizabeth's assault, was there someone you thought might have been spending too much time around Elizabeth and her friends? An adult or older teen who was maybe too friendly?"

"You sound like my late husband." Rita's laugh was a hollow one. "He was a member of the SBCA, and at first, he suspected it might have been one of them. They were all such big supporters of the activities the girls were involved in. But then . . . then he became convinced it was more personal."

"How so?"

"Bert started thinking it was someone—I know this sounds absurd—someone who was mad at Elizabeth. Maybe a boy who liked her but she didn't like back. Then, he decided it was someone who had it in for *him*—someone maybe trying to get to him through our daughter." Rita sipped her tea for a few seconds, then put the cup back on the table with a clatter; her hands were shaking.

"This is a rather difficult conversation for me." Rita caught Davina's eyes and smiled apologetically. "God, I need a drink."

Davina sighed. "It's okay, I understand."

"No, we're going to be good today. Promised myself," she said after a moment. "Bert didn't like Doctor Fidanza."

"Did he ever say why?" The doctor's name made Davina's skin crawl.

Rita reached for her cup. She didn't drink, instead clutching it in her hands as though trying to warm them. "Bert accused Doctor Fidanza of . . . of inappropriately touching Elizabeth."

"Oh my God." Davina recalled the conversation she'd overheard at Joy's wake.

Rita began to cry, tears slipping silently down her cheeks. "At the time, I told Bert he was mistaken. He was being overly protective of our girl and had been influenced by things he saw in the news. Now I . . . regret doing that."

Rita began to weep in earnest, and Davina got up to search for a tissue. She found a box on the kitchen counter and brought it back to the distraught woman.

"Thank you." Rita took a tissue from the box.

Davina wanted to comfort the woman, but it didn't come naturally to her. She realized, with a jolt of epiphany, she was unable to give Rita Pine what she, herself, had longed for all those years ago—comfort and some validation. Well, she could at least listen and do her best to say the right things. She sat down next to Rita on the sofa.

"Don't be hard on yourself—we all make mistakes."

Rita's voice was soft, barely discernible. "Thank you. But that was bigger than just a mistake."

"Did Elizabeth say anything about Dr. Fidanza?"

Rita shook her head. "No, it was something Bert thought he saw when he took Elizabeth in to have her tonsils checked out. He confronted the doctor about it and . . . well, you can imagine what happened. Dr. Fidanza was angry, insulted. I had to move Elizabeth to another practice."

"And Bert thought Fidanza might've taken it out on Elizabeth?"

It was hard to believe such a thing of the caring Dr. Fidanza, but Davina knew from bitter experience that people were often not what they seemed. The two sat in silence for a moment, then Davina asked, "Did your husband have bad blood with anyone else?"

Rita scowled. "Sean Delafield. Bert did the plumbing work on one of his biggest construction jobs—gave up a lot of his other clients to do it." Rita's eyes settled on the mantel and the framed picture of her husband.

Davina followed her gaze. Bert Pine was an affable-looking, square-jawed man with a head of thick, wavy brown hair and mellow smile. "I'm guessing it didn't work out."

"That man claimed Bert's work was shoddy and refused to pay the majority of what he owed him. We were carrying a second mortgage from Richmond Savings, and we lost our home to foreclosure."

I can't believe how many people have been fucked over by Sean Delafield. My father included. "That's horrible," Davina said.

"Bert took action, of course. There were suits and countersuits, and when it finally looked like we were going to get the money Sean owed us, Elizabeth . . ."

Davina was struck dumb. That couldn't be a coincidence. It just couldn't.

"Did . . . did the suit go through?"

"No. We dropped it. Elizabeth needed our full attention after she was attacked."

Jesus Christ.

"You have to understand. Nothing mattered to us after that—and we were getting anonymous threats."

"By phone? Email?"

"Both." Rita wiped her eyes, destroying what was left of her makeup. "The police looked into it, but they said the numbers were hotel phones. A whole string of them. They weren't even all from Staten Island." She took a deep breath. "Ten months later, Bert died. The stress of everything was too much on his heart."

And what, Davina wondered, had been too much for George Modica's heart? Keeping dark secrets? Or thinking someone was about to spill some?

"I'm so sorry. After what happened to Elizabeth, that must have been crushing."

"It was. But I . . . got us through it. Somehow." She paused for a moment, deep in thought. "You know, I didn't always go along with my husband's opinion about things, but I never trusted Sean Delafield or his promises of future work with Delafield Enterprises. I didn't like the way he treated my husband—even before he stiffed him for all that money. I didn't want Bert to take that last job. Sean Delafield has a very punchable face, Miss Speers."

Davina had no argument with that.

"We had a nice business, you know? It was small, but we did all right. We had a simple life, but Bert always wanted better for us. Better for Elizabeth."

"Bert sounds like a good man."

"He was, but he wasn't the kind of man you screwed over. If you wronged him, he went after you, no matter who you were. He was like a gentle bear or a bulldog, maybe."

"Did you ever question the timing of Elizabeth's attack?"

"You mean because of the lawsuit? Of course, we—" Rita stared blankly into the distance. "I questioned many things. But after Bert died, everything became so overwhelming I couldn't wrap my mind around any of it anymore. I guess I just lost the will to fight."

Davina sighed. Yet more pieces to the puzzle and no fucking way for her to put them together. Had Elizabeth been attacked as retaliation, or was the timing random? Was there a pattern here, or had Davina started seeing patterns where there were none? After all, what could George Modica's death possibly have to do with Bert's—or Elizabeth's rape?

Davina's phone buzzed. It was a text from Nick. Shitty timing.

> Hey, you up for a soda and a slice?

> Can't now.

She supposed the request was innocent enough, but after her conversation with Rita Pine, Davina wasn't sure she was in the mood to see any Delafield.

> You can't say no to your big brother. ☺

> I have class this afternoon.

She thought that was it, but Nick was persistent.

> Real fast. Poppa's Brick Oven. Be there in 20.
> Please?

Davina didn't realize she'd sighed aloud until Rita said, "Someone demanding your presence somewhere you don't want to be?"

Davina was surprised how close Rita came to what she was feeling. Why did she feel compelled to give in to Nick Delafield? "Something like that," she said. "I really don't need to go."

Rita gave her a shrewd look. "I'm fine. In fact, I think the cry did me good. You will try to see Elizabeth again, won't you?"

Davina smiled. "Try and stop me."

"So many mistakes in this life." Rita turned her gaze back to the mantelpiece. "And Elizabeth was the one who paid."

The Elizabeths of this world always pay. They always suffer without ever understanding why.

Outside, in her car, Davina studied the string of texts on her phone. It had been ten minutes since Nick's last message, and she was trying to imagine how he'd feel when he got to the pizza parlor and she wasn't there.

The other Davina—the one who still looked up to Nick Delafield like the big brother and out-of-reach older guy her adolescent heart had crushed on—ran through a litany of devil's advocacy: He's practically family. He's not his father. He did say, "Please."

She texted back:

> Mushroom & linguisa. DP. On the table when I get there.

CHAPTER FIFTY-THREE

FRIDAY, OFFICES OF THE STATEN ISLAND ADVANCE

Geoff Wong played the video over and over again.

It seemed almost perverted at first, given the subject matter, but he was trying his damndest to figure what had been doctored out. In the video, blown up to the full size of his iMac's twenty-seven-inch display, Sean Delafield was listening to Jimmy Buffett's "Margaritaville" and swaying drunkenly. There were male voices in the background, although no one else was visible. The movie was taken from an odd angle, the upper quarter of the right side obscured by the bell of a half-filled wine glass. It looked as if someone had propped their phone on the table, set it to record Sean Delafield's cavorting, and gone off to party. The bottom of the frame showed several lines of coke on the gleaming tabletop, and on a side table was a collection of colorful bottles—some empty and lying on their sides.

Sean held onto a cocktail that was all but escaping the glass as four nubile young girls danced around him; not one looked to be of an appropriate age to be frolicking all but naked with a bunch of middle-aged men. They twirled around Sean, their faces quick blurs as they danced and gyrated, while he groped them, grabbing one by the breasts and reaching for another's crotch.

That was the girl that looked a hell of a lot like Davina.

Trying to elude Sean's touch, the teenager executed an off-balance pirouette, stumbled, and almost fell. Her face, half turned toward the camera, screwed up in revulsion when his fingers probed at the bright orange thong barely covering her crotch.

Sean wasn't about to let his little odalisque escape quite so easily. He made a drunken pounce, spilling half his drink, and grabbed the girl by her latex thong. Then, he hooked an arm around her waist, pulled her against him, and ground his all-too obvious erection into her hip.

The girl gyrated suddenly, wildly, in her struggle to be free. Her elbow connected with Sean's chin, and her hip thrust back with enough force to loosen his grip. She leapt away, and the mighty Sean Delafield hit the floor, laughing. The song ended, and several of the girls gathered to help Sean wobble to his feet; the one Geoff thought might be Davina was not among them.

The video made Geoff sick. The sight of Sean Delafield flushed, sweaty, boozed up, and rubbing on underaged girls was enough to turn any sane human's stomach. *I didn't know it was possible to dislike this motherfucker even more than I did.*

Geoff considered his next move. If the video were leaked, Delafield and his political aspirations would be toast. Once out there, the news would spread like wildfire, and that would be that. But what about the other guys at that party? No way could they be allowed to get away with it—they were all equally culpable as Sean. Geoff wanted to take them all down.

He wouldn't take any such action before talking to Stan. As the managing editor, Stan was the gatekeeper, and Geoff valued his opinion. Picking up his phone, Geoff got up from his desk and made his way over to the corner office. He poked his head into the open door and rapped gently on the doorframe. "Stan."

"Wong." Stan put down the newspaper he'd been reading.

"You got a minute?"

"Always."

Geoff sat himself down. "I'm surprised it doesn't smell like burgers and fries today." Geoff noted the huge stack of papers on Stan's desk.

"Didn't have time to go out." Stan reached down into his drawer and took out a massive bag of Twizzlers. "So, I make do."

Geoff slid his phone across the desk. "I've got something for you."

"Great. Then I don't have to fire you today." Stan chewed on his candy and picked up the phone.

"The video is all queued up."

Stan pressed play. His facial expression went from curious to aghast to repulsed.

Glad we agree.

"You made me watch this while I'm eating?" Stan put the phone down. "For Christ's sakes, Wong."

"This is huge, Stan. There's no denying that footage. It's the end for Sean Delafield."

"When did you get this?"

"Twenty minutes ago." Geoff took his phone back.

Stan leaned his elbows on the desk and scratched at his chin. "Well, this proves the blackmail email was legit. Come from the same email address?"

"A different one. I'm pretty sure the accounts got deleted right after sending."

Stan smiled. "So, we've got a video depicting Sean Delafield, and *only* Sean Delafield, at the mother of all skeevy parties. Whoever edited it was damn clever."

"That's what I was thinking. It was obviously cut to show only Sean, the booze, drugs, and underaged girls. But it's obvious he isn't the only one there. If you look real close, you can barely make out a reflection in the side of the wine glass."

Geoff took up his phone again and fast-forwarded to the part he was talking about. He froze it so the distorted image of the man was visible and handed the phone back to Stan.

Stan held the phone so close it almost touched the end of his nose. "That's fucking creepy."

"Yeah. I can't tell if he's one of Sean's regular cohorts. But then again, it's hard to tell. The glass acts like a fun house mirror."

"Yeah, I see that." Stan squinted at the image. "Too blurry to guess who it might be. I can't even make out the girls' faces."

"They look young—*really* young." Geoff cleared his throat. "I think that Goth stripper is definitely Davina Speers."

"You talked with her about this?" Stan seemed surprised.

"She says she doesn't remember being there. I can't imagine she'd *want* to remember. I'm not sure about showing her the footage, but I guess I'll have to."

"Understood."

"So, what next?" Geoff knew what he'd do if left to his own devices, but the situation needed his boss's steady hand.

"I'd love to run it on tonight's front page." He laughed. "But, for now, let's keep a lid on it—in-house. Get it over to Steve Watson in the publishing department. That guy's a genius when it comes to stuff like this, and he dabbles in filmmaking—he does a lot of the promo videos for the Historical Society."

A knot formed in Geoff's stomach—the thought of anyone else having the video terrified him. "This could be the biggest scoop of the year, Stan," he said. "Can Steve be trusted?"

Stan's forehead crinkled. "I trust the guy with my daughter, Geoff. I think I can trust him with this."

Of course! It had slipped Geoff's mind that Steve Watson was Stan's son-in-law. It was how he'd gotten the job putting the paper together in the first place; nepotism was alive and well at the *Staten Island Advance*.

"Good enough, Stan," Geoff said, still with some reticence. If he had the software and the skills, he'd much rather do whatever needed to be done himself. "I'll email it straight over to him."

"Don't look so worried, Geoff," Stan did his best to reassure. "I'll make sure Steve knows it's for his eyes only—nobody's going to steal your thunder on this one. If anyone can make something of that face in the glass, it's him." He passed the phone back over the desk.

"I was thinking I'd approach Davina with it. Maybe seeing the video will spark a memory or two about that night. Who else was there."

"That's *if* she was there, of course," Stan said, his eyes reading Geoff's face.

"Of course." Geoff took a deep breath. "Whoever sent us the video is trying damn hard to look innocent, which could be a smokescreen. I mean, what if they're even more fucked up than Sean Delafield? Someone even more corrupt trying to push him out of the way for their own means? If that's what this is, I want *that* guy to go down too."

Stan pointed his Twizzler at Geoff. "Everything makes you suspicious, Wong."

"That's what you pay me for, Stan."

Walking back to his office, Geoff considered the best way to get Davina to see the video. He didn't want to risk sending an email with the thing attached: The information was too sensitive and he'd *technically* be distributing child pornography.

If Davina recognizes herself, it's gonna change everything.

CHAPTER FIFTY-FOUR

FRIDAY, DONGAN HILLS, ORIGINAL POPPA'S BRICK OVEN PIZZA

Before stepping into the pizza joint from its air-conditioned foyer, Davina took out her notebook and jotted down a few thoughts.

- *Elizabeth Pine and I were attacked* after *an arrest was made—meaning they didn't get the right guy.*
- *It was a blood choke, not a chokehold that cuts off air—or a plastic bag.*
- *Chokehold commonly used by cops. Less since the killing of Eric Garner.*
- *Sean Delafield real estate interests coincide with some attacks.*
- *Two took place in private homes—why?*

She shoved the notebook back into her fanny pack and entered the restaurant. It was past noon, but Poppa's Brick Oven Pizza was still bustling; the smell of cheese, baking dough, and marinara sauce filled the air. The rows of old Formica tables were all occupied, one by Nick.

"Davina!" He waved her over.

When Davina got to the table, Nick got up to kiss her.

"Wow." She turned her face away to avoid her lips meeting his, ostensibly to check out the crowded dining room. "This place is hopping."

"Good pizza and great location. It's surrounded by office buildings, and you know the old saying about real estate: location, location, location." Nick spoke quickly, his smile tight.

Davina assessed the guy as she took her seat. There was something off about him. Something different, something . . . *edgy.* "Yeah, I guess you're right."

"I know you're in a hurry, Davina." Nick grinned at her. "So, I ordered your half pie—mushroom and linguisa with extra cheese." He slid over a can of Dr. Pepper and a glass.

"Thanks." Davina popped the tab and took a long, much-needed drink straight from the can. "So, what's up?"

The server brought over the half pie on a round tray, along with a couple of paper plates; the aroma made Davina's mouth water.

Nick grabbed a slice for himself. "I thought you might be freaked out about George dying, so I wanted to make sure you're okay."

Was Nick projecting? He'd known his father's old associate most of his life, and now George Modica was dead. "That's sweet. Yeah, I'm fine, I guess. It came as a shock. Especially with everything we talked about last night. The timing was unsettling."

"How'd you find out?"

Davina swallowed a bite of pizza. "Gerry got a text from the SBCA."

Nick nodded. "So, she ended up joining. I figured she would." He hesitated. "She, um, she gets pretty heated."

"Gerry is passionate about Staten Island."

Nick's eyes met Davina's. "Are you?"

"Not as much as Gerry. She's very politically minded, but *everyone* is politically minded with the election coming up."

He made a face. "I guess I'm kind of used to it all. Growing up with my father will do that to a person."

"That makes sense." Davina could no longer think about Sean

Delafield without also thinking about Son of Cropsey. "Um, I was just talking to Rita Pine. Do you know her?"

"Of course. The crazy mother of the girl that was raped. She's a crackpot. And a drunk." Nick bit into another slice of pizza. "Her *and* her husband."

Davina bristled. "That's harsh. Mean, actually. Bert Pine is dead."

Nick cleaned his hands with a napkin. "Probably gave himself a heart attack—like George."

"That's fucking insensitive, Nick."

Nick swigged at his soda. "What's fucking insensitive is doing shitty work for my father, and then demanding more money for it."

Davina didn't know whether to believe him about the quality of Bert's work. After all, there were always two sides to every story. "Is that right?" she said.

Whatever Nick saw in Davina's face brought about a distinct change in his demeanor. He took a deep breath. "I'm sorry. That was way out of line."

"Yeah, it was."

Nick seemed unable to meet Davina's gaze. "Sorry for the rant. My father is not a pushover, and Bert Pine knew he'd done a crappy job. The man pushed his own ass into a corner."

"Rita said Bert gave up his other clients because your dad demanded that he be exclusive. So, maybe he had some help getting into that corner."

Nick ignored her. "We had experts ready to testify, but it never came to that. They backed off—like people do when they're wrong and have their bluff called."

Davina placed the crust of her pizza slice on the plate. "They backed off because their daughter was brutally raped and their lives fell apart, Nick."

Nick shook his head. "You know why they *really* backed off? Because they couldn't support their lies. Don't get me wrong, the whole thing with Elizabeth Pine was a shame." He took a large bite of his pizza slice.

"Yeah, a real shame." Davina repeated Nick's words softly. "I met Elizabeth. Her whole life is destroyed. She was an innocent girl, and now she's in an institution bouncing backward and forward in time."

"Like I said . . . a real shame."

Biting her tongue, Davina decided to take the conversation in a different direction, determined to get something, *anything* out of Nick. "I think the cops arrested the wrong guy for the Son of Cropsey rapes and left the real rapist on the loose. I also think they're wrong about how he targets his victims."

Nick stared blankly at her. "What d' you mean?"

"Well, they thought the attacks were random. I think they're not."

"Why?" Nick stared intensely at Davina; his eyes fixed on hers.

Davina was confident about her evolving theory, but was suddenly uncertain Nick was the right one to hear it. "No, forget it. You'll tell me I'm crazy."

"Try me."

Davina stared down at the crust on her plate and considered her next words carefully. "Timing. Some of the rapes *benefited* people. And there's an odd connection to real estate."

"You're cute." Nick dismissed Davina like she was some crazy, tin-foil hat conspiracy theorist.

"Never mind. I gotta go." She took one final sip of her DP and got up from the table. "Thanks for the slice." *And for revealing yourself, asshole.*

"Whoa!" Nick sprang out of the booth. "I want to hear more about your theory."

Davina stopped. "So, you can tell me I'm cute again?"

"So, I can help." Nick reached over the table and grabbed Davina's wrist. Her body tensing, she sucked in a deep breath and yanked her wrist away.

Nick gave her a quizzical expression. "Seriously, Davina. I mean it. I want to help. If your thoughts about timing bear out and this is connected to real estate, I might be an asset to you."

An asset or . . . "All right. Let's brainstorm this evening."

"Sure."

"I'm gonna call Joe, and Geoff Wong. I'll pick up Chinese, and we can all try to put the pieces together. My place. 6-ish?"

"I'll be there, Davina."

Nick switched on the earnest with ease—could be he's just trying to get into my panties.

Davina dismissed the thought and left Nick standing in the pizza parlor while she returned to the muggy afternoon heat; if he was trying to fuck her, it gave her an advantage. On her way to the car, she fired off a quick text.

> Up for Chinese tonight?

Joe responded within seconds.

> Yes. I've been missing you.

> We saw each other yesterday.

> Feels like a week.

> A lot has happened.

> I want to hear all of it.

> You will. So will Geoff Wong and Nick. Tonite we brainstorm.

Radio silence.

A couple minutes later, Joe texted back:

> I'll be there.

CHAPTER FIFTY-FIVE

FRIDAY, DARREN'S APARTMENT IN ST. GEORGE

DARREN HADN'T RETURNED TO THE BANK AFTER LUNCH. HIS secretary said he'd missed an important meeting and wasn't picking up his phone. Kevin Monaghan was concerned Darren might be the next one of their circle to have a "heart attack."

George had been perfectly fine the night before at the SBCA meeting, if a little drunk and agitated—there was no way he had just dropped dead. Kevin smelled a rat, and his instincts were never off.

Hell, I'm living in a fucking den of rats.

Route 439 was packed because it was Friday; folk were fleeing the city early in their hurry to have the week over and done with. Kevin knew the feeling: as majority partner in Monaghan Security Systems, he felt the grind all too much. Back when he was a cop, Kevin could work all day, all night because the work excited him. Dealing with the private sector with their entitlement and general stupidity, he, too, found himself working for the weekend.

Kevin's phone buzzed on the windshield mount of his Dodge Ram. He leaned in to see who it was. His fucking ex-wife. He could just imagine the message: *Why aren't you answering my lawyer's calls? Where's last month's check?*

Kevin ignored her.

His ex was a high-strung woman. High maintenance, too. And that's why the marriage hadn't worked. Kevin had a solid job, provided well for the woman, even took her out on date nights from time to time, but Sandy Monaghan had turned into the kind of woman Kevin despised: a crazy bitch. But they were all crazy, weren't they?

He finally made the exit for the Seaview Apartments, a luxury building only someone like Darren Rivers could call home. It wasn't Kevin's style. He preferred old, shabby Staten Island—it felt like *home*. He loved the dirty, fucked-up streets. They were his bread and butter.

Kevin parked and made his way by the topiaries flanking the automatic entrance doors. He stepped inside where the air was cool and dry and the elevator Muzak gave off a peaceful, bougie comfort. He felt the irony that one of the only Black guys in the SBCA lived better than most of the Whites. Still, knowing what Kevin knew about Staten Island, Darren probably lived there so he wouldn't suffer death by cop. Couldn't begrudge him that.

Kevin approached the concierge and tapped a finger on the granite counter. "I'm here to see Darren Rivers."

The concierge checked a ledger, then looked up at Kevin from beneath her overly long lashes. "Is he expecting you?"

"What is this, fucking corporate headquarters?" Kevin laughed.

The concierge wasn't amused. "His assistant just went up."

"I'm a friend." Kevin pulled out his old police badge. It was expired and he wasn't supposed to have it, but who the fuck could tell? He used it all the time.

"Number ten, tenth floor."

Kevin gave the girl a wan smile and put the badge in his back pocket. Across the foyer, he stepped into the elevator and pressed for the tenth floor.

Kevin stepped out and noted the navy-blue carpet in the hallway was pristinely clean. Kevin examined himself in the mirror and smoothed his mustache down. He walked over to #1010 and knocked.

No reply.

He knocked harder.

A busty Black girl with a cell phone in her hand pulled open the door; Kevin recognized her as Darren's assistant. She looked like she was in the middle of a panic attack.

"Who are you?" she demanded. Her voice was shaky and tears stood out in the corners of her eyes.

Jesus, what's the guy gotten himself into now?

Kevin shoved past the girl. "I'm Kevin Monaghan. I'm—" Darren lay facedown on the floor. "What the fuck?"

Behind him, the girl melted down. "I don't know what happened. I got here and—and he was like this. I was calling the cops." She began to sob.

Kevin put up his hand. "Don't. I'll take care of it." He knelt beside Darren and felt for a pulse on his neck.

Nothing.

First George, now this.

An icy chill of fear stirred beneath the ex-cop's breastbone.

"Mr. Rivers didn't come back to work for a meeting, and there were papers he needed to sign, so I . . . I brought them."

"Goddamn it." Kevin saw the open laptop on the coffee table along with two empty wine glasses. Darren evidently had had a party that didn't end well. Kevin sat down on the sofa and woke the computer up.

The assistant protested. "Don't touch that! It's bank property!"

"Don't tell me what to do." Kevin took his cop badge out of his back pocket and threw it on the table. The assistant clammed up. "One of these wine glasses yours?" There was no reason not to suspect the assistant of foul play. Maybe Darren had gotten a little too frisky with her?

"No! I just got here. *Literally* a minute ago."

"He gave you a key to his place?"

"Sometimes I deliver files when he's not home."

Kevin ignored the sniffling girl and got to work. He went straight into

Darren's email to check for anything suspicious. There was nothing but bank correspondence and the occasional email from Nick Delafield. Most of those were campaign emails, except for one with the subject heading: *I'm sorry about last night.*

Kevin clicked on it. The content of the email was a broken heart emoji. Kevin furrowed his brow. What the fuck did that mean? Something wasn't right.

He speed-dialed Detective Riley, who picked up after three rings.

"Tom, we've got a situation."

CHAPTER FIFTY-SIX

FRIDAY, DAVINA'S APARTMENT

Davina stepped into her kitchen carrying two large bags of Chinese food. The lights were dim and Joe was already seated at the table.

"Oh, shit." Davina brought a hand to her chest. "You scared me." She reached over and turned on the light.

Joe got up. "Sorry, I didn't mean to. You *did* give me a key. You okay?"

Am I okay? Davina put the bags down on the counter. "Yeah, all good, Joe. I'm glad you got here before everyone else."

Joe smiled. "Me too. Gives us a chance to talk."

"I feel like I'm neglecting you. What you did for me—going to Tampa, paying for it . . . that was above and beyond."

He touched her cheek. "No, it wasn't."

Davina placed a hand on Joe's chest. "Things are starting to come together in my head, Joe. I had lunch with Nick today—kind of spur of the moment. I wanted to run something by him and see how he'd react to my ideas about the connections between Son of Cropsey and his father's real estate and development businesses."

He frowned and shook his head. "What connections?"

"Most of the Son of Cropsey attacks took place on properties Sean Delafield had interest in . . . and several of the victims' fathers worked for him. Including mine."

"Okay. That's unsettling. So, how did Nick react?"

"He pretty much laughed at me," Davina said. "He actually told me I was 'cute.'" She made air-quotes.

"And that's why you invited him tonight? To put the pressure on him?"

She nodded. "He insists that he's my friend. Almost family. I'm not buying that."

"I don't blame you. But the guy's right about one thing. You are cute. And I missed you." Leaning in, he kissed her.

He knew not to put his hands on her, but Davina's hips were pressed against the counter. Although it triggered a little anxiety, Davina reminded herself that she was safe with Joe.

"That feels good."

Joe rested his forehead against hers. "More?"

She nodded and closed her eyes.

Joe brought a hand to Davina's hip and kissed her again. "Is this, okay?"

"Yeah." She was surprised at how safe she felt with Joe, how badly she wanted him. She moaned softly as he kissed her neck and reached down to grab her tank top. He pulled it up her torso and it was just clear of her breasts when Millie walked in.

Shit.

Millie threw up her hands in mock horror and cut loose with laughter. "*Mercy me!*"

"I thought you were going to be late." Davina pulled her tank back down, her cheeks flushed. Joe pretended to stare out the kitchen window.

"Yeah, I see that." Millie walked to the kitchen window, reached past Joe, and opened it. "Just airing out all the sex in here."

Davina laughed. "We didn't *actually* do anything."

"We never do," Joe murmured.

"Funny," Davina said, though it wasn't at all funny, and she wasn't sure if Joe had intended it to be. She watched him walk away, head down like a little kid moping because he didn't get ice cream.

"Let me help you with that." Millie took plastic containers out of the takeout bags. "Damn, this smells good!"

Joe opened the fridge. "I'll get drinks."

"When are the others getting here?" Millie grabbed some large serving spoons from the drawer.

Davina checked her phone. "Any time now."

They finished setting the table moments before a knock sounded; Geoff Wong and Nick Delafield arrived at the same time.

"I'm here for the free food." Nick gave a brittle laugh as he strode into the kitchen. He stopped dead in his tracks when he saw Joe. "Hey, long time."

"Yeah, long time." Joe chugged his Diet Coke.

Geoff made his way around Nick. "Sorry I didn't bring something—late day at the office."

"That's fine, Geoff." Davina took the lids off of the food and everyone dug in.

Plate full, Joe turned to Nick. His voice was flat. "Davina told me she bounced some interesting ideas off you today at lunch."

Davina stopped, clutching a serving spoon full of kung pao. She eyed Joe warily.

"*Interesting* is one word for it." Nick gave Davina a side-eye and a crooked smile.

"She said you dismissed her."

Nick gave Joe a level look. "I would never dismiss Davina. She's too important to me."

"As important as Alessandra?"

Davina held her breath. *Jesus, Lord. What's he doing?* Was that jealousy or suspicion in those blue eyes? What point was Joe trying to make, and with whom?

Geoff plucked a can of sparkling water from the middle of the table. "Sorry, I'm not up to speed. Who is Alessandra?"

Davina made a mental note to thank the journalist later for breaking up that . . . whatever *that* was. "My older sister."

Geoff nodded his acknowledgement. "Right."

"Okay." Davina clapped her hands together. "First of all, I want to thank you all again for coming,"

"Thank *you* for the food." Nick held up a piece of General Tso's chicken in his wooden chopsticks.

Davina felt the mood lift a little. "Okay, I'm going to dive right in. I don't think Son of Cropsey's attacks were random. I'm convinced more than ever the whole thing is connected to the real estate and development businesses on the Rock."

Nick spoke up, "You hinted about that at lunch. What makes you think that?"

"Because most of the attacks happened on real estate connected to your dad, Nick," Joe ventured, clearly happy to get the dig in. "And apparently, some of the victims' parents worked for Delafield Enterprises and had a falling out with the company."

Nick put down his chopsticks. "You're kidding me, right?" He turned to Davina. "Tell me he's kidding?"

Davina shook her head. "I mentioned it at lunch, Nick. So, no. The connection's obvious, but the cops missed it. Riley only saw what he wanted to see."

"What you're saying is my father is Son of Cropsey?" Nick scoffed.

"Could be a frame-up, I suppose," Joe offered. "By somebody who really doesn't like your dad . . . which is gonna be a pretty long list."

Nick opened his mouth, closed it, then shrugged. "Yeah. He rubs a lot of folks the wrong way. But Son of Cropsey is behind bars."

Davina was shaking her head. "No. No, he's not. There's no way Rob Cox was the rapist. For a start, the rapes continued after he was behind bars, and the latest attacks have exactly the same MO."

Nick crunched into an egg roll. "How are you so sure?"

Davina put down her chopsticks and massaged her temples. "First, all but two of the attacks took place on property slated for development by Sean. Of the ones I was able to get information on, he either owned outright, was trying to purchase, or was bidding on development contracts. Then, there's the work-related connection. My dad, for one. Bert Pine, Elizabeth's father, was a plumber on one of Sean's biggest jobs. He was suing Delafield Enterprises for breach of contract when Elizabeth was attacked, forcing him to give up the lawsuit."

"I told you—"

"Yes, I know, it was all Bert Pine's fault. Just like what happened with my dad was all his fault, too. Being connected with your father's business has destroyed more than one family, Nick." Davina knew her words sounded harsh. She told herself she couldn't allow herself to care, even if Nick was supposed to be a friend.

Nick laughed. "So, you're *really* saying my father is behind it? He's always to blame for everything, isn't he?"

"I'm not saying your father is behind this. But he's . . . *connected* to it."

"I get it, now. This is all about your dad losing his job and me dumping Allie and you ending up on the street." Nick's face reddened. "You blame my dad because your family was fucked up. This is about *revenge*, Davina."

"Absolutely. But not mine, Nick. The rapes were about revenge."

"Bullshit," Nick snarled.

Davina put up her hands, palms facing out. "I need everyone to listen before you judge. The business connections are too many to be coincidental. Add to that the fact the attacks continued—are *continuing*—"

"More bullshit," said Nick. "It's a copycat."

Davina faced him. "A copycat wouldn't get the MO precisely right. At least not the parts of it the police didn't release. Originally, they said the victims were asphyxiated with a plastic bag, but they knew it was a blood choke."

"How do you know that, Davina?" Nick put down his chopsticks.

"Detective Packer," said Joe. "He was lead on the case until Riley produced a perpetrator and things got hinky. Then he suddenly retired and Riley got to play hero."

"Earlier this week, I was attacked by a man who tried to get me in a blood chokehold," Davina said quietly, her voice faltering. "At Great Kills train station."

"We were following up a lead on Joy Sheridan's death," Geoff filled in. "She and Elizabeth Pine were both attacked at Great Kills—*after* Cox was already in custody. The attacker put them both in chokeholds."

"What's it got to do with your dad losing his job ten years ago?" Nick threw in.

Davina felt all eyes on her.

"Tell him," said Joe. He went to the fridge to grab another soda.

Davina took a deep breath. "*I* was one of Son of Cropsey's victims."

"What?" Nick glanced around the table at the others, his face bone white.

Joe returned to the table. "Two attacks, ten years apart. The guy raped Davina back then, and this time, he tried to kill her."

"Then who'd Riley put away?" Nick asked.

"Some low-life drug dealer who copped a plea deal to keep him from facing a homicide rap," Geoff told him.

"Every single victim was attacked using a blood choke," Davina explained. "It uses the arm's strength to cut blood flow to the brain. The victim loses consciousness in seconds. It's the same guy using the same method."

"Or someone who read the real police report—or a cop," argued Nick.

"But they didn't release the description of the rapist's signature." Davina's words dropped into the tension, leaving silent ripples. She pointed to her forehead. "I had the Greek letter theta written on my forehead in Allie's lipstick. Elizabeth Pine had something carved into her forehead with a sharp point. Detective Packer confirmed it when Joe and I went to Tampa to see him. All the girls I've been able to talk to had some sort of mark on their foreheads."

"What does it mean?" Millie wanted to know.

"Packer said the cops thought it meant 'nothing,' at first," said Joe. "As if the rapist was saying the girls were nothing. But it also means—"

"Death, or maybe divine," said Geoff Wong. He shrugged when everyone turned toward him. "I Googled it."

Nick appeared stunned. "So, if there's a copycat, it'd have to be someone who knew what the police were concealing from the public and the press. I see how that's a long shot, okay? I see how you're thinking they just got the wrong guy. But I still don't understand how my dad—"

Davina held up a conciliatory hand. "Not just your dad, Nick. The other businessmen, too. Members of the SBCA."

Nick scoffed, "They're *all* rapists?"

"I don't know what the connection is," Davina admitted. "I just know there is one. Whoever was—*is*—doing this, may be using the victims to get to their parents. My dad was run out of town on a rail, essentially. He'd never been a quitter, always stuck things out. But he quit back then, right after what happened to me. You quit too, Nick. You gave up on Allie—and me—when you pulled your vanishing act."

Nick grabbed the carton of kung pao pork. "My father wasn't keen on me being in a relationship with the daughter of the guy who burned down his warehouse. You're suggesting that he hired someone to rape you and that other girl because your parents might cause trouble? Because they *knew something?* What about all those other girls, Davina? What did their parents do?"

"I'm not saying they're *all* tied into development on the island," Davina replied. "Some of them might have been crimes of opportunity. Fun for a sadistic bastard. But . . . Joy's mom was a Delafield real estate agent. Mary Lamont's uncle is a county building inspector."

"Oh, c'mon!" Nick threw up his arms in a wildly exaggerated gesture.

Davina leaned toward Nick across the table. "Here's something else I know, Nick. I know there's something weird going on in the SBCA. I felt it at Joy's wake and again at the meeting. I'm surprised you didn't pick up on the dread filling that room—you could almost *smell* it. George Modica was wigging out—I've never seen a man so soaked with sweat. And the way he kept staring at me . . ." Davina shuddered.

"The poor guy was working on a heart attack," Nick reminded her.

Geoff spoke up. "I'm gonna play devil's advocate. The real estate development connection could be just a weird coincidence—Sean Delafield is a real estate guy with fingers in practically every pie on the island. It's kind of inevitable there'll appear to be some connection, even if there isn't one."

Davina raised her eyebrows. "The Todt Hill victim's father works at the Department of Urban Development. He's one of the guys who has to put his stamp of approval on precisely the sort of work the SBCA has interests in. Somehow, then and now, business interests—Sean Delafield's and possibly others'—are driving the crimes. Detective Packer made a sideways reference when Joe asked him who'd be on his list of suspects if he were still investigating the case."

"The butcher, the baker . . . the *banker*. He made a point of it." Joe was pensive. "Packer also talked about Sean getting a 'sweet mortgage deal' from Darren Rivers."

"Darren Rivers is—" Nick cut off. "He's too prissy to get his hands dirty."

"Packer singled him out for some reason," Joe replied. "And his bank is the beating green heart of the business association."

"It's also involved in activities most of the girls were doing after school. Sports, clubs, Girl Scouts. They were all supported by the bank." Davina pictured the cutesy display she'd seen at the bank—all those young girls in tight swimsuits.

Millie raised her hand like she was back in third grade. "Okay, supposing Son of Cropsey *isn't* in jail, why'd he take such a fucking long vacation?"

"Maybe he left town to avoid detection. Maybe he realized that, with someone in jail, people would soon realize the cops had arrested the wrong guy. If he went somewhere else. . ."

Geoff pushed his plate away. "If that's the case, he might've left a trail."

Joe shook his head in frustration. "Why are we not talking about the fact Sean Delafield spent time in jail?"

"*Fuck you*." Nick was incensed. "That was for tax evasion, a white-collar crime. He's a prick, but not a violent prick."

"Then how about we talk about the fact that when I worked for your father, I saw him punch one of his employees?"

Nick raked his fingers through his hair. "The guy was drunk."

"He was trying to tell your old man about stuff going missing from the warehouse."

"Who'd he hit?" Davina asked.

Joe shrugged and gave Davina a lopsided smile, as if by means of an apology. "Your father."

A cell phone began to play "If I Only Had a Brain" from *The Wizard of Oz*. Geoff Wong jumped and pulled the device out of his pocket. "Sorry. That's me."

Nick picked up his plate and took it to the sink. "Appropriate."

Davina was reaching for the nearly empty container of white rice when Geoff's words stopped her.

"Darren Rivers is dead."

"Shit," said Millie.

Nick's face drained of color. Getting to his feet, he shoved his chair away from the table and went over to the sink—like he might lose his kung pao.

Geoff put his phone away and rose to leave. "I gotta go. I have a source I need to meet. Thanks for dinner." He let himself out.

"Sure." Davina's voice was hushed. Moments ago, Darren Rivers had been a top suspect—and now he was dead.

"I've got a campaign meeting." Nick rushed to the door.

Joe eyed him with suspicion. "That was sudden."

Nick opened the door and held onto the knob, his back to the room. "What you said about my dad and Davina's father? It didn't happen, Joe."

"Sure, Nick. I just imagined it, right?"

Nick slammed the door behind him and was gone.

Davina sat there unsure of what to do next, while Millie bustled around her, tidying away the suddenly abandoned meal.

Joe kissed Davina's forehead. "You okay? I have a client meeting in the morning to prep for."

Davina tilted her head up, willing Joe to kiss her on the mouth. He did so, softly.

"I think I'm okay." She wrapped her arms around herself. "I'm supposed to meet Gerry later."

"Tell her I said hi." Just like that, Joe was gone, leaving Davina and Millie alone in the apartment.

Millie continued to clean, carrying plates to the kitchen. "D, this is deep. I'll have trouble believing it if they try to tell us this was another heart attack."

"Do you think it's true, Mil? That Sean punched out my dad, then falsely accused him of negligence to shut him up about it?"

Millie thought for a moment. "At this point, anything could be true, D."

"Yeah."

"You say you're going to the gym tonight?" Millie tossed takeout cartons and chopsticks in the trash.

"I promised Gerry I'd help her clean up after the construction crew. They've been doing work downstairs and left it in a real fucking mess. First, though, I have to finish a paper for my forensics class." Davina rubbed at her aching temples. How the hell was she supposed to concentrate on schoolwork with so much running through her mind?

"Do what you gotta do. When I'm done with this, I'm going to my room to sext my hot girlfriend."

Davina gave her roommate a faint smile. "So, she's *girlfriend* now?"

"I'm doing my damndest to make it that way."

In her room, Davina sat at her small desk and turned on the lamp. Staring down at her computer, she inhaled deeply, then exhaled and willed herself to get to work.

It just wasn't happening.

I have to keep moving. If I sit here, I'll go insane.

At close to 8:00 p.m. Davina closed her laptop and got up from her desk. Walking down the hall, she called, "I'm heading out!"

Driving to Dobson's, Davina's whirling brain homed in on Nick's throwaway comment: *someone who read the real police report—or a cop.* It wasn't too much of a stretch to believe Riley was capable of brutal rapes— and murder. But even if he wasn't, Davina was convinced he was somehow at the center of the Son of Cropsey case. Riley, who had kept an eagle eye on her since her father left, who had been the first person to say she was acting out and made up a story about how Allie's lipstick got on her forehead. Riley, who'd offered some drug dealer a deal to take the rap and driven Packer off the case. He was like a big, malevolent spider at the center of a web of chaos and cover-ups.

Maybe, just maybe, he *was* Son of Cropsey?

Whatever Riley's involvement, one thing was for certain; someone had taken Darren Rivers off Davina's suspect list.

CHAPTER FIFTY-SEVEN

FRIDAY, DOBSON'S GYM

Gerry's car was the only one in the parking lot when Davina reached the gym. The main level lights were off and the door was locked. Davina figured she'd gone over to her favorite taco stand a block up the street.

Davina unlocked the door and let herself in.

Gerry's office looked like a tornado had swept through it. Papers and files were strewn all over and the wastepaper basket was upturned, as was the chair behind Gerry's desk. The phone's line had been ripped out of the wall.

Fear hit Davina like a sickening blow to the stomach; something was terribly wrong. She moved swiftly, silently to the top of the stairs that led down to the locker rooms. There she paused, taking shallow, trembling breaths and listening. Except for the soft exhalation from the A/C, the darkness was silent.

Cautiously, she made her way down to the women's locker room. It was dark—the only illumination came from a couple of safety lights low on the wall at the entrance to the showers. With a constant eye on her surroundings, fists raised and ready, Davina espied what she thought at first was a heap of discarded towels.

God, no. God, please, no.

In a blind panic, Davina eschewed any attempt to be quiet or careful and crossed the room in seconds.

She knew in her pounding heart the heap was a body—Gerry's body.

Dropping to her knees, Davina pulled out her cell phone, thumbed on the flashlight app, and placed trembling fingers to her friend's neck to check for a pulse.

There was none.

Gerry's eyes stared up, glassy and half-closed, at Davina; her body was warm and limp: the murder had just happened.

Davina didn't realize for a moment that her knees were wet: she was kneeling in a wide pool of Gerry's blood. Numb with grief, tears welling in her eyes, Davina began to dial 911.

But before she could tap send, Davina caught a whisper of sound from among the lockers.

Whoever killed Gerry was still down there.

Davina sprung to her feet, pivoting as she rose. The glow from the safety lights glinted off the blade of a knife, roughly three feet and some change away. Davina turned her pirouette into a roundhouse kick that sent the knife flying from her assailant's hand. She'd crouched to leap after him when a second man came at her from behind. She used his momentum to flip him, breaking his hold and sending him to the concrete floor with a gratifying thud. He groaned and struggled to rise.

Two more figures emerged from the darkness, and Davina pressed her back against the wall—there was nowhere to run.

One of the dark shapes slashed at Davina with a knife, and the other took a wide swing with an aluminum baseball bat; it flashed silver in the dim light as it arced toward her head. She was able to duck the baseball bat, but the knife scored her left arm just below the shoulder.

Adrenaline hit so hard, she barely felt it. She came out of her crouch right at the bat-wielder and managed to land a flurry of blows to his stomach before delivering an uppercut to his jaw that decked him.

The guy's skull hit the ground with a sharp, wet *crack* and he lay still.

Davina spotted the knife on the floor between two rows of lockers and leapt at it. Landing in a crouch, she scooped up the knife and spun to face her three attackers. The first she'd put down was back on his feet. In the narrow aisle between lockers and benches, the dark-clad men were forced close together, which made them better targets.

She could do this.

Davina took full advantage of the darkness and confined space to launch a chaotic attack—slashing, kicking, punching, then slashing again; she kept the three at bay and scored hit after hit as she backed herself toward the doorway.

One of the men disappeared behind the end of the lockers closest to the shower. Davina knew he'd be circling around to get behind her; it's what she'd do. Taking advantage of his absence, she delivered more slashes and punches to the remaining two, and added a high kick that had one of them screaming out loud in agony. The guy doubled over the other one to topple like a felled tree.

As the men hit the floor, their buddy rushed Davina from behind, swinging the baseball bat.

Davina lashed out backward with her left foot, catching the guy square in the groin before he could connect with the bat. She was sure she felt something *pop* beneath her heel. With a breathless yelp, he lost his grip on the bat midswing and crumpled. The loose bat smacked Davina's upper thigh, but with only a fraction of the force had it still been in her attacker's hands. Bouncing from her taut quad, the bat clattered noisily to the concrete floor and rolled away.

The locker room fell silent, still but for the wild beating of Davina's heart and the groans of her would-be killers. She bolted for the stairs, legs shaking so badly she had to climb on all fours. The four men who'd attacked her, who'd killed Gerry—*killed Gerry*—were still alive, which meant she had to reach her car before they could catch up to her. She staggered across the gym, tripping on mats, blundering into random machinery, and reached the front doors, panting. She threw her entire weight against the release bar and flung the doors wide open, all but falling out into the balmy night air.

The relief she felt at the sight of her car made her want to weep. She took a step toward it, only to see a backlit figure rise from its dark bulk to loom before her. She screamed, thrusting the bloody knife out in front of her. The figure wavered but took a step forward into the light of a fixture over the doorway.

"Davina." The voice was unexpected but welcome.

"Nick?"

CHAPTER FIFTY-EIGHT

FRIDAY, DOBSON'S GYM

NICK STARED WIDE-EYED AT THE KNIFE AIMED DIRECTLY AT his heart. He raised his hands in a gesture of surrender. "Davina? What the fuck?"

"*Nick?*" Davina was overcome with relief; she dropped the knife. "Nick."

He lowered his arms, eyes fixed on the knife. "Are you okay? What the hell is going on?"

Davina looked over her shoulder at the gym's dark interior. All was still. Who were those guys? How badly had she hurt them? Had she killed any of them?

"Gerry is dead," she said, her voice eerily calm with shock. "Call 911, Nick."

"Sure, D. Sure." And then Nick's arms were around her in a tight embrace. Davina barely noticed.

"Why is everyone dying?" Davina trembled, tears streaming down her face. She felt weak, dizzy. Was she bleeding?

"Okay, breathe, Davina. Just breathe."

The blood on Davina's hands and arms stained Nick's button-up white shirt in a matter of seconds. "They're still down there. I hurt them, but they're still alive."

"I'm gonna put you in my car, okay?" As Nick maneuvered Davina across the parking lot, she stumbled as her legs wobbled beneath her. In one swift, reflexive motion, Nick swept Davina up into his arms and carried her to the car, cradling her against his chest. He slid her into the passenger seat, then went around to the driver's side and got in, locking the doors.

"Gerry's still down there." Davina's voice was a whisper. She felt freezing cold; her teeth began to chatter.

Nick dialed 911. "The police will take care of everything."

Yes, because they're good at taking care of things. "I think those were Riley's thugs."

Nick pressed his phone to his ear. "I'm Nick Delafield. I'm at Dobson's Gym. There appears to have been a break-in. There's at least one fatality."

"I can't believe this is happening." Davina stared out the window at Dobson's. There was still no movement.

"The address is 15 Clifton Avenue. We're in the parking lot in my car. Okay, yes. We will." Nick ended the call.

Davina's head began to clear. "Nick, what are you doing here?"

"That's not important right now. You're bleeding." Nick reached to the back seat and grabbed his jacket. He plucked a handkerchief from the breast pocket and pressed it to the center of the spreading patch of blood on Davina's shirt. "I need to get you to the ER. This might be serious."

"I want to wait for the police, to tell them everything."

"You can tell them later."

Davina pushed away his hand; pain flared up her arm and across her chest. She ignored it. "I'm fine." In the dim cabin light, Davina examined her wounds and willed herself to breathe and relax her jaw. She had a few shallow gashes below the collarbone and what appeared to be a deep one just above her left breast. The wound on her arm was still oozing blood.

"Whatever you say." Nick sighed. "Can you tell me what happened in there?"

Davina dropped her chin to her chest. "I-I found Gerry's body in the locker room. There were four guys, dressed in black, faces covered. One had a knife. One had a baseball bat. I don't know why anyone would go after Gerry. There's no reason to kill her. Maybe they thought she was me. Or maybe it was a warning or something."

"Aren't you taking all of this too far?"

"Taking what too far?" Davina turned in her seat to face him. "Nick, Gerry's down there, dead in a pool of blood."

"And you kicked the living shit out of them, I gather."

Was he *smiling?*

"This isn't funny. It was pitch black down there. I just got the knife off them and went on instinct." Davina swallowed the lump in her throat.

Nick gripped the steering wheel and stared out the windshield at the dark lot. His hands kneaded the leather wheel cover. "This is fucked up."

"More fucked up than any of us know. I gotta call Joe. Where's my phone?" Davina searched through her pockets.

"That's a bad idea, Davina. We both know Joe can't keep his cool."

"That's not true."

"Those things he said about my father. And *your* father. None of it was true."

"So, I shouldn't believe Joe? He's lying to me?"

"Joe's *jealous*, D. Believe *me*." Nick grabbed hold of Davina's bloody hand. "I'm still your big brother, right? You could trust me back then, and you can trust me now. I'm always here for you." He smiled, his teeth flashing perfectly white in the parking lot lights.

"Are you?"

Nick took his jacket and wrapped it around Davina's shoulders. "Of course. Put this on."

"I'm covered in blood."

"Don't worry about that." Nick lifted up his phone. "If you want me to call Joe, I will."

Davina thought about it. Yes, Joe needed to know. Maybe he'd come, and she desperately wanted to see him. She didn't trust Nick, but she *wanted* to trust him. That was a problem in and of itself. She willed hard for the needy twelve-year-old Davina to stay out of it.

"Yeah, I want you to call Joe."

"Okay, Davina." Nick pulled up the number and tapped on it.

CHAPTER FIFTY-NINE

FRIDAY, BLUE STAR GROCERY

STEVE WATSON—STAN'S SON-IN-LAW—HAD PULLED OUT THE trump card with the anonymous party video. In a meeting back at the *Advance*, using a hell of a lot of tech speak that was lost on Geoff, he'd explained with great patience how editing digital movies worked. Apparently, Steve had told Geoff and the equally bewildered Stan, when a digital film is spliced using most typical applications, there are always a few frames left on either side of the cut. The frames represent fractions of a second and are only detectable by the trained eye.

That was to be the downfall of Sean Delafield and his cronies who'd enjoyed the coke, MDMA, and underage hookers at the party someone had thoughtfully decided to film.

Geoff now knew who that somebody was: Gino Romano. For, not only was it glaringly obvious the party had taken place at Stavros Scala's house, but the recovered secret frames had shown Gino's reflection in a wine glass as he'd watched Sean manhandling the young stripper. Another of the frames, at the end of the video, had also given up a couple of the other revelers, members of the SBCA, and that's what Geoff intended to discuss with Mr. Romano.

Geoff was well aware that if the video leaked, it would cause serious damage to some of the leading businessmen on Staten Island. *I wouldn't shed a tear.*

Geoff had texted Gino as soon as he got through with Steve and asked to meet him at Blue Star Grocery. He hoped the guy, once presented with irrefutable evidence, would oblige by being willing to talk openly about the night of Scott's bachelor party.

As he stepped into the grocery store, blinking under the harsh fluorescent lights, Geoff thought about Davina's apartment overhead; maybe he'd pop in to say hi once he'd finished up with Gino.

The Blue Star was all but empty of customers, and the staff were busy stocking shelves for the weekend rush. By Geoff's watch, the place would close in roughly fifteen minutes. He spotted Gino in the meat department, arguing with the butcher.

"You're not pushing any of my best cuts," Gino was saying.

The butcher shrugged. "Folks don't want the best cuts. They wanna save money."

"If they want to save money, they can go to Food Town. I only sell the good stuff."

"Pardon me, Mister Romano." Geoff waved.

"Mister Wong." Gino wiped his hands on his white apron and scuttled around the display case.

"Thanks for meeting me." Geoff shook Gino's hand.

"No problem." Gino led the journalist to the back office.

Geoff had expected old and dingy. It wasn't. Gino's office was light, bright, and furnished by IKEA.

Gino seated himself behind a light-wood, minimalist desk; it had only a laptop atop it, positioned to the right of center. "You said you had a story I can contribute to. I'm intrigued. Have a seat."

Geoff took the only other seat in the office, a high-backed, padded armchair that matched the desk.

"You heard about Darren Rivers, I suppose?"

Geoff studied Gino's face. "I got the news about two hours ago. How did you hear?"

"Friend on the force. First George, now Darren." Gino shook his head.

Geoff took out his phone and placed it on Gino's desk. "You think it's more than just a coincidence?"

"You reporters. You're always looking too deep into things."

Geoff chuckled. "That's literally what I'm paid to do."

Gino sniffed. "Yeah. I get it. What do I think?" A shrug. "I think George had a heart condition and Darren—"

"Didn't?"

Gino rubbed his hand along his bald head and wiped off some sweat. "Exactly. It's sad. They were good men. Who the hell is going to be next?" Gino appeared agitated.

Geoff cleared his throat. "That's not the story I'm here about."

"Okay." Gino stood up and walked over to the mini-fridge. He pulled out a beer. "You want one?"

"No, thank you."

"Don't mind me." Gino popped the bottle cap with an opener attached to the side of the fridge. "Been a long day."

Geoff waited patiently for Gino to return to his desk. "Someone sent an anonymous video to the *Advance*. It shows Sean Delafield falling-down drunk, coked-up, and surrounded by underage girls—strippers, to be exact."

Gino took a long, hard slug of his beer and toyed with a pencil on his desk. "I see."

"Does that ring a bell?"

"Why should it?"

"Just asking."

Gino snorted. "That man has a lot of enemies. Throw a rock anywhere on Staten Island and you'll hit one."

"The video has been cleverly edited—and it's an impressive job—to conceal everyone but Sean and the strippers. But whoever edited the film missed the wine glass."

Gino made a face. "Wine glass?"

"That's right. There's a wine glass just to the right of the camera—most probably a cell phone—and faces are reflected in it. It's amazing what can be done with a laptop nowadays—suddenly everyone is Steven Spielberg. We have a guy at the office who knows his way around movies. He paid a small fortune for Final Cut to edit the short films he makes for kicks and pocket money. Did you know that an edited digital movie always has a couple frames left on either side of the cut?"

Slowly, Gino shook his head.

"Our tech guy was able to enhance it, clean it up, and enlarge it enough to make out a couple of images."

"What images?"

"For starters, there are several pictures of Greece on the wall opposite the camera."

"So?"

"I can't think of too many of Sean Delafield's friends who would hang pictures of Greece on their wall. Stavros Scala is one of them."

Gino scratched at his forehead. "Could be anybody—a lot of people love Greece."

"Yeah, it could be, but there's only one person's reflection in the glass." Geoff leaned forward. "You wanna guess who that person is?"

Gino met Geoff's eyes.

Geoff picked up his phone, swiped to the Photos app, and showed Gino the enhanced image. "That's you, isn't it?"

"I don't socialize with Sean Delafield."

"Well, it looks like you did the night of Scott Kantor's bachelor party —along with George Modica, Carlo Donato, Kevin Monaghan . . . you get the picture, Gino. No pun intended." Geoff put his phone back down on the desk. "Now, whoever sent this wants me to think it came from one of the strippers, but I'm not buying it. Can you tell me what's going on and why I got this video?"

"How would I know?" Gino swiveled his chair from side to side. "Maybe you edited the video to make it look like I was there—it's amazing what can be done on a laptop nowadays."

Okay, tough guy. "Mister Romano, let me be clear about this. Right now, it's just me and you talking, entirely off the record. Nobody else knows about this video, apart from my editor and the tech guy. No cops, no authorities, no one in the public. But that could very easily change, and this could explode. It may well become evidence in a criminal investigation, since the girls involved are undoubtedly underage. And you know how the media loves a good criminal investigation, especially one involving sex and young girls. Just look at the meal they made out of Ghislaine Maxwell. This video might even make the national news—suitably censored, of course." Geoff sat back in his chair. "So, it's entirely up to you whether you choose to be an upstanding citizen or a corrupt businessman who likes girls young enough to be his daughter."

Gino stared him down. After several seconds he broke the loaded silence. "Off the record?"

"You have my word."

"Only if you have a beer." Gino lifted his bottle. "I hate drinking alone."

"Sure."

Gino retrieved another bottle of Michelob from the mini-fridge and twisted off the top. "These are cold beer times."

Geoff smiled. "Indeed they are."

Gino walked back around his desk and sat. "I'm gonna start by saying this. Sean is a liability to the party, a danger to Staten Island."

"I've seen the video—that much is clear."

"If I tell you everything I know, how can I be sure it's off the record?"

"Because not everyone has Sean Delafield's questionable morals, and because I'm not here to run this story," Geoff told him. "I'm here to understand what's going on."

"Why should I believe that? You're a fucking journalist."

"Because this case has become personal for me." *Don't ask me why the hell that is, because I don't exactly know.*

Gino looked him up and down and then said, "Okay, Wong. You ask your questions, I'll answer them. Off the record, of course."

CHAPTER SIXTY

FRIDAY, DOBSON'S GYM

DOBSON'S HAD BEEN HER REFUGE, THE ONE PLACE DAVINA could escape the utter chaos of her life. Now it had become the epicenter of the worst kind of chaos. Inside, Gerry Dobson was alone and dead, her body cooling on the concrete floor. She'd fled to some unreachable place, leaving her broken shell behind.

Leaving Davina behind.

"Joe's coming." Nick slipped his cell back in his pocket.

They'd heard sirens, and Dobson's parking lot flooded with the flashing red and blue lights of police cruisers.

Davina grabbed the door handle and pulled it.

Nick reached across to stop her from opening the door. "Let me do this."

"Nick, I—"

He put a firm hand on her arm. "Let me—please."

She was still shaken, her body cold and trembling from shock. Davina slumped back into her seat and let Nick go deal with the cops.

From her window, Davina saw Detective Riley climb out of an

unmarked black Suburban. Of course, he'd be there. The cop knew Gerry Dobson was connected to Davina, and likely knew she was Davina's surrogate mom—he was a stickler for digging for details when it suited him. Had Riley set up the hit with the intention of getting to Davina, or had Gerry been the target?

If that was the case, *why?*

Nick approached Riley and spoke to him with urgency. When Nick motioned toward the car, Riley's gaze snapped to it. Davina made eye contact with the cop. She hadn't meant to. Hadn't *wanted* to.

Too late, she looked away. *I gotta confront that asshole. Now.*

Davina pushed open the car's door and got out into the balmy night air. Nick put up a hand, halting her.

"What the fuck?" She sat back down but kept the door open so she could watch Nick and Riley—the two seemed thick as thieves.

After a few minutes, Nick returned to his car and squatted in front of her, effectively blocking her from standing. "They're going in."

"Okay." Once again, Davina tried to get out of the car, and once again, Nick stopped her. This time he put a hand on her shoulder.

"Chill. Okay?"

A deep, weary breath. "Okay."

They watched together as cops milled in and out of the gym and yellow tape was unfurled like grim bunting to block off the doorway. Father Stephen appeared as if from nowhere—bad news sure as hell traveled fast on the Rock—and was deep in conversation with Riley. The coroner's van arrived and parked diagonally to the door. Gurneys trundled in and came back out carrying sleek black body bags, which were loaded into the van. Had she really killed all four of them?

Surely not.

Last out of the building was Gerry's body, so much smaller than the four men who'd murdered her in cold blood.

Rage struck Davina like an electric charge. She jumped to her feet, forcing Nick to move. He grabbed her arms; pain flared through her body. "D, you really can't. This is a police matter now."

"Yeah, and I'm a material witness."

She broke Nick's grasp, shoved him roughly aside, and strode up to Riley to get in his face. "You got the wrong one, *asshole!*" She pointed to Gerry's body on the gurney.

Riley's voice was cold, measured. "What do you mean by that, Davina?"

"You got the wrong fucking woman. You wanted your goons to kill me, and instead, they killed an innocent woman. *They killed my fucking friend!*"

Father Stephen spoke softly. "Please, Davina. You're very upset—"

"They were day laborers. The kind you pick up at Home Depot. Gerry hired them, and I guess they figured they'd rob her."

"Fuck you, Riley. She hired a local company—"

"Did you see their faces?"

"It was too dark."

Riley moved in close; Davina smelled his cheap aftershave. "Then how the fuck do you know who they were, Davina?"

"I know the contractors Gerry hired, and that wasn't them." Davina steadied her voice. "And why the fuck would they kill the woman who was paying them?"

Father Stephen placed a hand on Riley's shoulder. "We can all use a moment to calm down. This is a fraught situation for Davina, Tom. She's just lost a dear friend."

"I know you're all after me." Davina watched over the cop's shoulder as Gerry's body bag was lifted into the van. "I'm not stupid, Riley. I *know* you're behind this."

Riley's jaw clenched, and the sinews in his neck stood out. "You listen to me," he said in a gruff tone. "I'll grant you a small degree here for shock, but don't push it or I'll drag your ass outta here in cuffs. Are we clear?"

"Crystal."

"Gerry liked to hire street scum to give them a break. They wanted money, and it went bad. Your boss's Good Samaritan act caught up with her. Period. Go home."

"I'm a witness, Detective. I fought them."

Riley's lips twitched. "Right. You killed four grown men. All by yourself."

Davina shook her head. "Honestly, I'm pretty sure I didn't. They were still alive when I left the locker room, and if I didn't kill them, who did?"

Riley ground his teeth. "I said, go home." He walked away.

Davina spat on the ground by the cop's feet. "Liar."

"Jesus, Davina." Nick was visibly shocked.

"Now, everyone, calm down. Please." Father Stephen stepped in.

Riley stopped in his tracks and slowly turned to Davina; his face flushed. "That's your last fucking chance. Don't leave town, Speers."

The cop was barely a handful of strides away when Geoff Wong appeared.

"Fuck, who the hell called the press?" Riley snarled and quickened his step toward his car.

Geoff got to Davina as Father Stephen set off after Riley. "I heard the call over the police band. Are you all right, Davina?" He eyed her blood-covered shirt and hands with concern.

"Not really." Davina wrapped her arms around herself and shivered; she wondered if she'd ever feel warm again.

"Has anyone checked you over? One of the EMTs?"

"I want to take her to the ER," Nick said. "But she won't go."

Geoff finally acknowledged Nick's presence. "What are you doing here? I thought you had campaign things to do."

Davina had wondered the same thing. Had Davina mentioned she was going to help Gerry with the cleanup, or had Nick thought Gerry would be at the gym alone that evening?

"I finished up early and thought I'd come by and help unpack the new equipment," Nick replied.

Wait, what?

Geoff scowled, "That's nice of you, Nick."

Nick opened his mouth to reply, only to be interrupted by a sudden commotion over by the coroner's van. A cop yelled, "*Stop!*" and Joe Kelley appeared at a dead run, heading straight for the gym's entrance. Spotting Davina, he made a beeline for her, arms open.

Davina fell into his embrace, letting him wrap his arms completely around her. She felt no sense of capture or restraint.

She simply felt safe.

"You . . . you're bleeding, Davina," Joe said softly.

"Gerry's dead, Joe." *Maybe if I keep saying it, I'll be able to believe it.*

Joe looked from Nick to Geoff and back. "What the hell happened?"

"I just got here," Geoff told him.

Nick shook his head. "I showed up to help unpack equipment and Davina was running out of the gym. The cops say a bunch of bum workers killed Gerry for money and . . . uh, somebody killed them."

"And then disappeared?" demanded Davina. She struck her chest with a clenched fist. "*I'm* the one that fought them. The last time I saw them they were *alive!*"

"Maybe they turned on each other."

"Sure." Joe glared at Nick and grabbed Davina by the hand. "I'm taking you to the hospital."

Davina allowed Joe to lead her to his car. Although she wasn't convinced that she needed a hospital, she wanted to be away from Dobson's.

"Those weren't our construction guys, Joe," Davina said quietly as Joe pulled out of the lot to wait at the red traffic light.

Joe placed a hand on her knee. "This has gone too far."

"Riley's behind it. I just *know* it. They were *his* guys—he lied about them. He said they were the workmen Gerry hired to fix up the locker rooms and showers." Davina paused, fighting to form the right words. "The guys she hired were small, Latino. Gerry's killers were bigger, *much bigger*. And they were White. Also, there were no EMTs, Joe."

"What?"

"Nick called in the attack at Dobson's with people down, and Riley turned up with the coroner's van and a bunch of cruisers—and no ambulance."

"Maybe because they were all dead?"

Davina couldn't hide her frustration; it was as if Joe was being deliberately stupid. "For the love of God, Joe! Riley didn't know that. I'm damned sure I didn't kill four big-assed thugs—I'm not even sure I killed *any* of them."

"Well, if you didn't . . . Jesus, Davina, do you realize what you're saying?"

"Either the guys who killed Gerry and attacked me aren't actually dead and Riley wants us to think they are. Or . . . or they *are* dead, and somebody other than me killed them."

Joe let out the breath he'd been holding. "Why would somebody do that?"

"All part of Riley's cover-up—his hired assassins became collateral damage, people who knew what he'd done."

Joe put a hand on Davina's cheek, a loving gesture. "This is out of hand, D. Not only is it hurting you, it's hurting the people you love. It's time to back off before you get yourself killed. We'll make sure Riley knows you're letting it go—"

"No, Joe." Davina rested her bloody hand on top of Joe's. "I gotta take this to the end. It's not just about me, it's about all the girls whose lives have been shattered. Riley *knew* he didn't have the right guy back then. Think about that. The cop's been actively protecting a serial rapist."

Joe shook his head. "He's been protecting his job and reputation."

"That's what I thought too, for the longest time. But now I honestly think Riley is protecting something else—and I think George Modica, Darren Rivers, and . . . Gerry died because of it."

The lights turned green and Joe pulled away, leaving the flashing lights in the rearview.

Davina stared blankly out the window at Dobson's Gym. *That was my home.*

CHAPTER SIXTY-ONE

FRIDAY, DOBSON'S GYM

ONCE JOE AND DAVINA HAD DRIVEN OFF, NICK LEFT THE Dobson's lot and drove around aimlessly for a while. He needed time to clear his head, to think. But spent much of the time stewing rather than actually thinking.

He lost track of time, eventually coming to realize he'd driven all the way to Darren Rivers's neighborhood. There, the landscaped lanes were crowded with people driving, walking, chatting on the sidewalk, and sitting on wrought-iron benches dotted around the neatly manicured foliage.

Why the fuck are so many people out tonight?

He'd forgotten it was Friday—the beginning of the weekend and a warm summer evening. Of course, folks would be out. Add to that the fact one of the upscale condos had become a crime scene. Nick imagined the ghoulish conversations taking place—people just *loved* a good murder.

Nick then wiped his eyes on the sleeve of his bloodstained dress shirt.

Darren was dead.

His Darren.

The realization hit Nick in a way it hadn't when the words had first come from Geoff Wong's lips, when he'd set off from Davina's apartment to get to Darren's place, only to find the lane leading to it blocked off.

It was no longer blocked, but the strip of visitor parking in front of the building was still host to two police cruisers. The CSI van was gone, leaving behind the yellow tape around the condo's front door, by which stood a solitary cop.

Nick parked the Beemer at the end of the guest parking area and contemplated approaching the cop.

For what purpose? To gain entry to Darren's apartment to take one final look around? To relive the last moment he'd spent with a living, breathing Darren—one in which they'd argued bitterly? Or to snoop around to see what Darren may have been up to behind his back?

After ten minutes or so of fierce internal deliberation, Nick decided against it. If his father found out he'd been at Darren's apartment, Nick would be peppered with far too many questions he wasn't prepared to answer. And, given he was covered in blood from playing hero to Davina, Nick's common sense told him the best thing to do was abandon any thoughts of getting into a crime scene.

He should just go home. It had been a long, draining night.

Reaching his apartment, Nick opened the door to silent darkness. He flipped on the lights and peered at the framed picture of him and Darren on the mantel; they'd taken it on their hiking trip in the Adirondacks the year before. Just a couple of guys out being guys in the great outdoors.

Right.

Nick stared at the photo for a moment or so before depositing his briefcase on the kitchen table and grabbing a beer from the fridge. Then, he fired up his laptop and sat down with it in the living room. His news feed was already filled with articles and speculation about the untimely demise of Darren Rivers of Richmond County Savings & Loan.

There was one particular photo of Darren circulating: he was smiling in the sunshine as the Hudson River rolled majestically in the background. Nick had taken that photo, and he was struck by a wave of grief he'd not felt since his mother passed away. Darren had been many things to Nick—a challenge, a mission, a lark, a campaign, a bold sexual adventure; Nick truly hadn't expected such an immense, growing sense of loss.

Nick put his beer down on the table and held his head in his hands. It was all too much. The idea of never seeing Darren again—of never *being with* Darren again—was devastating. Picking up the phone, he called his father.

"You heard about Darren?" Nick asked—no time or mood for niceties.

"Monaghan called me." Sean's reply was followed by a long, wheezing exhale. He was smoking a cigar.

"And you're celebrating?"

"What kind of question is that?"

"It's one less headache for you and your campaign: Darren wasn't on your side. I know you weren't on his."

"He made some stupid decisions," Sean growled. "And I did him a lot of favors."

"He did quite a few for you, Dad."

Sean was silent for a beat. "Why are we having this conversation right now, Nick?"

Nick pulled the phone away from his ear. Did he have the balls to tell his father about his relationship with Darren? He was certainly in the right kind of belligerent mood, and nothing he could say would hurt Darren.

"I don't know," was all Nick could manage to say. His heart was breaking; pissing off the old man could wait.

"Good. See you tomorrow." Sean ended the call.

Nick set his phone on the coffee table. Sean Delafield would never know what he and Darren had shared.

No one would.

Nick went into the living room and collected every photo of Darren he had—pictures taken at SBCA events, scholastic awards ceremonies, and the two of them in the Adirondacks. He yanked them from their frames and shredded every last one in his home office. Next, Nick grabbed

a black trash bag and began collecting everything Darren had given him—
a set of ornate wine bottle stoppers, a pair of hiking shoes, a wrist watch,
and a collection of bejeweled butt plugs. It all went into the trash bag,
which went into the kitchen compactor in his kitchen.

Nick took little pleasure in hitting the compactor's switch.

CHAPTER SIXTY-TWO

FRIDAY, RICHMOND UNIVERSITY MEDICAL CENTER

DAVINA SAT ON THE EDGE OF THE EXAM TABLE WHILE A WHIP-thin male doctor tended to her wounds. The worst of them—the deep slash to her upper left arm—he sealed with Steri-Strips, and a few of the others he coated with a cold liquid that would dry to make a flexible bandage.

"No serious damage," the doctor told Davina as he typed up his notes on a hospital-issued iPad. "You were very lucky, young lady."

"I told you I was okay," Davina chastised Joe, who watched patiently from a plastic chair in the corner. He still seemed concerned about her.

The doctor went on, "We don't want those strips to let go, so you need to take it easy for the next few weeks. Okay? No kick-boxing. No martial arts of any kind. And I'd like both of you to keep an eye out for evidence of post-traumatic symptoms such as bad dreams, issues with being in a crowd, or seeing people coming at you in your peripheral vision. You might be overly sensitive to those triggers even if you don't have PTSD, but better safe than sorry. I'd like you to reconsider talking to the trauma counselor, Davina."

Davina peered out through the gap in the emergency room curtain. There, she saw Angela Donato sitting alone in the waiting area and wondered if the woman realized she was akin to a portent: She only turned up when bad things happened.

"Thank you, no." Davina hated to sound ungrateful. "I'm okay, really —and I'm not . . ."

. . . *twelve anymore?*

As the words went unsaid, Davina's mind tormented her with the time she'd spent with the therapist, and how Angela had been the only one to believe her about the rape, the only one to actually *listen*.

Joe stood. "Is she free to go home now?"

The doctor smiled and gave a thumbs-up. "Remember, take it easy for at least two weeks. If you experience any unusual pain or swelling, call."

————

The ride back to Davina's apartment was mostly silent. She kept replaying the events of that night in her head: Darren dead. Gerry. The dark locker room. The attack she'd fought off. How'd she managed to survive that?

And, more importantly, why hadn't Gerry?

The lights were off inside the Blue Star Grocery when they pulled up. Above it, Davina's kitchen light was on.

"Oh my God, I forgot to call Millie."

"I texted her." Joe helped Davina out of the car and closed the door.

"Of course, you did." Davina gave Joe a pained smile. "She's waited up for me, bless her heart." Davina hugged herself; she still felt cold.

Joe draped his jacket around her shoulders. "Or she had another date."

They climbed the stairs and Davina put her key in the door. It was unlocked. She pushed open the door to see Millie sitting at the kitchen table, nursing a mug of cocoa.

Millie ran over. "I've been sitting here scared to death."

"Tell me about it." Davina threw her keys down on the entry table and dropped her fanny pack beside them.

"Shit, look at you." Millie pointed at the dried blood on Davina's clothes.

"Most of it's not mine." Davina's voice was soft, empty. "It'll wash off. I'll heal."

"Sit down. Let me get you something." Millie walked over to the kettle on the stove. "I can make you tea, coffee, or whatever you need."

"Is that cocoa?" Davina sat at the kitchen table.

"You bet your ass."

"I'll have some of that, Mil."

"Joe? Anything?" Millie offered.

"I'm good, thanks." Joe sat beside Davina and placed a hand on her knee. "I'm proud of you."

Davina met his eyes. "Why? I'm not. If I'd saved Gerry, then I'd be proud of me."

"There was nothing you could do," Joe soothed. "She was already . . . *gone* when you got there."

"She was like a mother to me, Joe. Gerry got me off the streets. She put a cot in the back of Dobson's and let me live there while I cleaned up. She put me in NA and made me go to school. Gerry gave me everything, and now she's dead because of me. If she'd been the target, they'd have been in the next borough by the time I got there."

Millie returned to the table with a fresh mug for Davina. "This is some fucked-up shit," she said. "I honestly didn't know how deep it all went."

"I did." Davina wrapped her fingers around the mug, warming them. "My childhood nightmares, the extreme anxiety, my fucked-up past. I've known for a while now just how deep this goes."

Joe removed his hand from Davina's knee and scratched his head. "How was it Nick just happened to be at Dobson's tonight? I really don't buy his bullshit story about unpacking equipment."

"You think he knew something?" Millie asked Davina.

Davina sipped her cocoa. "I can't believe Nick was there for any shady reason. But you're right, it doesn't make sense. He didn't know I'd be there."

Joe corrected her. "He *did* know. You told everyone after dinner you'd be heading to the gym to help Gerry."

"Shit," Davina said. "Then maybe he just wanted to see me?"

"Did anyone else know?" Joe asked.

"Just you and Millie, and Geoff. Gerry, of course." Davina looked to Millie and Joe for reassurance.

Joe chimed in, "What about Detective Riley?"

"Yeah." Davina took another sip. "There's a good chance he knows my every move. I wouldn't put it past him to put a tail on me."

"Seriously?" Joe said.

"How else would he show up so fast? He lives in Tottenville."

"Maybe he was working the night shift." Joe shrugged his shoulders. "Or maybe he was out to dinner or something. If you apply Occam's razor, the simplest explanation is the most likely."

"Joe, he showed up in minutes with three cruisers and the coroner's van prepared to collect corpses."

"If that's right, you're in serious danger, Davina." Joe was terrified. "You need to wash your hands of all of this before . . . before it's too late."

Davina glanced down at her hands; there were still spots where Gerry's blood clung to her skin. "I wish I could, Joe."

"I gotta go to bed." Millie got up and placed her mug in the sink. "If I keep on drinking this, I'm going to be up all night."

As Millie left them alone, Davina turned to Joe. "Thanks for being here."

"That's my job."

"Will you stay tonight?" Davina blurted out the words before she could change her mind; they hung in the silence between her and Joe.

Joe cocked his head. "Do you even need to ask?"

"No," Davina said and went to wash away Gerry Dobson's blood.

CHAPTER SIXTY-THREE

SATURDAY, DAVINA'S APARTMENT

Geoff's palms were sweaty. After he'd gone back to the *Advance*, after he'd tried to focus on all the moving parts and bizarre angles in this whacked-out, snowballing mess, he'd texted Davina and received no answer. Her lack of response troubled him.

She's probably in bed with the boyfriend for some life-affirming sex. And why the hell do I care?

Geoff tried to convince himself everything Gino Romano had spilled earlier that night couldn't wait 'til morning. But the pieces were coming together, and he reckoned Davina needed to know. Also, it was possible something Gino had told him would jog her memory.

Geoff wasn't the least bit surprised when Joe opened the door.

"I'm sorry it's so late," Geoff said by means of a greeting. "Can I come in?"

"Sure." Joe stepped aside to let Geoff in. "Davina is just showering."

Geoff followed him into the kitchen, watching him open the fridge.

"Care if you sleep tonight?" Joe asked.

"Oh, uh, one of those sparkling waters—if there are any left."

Joe pulled a can of pomegranate seltzer water out of the fridge and handed it over.

"How is she?" Geoff sat down at the table.

"I guess she's okay—*physically*." Joe sat opposite the reporter. "The hospital said there were no major injuries."

"She's a tough lady."

"Sometimes *too* tough." Joe took a sip of his drink and set the can down. "I wish she'd let me take care of her."

"Modern women aren't into that whole knight in shining Armani thing."

Joe smiled crookedly and shook his head. "It's in her somewhere. Something more traditional—and I'm going to find it."

"Good luck with that." Geoff raised his drink. "To fishing."

"To fishing." Joe tapped Geoff's can with his own.

Davina emerged from the hallway, a blue towel wrapped tight around her body, shoulders bare. Her skin glistened with shower dew.

"Geoff?" Davina pulled the towel tighter.

A wave of unexpected embarrassment spread beneath his skin. "I'm sorry. I don't mean to intrude."

"It's fine, um . . ." Davina pulled a hand through her damp hair. "Just let me get dressed." As Davina tip-toed back down the hall, Geoff turned to Joe. "You're one lucky son of a bitch, y'know?"

Joe smiled. "She'll only be a minute."

Joe wasn't wrong, for moments later, Davina reappeared in a pair of panda bear pajama shorts and a white cotton T-shirt. Joining them at the table, she pulled her wet hair back into a bun and expertly fixed in place a plain black scrunchy.

Geoff let out a weary sigh. "I'd have come earlier, but I had to go back to the *Advance* to finish Darren's story . . . and yours."

Davina's eyes sharpened, and she leaned her elbows on the table. "What's the official word on Darren?"

"It looked like a heart attack at first, but it's since morphed into a criminal investigation. I guess after George Modica's death, somebody saw more than a coincidence."

"Makes sense," Joe said.

"Not like the cops are going to say. Whatever caused the shift, the docs apparently didn't catch it right away," Geoff explained. "Maybe drugs in the system, wounds that were hard to see until they got Darren on the slab. Frankly, I didn't believe it was a heart attack. Darren Rivers was a young, healthy guy."

Joe lifted a brow. "There's always the possibility of underlying health issues."

"Possible, sure." Geoff took another sip of his drink. "Look, the reason I'm here is because I met with Gino Romano last night. He told me some things . . . Well, I felt a bunch of texts wasn't the appropriate way—"

"It's okay." Despite everything she'd been through, there was warmth in Davina's eyes. "You don't have to apologize for being here. You're not bothering me. You're helping, Geoff."

"The skinny on the Sean Delafield video, Davina, is that it was filmed six years ago." Geoff paused to get his thoughts in order. "It was filmed in Stavros's basement rec room, and pretty much everyone in Sean Delafield's collection of skeevy businessmen was there."

"Riley?" Davina's voice was hushed, her eyes dark.

Good question. "That's the one person Gino didn't mention."

Davina scoffed. "Convenient."

"Kevin Monaghan was the one who made the video—apparently at Darren Rivers's request. Even back then, Darren was using him as his fixer." Geoff fiddled absently with his seltzer can. "The next point of interest was that the video sent to the *Advance* was carefully edited to *not* show any of the other partygoers. That was Darren's idea, sanctioned by Scott Kantor. Without our tech guy knowing about the hidden frames on either side of a cut, we'd never have recognized Gino's reflection in the wine glass, or the others'—or the telltale pictures of Greece in the background."

"I wonder if that was on purpose," Davina spoke up. "Subliminal finger-pointing?"

"If you ask me, it was down to ignorance," Geoff countered. "They obviously didn't know the finer details of digital movie editing."

"Isn't Kantor a political guy?" Joe asked.

"Yes." Geoff nodded. "He's the chairman of the Staten Island Republican County Committee. Both he and Darren were convinced Sean Delafield didn't stand a chance in the council race. The idea of doctoring the video and using it as a weapon against Sean was Darren's idea—but everyone was on board."

Davina's eyes widened. "I saw them all together at the bank Thursday. Darren and the rest of them came out of the bank's conference room. I'll bet they were hashing all this out."

Smart girl. "I'd say so." Geoff paused as an ambulance siren dopplered by the apartment; red, flashing lights briefly lit up the room and splashed across the ceiling.

Davina tensed and clenched her fists. "I hate that sound," she murmured.

Joe put a protective hand on her shoulder.

"So," Geoff continued, keen to get everything he'd learned out in the open. "Kevin Monaghan fired off the first teaser email to me and copied in Sean. He used a burner email account and a personal VPN; hence it couldn't be traced. Sean didn't bite, and that's why the video was eventually sent to the *Advance*. Davina, I have a question: If you saw the video, and you were in it, do you think you'd recognize yourself?"

Davina was taken aback. "I don't know. I was constantly high back then; it's mostly a complete blur."

"If you did recall being there that night, it would make a huge difference to our story." Geoff slipped his cell phone from his pocket. "Are you willing to at least take a look?"

Davina glanced sideways at Joe for support. Joe was so grim, Geoff thought it comical.

"Okay," Davina said quietly.

Geoff pulled up the video and handed Davina the phone. He studied her face as she watched the footage, as did Joe.

The video finished and Davina handed back the phone. "It *could* be me. I just don't know. I *honestly* don't remember."

"Although the girls are clearly underage, if there's no substantial evidence to put you there, it'll be difficult to prosecute Sean Delafield. Unless, of course, we can track down one of the other girls and get her to testify she was underage at the time. It's not illegal to have a private party with exotic dancers, and there's no way of proving from the video if sex was paid for. The video would impugn Sean's character, but it wouldn't put him in jail."

Joe said, "There's nothing wrong with impugning his character if it keeps him off the city council."

"Yes, but if Sean is really the corrupt individual that we think him to be, getting him behind bars is definitely more appropriate. I'm wondering if Sean found out who orchestrated leaking the video and ordered punitive action."

Joe's eyes narrowed. "You're suggesting he might be guilty of more than partying with underage girls?"

"It wouldn't surprise me in the least." Geoff's reply hung in the air.

"Riley's the one who should be behind bars." Davina's voice was almost a growl.

Joe got up and threw his soda can into the recycle bin. "You're back on Riley again?"

"Do you blame me? You heard what Packer said."

"But does that make Riley a rapist?" Joe confronted Davina. "Yeah, he's a piece of shit cop. Hell, he's a fucking *shark*, but we gotta be careful. He's already looking for excuses to harass you, D."

Davina wrapped her arms around herself, drawing Geoff's gaze. Vulnerability haunted her eyes, the set of her mouth, and her submissive posture. It was not the Davina Speers he'd gotten to know, and Geoff didn't much care for this version.

"Guys," he said, "this is bigger than a piece of shit cop who harasses innocent people."

Davina frowned and shook her head. "What do you mean, bigger? Bigger how? Bigger than a serial rapist? You think politics is a more important story than a guy who methodically destroys lives?"

CHAPTER SIXTY-FOUR

SATURDAY, DAVINA'S APARTMENT

CONFUSION LEFT A BITTER TASTE IN DAVINA'S MOUTH. GEOFF was a reporter and it was his job to expose corruption, but . . .

His eyes met hers. "I know catching the *real* Son of Cropsey is important, Davina. I genuinely empathize with that. What you and those other girls went through is deplorable, but this is a bigger, broader story about corruption destroying the systems we all depend upon."

Joe was perplexed; he really wasn't following.

Geoff's eyes burned bright with journalistic zeal. "This could be the biggest story of the decade. It's a game changer. It'll bring Staten Island to its knees."

Davina's voice came out as a ragged growl. "So, this is just about breaking the big story for you? The *story* is only important if it brings Son of Cropsey to justice, Geoff. I won't be able to rest until he's in jail, and neither will his other victims. They're all scarred—deeply, and in more than the physical sense."

"Do you think having the real perp behind bars is going to somehow magically heal you, Davina?" Geoff snapped his fingers. "Just like that?"

"What the hell, Geoff? This is not just about finding closure for some past trauma. The guy is still out there ruining lives! Just ask Mary Lamont, Jessica Balducci . . . or Mariah Washington."

The journalist flinched as if she'd slapped him. "I'm not arguing against naming and nailing the rapist, Davina. I'm just suggesting your fixation with Riley is clouding your judgment. You don't seem to be able to separate the two things."

"Maybe they shouldn't be separated. Maybe Riley is the rapist."

Geoff sat back in his chair. "Do you really believe that? He was around you all the time back then. Don't you think you would've known if it was him?"

It was Davina's turn to feel slapped. Wouldn't she have known if Riley had raped her that night—recognized the stink of the cheap aftershave? "Maybe," she argued, "but if he wasn't . . . involved in some way, why the insistence my story was made up? He wasn't just skeptical. The asshole was *adamant*."

"Davina," said Joe quietly, "think about it. If Riley ever admits you're telling the truth, he admits he bagged the wrong guy. And if he does that, his incompetence will be exposed—and just think of the lawsuits for negligence against him and the city."

Geoff leaned forward once more. "Davina, you were assaulted and left traumatized. You've done a hell of a job putting your life back together, and you're stronger now than you've ever been. Riley may be a shark, but you're a fucking killer whale. A powerful, smart woman. I think—no, I *know* you're smart enough to see this is bigger than Riley's corruption. Joe's right—he may be just covering his ass, nothing more."

"And what do you want out of this, Geoff? A Pulitzer for breaking the story of the decade?" Davina asked.

Geoff clenched his fists, his eyes angry. "I don't want a fucking Pulitzer. I want to bring down a racket that has killed people and their political manipulation of laws and lives that are affecting the entire community of Staten Island. If this is connected to the Son of Cropsey case, then we'll get that bastard, too. And, if not, it still needs to be exposed before anyone else gets hurt. C'mon, Davina, think. Gerry

Dobson was one of the people caught up in this thing with Delafield. No way she died because Riley got the wrong man."

Tears sprung to Davina's eyes. "She died because of *me!* I was Riley's target!" She pounded her chest with a fist. "*Me!*"

"Maybe so," Geoff conceded. "But if you were, it wasn't because Riley arrested the wrong Son of Cropsey. It's more likely because you may just be one of the girls in Monaghan's video, which means you could topple some powerful men."

"Jesus," murmured Joe. He stretched out his arm across the table to Geoff. "May I see it?"

Davina stared at him. "Are you sure?"

"Yeah."

Geoff cued up the video and handed over the phone. He said to Davina, "You genuinely have no memory of that party?"

Davina willed herself to breathe. "What do you want me to say, Geoff? Yeah, I honestly, truthfully have no memory of it. If I was at the party, I'd have been too shitfaced to know my own goddamn name. You're right about all the corruption, and I get why that's your focus. But *my* focus has to be on what it means to Son of Cropsey's victims that he's obviously still on the island and back to his old tricks while Riley walks around acting like he's the right hand of justice—it's like our rape just goes on and on. That's why Joy Sheridan killed herself. It's why Elizabeth Pine checked out of the real world and has nothing to look forward to but people bringing her M&Ms."

"Fuck," said Joe quietly.

Davina and Geoff both turned to look at him.

"What?" said Geoff.

Joe set the phone in the middle of the table; the video paused. "That." He pointed.

Davina and Geoff both leaned closer to see what he was pointing at. The little Goth girl was executing the pirouette that had set Sean Delafield on his ass. Her bare arms were outflung, revealing a bruise on her left wrist.

Joe enlarged the image with a flick of his fingertips, and the bruise took on form and definition. Davina saw it wasn't a bruise at all—it was a tattoo of a flower.

A chrysanthemum.

Davina felt the blood drain from her face. "I-I don't remember."

"I think," said Geoff, "somebody does." Pausing, he raised his hands as if to push his thoughts back into line. "Okay, you focus on what you have to focus on. I gotta find out more about the guy who made the video—Kevin Monaghan. All I know so far is he's a retired narco detective who went through a messy divorce and now he's a security contractor."

Joe added, "I've met the guy a couple of times. He seems like a bully—a lot of bluster—you know the type."

"He's Riley's fucking Mini-Me." Geoff threw back the rest of his drink. "I'm gonna talk with some cops tomorrow. Probably ring Packer, too—see if I can get more from him on the Son of Cropsey bust."

Davina imagined she saw something in the journalist's eyes: *I'm not giving up on you.* She took another deep breath and forced herself to let go of her remaining anger. If one of Sean Delafield's cronies *was* the rapist, or was covering up for someone who was, then Geoff's line of investigation could get them closer to the truth. It made sense to do everything she could to help.

"What's the guy's ex-wife's name?" Davina asked. "I'll try making contact with her in the morning."

Geoff's nostrils flared. "Good thinking. It's *Sandy* Monaghan—or maybe she's back to being Sandy Burke. Anyhow, she still lives on Staten Island. I'll get you a phone number tomorrow. She's a hairstylist." Geoff got up from the table and walked his can to the recycles. "I gotta go. It's a busy day tomorrow—the Lady of Mount Carmel Feast. You going?"

What the hell?

"I wasn't planning on it, even before . . ." Davina was unable to finish the sentence.

Joe shot Geoff a worried glance. "With everything that's happened, you're taking in a street fair?"

Geoff gave a wry smile. "Because all our local political movers and shakers are gonna be there—it'll be a good place to hear things, to watch our key people interact with each other . . . and *you*." He pointed at Davina. "You really have to go—with Joe. I'm not sure any of us are safe on our own right now. Meet me tomorrow morning at the shrine? 9-ish?"

"I have NA tomorrow morning," Davina told him. "And I really *do* need to go."

"Understood. 11-ish, then?"

When Geoff had gone, a chill came over Davina, sweeping her up into a fugue of fear and darkness. *I'm not sure any of us are safe anymore on our own,* the journalist had said, and it echoed just how she'd felt since the first time Son of Cropsey had lain on top of her, choked her, marked her.

Her throat tightened at the thought as tears pressed for release. How the hell was she supposed to go on without Gerry? Maybe it was time to give up, to admit defeat and surrender, to just save herself and leave Staten Island.

Maybe.

But maybe she had to dig a little deeper. See it through. If she gave in now, what would Gerry think?

Joe stood in front of Davina. He put his hands on her shoulders and squeezed them gently. "Let's get you to bed. You look done in."

"I am."

Joe pulled Davina to her feet and wrapped his arms around her— gently, loosely, hands resting on the small of her back. Davina leaned her head on his chest. He reached up and stroked her hair.

"You don't have to go to the festival tomorrow if you don't want to," Joe said.

"I want to. Geoff's right. Maybe we can pick up some information. With George and Darren dead, there'll be some raw nerves. And there's this." She raised her left wrist.

Joe kissed the chrysanthemum tattoo, then escorted Davina down the dark hall past Millie's bedroom door. The floorboards creaked, and Davina hoped they wouldn't disturb Millie, if she was even sleeping at all.

In Davina's bedroom, Joe flipped the light switch, turning on Davina's bedside lamp. Davina shuffled to the bed, pulling off her top as she went, leaving on her sports bra and pajama bottoms. She folded down the comforter and climbed in beneath the light summer blanket. Her damp hair wet the pillowcase.

As Joe undressed, Davina admired his body: powerful, lean. Why was it so hard to be intimate with someone so damn hot?

Stupid question. Davina knew why. It was a deep-rooted problem she was desperate to conquer.

Joe pulled off his pants, revealing black boxer briefs distorted at the front by his growing erection. He climbed into bed, lying face-to-face with Davina; it'd been weeks since he'd spent the night in her bed, and she realized how much she needed him.

He placed a hand on her hip, which Davina covered with her own, their fingers entwining.

Joe touched her cheek with his other hand. "I love you."

Davina's mouth went dry. Why was it so difficult for her to respond when Joe told her he loved her? She loved him deeply, but by repeating those words, Davina feared she'd make an implicit promise she wasn't sure she could keep. If life had taught her one thing, it was how ephemeral it could be. How changeable.

Instead of a reply, Davina kissed Joe's parted lips and flicked her tongue across them. He moaned. Davina pressed her mouth to his, the kiss urgent, her tongue probing, searching for his; at that moment, all she craved was physical and emotional connection, intimacy.

Davina kicked off her pajamas, then sat up and straddled Joe's hips, placing her hands flat on his muscular chest. She felt him hard and hot beneath her. Heeding the answering flush of heat between her legs, she pulled the sports bra off over her head.

Joe's hands skimmed Davina's breasts before pulling her down for another kiss. She wasn't afraid of Joe's arms around her—they didn't feel suffocating like so many times before. They felt *liberating*.

CHAPTER SIXTY-FIVE

SATURDAY, DAVINA'S APARTMENT

Having made his way out into the night, something made Geoff swing by Dobson's on his way home; he expected to see a police presence there. There wasn't. The parking lot was empty, dark, silent. Geoff thought about what had happened there that night, and about what it had done to Davina—about what might have happened to Davina had she not been so adept at defending herself. He also considered what might happen to him if he kept after the Delafield party story. Should he buy a gun? Carry Mace? Hire a bodyguard?

Arriving at his apartment building, Geoff pulled into the parking garage. Glancing into his rearview mirror at the automatic gate, he saw a dark figure slip through as it closed.

Fuck.

Terrified, Geoff turned off the car and sat in his designated parking space with the doors locked. He scanned the dimly lit garage for signs of movement.

Nothing.

The minutes dragged by and Geoff detected no noises, no movement.

He considered calling the police before convincing himself he was being overly paranoid and what he'd seen had been nothing more than a shadow. Also, he realized he couldn't stay in his car all night and allow fear to rule his life.

He got out and locked the car.

Walking quickly, Geoff carried his briefcase in one hand, his suit coat draped in the crook of his arm and his cell phone in the other hand. Over in the corner, between the elevator and the stairwell, was the bright blue light of the panic phone. It offered some comfort.

To Geoff, his leather-soled dress shoes sounded absurdly loud on the cement floor as he strode with purpose toward the elevator. Each car he passed, Geoff peered into the shadows surrounding it, expecting the sinister black figure he *thought* he'd seen to leap out and choke the life out of him. Davina's story really had gotten to him.

Almost at the elevator doors, he heard a low, metallic scraping sound from behind. Heart pounding painfully in his chest, Geoff's walk became a sprint as he abandoned the idea of waiting for the elevator and bolted to the stairwell door. He shoved it open and vaulted up the stairs two, three at a time to the ground floor. There, he rammed the second door open with his back.

Someone stood on the other side of the door, as if he'd been waiting for Geoff. He was a hefty guy with a long, brown beard and a scruffy Metallica T-shirt.

"You okay, dude?" His voice was gruff, gravelly.

"I . . ." Geoff glanced down the stairwell. "Just a little paranoid. Thought I saw someone sneak in down there."

"Huh. Hope you're wrong. But if you're not . . ." The bearded rammed a pudgy fist into the opposite palm. The smacking sound made Geoff jump. "Dude," he said, "you look like you could use a drink." He skirted around past Geoff and disappeared into the stairwell.

I'm gonna puke.

Geoff's legs shook so badly he spent a couple minutes leaning against the wall. There was no one in the corridor that led off to the lobby. And always , Sid the security guard sat behind his desk reading a gun magazine.

Sight for sore eyes—all six-foot-five, 260 pounds of him. Geoff allowed himself to relax and made his way down the hallway.

Sid smiled. "Good evening, Mr. Wong."

"Good evening, Sid." He sketched a salute as he crossed to the elevator and prodded the up arrow. Waiting, he glanced around the quiet lobby. He was safe and fully prepared to accept that his mind had played tricks on him down in the garage. It was late, he was tired, and it had been one hell of a day.

The elevator arrived and Geoff stepped in, breathing easier as the car climbed. The third-floor hallway was empty and eerily quiet. It was 2:00 a.m. when Geoff finally entered the sanctuary of his apartment. He double-locked the door and slotted on the security chain for good measure.

Although he was exhausted, Geoff took his Metallica-loving neighbor's advice and poured himself a tall scotch. Then, he opened the fridge and pulled out a block of cheddar cheese, which he put on a plate with a knife and crackers.

Geoff sat with his food and booze at the kitchen counter, where he set up his laptop and composed an email to his editor.

———

Stan,

I know you're a night owl, so you probably heard about the incident at Dobson's Gym. What you may not know is that not only was Gerry Dobson murdered, but Davina Speers was almost a victim of the same assailants. The police say they are all dead. Davina doesn't think she killed them. In fact, she's sure of that. Just wanted you to know I'm on it. Spoke to Gino Romano, and have a lot to share. Hope you're bringing donuts to the office tomorrow, 'cause it's going to be a doozy of a day.

Not sure, but someone may have been following me tonight. Or I'm just losing my fucking mind. Either way, keep an eye out. You know as much as I do.

Geoff

He pressed Send, listened for the confirming *whoosh*, and closed his laptop. That really was enough for one night.

Davina was right: all shit had broken loose after Joy Sheridan's death, and not on its own. Davina was bringing things to the surface that had been long buried. Geoff was grateful she'd come to him with her story, but he was beginning to wonder if his involvement might eventually cost him his life.

Geoff's phone lit up. A text from Stan.

Just read your email. Stay safe, comrade.

CHAPTER SIXTY-SIX

SATURDAY, FEAST OF OUR LADY OF MOUNT CARMEL

BY NOON, THE FEAST OF OUR LADY OF MT. CARMEL WAS WELL underway. Located in a historical district on Amity Street in Rosebank, it was a place out of its time and completely alien to its urban American location. The shrine itself was like a doll house version of a European cathedral with its ornate chambers open on one side to the penitent worshippers and admiring crowds attending it during the three-day festival in honor of the saint.

A statue of the Virgin Mary in her traditional blue-and-white gown stood among the shrubs next to the shrine, reminding Davina of a little statuette she'd seen in Elizabeth Pine's room at the nursing home. Did Elizabeth pray to the Blessed Virgin every day?

The shrine's structure was decidedly organic—as if it had grown up out of the earth in a green, tree-shrouded grotto—and it reminded Davina of Antonio Gaudi's great cathedral in Barcelona. Much like Gaudi's works, Our Lady of Mt. Carmel's shrine was inlaid with polished stones and inhabited by figures of the divine. It had been the creation of Vito

Russo, once president of the Our Lady of Carmel Society, a mutual aid society founded by Italian immigrants.

On a regular day, the grotto and surrounding park was quiet and sparsely attended by the faithful . . . along with the ubiquitous tourists, of course. But on the Feast Day, it came alive with food kiosks, artisans' stalls, and game booths that overflowed to take over the surrounding streets. There was a stage where bands played, competing with the myriad performers who set up impromptu street concerts here and there.

Davina had never been a religious person but understood how such beauty might inspire faith and hope and a certain quivering sense of awe and peace. She had been raised going to St. Mary's Roman Catholic Church on Sundays. All of that changed when Davina's mom hit the bottle and gave up on God. Davina wondered sometimes if that was why she'd given up on him herself.

Joe appeared with an Italian ice in hand. He handed it over, along with a tiny spoon. "So, you weren't kidding when you told me you've never come to the shrine before?"

Davina shook her head.

"I want our children to go to church."

Davina found the statement oddly comforting. Smiling, she spooned some of the red ice into Joe's mouth. He scooped a spoonful himself and popped it in Davina's mouth; it was lovely, cool, and refreshing.

"*I* want a slice of pizza," she said.

Joe made a face. "There's an infinite array of authentic Italian food, and you want pizza?"

"I'm a pretty basic girl."

Joe laughed. "No, you are not."

They wandered over to one of the countless pizza booths, one with a jolly red, white, and green sign. The smell was delectable; it wasn't the kind of pizza to be found at one of the chains—it was authentic Staten Island pizza at its best.

The pizza vendor leaned over the counter. He had tomato sauce stains on his white apron. "What'll you have, miss?"

Davina held up her finger. "One slice, please. White."

"One white pizza, coming up." The vendor placed a slice on his paddle with expert ease, then shoved it into his oven. "Two minutes. That'll be four dollars."

Davina contemplated Joe as he fished out a handful of crumpled dollar bills from his pocket and handed them over. Their early morning hours together had been perfect; it had been the freest and most intimate Davina had ever allowed herself to be. What had helped her to open up? Perhaps it was a growing trust. Joe was helping her through her journey, helping to piece her back together.

Her tickle of affection faltered as a small, wiry woman in purple and black workout gear jogged by. Davina grimaced. Nothing would ever bring Gerry back—she was gone forever.

Then came the unwelcome but inevitable question: Would Davina be able to set foot in Dobson's again? Once Gerry's death had sunk in, it had occurred to Davina that she no longer had a job—unless there was some way that she could keep the gym open herself. Dare she hope Gerry had made provisions for that in her will—if she had one?

Davina sighed. On Monday, she was just going to have to bite the bullet and talk to the police and the bank—and attempt to find another gym to take her on.

"White pizza!" the pizza vendor announced, sliding Davina's slice across his narrow counter.

Davina grabbed the paper plate and told the man thank you.

"Let's go find some shade." Joe pointed to a wooden bench some yards away. Heat wave over, it was now in the mid-seventies, but direct sun could still be unpleasantly warm.

"We'll have to keep an eye on the grotto for Geoff."

Beneath the shade of a big old chestnut tree, Joe finished the dregs of his red ice and Davina took her first bite of pizza; it was the only thing she'd eaten so far that day—with the exception of half a cake donut—and it tasted appropriately divine.

In the distance, a Frankie Valli cover band played "Sherry Baby," and people young and old danced.

Davina was enjoying herself. She felt as relaxed as she could be. The warm breeze ruffled her hair, people all around wore smiles, and though Davina was painfully aware of the spreading darkness just beneath the shiny surface, she refused to think about Gerry.

That would come later, when she had time to grieve properly.

As Davina finished her pizza, she spotted Geoff by the grotto. He wore a pair of black aviator sunglasses. That, combined with the white button-up shirt and slacks, gave him the appearance of an undercover cop. She waved him over.

"Sorry I'm late. Had to make some phone calls."

Joe asked, "Anything?"

Geoff grimaced. "Lips are suddenly very tight. I don't know what I would have done without Gino Romano spilling."

"He's a good guy." Davina placed the paper plate on her lap. "Now I hope he's good enough to forgive my rent since I'm now unemployed."

"I'll hope right along with you," Geoff said. "Look, I'm gonna go grab a slice, okay?"

Davina's cell dinged in her fanny pack. She nodded absently at Geoff and fished it out. The text was from Nick.

U around?

At Mt. Carmel Feast w Joe & Geoff.

How very Staten Island of you.

Ha.

Joe gave Davina's phone a sideways glance. "Who's texting?"
"Nick."
"Really." Joe got up to throw his ice cup away.

Got some hot news.

?

Learned something about the link between Gerry's murder and Cropsey.

Davina's eyes widened; it really wasn't the conversation she wanted to have via SMS.

Call u?

Not alone. But sweet u need to hear my voice.

Davina ignored Nick's inappropriate remark.

What news?

Know the guys at gym last night.

Davina's heart felt as if it had been stuck in a deep freeze.

????

Promise u won't get any wild [lightbulb emoji] when I tell you.

Tell!

K. They were on dad's payroll once, but

He stopped typing.

Davina waited a second or two then pummeled her cell phone's screen.

R u you kidding me?

Not this way. Need to get everyone together again. Lots to discuss. Can y'all meet me at Battery Weed in 30?

Davina typed "K" then looked around for Joe and Geoff. Geoff was approaching, pizza slice in hand. He sat down next to her and took a bite, giving a blissful roll of his eyes.

Davina eyed the slice skeptically as she switched off her phone. "I'm surprised they have Hawaiian pizza at an Italian festival."

"Don't judge me."

"Not judging. Just surprised."

Geoff gazed around. "I gotta admit, I'm not seeing anyone here that I expected to see. Scott Kantor, Kevin Monaghan…"

"Sean Delafield?"

"That is a surprise." Geoff took another bite of pizza. "Given he's campaigning for office."

"Nick just texted me," Davina told him. "He wants us to meet at Battery Weed in thirty minutes."

Geoff's brow furrowed. "Why?"

"He said he scored information about Gerry's murder and how it's connected to Son of Cropsey. He said he knows the guys who killed Gerry."

Geoff dabbed at his lips with a paper napkin. "Okay, then let's go."

Davina stood up from the bench as Joe arrived back. "We're leaving," she told him.

"Now?"

"Yeah," said Geoff. "Nick apparently has some information about Gerry's murder."

"What could he possibly—?"

Davina cut him off. "He claims the guys who did it worked for his dad at one time. Wouldn't tell me more over the phone."

Joe shook his head. "Could this get any stranger?"

"We can take my car," Geoff said. "It's just across the park. And please don't say things like that. I think it's bad luck."

CHAPTER SIXTY-SEVEN

SATURDAY, BATTERY WEED, FORT WADSWORTH

Standing atop the third-floor roof of Battery Weed, Sean Delafield gazed out at the Atlantic Ocean. Barges navigated the distant waters, and the sun played hide-and-seek with the clouds, fitfully illuminating the raucous seabirds wheeling overhead. The Verrazzano Narrows Bridge loomed just south of the fortifications, spanning the glinting waters to the opposite shore where Fort Hamilton—still an active army installation—stood sentry over the Narrows. The weather was wonderfully mild, the sea breeze most pleasant.

The roof of the old battery was overgrown with wild grass and weeds, and littered with chunks of crumbled concrete that scuffed his Ferragamos, but Sean had to admit the views were killer. In private hands, the place would make a great venue for picnicking tourists, concerts, or some other revenue generator. The federal government—with its usual ineptitude—was making a hash out of exploiting the commercial capacity of the properties around Fort Wadsworth. Now, if *he* owned them—

"Done." Standing next to his father, Nick finished up a text message and fumbled his phone into his back pocket.

The two Delafields were alone at the top of the fort. It was closed to the public for the week for maintenance—although the top level was *never* open—but Sean had slipped the security guy a few hundreds to let them in and make himself scarce. For some dumb reason known only to himself, Nick had insisted they climb up through the defunct lighthouse, which pissed Sean off. His new suit—a suit so new he'd only pulled it out of the Nordstrom garment bag that morning—was smudged with dirt and moss stains from the walls of the stairwell.

"Why are we here, Nick?" he asked.

Nick made a loopy face, lifted his arms high in the air, and did a 360-degree turn. "Just look around you, Dad."

"Yeah, the views are great." Sean's tone was flat, bored—he had places to be, people to schmooze.

Nick's frustration showed. "You talk about recreating Staten Island, but you've ignored one of its most important locations. Just think about all the things this could be."

"Unfortunately, it's federally owned." *The kid is more ambitious than I am.* Sean had to admit, the thought was not displeasing, even if Nick's enthusiasm was misdirected.

Nick took a step toward his dad, his eyes alight, perspiration standing out on his upper lip. "What if it wasn't? Can you imagine how much condos would go for in the shadow of this fortress? Maybe if we got the lighthouse working again? Opened up the grounds for big events?"

"The yuppies would go wild over it," Sean admitted. "But I've got too many other things on my plate right now, Nick. I don't have the time to kick off a campaign to get developers interested in something like this. You're jumping the gun, boy." He gave his son a narrow-eyed once-over. "In fact, you're *jumpy*. And you're sweating like a pig—you on something again?"

Nick's laugh was hollow, mechanical. "If I show enthusiasm for the family business, I must be high? I can't understand how sometimes you think big and sometimes you can't think at all." Shrugging off his coat, Nick draped it over the stone parapet.

"Fuck this." Sean began walking away. "I'm going to the Mount Carmel wing-ding for a calzone."

Nick grabbed the back of his father's shirt. "Don't walk away from me!" His voice tone demonstrated anger and desperation.

Pulling free, Sean spun around. "How *dare* you put your hands on me, you fucking punk. What the hell has gotten into you? You've been acting like some psycho—I don't even want to know you right now."

Nick cringed visibly at the cutting remark, anger flashing in his eyes. "You never listen to me. All I ever wanted was your fucking approval, and you treat me like the competition. I'm working full time on your campaign—"

"That's right. *My* campaign. You seem to forget that, Nick. It's like you're trying to take me down, not help me win. Well, you're not gonna do it without a fight." Sean raised a fist. "Just 'cause you're my son doesn't mean I won't plant this in your face."

Nick's countenance darkened. "Don't. Threaten. Me."

"You weak little pansy," Sean snarled; the kid didn't have it in him to take anyone on, let alone Sean Delafield. "Two weeks till the primary and that fuck Darren dies on me. I needed his support, damn it! If losing that wasn't enough, I got you laying this-this dumbfuck pipe dream on me? You think I don't have enough on my mind?"

Nick laughed in his face. "You're so fucking ignorant."

Sean was taken aback. In all the years they'd worked side by side, his son had never spoken to him that way. "What the hell did you just say to me?"

"I said, you're *ignorant*. You believe what everyone tells you. Darren *pretended* to be back in your corner just to play into your fucking ego. Behind your back, he was finding ways to get you out of the race."

"Bullshit."

"*Bullshit?* It was Darren who sent the video to the paper. He was the fucking ringleader of a conspiracy to get you out of the council race. Your so-called friends and supporters—they all want their piece of what you've got to give, but they've turned their backs on you. *I'm* the only one in your corner now." Nick jabbed a thumb into his own chest. "*Me.*"

Sean took in a deep breath and exhaled loudly. The boy had to be lying. The team was with him 100 percent of the way. Sure, Darren had gotten cold feet for a short while, but Sean knew he'd win him over. "And you know all this—how?"

"Darren told me."

"On his death bed, no doubt?"

"Ask Geoff Wong. He knows."

Sean waved a dismissive hand. "That fucking Slant? I don't care how he got that fucking video—it's not going anywhere. Wong called me himself to say he's not gonna leak it. He only wanted to know who sent it. I didn't know then, and I don't know now."

Nick's mouth twisted as if something bitter had filled it. "Is Davina Speers the girl in the video?"

"Why do you care who's in the video? That girl's nothing, she's damaged goods, fucked in the head. But yeah, now you mention it, it is her—how could I forget that sweet little ass?"

Nick closed his eyes. "You're *sure?*"

"Sure, I'm sure." Sean was puzzled. Why the fuck was his son so bothered about his ex-girlfriend's little sister? "She had a flower tattooed on her wrist. What did your mom used to call 'em? *Mums.* Chrysanthemums. The dumb little slut. So, what if she was there? We partied, she and her friends all got paid—everyone was happy."

"You think you're fucking indestructible," Nick snarled "News flash, Dad—you're not."

"Bullshit. And it's bullshit Darren sent the video. It was probably that little slut—she and her fucking boss were sniffing around the business association. Who the fuck is going to listen to some junkie stripper anyway?"

"Wong is listening to her. The *Advance* is listening to her."

A cold tingle of fear stirred and began crawling up Sean Delafield's spine. "This is why you brought me here, isn't it, Nick? Fort Wadsworth condos were just a come-on. What you really want is to fool me into believing my associates are doing shit behind my back, just so you can be the Man. Fat fucking chance."

Nick shook his head. "Actually, I wasn't going to bring it up. I was hoping to get you all fired up with a new project. Distract you. But it's fucking obvious you need to know who's *really* in your corner, Dad." Stepping closer, he lowered his voice. "Don't worry, I'm taking care of things."

Sean didn't much care for the unhinged look in his son's eyes. "*Taking care of things?* What the hell does that mean, Nick? What the hell have you done?" He folded his arms across his chest, a symbolic barrier between him and his son. He'd never seen the kid with such raw, nervous energy before, even when he was using.

"Darren *never* supported you. He never shut up about how you should be stopped from ever holding office again. Even when we were in bed together."

Nick's supposed revelation came as little surprise to Sean. His snoops had told him about his dalliance with Rivers back in its early days. What did surprise him was Nick had waited so long to taunt him with it. "So what? The guy's dead—can't do squat now."

"I did it for you, Dad."

"Did what, son?"

"I killed Darren to get him out of the way—so he wouldn't get in yours."

Scared now of his own flesh and blood, Sean backed up a step, hands raised, palms out. "What the fuck, Nick?"

Nick stepped closer, smiling. "There's nothing for you to worry about. I'm handling everything."

"Stay away from me, Nick." Sean turned and ran back toward the lighthouse. Stumbling through the grass, he heard Nick's footfalls close behind.

"*Dad!*"

He knew he had no chance of outrunning the younger, fitter Delafield, so Sean stopped and turned, fists clenched and at the ready. As Nick caught up, Sean threw a punch, which landed on the side of Nick's head. Nick toppled over, clutching his jaw. Sean dropped to one knee and punched him hard in the ribs.

"They'll put you away for life, you fucking idiot!"

Coughing, fighting for breath, Nick sputtered, "It needed to be done."

Sean stood back up and paced, hands pressed to his face. "I can't believe this. *I can't fucking believe this.* This is your sick way of protecting me?"

Groaning in pain, Nick sat up, holding his side. "Yes. Which is why Davina has to go, too. I've made plans."

"You made *plans?* Your plans are going to fucking ruin me!"

Nick ignored his father's anger. "She's your biggest threat. Taking out Wong would be too obvious, but she's pursuing her Son of Cropsey bullshit and getting into Riley's head which could actually help us. Everyone's seen the way he's gone after Davina since Joy Sheridan's funeral—I'll make it look like he killed her to shut her the fuck up."

"Listen to yourself, Nick!" Sean quit pacing and faced the sky in despair. The sun reflecting through his tears blinded him. Sweat trickled down Sean's face and back, making his skin creep.

"I'm going to feed her a bunch of crap so she thinks she's close to breaking the Son of Cropsey case. Then I'll take her to the boat graveyard to see a crucial piece of evidence." Nick gave his father a conspiratorial smile.

Sean was aghast. "You're actually *enjoying* this?" *Who is this person? This isn't my son.*

"I'm enjoying doing what needs to be done if that's what you mean. No one is doing as much for you as I am."

Sean stared blankly at Nick. He saw the fat tears in his son's eyes. How could he have such a fucked-up kid? Had he made Nick that way?

"Get up," Sean growled.

Nick put out his hand for his father to help. Sean took a step backward, his pulse hammering in his ears.

Lowering the hand, Nick slowly levered himself off the ground and stood to face Sean. "I imagined this would go differently," he said.

"What did you expect, son? You murdered Darren Rivers."

Nick's eyes fixed on his father's. "You've messed up, too."

"Christ, I didn't *kill* anyone."

"You've killed me a million times in a million different ways, Dad. And you don't even see that," Nick rasped. "Nothing changes. I fight for you. I try to make you see that I love you—that I'm your fucking son."

"No," Sean said quietly, calmly. "You're crazy. God, how the fuck will I clear my name? I need to report you myself. What you've done—"

"For you! Everything I did, I—"

Sean jabbed a finger into Nick's chest. "*I didn't ask you to commit murder.* There's no coming back from that. I have no choice but to disown you—loudly and publicly. Don't you see the line you've crossed?"

"The same one you crossed the first time you hit Mom?"

Sean stiffened.

"You beat the living shit out of her, Dad."

Sean smarted at that comment. He'd never raised a hand to his wife—not when the boy was around. "She told you that lie?"

Nick laughed. "I *saw* you. More than once. I saw the black eyes she tried to hide with makeup. I remember all the times she ended up in the hospital. That one time when you broke her face so bad I didn't even recognize her. She told me she walked into a tree branch in the backyard."

Sean put up his hands. He'd no idea Nick had seen any of that. Lara had always been so clever at concealing any damage he caused during their . . . disagreements. Except for that one time . . . "Look, kid, my marriage to your mother is over. That was then—this is now."

"*Kid?* Yeah, I guess I am to you. It's hard to really grow up when you've seen your mother thrown across the room. Makes you afraid of what you might turn into if you grow up."

"So, you became a murderer?"

"You know what else I became for you? I fucked him to gain his trust so he'd tell me what he really thought about you and your political aspirations."

Sean felt the blood drain from his face. "I thought you were angling after the Speers girl."

"Variety is the spice of life, Dad," Nick smirked. "And angling is exactly the right word because *everything* is about angles. How to get leverage, how to get behind someone's defenses, gain their trust . . . their *love*. I have you to thank for that lesson."

"Jesus. What kind of monster are you?"

Nick's eyes blazed. "Exactly the kind you made me."

Nick moved swiftly, and with no warning. Sean was caught completely off guard. Before he knew it, he was flat on his back on the ground with Nick looming over him. As Nick raised his hands and stepped closer, Sean shifted his hips to one side and pulled out the police-issued Glock .45 he always carried nestled in his waistband.

He aimed it at Nick's torso.

Nick raised his hands but didn't step back.

Sean felt a surge of fierce adrenaline. He bared his teeth. "You forgot that I carry this?"

"Of course, I didn't forget." Nick's heart pounded hard, the ringing in his ears intensifying.

"Let's not have *two* murderers in the Delafield family, son. Back off." Sean rolled back onto his feet. "Let me tell you something about your precious mother. Let me tell you why she kept getting the shit beat out of her. She was a cheat, Nick. A two-faced, prick-chasing slut. She was exactly the type who deserves everything she gets."

His dad's words rattled him, and Nick was forced to consider that they were the truth. Or was it Sean Delafield blaming the victim of his foul temper? Nick's mouth felt like it was full of ashes. His entire life he'd striven to please the man who had terrorized his mother. Why had he done that? Was it fear? Guilt?

Or the niggling feeling his father must have had his *reasons?*

Nick's thoughts were dark and chaotic. His eyes spilled tears that refracted the fitful sunlight and made his father a blur of light and shadow. "All I ever wanted, Dad," he said, "was for you to love me."

"You're just like your mother. Both of you working overtime to make me look like a fucking idiot."

Nick put his hands to his face. "Don't say that."

"I'm no idiot, boy. I'm a fighter. I've been fighting my whole life to make a name for myself, and I'll be damned if I'm gonna let you harpoon that name. You'll shut the fuck up about all of this and get the hell off Staten Island. Out of New York. Off the fucking *continent*."

Lowering his hands, Nick stared up at his father as he stood there, gun lowered, contempt oozing from his every pore. All the work he'd done his whole life to get his father to love him had been a meaningless waste.

The father he needed so desperately to love him had used him and tossed him aside just as he had every other person in his warped, narcissistic life.

Nick doubled over, hands on his knees, fighting to catch his breath to clear his head.

"So now you're gonna snivel like a goddamn baby? Stand up straight like a fucking man and get out of my sight."

Nick straightened, his eyes on his father's gun. Half upright, seemingly unsteady on his feet, Nick's hand shot out with lightning speed and ripped the weapon from Sean's hand.

"*Son of a bitch!*" Sean snarled and backed away as Nick aimed the weapon at him. "So, Nick," he said, "this is how it ends, then."

Nick held the gun steady. He willed himself to breathe, to ride the adrenaline high coursing through his body. There were things he wanted to know. Things he needed to understand.

"Why did George Modica die?" Nick took a step toward his father.

"He had a bad heart."

"That I believe. But that's not what killed him. The night before, he was freaking out about the video—he recognized Davina from it."

Sean's eyes widened. "Davina Speers killed George because he saw her at the party?"

"No." Nick kept his words slow, deliberate. "George died because he knew *your* connection to Davina's rape. To *all* of them."

Sean's expression was one of pure fury. "You really are fucking crazy. How the hell did I not know how sick you are?"

"Davina's right—too many of those girls had parents that worked for you for it to be coincidence. Any of them could have made trouble for you if they, say, went to the police or the press or took you to court. Ray Speers, Bert Pine, Mark Balducci. Maybe others. Ray Speers knew there was stuff disappearing from your warehouse. He probably thought you'd be pleased he reported it. But you weren't pleased, because you most likely had some crooked side deals going on. So, you punch the guy out and the warehouse mysteriously catches on fire. Then Speers gets his ass fired, and the insurance company pays for the missing stuff. What did George have on you? If he'd had a teenaged daughter, would she get raped too?"

Nick saw contempt on his father's face; it hurt more than the lack of love. "Supposing you're right," Sean offered. "Let's say I have never asked anyone to intimidate families by . . . in that way, but I have a . . . a warped guardian angel who takes care of things in his own, imaginative way. And let's say Davina Speers *is* now a threat and the attempts to remove that threat have failed. You've always wanted to be my Number One, Nick—I can see how you'd think removing Davina Speers would get you there."

Ah, yes, he could see it now—the cold, hard gears of calculation turning behind his father's eyes.

"And would it?" asked Nick.

Sean smiled and shrugged. "Why not?"

The trite non-answer killed every last illusion Nick harbored about his old man. "You fucking, arrogant bastard," he said. "She knows. Everything I just told you, everything you just told me, she *knows*. Davina Speers is your worst nightmare, and I hope she fucking finishes you."

Nick Delafield put the barrel of his father's Glock in his mouth and pulled the trigger.

CHAPTER SIXTY-EIGHT

SATURDAY, BATTERY WEED, FORT WADSWORTH

"Battery Weed, of all places?" Geoff steered his car onto the verge along Weed Road and pulled up behind Nick's Beemer. The only other car there—a Mercedes sports coupe—was parked on the opposite side of the avenue.

Davina, who'd ridden shotgun mostly gripping the "oh, shit" handle above the door, glanced down at her phone. Nick still hadn't responded to her last text.

Joe snorted his derision. "I'm sure it's just another of Sean's prospects —Disneyland, Staten Island. They could create a dark, scary ride through the fort."

"As wack as that sounds," Geoff said, "I really wouldn't be surprised."

Davina slid out of the car, her legs shaking a little. Geoff's driving really was . . . adventurous. "I don't think it's about Sean's real estate deals. I'll bet Nick chose here because there's not a chance in hell anyone will overhear anything we have to say. I'm hoping he'll be able to . . ." She stopped herself. What was she hoping, really? That Nick would corroborate her suspicions about Son of Cropsey's connection to Delafield

Enterprises? Or that he might have facts related to Gerry Dobson's death?

Geoff and Joe had gotten out of the car and were checking out the area.

"Battery's closed to visitors," Geoff said, nodding toward some signage on the front gate that announced a maintenance closure. "But the gate's open." He turned to Davina. "It's a big place. Did Nick say where he'd be?"

Davina checked her phone. Still no text. "He just said Battery Weed. I guess we just go in and find him."

Davina had expected the old fortress to look cold and forbidding, but blanketed with sunlight, the front-facing stone wall was warm and mellow. It concealed the parade grounds and three-story battery that faced the sea, and belied the fact Battery Weed was colossal. She hoped Nick would be looking for them or waiting someplace obvious.

The three had just entered the open sally port, when they were brought up short by the discordant sound of an argument. Voices echoed off the stone—angry tone clear, words unintelligible.

Joe stopped, listening. "I figured Nick would be alone."

"That was the impression I got," said Davina.

The resonant crack of a gunshot split the air.

"Shit." Geoff jumped.

Joe broke into a dead run.

Davina and Geoff followed him through the vaulted sally port and into the empty parade grounds. Inside, Joe hesitated, his gaze sweeping the grounds. He froze momentarily with his eyes fixed on the roof of the battery just to the right of the old light, then took off again toward the access at the base of the adjacent tower.

Davina, close on Joe's heels, could only repeat what she knew was a prayer chanted by her entire being: *Don't let this be what I think it is.* She'd experienced enough horror in the past few days to last a lifetime.

Joe vaulted up the spiral staircase, taking the steps two at a time. From behind and just below, Davina saw him break out into the sunlight atop the grassy rooftop and stop dead in his tracks. She slowed, vaguely aware of Geoff skimming past her on the stairs and following Joe out onto the roof. He, too, stumbled to a halt, staring in the same direction.

Davina threw herself back into motion, bursting from the exit behind the two men. Her lungs ached from the exertion and pain flaring up in her wounded shoulder; she could hardly breathe.

"Don't, babe." Joe turned back to physically restrain Davina and block her view of whatever had Geoff Wong doubled over and puking up his pizza slice.

"What is it? What?"

Joe wrapped his arms around Davina and pulled her against his chest. Then, he allowed her to see.

Davina quit struggling when she saw Nick's lifeless body facedown on the grassy rooftop just yards away. Much of the back of his head was gone, pink-gray brain tissue and splintered shards of skull glistened in the grass and weeds, and a spreading pool of blood blossomed around his face.

And, to complete the grim tableau, Sean Delafield stood over his son, trembling and weeping. As Davina looked on in horror, Sean turned toward her with pain and confusion in his eyes.

Davina's mind raced to make sense of what she was seeing. No way would Sean have shot his own son—and he had no weapon. Yet the thought of Nick killing himself . . . A hot, sticky wave of nausea swept through Davina, and for a moment she thought she was going to throw up. Her legs wobbled, and had Joe not been holding her up, Davina knew she'd be on the ground with . . .

Nick. Poor, big brother Nick.

Stomach empty, Geoff stepped away from his puke and stabbed a trembling finger at his phone.

Sean finally acknowledged Davina, Nick, and Geoff. "What the fuck are you doing here?"

"What did you do?" was all Davina could think of to say.

Sean crumpled, dropping to the ground, shaking his head. For such a powerful man, the scene was heart-wrenching to witness.

Joe loosened his grip on Davina. "We should wait outside for the cops."

"Sean. What did you do, Sean?" Davina demanded again.

Sean ignored her. On all fours, he crawled over to his son, sobbing, gasping for breath. Davina wriggled from Joe's slackened grasp and stumbled to Sean's side, where she dropped to her knees. She saw death on Nick now—the one sightless, glassy eye she could see from the side; his bloody mouth; the gun that was still in his hand.

In an instant, Sean snatched up the gun and trained its quivering muzzle on Davina. "Get away from me! Get away from my boy!"

"*Sean!*" Hands up, Joe took a step toward him. Sean waved the gun in his direction.

"Don't," Joe said. "Don't do this, man."

Sean swung the Glock back toward Davina and her stomach churned. "This was all your fault. *You* did this with your goddamn scheming. My Nick took his own life because you're a meddling whore who can't get her shit straight."

Davina remained silent and allowed the grieving man's condemnation to roll over her.

Slowly, Joe took a step closer. "Put down the gun, Sean. This isn't Davina's fault."

Sean turned on Joe. "And you, you fucking idiot! You've been against me from jump. And I gave you your first fucking job! *Everyone* is against me! They took my campaign away from me . . . and now my son."

Geoff chanced a step toward Sean. "The police are on their way." He spoke calmly, deliberately.

Snarling, Sean whipped the gun in Geoff's direction and fired off a shot. It hit the stone parapet above Geoff's head in a puff of dust and ricocheted away.

Geoff dropped to the ground.

Davina screamed.

"I'm gonna have to explain all this to the cops." Sweat covered Sean's face in a shining veil. "About how Joe killed my son . . . out of—out of *jealousy*, and I had to defend myself against the three of you."

"C'mon, Sean," said Joe, his voice shaking. "Even Riley won't believe that."

"Riley will believe whatever I tell him to believe," Sean snarled.

Davina found her voice. "None of us is armed, Sean. And there's only the one gun with Nick's prints on it. And yours."

"Listen to her," Joe added. He'd taken another step forward, hands still raised.

Sean laughed. "Listen to that dumb slut? She started this whole thing."

"Don't call her that."

"You're just as dumb as your girlfriend," Sean continued his tirade. "You were a bright, promising kid, Joe. Not as promising as Nick, but still. I really thought you were going to make something of yourself, but you couldn't hack working for me 'cause you weren't tough enough. Then you start fucking the stupid whore who's out to ruin my life!"

"Sean, stop. Put the gun down," Joe urged.

Sean gave him a lopsided, maniacal grin. "You going to do something about it? Go ahead—give me a good reason to defend myself." He aimed the gun at Joe's face.

Davina thought her heart would stop. She couldn't just stand by and let Sean kill them all.

Taking advantage of Sean's attention on Joe, Davina leapt from a crouch and aimed a kick into Sean's gut.

Too late.

Sean pulled the trigger just as her foot connected, and Joe went down in a spray of blood.

Sean doubled over. He was still in possession of the Glock, so Davina focused her entire being on the gun. In one swift, smooth motion, she grabbed Sean from behind, put one arm around his neck, the other in a death grip on his wrist. She then wrenched him upright, digging her nails into the soft underside of his wrist.

"*Let go, bitch!*" Sean gurgled as she choked him.

Davina would not let go. She dug her fingertips deeper into Sean's wrist, which finally forced him to let go of the gun; it thudded harmlessly to the rooftop. Sean let out a strangled roar of rage, then, gurgling and spitting, fought to pry Davina's arm from his throat. He was strong, but Davina had the advantage of training and her own wiry strength. She hung on to Sean with dogged determination, using one of her legs to destabilize his. Eventually, the tactic paid off and Sean Delafield toppled to the ground, dragging her with him.

Ignoring the searing pain in her shoulder, Davina straddled Sean and pummeled his head and upper body to subdue him. Beneath her, the man could do nothing more than cry out in pain, wriggle to be away from the onslaught, and try his best to fend off the blows.

No mercy came from Davina, just a pure, undiluted hate, the likes of which she'd never felt before—even for Riley, even for Son of Cropsey.

Geoff called her name, his voice urgent, desperate.

"Davina! For Christ's sakes, stop!"

Then the journalist's hands were on Davina's shoulders. Twisting, she shook him off and continued to pound her fists into Sean's shoulders and face. "You did this! You did *all* of it, you bastard!"

Not giving up, Geoff threw his arms around Davina's shoulders. He squeezed until she quit her merciless assault. Putting his lips to Davina's ear, he spoke softly. "We need to get Joe to the hospital."

Joe. God, Joe.

The fight out of her, Davina allowed Geoff to pull her off Sean's twitching body. She then staggered over to where Joe lay, eyes closed. Geoff had used his own shirt to staunch a wound in Joe's shoulder and was clad only in jeans and a sleeveless T-shirt. Davina knelt at Joe's side and put a hand to his chest to reassure herself Sean Delafield hadn't killed him. She was relieved to feel Joe's ribs rise and fall with each ragged breath. But the bullet wound was bleeding too freely; Geoff's shirt was already sodden.

"Joe?" Davina shook his unwounded shoulder gently.

Joe opened his eyes a crack and said, his voice barely a whisper, "I'm okay, babe."

"I'm so sorry." Davina's tears dripped onto Joe's cheek.

"I've got the gun." Geoff was pacing. "We just have to wait for the cops. What the fuck is taking them so long?"

Joe managed a shallow laugh, his face screwed up in pain. "It's Staten Island, Geoff."

Behind them, Sean stirred with a loud groan. Davina tensed, but Geoff was already on it—he stood over the politician and aimed the Glock at his chest.

"Stay down, man, or I'll give you back to Davina."

Sean moaned, spat out a thick wad of blood, and rolled onto his side.

Davina rested her head on Joe's chest. He stroked her hair. "You kicked the shit out of him?"

"Yeah. And I'd do it again."

"That's my girl."

As they waited for the ambulance and police, Davina took delight in every breath Joe took. She kept her focus on him, willing herself not to look over at where Nick lay dead on the ground. It was impossible to believe he was gone.

CHAPTER SIXTY-NINE

SATURDAY, STATEN ISLAND UNIVERSITY HOSPITAL

THE THIRD-FLOOR WARD OF THE TEACHING HOSPITAL REEKED of lemon and antiseptic. Geoff found it suffocating. He had spent enough time in hospitals to acquire an ingrained dislike of their sights, sounds, and smells. They reminded Geoff too much of loss and people with pink ribbons pinned to their clothing. Mom had never gotten to see him graduate with honors and a shiny master's in journalism, much less become a successful journalist who'd even appeared on TV news. She'd have been especially proud of the latter.

The door to Room 347 was open. Geoff poked his head in. There were two beds: Davina sat on one, and the second was vacant. "You okay?"

Davina gave him a crooked smile and stood up. "Second time in the hospital in forty-eight hours—what do you think?" Wobbling, she held onto the side of the bed to steady herself.

"Sit down, woman. You're not Supergirl."

Davina did as instructed. Geoff sat himself down in the white plastic guest chair. "Where's Joe?"

"Surgery."

"Any news?"

"Apparently, it's not as bad as it looked." The relief in Davina's voice was encouraging to hear. "Through-and-through just below the collarbone. Missed everything important. The bullet almost nicked an artery, though—Joe's a lucky guy. They said he'll be out soon. How'd you do?"

Geoff shrugged. He'd spent the past few hours with Sean Delafield at the 120th Precinct, and then he'd been on the phone with Stan at the *Advance* to fill him in. "The cops are dealing with Nick's death as a suicide. They have to wait on the autopsy, but the cops seemed pretty sure."

"Suicide." Davina looked gutted. "I can't believe Nick would ever do such a thing. He always had his shit together."

"Sometimes it's impossible to see what's beneath the surface," Geoff told her. "Nick . . . well, I think he showed people the Nick Delafield he *wanted* them to see."

"Even when he was dating Allie, Nick was always so confident—arrogant, even. Something awful must've happened between him and his dad. I know Sean is . . . well, I've seen him tear Nick apart in public a few times."

"You only saw things from the outside, Davina. Nick had been suffering his father's dickishness his whole life."

"Then why work for Sean's campaign? Why not just get the fuck off Staten Island and find a better life?"

"Can't you ask the same question of yourself?" The words were barely out of Geoff's mouth when he regretted them. *Shit, that was going too far.*

Davina didn't bristle. She simply studied the toes of her sneakers and shook her head. "Maybe you're right, Geoff. I'd be better off right now if I'd just left the second I could. But, here I am. What do they call that?"

"Learned helplessness," Geoff said. "Or maybe just a desperate need for approval."

"Yeah. Maybe that's what Nick was going through, too. I guess it doesn't matter anymore. Now, I just want answers." Tilting her head to one side, Davina's brow furrowed. "Sean said it was my fault—my meddling cost Nick his life. How?"

"Do you think Sean is Son of Cropsey?" Geoff chanced the loaded question.

But before Davina could answer, a nurse came in carrying a small tray with a glass of juice, a sandwich, and an apple. The nurse placed the food on the bed's table tray. "They're just finishing up with your friend. Thought you could use some fuel."

"Thank you," Davina said and gave the young woman a grateful smile.

"He's going to be just fine. Dr. Crenshaw is a wonderful surgeon." The nurse returned the smile and bustled from the room.

Davina picked up half the sandwich. Tuna salad. Geoff could smell it, and it made his mouth water. As if she'd read his mind and heard his stomach growl, Davina handed the first half to Geoff and grabbed the second.

"No. I don't think Sean Delafield is a serial rapist," she told Geoff, then bit into the sandwich.

"Okay . . . why not?" Geoff said through a mouthful of sandwich; it tasted like heaven.

"For one thing, he doesn't give me that vibe. I know that's hardly scientific, but it is what it is. The guy's creepy, sure, but in a different way. He's too . . . *entitled*. Too likely to say what's on his mind because he believes he can. Sean may hide his business activities, but he doesn't hide his contempt for everyone around him. And frankly, he's physically weak. He was far too easy to overpower."

"And your guy . . ."

"Strong. And practiced."

Geoff nodded. "What about Darren?"

"Don't think so. Though I wonder if he didn't have some connection to Son of Cropsey. He was up to his neck in Sean's political and business ventures and active in the SBCA. Gino said Darren was the one who did all the cleaning up, using Monaghan as his fixer. What scares me is . . . Nick. How badly I wanted to trust him—*did* trust him at first. But what happened on that rooftop . . ."

Chewing on his tuna, Geoff pondered a moment. "It does beg the question: Who really set up that meeting? Sean or Nick?"

"Only Sean knows the answer to that," said Davina.

"While Kevin Monaghan has the answer to so much else… It's interesting that he's the only one who has gone incommunicado. I've spoken with Gino Romano, Scott Kantor, and Stavros. Monaghan, I haven't been able to nail down. He's not answering his phone, hasn't been into his office since yesterday morning—and no one's heard from him since then, either. I'd love to know the exact genesis of that party video. I'm guessing Darren had it made to provide leverage over . . . well, whomever he needed leverage over. I wouldn't be surprised if Monaghan has the master file stashed somewhere—the one showing everyone in SBCA leadership who was there that night."

"Maybe that's why he's dropped off the map. He's holding the grenade, and George and Darren's deaths must have him looking over his shoulder. Did you give a copy of the video to the cops?"

"My editor did. And he let them know it was just a copy—I think Stan forgot to mention we'd managed to get a peek around its edges."

Davina wrinkled her nose. "At least Riley can't just deep-six it."

"Bingo. That video exposes the rest of the SBCA honchos just as vividly as it does Sean. I'm convinced now it was meant to kill two birds with one stone. Staten Island's business community has a vested interest in having Sean Delafield revert to being their pot of gold behind the scenes, even if it means him ruining any hope he may have of getting back into office. His insistence on staying in the council race exposes all of them, as well as hobbling the local party for the foreseeable future." Geoff polished off the half sandwich with a sigh of satisfaction; it definitely hit the spot. "If Sean is in the race, the party loses. If his buddies force him to quit, bye-bye cash cow."

Davina gazed up at the ceiling for a moment. "So, let's say Sean and his cabal use rape as a punishment or a deterrent. Why would they stage the attacks on properties so easy to connect to him?"

Geoff considered his reply. "Leverage? That's the first thing that comes to my mind. You have to admit, though, some of those connections are tenuous, to say the least. Not all the rapes were committed on properties Sean had an interest in—yours and Jessica Balducci's, for example."

"True, but we both had fathers who were involved with Delafield's construction businesses. Still, it might have been a way to make it appear to be a frame job if anyone did connect Sean to the rapes. I mean, he'd have to be a complete idiot to commit serious crimes on properties connected with him—right?"

Geoff nodded. "Yeah, and he's got alibis for the recent attacks. I checked."

Davina's body language changed: It was like watching a hunting dog go on point.

"What if Sean's not the rapist, but he knows who is?" Davina said.

Sobering thought. "An attack dog."

"Yeah, but what if it's not as simple as a hit man who does little girls on command?" Davina shivered. "What if the rapist is someone not even Sean Delafield can completely control? That could possibly explain the locations. Perhaps it's Son of Cropsey's way of exerting his own control."

Geoff lifted an eyebrow. "A sick, symbiotic relationship?"

Davina nodded. She picked up her apple, tossed it into the air, caught it, and tossed it again. "My money's still on Riley. He's an attack dog who hates taking orders."

"Huh. You think salvaging his career wasn't enough of a motive for falsely arresting Rob Cox? He just arrested *someone* to cover his own ass?"

"Geoff, these guys are all connected. They run this town. Whatever Sean Delafield is covering, I have to believe George and Darren knew, and that the rest of them know. If we could just get one of them to crack."

"Good point." Geoff hoisted himself onto the vacant bed. "I agree Riley fits the bill in many respects. Maybe I should talk to Romano again? He gave up the video without too much pushback—maybe he'd roll over on this, too."

"You know something strange?" Davina tossed the apple to Geoff. "Riley didn't show up at Battery Weed this afternoon. Someone would have informed him if the Delafields were involved in a shooting. You didn't make a secret of that when you called the cops."

Geoff had to admit that, yes, it was a little odd. "You think he may have known what was going down? Seems a little far-fetched to me, Davina."

A knock sounded at the door.

A tall, officious-looking woman wearing a white coat stepped into the room. She studied the clipboard she held in both hands. "Davina Speers?"

Davina slid off the bed, a worried expression on her face. "Joe?"

"Dr. Crenshaw wanted me to let you know that Mr. Kelley is out of surgery and has gone to recovery. They'll take him to ICU after that—rather than bringing him down to the ward."

Davina paled. "Is he worse than they thought?"

"No, but Mr. Kelley's medical records note reactions to anesthesia in the past, and Dr. Crenshaw would like to keep him under observation 'til morning. He'll be sleeping for a few hours, so you should go home and get some rest. Come back this evening when he's awake."

Nodding, Davina grabbed her fanny pack from the bed.

Geoff walked Davina out of the hospital. "You're *really* going home to rest up?"

"And take a shower and change clothes," Davina replied. "Although, I did promise to go speak to Monaghan's ex-wife in Tottenville."

"Ah, the start of a great investigation." Geoff chuckled. "Here's a wild idea. Why don't you just go home? Shower. Eat. Rest. You can get your hair done tomorrow."

Davina opened her mouth to object, but Geoff cut her off. "Trust me —food and sleep are essential to a successful investigation. And coffee. Most of all, it's coffee."

"But—"

"Joe will be in the hospital at least until tomorrow afternoon. It takes longer to check out of these places than it does to have surgery."

"Okay," Davina conceded. "Are *you* going home to rest?"

Geoff shook his head no. "I'm going to find the disappearing ex-cop security expert—if he can be found. I also wanna see if maybe I can talk to Sean Delafield. You gotta wonder what stories he's telling the cops about his son's death."

Out in the parking lot, as the two prepared to go their separate ways,

Davina rested a hand on Geoff's shoulder. "Thanks for everything, Geoff. If you hadn't been there today, I think I might've killed Sean."

Geoff looked deep into Davina's beautiful eyes and said, "Nah, you'd have gotten control of yourself before that happened." And even as the words tumbled from his mouth, Geoff doubted them.

CHAPTER SEVENTY

SUNDAY, HUGUENOT HAIR AND NAILS, TOTTENVILLE

Huguenot Hair and Nails was located in an upscale strip mall. Yelp reviews gave the salon high praise and mentioned Sandy Burke specifically by name as a skilled stylist and someone who was "comfy" to chat with. One commenter said she felt as if she'd known Sandy for years after just one haircut and blow dry. That boded well for Davina if she could get Kevin Monaghan's ex talking about the right subject. Davina had called the salon the evening before, made sure Sandy would be working Sunday, and asked for an early appointment.

When Davina entered the salon, tepid Starbucks cup in hand, a little bell over the door jingled merrily; all eyes turned toward her. The salon was generously sized, with a waiting area in front, six stylist stations in the middle, and four sinks at the rear. A quartet of manicure tables were placed artfully along the walls. The decor was decidedly Frenchified, with colorful prints of famous Parisian tourist spots decorating the cream-colored walls.

Beneath a huge print of the Eiffel Tower sat a woman with aluminum foil on her head. Two more ladies occupied manicure tables, with their hands in the care of the beauticians on the other side, while a fourth was having her long brown hair blow dried by a stunning woman who perfectly fit the description Davina had of Kevin Monaghan's ex-wife.

"How can I help you?" The receptionist had perfect makeup and enviably glossy raven-black hair.

"I have an appointment with Sandy. I'm a bit early."

The receptionist tapped away on her iPad, then called across the salon, "Sandy!"

Davina was right; the gorgeous stylist wielding the blow dryer was, indeed, Sandy.

"Your 9:30 is early."

Sandy flapped a hand and offered Davina a smile. "I'm almost done."

The receptionist turned back to Davina with a brilliant smile. "It pays to be early! Please, have a seat."

Davina made herself comfortable in the cozy waiting area and sipped her coffee. She pulled out her phone to catch up on anything the press and police had to say about Nick Delafield's death and his father's possible involvement. Oddly, the local news was absurdly spare. It consisted of several breaking news notices about an incident involving a fatality at the old battery the day before, but nothing beyond the perfunctory police presser. Given the Delafields' high profile on the island, the lack of coverage struck Davina as odd. Only the story in the *Advance* mentioned names, and even then, there was no mention of suicide, and nothing at all about Sean being taken in for questioning.

Someone had put a lid on it.

Riley?

Geoff must be pissed.

Davina had just finished her coffee and tossed the cup when she received a text from Joe.

They're letting me go in an hour.

Great! I didn't expect to hear from you 'til this afternoon.

Bounced back real fast. Woke up feeling like I've gotten a year's sleep. Police want to talk to me.

Why haven't they asked to speak to me?

Kind of stuck where I am. Getting a trim from Kev's ex. Questions to ask.

There was a moment of inaction before Joe replied.

Do you ever quit?

Sorry, no.

Especially not now.

I'll come by and get you when I'm done with Sandy.

Maybe it seemed ridiculous to Joe, but Davina *had* to push ahead. With people dying right and left, plus the attempts on her own life, she knew it was not the time to take a breather. If she were anywhere else with the same crap happening to her, she'd have asked for police protection. On Staten Island, however, the thought was ludicrous.

"Miss Speers? I'm ready for you now."

Looking up, Davina saw Sandy Monaghan-nee-Burke at the edge of the waiting area. She held up a black plastic cape with "Huguenot" emblazoned on it in stylish gold letters, and gestured toward the chair her previous client had just vacated. Sandy was petite with a trim, narrow waist and an ample bosom fetchingly set off by a white low-cut, V-neck blouse. Her honey blonde hair was fashioned into an eye-catching, asymmetrical bob, and her makeup was expertly done and fresh. At once, Davina became a little self-conscious of her own *au naturel* appearance. She'd hastily applied some face powder, blush, and mascara, but that had been the extent of it; she felt entirely inadequate.

"Good morning, Miss Speers," Sandy said as Davina climbed into the chair.

"Call me Chrissy," Davina lied—it was the first name that came to mind.

"Well, good morning, Chrissy." Sandy shook out the cape and draped it over Davina's chest. She fastened it behind Davina's neck and fluffed her hair with both hands. "Your hair's a beautiful color. Natural, right?"

"It is."

"So, what can I do for you this morning?"

Davina had been so focused on what she was going to say to Sandy, she'd not even thought about hairstyles. So, she blurted out the first thing that popped into her head. "I *love* your bob. Could we do that?"

Sandy nodded. "With your face shape, you can totally pull it off. Let's do it." She ushered Davina to the wash basins. There, she washed and rinsed Davina's hair, towel-dried it, and massaged a conditioner into it that smelled of honey.

"Can you believe all this stuff that's going on?" Davina nodded to a half-folded newspaper on a low table by the sink; the headline was about the Farm Colony rape.

Sandy followed her gaze. "The attacks on young girls? Yeah, it's horrific."

"Two this week," Davina pressed.

Sandy sighed. "I know. The first one was a home invasion, and that one—I mean, that creepy old Farm Colony. What I'd like to know is what a girl that age was doing there in the first place. I hope she didn't do anything to provoke the guy."

Davina felt a stab of anger at the suggestion that poor Seraphina Bellano might have done something to provoke her own rape. A hazy memory from ten years before, of Detective Riley asking her, "*What did you do?*" flashed though Davina's mind. She fought the desire to pull Sandy Burke's silky blonde hair 'til it came out in clumps.

Can't think about that now.

Focus.

"It's crazy how it's happening again after Rob Cox was put away for the Son of Cropsey attacks," Davina said.

Sandy shook her head in disapproval. "It's always something on this island, isn't it? It's like living in the freaking *Twilight Zone.*"

Impatient, Davina took the plunge. "I was reading on my phone about Sean Delafield's son. He was killed yesterday—someone shot him. The guy was almost a celebrity with his father running for city council and all."

Sandy paused a moment. "I hadn't heard. Was it on the morning news?"

"It was in the *Advance.* It's been a weird week. My bank manager was found dead in his apartment a couple of days ago, too—Darren Rivers."

Davina, you're moving too fast.

Finishing up with the conditioner, Sandy checked her watch. "Ten minutes, then we'll rinse and cut. I know all those people," she said with a sad frown. "It's a twisted, sad world we live in. My ex was a cop, so I heard some pretty awful things."

"Really?" Davina hid her excitement; Sandy was opening up.

"Guys like Darren Rivers and the Delafields might appear to be grownups and respectable businessmen, but they act like horny teenagers. The way Kevin used to tell it, they had three brain cells between them and enough testosterone to sink a freakin' battleship." With a crooked grin, Sandy rinsed out the conditioner and walked Davina across to her work station.

"Your ex was a cop?" Davina picked up the conversation.

Sandy grimaced. "Yeah. Man, he was a piece of work."

"Sorry to hear that."

Sandy worked on Davina's hair, her movements deft and skillful. Hair clips seemed to appear out of the ether for Sandy to pin up the top layers while she snipped away at the bottom ones.

"Not as sorry as I was, honey," Sandy chuckled. "He was like they all are—sweet at first. Kev was a real charmer, swept me off my feet the first time we met. You know what they say about that honeymoon period, right?"

"I hear it happens to a lot of people." Davina wondered about her relationship with Joe: Was that still in the honeymoon period?

"Anyway," Sandy made a dismissive gesture with a hair clip, "he used to impress me with stories about his high-flying buddies and fellow cops. I still don't know why he hung around Delafield and his cronies so much, because he had no respect for any of them. *None*. He thought they were all pathetic, entitled morons. He was pretty sure they weren't blind to his opinion of them."

"Wow." Davina was astounded to hear that; she'd assumed Sean's inner circle were all best buds 'til the end. "So why include him in the business association? I went to an association thing with my boss one time, and there were business owners, doctors, and lawyers—even politicians there. Like the *real* movers and shakers. I mean, no offense, but where would a cop fit in?"

"It started when Kev was just a detective sergeant. He was a cop, so he was useful to the likes of Sean Delafield: DUIs, parking tickets, other minor shit—pardon my French—he could make things go away. I wonder how useful he is to them now that he's not on the force. Well, unless they need a price break on a security system. They probably have someone new in their pocket now."

"I guess he was on the force during the Son of Cropsey case."

"Oh, you bet," Sandy huffed. "I heard all about that sick bastard— stuff you'd never read in the papers or see on the news."

"Behind-the-scenes stuff?"

Sandy let down some of the top layers of Davina's hair and continued her precise clipping. "More like between Kevin's ears stuff. Kev liked to *exaggerate* things to make himself look like the big man. How great at his job he was, how crooked Delafield and his cronies were, how totally indispensable he was to the Son of Cropsey case. His partner at the time—what was his name? Yeah, Packer. He made some serious mistakes. According to Kev, Packer was convinced he knew who was behind the attacks, but Kev told him it was a crazy idea."

So, Packer *had* fingered someone other than Rob Cox? "Did he ever say who he thought it was?" Davina prompted.

"If Packer did, Kev didn't tell me. He told me all this when he was a little drunk, though, so some of the details got muddled up.Kev was especially grandiose when he was drinking. Mark my words, Chrissy, never marry a guy until you've seen him plastered. He said he knew all the stuff the police didn't tell the public."

"Wow. Like what?" Davina played the ghoul well.

"Yeah, I remember him telling me Son of Cropsey used to draw on his victims—how freaky is that? This is going to look great." Sandy stood back to admire her work.

Davina felt cool air on her nape and glanced up into the mirror. The shoulder-length hair at the back of her head was all gone. In its place was a thick, layered bob that tapered in toward her neck. She looked so . . . *different*. "Wow," she said again.

Sandy studied Davina in the mirror. "You've got a really pretty face, Chrissy. I bet people tell you that all the time."

"Just my boyfriend."

Sandy pointed an accusatory finger. "He'd *better* tell you that. That's his job."

Davina smiled. "He's a good guy."

Sandy let out a loud, world-weary sigh. "There are so few of those out there," she said. "Kev always said his partner was one of the good guys." Sandy got back to letting down each layer of Davina's hair and trimming it. "He said Packer just didn't understand how the world worked, is all."

"And how *does* it work?"

"According to Kev, their superior officer, Tom Riley, had a completely different suspect in mind for Son of Cropsey. Riley needed a win, Staten Island needed the case closed, so Kev was deputized to make sure Packer gave Riley his win. They handed the case to Riley, Riley arrested someone, and everybody was happy. Kev told me they called him The Fixer. He sounded more like The Lackey to me." Sandy shook her head; her pale gold curtain of hair swung about her beautiful face.

"The Fixer." Davina tried her best to sound impressed. "That's quite a title. He must have been—"

"Full of himself. That's what Kev was," Sandy growled. "He was useful enough for his powerful friends to arrange for Scott Kantor to represent him during our divorce. That's one freakin' relentless lawyer. I owned my own business when Kev and I got married—home decor. It took me years to build up a good client base, but by the time Kantor got done with me, I had to sell it and learn a new trade from scratch. Thank God, Kev and I never had kids."

"Sounds like that was for the best." Davina wasn't too sure of the appropriate thing to say. "You have your independence, a fresh start—and you're *really* good at this."

"I must admit I'm happier now. I never could've been happy with Kev —I know that now. Now I've got my space and my girls—that's all I need." Sandy looked around the salon like a mother hen surveying her brood.

"Light at the end of the tunnel," Davina said with a smile.

Sandy finished up cutting and applied styling lotion. She reached for the blow dryer. "It does make me a bit sad, though. There was a time when Kev was a good guy. We were high school sweethearts at Tottenville High. He played football, I was a cheerleader, yada, yada. Stereotypical stuff. Kev was sweet and *so* handsome. He'd send me flowers, and always bought me little presents. But, even back then, I saw there was a darkness in him."

"How so?" Davina was surprised how much Sandy was sharing. It was part of the hairdressers' shtick to exchange gossip, though—what was said in the salon, stayed in the salon.

"Sometimes he'd go all distant and far-off. I figured he was just being a guy doing the whole mysterious and moody thing and needed 'guy space.'" Sandy made air quotes with her pinkies. "I still don't know what it was all about, but it got worse when his sister died."

"That's really sad," Davina said.

"Yeah—she killed herself and no one knew why. A few months later, her boyfriend was found dead. They called them the Romeo and Juliet of Staten Island." Sandy's laugh was a bitter one. "It was all over the papers. There was even some speculation Kev had something to do with it—the boyfriend's death, I mean. Kev had kind of a weird relationship with his sister. Not creepy or anything, just way overprotective. I think I reminded him of her—she was a petite blonde, too."

Davina eyed her new look in the mirror. "That's such a tragic story."

"It gets worse." Sandy turned off the blow dryer and fluffed Davina's hair; she was chatting like they'd been best friends for years. "After we were married, I discovered Kev was sleeping around with hookers. Some were underage, I was told, but Kev would never admit to that—who would, though?"

"Who'd tell you something like that?" Davina wasn't as surprised at the revelation as she made herself out to be.

"Detective Riley. He said he was looking out for me and I had a right to know. That's when everything changed. I just couldn't do it anymore."

Underage prostitutes? Fuck. If that was true, it suggested something about the nature of Kevin Monaghan's loyalty to Riley. "Of course not," Davina said aloud. "I really don't blame you."

"Like I said, being a cop either brought out the dick in Kev, or it was already there waiting to be unleashed. He had this creed: 'Don't get mad, get even.' Once Packer was thrown off the Son of Cropsey case, the dick part of Kev grew out of control. Riley just fed it." Sandy fell quiet, as if she couldn't bear to relive the past anymore. In silence, she finished up Davina's hair, trimming a few loose ends and using an electric clipper to ensure the back and side undercuts were both crisp and clean.

"All done," Sandy declared. "Ta-da!" She whisked off Davina's cape. "What do we think?"

Davina found it weird, yet quite amazing, to have such a bold haircut—jaw length on the left side with a bright ruddy wing falling over one eye, and the pixie cut on the right. For the first time in a hell of a long time, Davina felt good.

"I've never had such a stylish cut in my whole life," Davina told Sandy in all honesty. "It's so cool. I really, *really* love it."

"It'd look even cooler with streaks," Sandy said, stroking at her chin. "I'm thinking orange . . . or even white."

Davina laughed. "I think I need to get used to this, first."

The haircut paid for and information gathered, Davina hurried out to her car and called Geoff.

He wasn't picking up.

Deciding to drive to the *Advance* and wait for Geoff to return to his office, Davina left a message to that effect. Her next call was to Ron Packer, who she hoped would give her the straight answers she yearned for. That call, too, went straight to voice mail.

Frustrated and antsy, Davina texted Joe.

Be there in about an hour, babe.

It's okay. I took the bus.

"Shit," Davina grumbled as she slammed the Jetta into gear and sailed out of the parking lot.

CHAPTER SEVENTY-ONE

SUNDAY, JOE KELLEY'S HOME, ROSEBANK

Joe lived in a picturesque two-story row house of tawny brick, which had been given a thoroughly modern interior—walls had been torn out to create a spacious, open living room, dining room, and kitchen area around a central staircase. Married to that was Joe's impeccable taste in interior design. Davina had fallen in love with the house at first sight.

She used the key Joe had given her to let herself in. The curtains were drawn across the big front window, and Joe lay on the *chaise longue* of his sectional sofa, fast asleep. Davina knelt next to him and placed a hand on his chest. Joe's eyes opened slowly, and he gazed at her through half-opened lids.

"You okay?" Davina asked him.

"I've had better days."

Davina grimaced. "I can't believe you took the bus, Joe."

A smile came to Joe's lips. "I lied. Geoff brought me home."

"I guess he's the superior girlfriend, then."

His smile died. "When's this going to end, Davina?"

"I wish I knew."

"It's insane. Why are we mixed up in all this?" Joe stared up at the ceiling. A stray bar of sunlight snuck through the curtains and fell across his face; it accentuated the big, blue eyes Davina had always admired. They had been the first things she'd noticed about him—how clear they were, how brightly blue.

"I'm sorry," she said caressing his cheek. "I don't know how many times I can say I'm sorry."

"How serious are you about . . . us?"

The question came as a shock: Was Joe having doubts? "I . . . I want to be with you, Joe. You know I do."

"But, are you sure you're ready for that? I know I am, Davina." Joe reached for her hand; the exertion made him wince in pain. "I want something serious with you, D. I feel like all I'm doing is chasing you from one crime scene to another and trying to keep you alive. What happened yesterday makes me think I'm not capable of that." He grasped her hand tightly. "You've got to let this go before it kills you, babe. What happened to you ten years ago was fucked up, but staying trapped in it makes things even more fucked up for you—and everybody around you. I wish you could see that."

"So, I guess *my* pain doesn't exist because it happened so long ago?" Davina pulled her hand away.

"I didn't say that. Your pain is very real—I see that every day. But by holding onto it, you're only perpetuating your victimhood. Worse, you're putting yourself in harm's way. You and people like Gerry who get too close."

Davina felt like the air had been punched out of her. How could Joe even say such a horrible thing? She wasn't being a victim—she was seeking justice.

"I'm not victimizing myself, Joe," Davina protested. "As long as *he's* out there attacking—*raping*—more young girls, he's victimizing me. That would be true whether I was trying to stop him or not. I just want justice, Joe. Not only for me, but for Elizabeth and Jessica and Joy—*all* of us. You understood that—or at least I thought you did."

"I thought I did, too. But then, this happened." Joe moved his wounded shoulder and cried out in pain. "Goddamn it! Get me some water, so I can take my pain meds." He gestured with his good hand to a small brown bottle on the coffee table.

Davina understood it was the pain barking orders, otherwise she'd have told him to get his own fucking meds. With a patient sigh, Davina got up and went into the kitchen. It was modern, a sophisticated setup in warm gray and cream—decidedly Joe's style; he had far fancier tastes than she did and the money to afford them. Davina opened the stainless steel, double-wide refrigerator and took out a bottle of Fiji water. The label was island-themed with a pretty pink hibiscus flower.

Fiji must be nice. I'd love to be there right now.

Anywhere but Staten Island.

Twisting the lid off the bottle, she handed it to Joe. She then shook a pill out of the bottle and gave him that, too; it was oxycodone. "Careful with this stuff, okay? I've known a lot of people hooked on it."

"Thanks. I'm going to switch to ibuprofen as soon as I can." Joe gulped down the pill with a hearty swig of water.

"I learned some things from the ex-Mrs. Monaghan," Davina ventured, keen to deflect Joe from the conversation about their relationship.

"Here we go." Joe took another sip of water. "Can you open the curtains?"

Davina threw the curtains wide, then turned back to Joe.

"Holy shit," Joe exclaimed. "I thought you'd just tied your hair back."

Davina smiled and patted her shorn locks. "I know it's a little extreme."

Joe eyed her with love. "No, Davina, you're beautiful. It's sleek. *Stylish.*"

"Now there's a couple of words I thought I'd never hear applied to me." Davina sat back down beside Joe. He reached up to caress her cheek, gently pulling her head down for a kiss. It was long and sweet.

"I guess you do like it, then," Davina murmured as she broke the kiss.

"It's a different you. A softer you. I like the new hair." Joe brushed a strand or two back behind Davina's ear. "It's sultry."

Davina's thoughts returned to Amber, the rape victim who chose to cover Son of Cropsey's signature with her hair and an illusion of wifely perfection. Perhaps Davina had it all wrong. Maybe she would be happier giving up and marrying Joe, having babies, and forgetting about her past.

But Amber hadn't forgotten the past. It was right there in her eyes, in the fragile tension in the air around her, in the camouflage she wore over the physical scar.

At least I don't have that to remind me every time I look in the mirror. Davina thought about what Joe said—that she was stoking the fire, putting all the people she loved in danger.

"Sandy told me Kevin was a real asshole. He was tight with Sean Delafield and the SBCA only because of his 'usefulness' as a police detective, and he knew they were using him."

"Riley," Joe said quietly.

"Yes. Riley, Darren, and even Sean. You remember how Packer told us he didn't think Cox was Son of Cropsey even back then?"

"Yeah."

"Well, according to what Kevin Monaghan told Sandy, Packer neglected to tell us he'd settled on a suspect of his own."

Joe's brow furrowed. "Who?"

"Kevin didn't tell her that. Not that Packer was necessarily right in his suspicions, but he *might* have been. Here's the thing—Kevin was deputized to talk Packer out of his line of inquiry, which caused him to dump the case in Riley's lap and retire not long after. The next time I see Mr. Monaghan, I've got a question for him."

"Why not call Packer and ask?"

"I tried," Davina said. "I got voice mail. He could've told us when we were there—and he didn't. I think maybe Geoff might have better luck, but I'll keep trying, anyway."

"D, this is major." Joe lay himself down with a grunt. "If you can find out who Packer suspected and why, this could all be over."

She tried hard to imagine that—having everything out in the open, the real Son of Cropsey arrested, his crimes stopped.

"Join me?" Joe scooted slightly to one side and gave Davina the puppy-dog look that was so hard to resist. Davina lay down and curled up to his side with an arm draped across his chest.

Joe yelped. "Ow!"

"I'm sorry." Davina moved her arm.

Joe turned his head to face Davina. "I need to ask you a question."

"Shoot."

"Did you ever have a thing for Nick Delafield?"

Davina didn't respond immediately. She'd known Nick half her life; something was definitely appealing about him, and Davina couldn't quite put her finger on it—some weird combination of big brother and guy you'd most like to turn from his rakish ways. She certainly had been pulled into his vortex. But was that a *thing*?

"I found him attractive and fascinating . . . back when I was in junior high."

"Did you ever sleep with him?"

"Joe! Jeez. Of course not. If it was a *thing*, it wasn't *that* kind of thing."

"Glad to hear it."

They lay side by side on the chaise for a while, silent, happy in one another's company. Joe's constant, regular breathing brought Davina comfort, just as it had at Battery Weed when she'd feared he was dying. She was grateful to have Joe in her life, but beneath her gratitude and love was a lingering fear she couldn't ever be what he needed her to be.

"I gotta try calling Geoff again." Davina sat up and rolled off the couch.

"Back to work, huh?" Joe's tone was cynical.

Davina chose to ignore him. "Can I get you something before I go?"

"Make me a sandwich, wifey."

Davina gave him a stern, schoolmarm stare. But, given his current situation and how she'd gotten him into this mess, Davina felt obliged. So she returned to the kitchen and threw together a turkey sandwich with mayo and mustard—just as Joe liked it.

Handing Joe the plate, she said, "I'm going. I'll keep trying Packer, too." She kissed his forehead and ran a hand through his soft blond hair. "I'll text you later."

"Okay." Joe took a bite of his sandwich.

Back in her car, Davina texted Geoff.

> I got dirt from Sandy & a new hairdo.

In mere moments, Geoff texted her back.

> Conga-rats. I've got some dirt too. I'm not sure Kevin is our guy. I'll come by tonight to explain

Davina put her phone into the dash cradle and started up her car. He was right; Kevin couldn't be the guy she was after.

And that left just one suspect in Davina's mind.

CHAPTER SEVENTY-TWO

SUNDAY, STEPHANIE'S LOVE SUPPLIES, 8TH AVE., BROOKLYN

Officer Karl Craigson huffed as he clambered out of his squad car in front of the adult store. He peered at the window display, which he was forced to admit was far more tasteful than he'd expected. A bright array of sparkly, skimpy minidresses, catsuits, and accompanying shoes with impossibly tall heels faced the street; Stephanie's could easily have been nothing more than a clothing shop for strippers.

Walking across the sidewalk to the door, he grumbled to himself about having been given the assignment. Of course, it was Riley's warped idea of a joke. Get the Christian gay cop to follow up the sex store lead on the Lord's Day and make him show the picture of the crude toy he had to put on his phone to the female proprietor. That asshat Riley had it in for Karl the moment he'd started at the precinct—even called him *God's fag* right to his face and nobody did a damn a thing about it.

Detective Riley, Karl had learned quickly, was pretty much untouchable. Rumor had it he'd shot his previous partner in the back and was transferred out quickly, and that was why the 120th Precinct was stuck with him. He'd made a big noise on a high-profile case the minute he'd set foot on Staten Island, made best friends with the Rock's key people, and that was that. Detective Tom Riley got to do whatever the heck he wanted.

Which included insisting the uniform he'd dumped the dildo follow-up onto *had* to personally take a picture of the thing in its evidence bag. Riley could have just texted him the image he had on his own cell phone, and that would have done just as well. But no, Riley had to have his fun.

The man was a hoot, all right.

"Pardon me, ma'am." Karl stepped into the store and was greeted by a slim, homely looking middle-aged lady. As he walked in, three customers walked straight out, trying to avoid eye contact with the officer. That left four others dotted about the place; each one eyed the cop with suspicion.

The store was pleasant enough inside—it was brightly lit and carried a smell that reminded him of the rubber gloves his mom used to wear to wash the dishes. "I'm looking for the owner—Stephanie?"

"There's no Stephanie." The lady stepped out from behind the counter. "I'm Claire, the proprietor of this fine establishment." She glanced around with pride at the mind-boggling array of leather, latex, and spandex clothing, DVDs covering every conceivable kink, and an eye-watering display of whips, vibrators, and myriad dildos.

"I'm hoping you can tell me if this is one of yours." Red-faced, Karl got out his phone, already displaying the diminutive fist-shaped dildo, and handed it over.

Claire eyed the photo a moment or two before handing the phone back carefully, as if it might break. "Looks like one from the stock I took off Stacy's hands—she couldn't sell 'em at her place," she said. "Did you speak to her already?"

Karl nodded. "A senior officer spoke to Ms. Abelman earlier this week."

"And he made you come all the way out here on a Sunday." Claire smiled.

"You're sure it was sold here?" Karl asked her as he tucked the phone back into his department-issued jacket.

Claire nodded and pointed across to a display of a half dozen or so identical sex toys on the wall opposite. "Yeah, that's one of mine, all right."

Karl felt an excited tingle in the pit of his stomach—he hoped it was something he'd never lose, even if he put in his full twenty-five on the job. "Do you think you'd be able to give me a list of people who bought one?"

"I'm sorry, Officer." Claire was genuinely shocked at the request. "But you must understand the sensitive nature of what we sell here—the anonymity of our clientele is paramount."

"The *toy* was found at a crime scene involving a young teenaged girl." Karl put on the pressure. "It fell out of her."

Claire's face paled noticeably, and Karl heard her swallow hard. "I'm sorry. I'd love to help, but without a warrant—"

The paperwork appeared in his hand as if by magic. "I have a warrant to search all your customer credit card receipts and CCTV footage." Karl deliberately raised his voice, and the quartet of the store's remaining browsers scurried for the door.

"Was that *really* necessary?" Claire huffed.

"Apparently so." Karl grinned at the woman; that would teach her to play hardball with the pros.

Resigned, flustered, Claire tapped at her keyboard behind the counter; her long, French-manicured nails rattled on the plastic keys.

"If the customer used a credit card, then we will have a record of the sale," she said. "If not, we'll have to go through all the CCTV footage since Stacy dropped off her dead stock."

Karl gave her a crooked smile. "I'm okay to wait while you look."

As it turned out, Officer Karl didn't have too long to wait at all.

"Here's your guy," Claire announced after ten minutes or so, and with relief in her voice. "Paid for the small black latex fist by Mastercard just over a month ago." She twisted the screen around for the cop to see the transaction record.

"Thank you, ma'am." Karl snapped a quick picture of the screen on his cell and dialed Riley as he made his way out of the store.

———

The Blue Star parking lot was almost empty. No surprise as the market didn't open until 1:00 p.m. on Sundays. So only Gino and a couple of the staff would be there. Millie's car was in her usual spot along the side of the building, but the door was slightly ajar. Davina bristled and walked over. How many times was she going to have to chastise her roommate about leaving the door propped open like that?

Davina closed the door properly and headed for the stairs that led to their apartment. A paper bag sat on the second stair; Davina riffled through the bag and found their usual groceries—eggs, milk, bread, Cheerios.

"Jesus, Millie."

Davina picked up the paper bag and made her way up the stairs. At the top, scanning the hallway, Davina saw the apartment door was open. Davina stopped dead as a chill sensation of dread creeped to the back of her skull. Slowly, senses alert, Davina stepped through the door and inside kitchen.

There, Millie lay facedown on the white linoleum.

CHAPTER SEVENTY-THREE

SUNDAY, DAVINA'S APARTMENT

"Millie!"

Heart pounding in her chest, Davina felt the bag slip from her hand. Blindly, she stumbled over the discarded groceries to where Millie lay.

Dropping to her knees by Millie's side, Davina felt for a pulse. But, before she could tell whether Millie was alive or dead, a strong, brutish arm whipped around her neck.

Davina gave out a loud, inhuman scream of fear and rage and clawed at the arm with her fingernails. The attacker hoisted Davina off the ground and tightened his grip around her throat, which had her gasping desperately for air. Instinct kicked in, and Davina let him have it with both feet. As her heels connected with his shins, she dug both elbows into the soft part of his torso.

"Fucking bitch!" he wheezed as the breath was punched out of him. In anger, he jerked backward, hauling Davina with him, the intention clearly to hurt her. It was a stupid move because it did nothing to keep Davina from stomping down on the bridge of his foot with her heel.

He screamed out in pain but didn't let her go. His arm did loosen enough, though, for Davina to twist her head around and clamp her teeth onto his biceps. Davina's assailant screamed again and his grip faltered. Davina bit down harder still and grasped his head with both hands, digging her nails into his face. She kept on biting down until he let her go, and when he finally relented, Davina leapt away, pivoted, and delivered a hard, solid jab to his stomach.

Davina fought for breath as the guy stumbled backward onto the kitchen counter; glasses and dishes clattered from the drying rack onto the floor. Davina raised her fists, ready to deliver the coup de grace, and as he straightened up, she got a good look at him.

Kevin Monaghan.

Seeing the retired cop didn't surprise Davina as much as she'd expected.

Recovering quickly from the blow, Kevin snatched the bread knife from the knife block and pointed it at Davina. The knife's blade was dull, the tip not designed for stabbing, but it was long and made for a perfect target. Davina's sudden, swift roundhouse kick sent the knife spinning right out of Kevin's hand.

Stunned, Kevin stood stock-still with his mouth open. "You some kind of fucking ninja?"

"I teach martial arts, Kev," Davina growled with a wry grin. "You picked the wrong girl to fuck with. What are you doing here, and what have you done to Millie?" She hated to hear her own voice shake, and she hated that tears blurred her vision.

"You see, that's your problem, Speers. You ask too many goddamn questions." Kevin's voice was a menacing snarl.

Davina plucked the knife from the floor and balanced it in her hand. Did he know she'd talked with Sandy that morning? Was someone spying on her?

Millie groaned and stirred, which sent a wave of relief through Davina. Thank God she'd turned up when she had—before Kevin could finish what he'd obviously come to do.

"Mill?"

"If I were you, I'd be more worried about myself, bitch," Kevin sneered, his lip curled at one corner.

"The bitch is the one holding the knife, remember."

Smiling, Kevin pulled a snub-nosed revolver from the front pocket of his jacket and pointed it in Millie's direction.

Davina's throat went dry, but she couldn't show the man her fear. "Put the gun down, Kevin. Unless you're afraid to fight like a real man."

"This *is* how real men fight." Kevin pulled the trigger, and the bullet tore into the linoleum mere inches away from Millie's head.

Millie uttered a stifled, mewling cry, and Davina flinched, almost dropping the knife from her trembling fingers. She hoped Gino or one of his stockers had heard the noise and called the cops, but knew she couldn't count on it.

Davina shook her head. "No, this is how cowards fight. You're just like Sean Delafield and all the rest of his buddies. Maybe even worse, Kevin— you made what they did possible."

"Sit down." The ex-cop waved the gun toward a chair.

"I'd rather stand."

Kevin fired another warning shot into the floor—even closer to Millie. "I said, *sit the fuck down*."

Davina had no choice.

There was a good chance she was about to die, and unless she chucked the knife at Kev, she had no way of fighting back. Davina knew if she did attempt to use the knife, he would shoot her before it even left her hand. So, she pulled the chair out from under the kitchen table and sat.

Kevin's gaze flayed her. "This is all your fault, you dumb bitch. Do you have any idea how much mess you stirred up this week?"

"I do—and it was for a good cause." Davina placed the knife on the table.

He sneered, "*Cause?*"

"To bring the real Son of Cropsey to justice. Along with the sick bastards who've enabled him."

Kevin stiffened, and his expression changed to narrow-eyed suspicion. "What the fuck are you babbling about? That case was closed years ago."

"You know it's still wide open better than anyone," Davina said.

"What—you think *I* raped all those girls?"

Davina shook her head. "No, Kevin, I don't think you did. But I'm pretty sure you know who did. Or at least you know who Ron Packer suspected. You were his partner—he must've told you." Elbow on the table, Davina propped her chin on her fist. "Who was it, Kev? Who did Ron think was the real Son of Cropsey?"

The ex-cop's jaw bunched as he ground his teeth. His cold, calculating eyes fixed on Davina as his face turned an unhealthy shade of crimson. Davina knew she was right on the button: Sandy had been telling the gospel truth.

"You're fucking certifiable," Kevin growled through clenched teeth. "So's your little piece of chocolate." He tilted his head toward Millie. "You two doing each other? I'd pay good money to see that. I gotta say, I gave it some thought myself—never had a Black woman." He grinned. "Day's still young, though."

Filled with rage, Davina jumped from her seat and reached for the knife.

Kevin cocked the gun with a loud, threatening *click* and aimed it directly into Davina's face.

"Sit the fuck down, *bitch*."

He's waiting for someone.

The realization hit so forcefully that Davina felt it in her bones. Riley? She sat down slowly and met Kevin's gaze. "Ron Packer figured out the real suspect, didn't he? My guess is it was someone in Sean Delafield's inner circle. Someone important, or maybe someone who had dirt on him. So, he had you convince Packer that his theories were all wrong. Except, Ron *knew* he was *right*. You must have really leaned hard to get him to drop the case and get out of the way."

Monaghan wiggled the gun a little and gave Davina a cocky smirk. "Interesting theory, Miss Speers. If you were as smart as you think you are, you'd have done the same thing a long time ago."

"No." Davina stared at him. "I want Son of Cropsey—the *real* one— to pay for what he's done to all the girls he raped ten years ago, and now. Who is he, Kev?"

"Shut up."

"Was it you who doctored the video from Scott Kantor's bachelor party? The one Darren sent anonymously to the *Advance*?"

Monaghan fell silent, his eyes fixed on Davina.

"You don't have to tell me. I already know the answer, Kevin. You left enough frames on it to give away most of the people there—including me. Why'd you do it?"

Kevin broke his silence. "Because the only bigger bitch than you on Staten Island is Sean Delafield. He took George down, then Darren."

Davina exhaled heavily. Had he also taken down his own son? "Sean killed them?"

"I don't fucking know." Kevin threw his hands in the air, the gun pointing at the ceiling. "I don't know why all these assholes are dying. I just know I didn't do it."

"Then who did?"

"Listen, Detective Slut." Monaghan stepped toward Davina and pressed the barrel of the gun to her forehead. "That's none of your fucking business."

The cold metal of the gun muzzle seemed to sear Davina's skin. She desperately wanted to pull her head away but feared Kevin would abandon his plan to wait for whomever and pull the trigger. Speaking softly, Davina said, "Put the gun down, Kevin. It's not worth pissing off your boss by killing me."

"My *boss?*" Kevin spat. "Nah. You got it all wrong, bitch. We're a team, a posse. I work for them, and they work for me."

They.

"Who did Packer suspect?" Davina demanded again.

"You're a stubborn bitch, aren't you? Gotta admire that. You want me to give you a secret to take to your grave, do you?"

Davina was preparing herself to knock the gun aside and fly at Kevin when her apartment door swung open.

Detective Tom Riley stood in the doorway, eyes cold and dark as a winter morning.

CHAPTER SEVENTY-FOUR

SUNDAY, DAVINA'S APARTMENT

With Kevin's gun still pressed tight to her forehead, Davina shifted her gaze to Riley.

"Put the gun down, Kevin," the cop said. He held his service weapon in his hand, finger alongside the trigger, aimed at the floor. He was relaxed; as if the weapon was a part of his hand.

Kevin straightened and stowed the gun in his pocket. "I was just joking with her, Tom. Softening the bitch up for you."

Riley stepped into the room, and three uniformed officers filed in behind him.

"*Joking,*" Riley mocked. "Then I guess you weren't really planning on answering her question."

Kevin paled visibly, and fat beads of sweat popped up on his forehead.

"Yeah," Riley said, "I heard you. You're like a bull in a china shop: Somebody's always gotta clean up after you." He shifted his chill gaze to where Millie lay; she was breathing heavily and uttering the occasional whimper. "What the fuck were you thinking, attacking this woman?

Firing your sidearm with a fucking market right downstairs? The damn stockers called 911. Fortunately, we were close by."

I'll bet.

Davina focused on the strained dynamic between the two men, seeking any opportunity to break free before things *really* got out of hand.

Kevin stepped away from Davina. He shook himself and plastered a crooked smile on his crimson face. It was spectacularly unconvincing. "Sorry, boss. But, hey, mission accomplished. I got the girl."

"You got sloppy." Riley turned to the uniforms. "All but Franco out. Guard the door—this is officially a crime scene."

Tensing, Davina knew things were about to get ugly. Hopelessly outgunned, she'd most likely die. Maybe that would be for the best. Maybe that would be the end of it, and no one else would have to suffer. But Millie didn't deserve to die for her roommate's actions.

"Kevin," said Riley, "let me make one thing crystal clear. Something you never seemed to understand. You *always* worked for *me*."

Before Kevin could reply, Riley raised his sidearm and shot him dead center in the chest. Blood blossomed on the ex-cop's shirt and he keeled over onto his back.

Riley stood over him, looking down. "You're a fucking idiot, Kevin. You deserve this." Riley unloaded four more bullets into Kevin's chest. His body jerked and twitched, and Davina's kitchen floor turned red beneath him.

Davina's breath came in ragged gasps as she tried to form words. Only one emerged from her lips. "Why?"

Riley turned to her; the movement reminded her of a hawk assessing its prey. "You should be more grateful, Davina. I just saved you from a hostage situation. Isn't that right, Officer Franco?"

The cop by the door—a young guy with a crew cut and wolf-bright gaze—nodded. "Right, sir."

Davina eyed Riley. "I don't—"

"This dumb piece of shit was threatening you." Riley nodded at Kevin's lifeless body and placed a hand over his heart. "I'm merely upholding the law. It's my job." His voice was calm, almost gentle.

It was the same tone Davina remembered from ten years ago when the cop had assured her she'd just had a bad dream, that she must have seen something on TV that frightened her—and that the vivid nightmare of being raped and suffocated in her bed was the result.

"You've never upheld the law a day in your life," Davina said. "You . . . this . . . you can't possibly hope to get way with this."

Riley squatted down in front of Davina's chair so they were at eye level. "Is that the way to talk to someone who just saved your life?" Reaching out, Riley ran his fingers through Davina's hair. "Pretty little damsel in distress. This is how I'm to be repaid?"

A thick wave of nausea roiled Davina's stomach as the cloying stink of Riley's cologne hit her. *That* cologne. That horrid, suffocating, God-awful smell. She coughed in his face. "If you're going to kill me—"

"*Kill* you? No, sweet girl. I can't do that," Riley said with a sinister grin. "I promised your mother I'd stay close to you. Look out for you. Believe it or not, I do actually keep *some* promises." Leaning in closer still, he placed a hand to Davina's cheek.

She wanted to puke. "I'll tell—"

"Who are you gonna tell? And what? That Kevin Monaghan claimed there was another Son of Cropsey suspect back in the day? *Kevin's dead.* He died trying to shut you up because you knew something about Sean Delafield that the SBCA didn't want widely known. You found out about Sean's behavior at a certain bachelor party—behavior unbecoming of a steward of industry and especially a city councilman. You knew about it because you were there . . . in the flesh." He smiled. "A whole lotta sweet young flesh, as I recall."

"I don't remember any of it."

The cop peered deeply into Davina's face, studying it as if trying to read her thoughts. "You don't *need* to remember. It's all on a hard drive— you can watch it anytime you like. And because of that, Kevin ambushed you in your own home. I'd say you were lucky I just happened to show up to interview you about what happened yesterday at Fort Wadsworth." Riley lifted his gun a little for emphasis. "Naturally, I was forced to act."

He turned his head to address Officer Franco. "Tony, what did you see here?"

"Kevin Monaghan was holding Ms. Speers and her roommate hostage. We stepped in and saved them both." His voice was firm, self-assured.

"And that's exactly what I saw," Riley said. "Thanks, Tony. Go fill the other guys in on the salient points of what went down here while I finish up with the witness."

Officer Franco let himself out into the upper hallway, closing the door behind him.

Riley returned his attention to Davina. "I should add that, when your friend wakes up, she's going to tell the same story. Kevin Monaghan came here looking for you and frog-marched her into your apartment with the intent of surprising you when you came home. He knocked her senseless, lay in wait, and ambushed you. As to how it ended, we have multiple witnesses—all fine, upstanding police officers. Case closed."

Davina's racing mind double-clutched. Riley was right. Millie hadn't been conscious of what had occurred after Davina's arrival. Her story would match Riley's in its essentials. Were she to say anything to contradict Riley's story, five people would proclaim her a liar, while her past on the streets—a runaway, a drug user, a teller of wild tales—would cast doubt on anything she said.

Davina whispered faintly, "Liar."

Riley smiled at her. "Pot, kettle, Davina. Do you think anyone will believe you? Well, I guess your boyfriends might, but who'd believe *them?*"

"Why are you doing this? Why have you busted my ass all these years?" Davina snarled.

Riley holstered his weapon, hauled Davina out of her chair, and pulled her roughly against his body. She felt his hard-on through his pants.

"Because there are things I'd rather do to your ass than bust it, but busting it at least meant I got to put my hands on you." To illustrate his point, Riley grasped Davina's ass with both hands and thrust himself against her, growling like an animal.

Davina felt like screaming, retching, and sobbing the way she had when Son of Cropsey shattered her young life. Had it been Riley, after all?

"You know when I started wanting that?" he asked with a lascivious growl. "After Son of Cropsey broke you in."

Davina opened her mouth to tell Riley what a sick fuck he was, but his words hit her like a freight train. "You fucking *believed* me! You told everyone I was lying! Was that because you had some poor bastard in custody already?" Davina shook all over with rage, uncontrollable tremors ran up and down her limbs, and she felt as weak and helpless as she had all those years ago.

"Smart and beautiful." Riley smiled down at her, his expression almost fond. "Before that, before him, you were just a little kid. Sophie's kid. After he finished with you, you were a woman."

Davina almost threw up in the cop's face. "Get the fuck out of my kitchen."

Riley ignored her. "You felt it, too, on some level. And you liked it. That's why you hit the streets. That's why you turned tricks."

"I never turned tricks, Riley. *Never*," Davina snarled, her spittle spraying Riley's smug face. "I stripped, I danced, I didn't let *anybody* touch me."

"I'm touching you, and from the way you're trembling, I'd say you *really* like it."

"No." It was the only word Davina could force from her mouth.

Riley's hands released Davina's buttocks and traveled up and around her torso to her breasts. She tried to pull away, but the table was in her way, pinning her against Riley as he kneaded her breasts. Leaning in close, lips to her ear, he whispered, "Now who's the liar, Davina?"

Snapping her head to the side, Davina tried to bite the cop's face. Laughing, he grasped the hair at the back of Davina's head and twisted her face away. He then bit her neck just below the left ear.

Davina yipped in pain.

"Explain that to your ever-loving Joe," Riley told her. "I guarantee he'll hear a different story from me. I'm looking forward to our next conversation, Ms. Speers. Ambulance is on its way, thanks to your downstairs neighbors. We'll be right downstairs to fill in the EMTs."

Riley's cell phone trilled; its ring muffled by his pocket. He let Davina go with a grunt and a hard shove that made her tumble over the table onto the floor. She crawled to where Millie lay and put fingers to her pulse; it was strong and regular. A gentle exploration of Millie's head and neck located a golf ball–sized lump at the base of her skull.

Stepping away from Davina, Riley took the call. "You did?" he growled. "Who was it?"

Silence followed as he listened to the caller, the voice too faint for Davina to make out. "You're *fucking* kidding me?" the detective spat, his mood darkening still further. "Are you sure about this, fag?"

A few more seconds of silence, then the voice spoke again.

"Do nothing, tell nobody about this—and don't you fucking dare pick up the suspect. This is one I'm gonna do myself." With that, Riley ended the call and stormed over to the apartment door and was gone. Davina heard the cop yell, "Franco!" at the top of his voice out in the hallway and then the downstairs door slam.

She found herself praying that the ambulance would arrive soon and settled in to wait, alone with Millie, Kevin Monaghan's corpse, and the knowledge that everything she knew and believed and had hoped to achieve was irrelevant. Her story wouldn't match anyone else's. Unless . . . unless she could convince Ron Packer to come forward. Clearly, Riley didn't believe he would.

Davina wondered if she had the strength left to convince him he must.

CHAPTER SEVENTY-FIVE

SUNDAY, PARAMOUNT THEATER

"THERE!" RILEY POINTED OUT THE WHITE SINGLE-DECKER BUS parked outside the old movie theater. The tour bus was decorated with pictures of smiling ghosts and grim-faced specters in period costumes and chains. Stretching all the way along the vehicle's side were the words: Staten Island Ghost Tour.

Officer Franco pulled the car up at a slant in front of the bus, although if the bus driver wanted to make a hasty getaway, there was no way a Crown Vic would stop it.

The theater was the third supposedly haunted stop of the tour.; Riley had arrived at the second stop to pick up the suspect the uniform had identified in the Brooklyn sex shop. Riley had put in a couple of calls on the way from Davina's apartment to people he knew in the Historical Society to find out which tour ran Sundays, and there he was—all primed and ready to sort out yet another fucking mess.

"You take the back," Riley barked at Franco as they got out of the car. "And don't call backup until I tell you."

"Yes, sir," Franco agreed without question. He'd worked with Riley a long time and knew better than to question Detective Riley's orders.

Riley made his way around the bus and to the Paramount just as the theater's door opened and a bunch of tourists spilled out onto the sidewalk. Behind the first batch of six or seven, the therapist who ran ghost tours, Angela Donato—clad in a neatly pressed, nineteenth-century dress and bonnet—ushered them toward the bus. And a little way behind her to ensure they got everyone safely out of the decrepit movie theater, Angela's husband Carlo was dressed in accompanying period garb.

"Carlo Donato." Riley reached for his card as he strode toward his target, who froze like a deer in the headlights.

"Can we help you, Tom?" Angela called over, all but shoving her tourists onto the bus.

"Carlo Donato, I'm arresting you on suspicion of the sexual assault of a minor. You have the right—"

Grabbing the tourist closest to him—a heavily pregnant young Asian woman—Carlo pushed her at Riley and darted back into the theater. The woman shrieked loudly in Riley's ear as he caught her and deftly moved her to the side. She was lucky he'd acted purely by reflex; otherwise, she'd have been flat on her knocked-up ass on the sidewalk.

Cursing beneath his breath, Riley set off after Carlo. He was in no mood for playing chase but was rather pleased Carlo had made the decision he had. It would make things that much easier.

The theater was bright inside, the holes in the roof allowing plenty of sunlight in to illuminate the sorry state it had fallen into. Riley wondered how the hell they allowed anyone inside—especially tourists—as the place was obviously a deathtrap. But the Historical Society held a lot of sway on the island, and the Donatos were prominent members, as well as in with Sean Delafield; with connections like those, nothing was impossible, and health and safety be damned.

A movement came from the left.

"Carlo!" Riley hollered, his voice resounding around the crumbling walls. "Give it up!"

Nothing, other than the sound of running footsteps and a door being forced open.

Riley headed toward the back of the theater, where the sloping floor led to the double exit doors. He was in good shape for a man of his age, which was just as well, because Carlo Donato was fucking fast.

As Riley shouldered his way through the exit doors, they creaked out their complaint on rusted hinges, and a cloud of thick, gray dust puffed out from the walls around the frame. One hearty shove and Riley reckoned the whole thing would come crashing down.

There, dashing along the hallway by the long-abandoned restrooms, Carlo was on his way toward a busted-down door. Riley thought the guy looked ridiculous in his off-white cotton shirt, thick brown pants, and peaked cap.

Riley followed Carlo through the STAFF ONLY door and up a narrow, dank staircase. Although the ceiling above it was largely intact, the light was poor there, making Riley uneasy. Sure, he could take care of himself, but there was no way of knowing if the perp was armed until he was on top of him. By then, it could be too late. Riley was banking on the element of surprise—Carlo had no idea he was about to be arrested that morning. And the fact it was highly unlikely meant chances were slim that Carlo was carrying a weapon to show a bunch of tourists where Staten Island's ghosts were supposed to hang out.

"You're just making this hard on yourself, Carlo!" Riley called out. "You should give up now. I can have the SWAT team here in ten minutes, and there's no place to run."

In his peripheral vision, in the gloom up ahead, Riley caught sight of Carlo slinking through one of the trio of doors at the top of the staircase; the guy obviously knew his way around the theater, and Riley wasn't sure what to expect. Of course, he really needed to call backup, likely SWAT, too, but he didn't care to take the risk of Carlo talking. All those years of Rob Cox rotting behind bars, Riley taking the glory of nailing Staten Island's resident rapist, and all the while, Carlo fucking Donato had been biding his time.

Fuming, his mind spinning with myriad scenarios of the repercussions of his secret coming out, Riley bounded up the remaining stairs and along the short hallway. He'd seen Carlo duck into the second of the warped, peeling doors on the right—it stood slightly ajar, as if the sick fuck was inviting the detective inside.

"This is your last chance," Riley growled; it irked him he'd actually socialized with Carlo on occasion, gotten drunk with him at Sean Delafield's parties. Of all the fucking people . . .

Riley found himself in the projection room. The projector was long gone, of course, as were the racks of reels that once adorned the walls. All that remained was an empty shell of a room, with holes in the wooden floor where the bolts holding the machinery once protruded. Riley paused a second for his eyes to adjust; the room was dim, the only light being what struggled to enter from the theater through the cracked, grimy window at its far end.

A shape appeared from the gloom: Carlo. His knees were bent slightly, arms held in a boxer's stance, fists clenched. He was not going to go down without a fight, not that it came as a surprise at all. Carlo knew what happened to people who crossed Tom Riley.

Riley pulled his gun.

Carlo leapt forward and sprung impossibly high into the air. A foot lashed out and, before Riley could react, it connected with the gun, cracking his fingers and knocking the weapon out of his hand.

"*Son of a bitch!*" Riley grunted and launched himself at Carlo, his fists aimed at the guy's face. Pain shot through Riley's knuckles as his first punch hit home, squarely on Carlo's nose. Cartilage crunched, blood flew from both nostrils, and the guy's head snapped back, eyes rolling.

Seizing his chance, Riley lunged again and clamped both hands around Carlo's throat. Carlo reacted in a split second, bringing both hands up inside Riley's arms and knocking them away with one solid, outward sweep. Riley's elbows let out an unearthly *crack* as the joints popped; a lesser man would have had them broken. The cop reeled backward, his feet threatening to trip him over; Riley fought hard to stay upright.

"Let me go, Tom," Carlo finally broke his silence. "You put your man away. Nobody has to know."

"*You* know," Riley sneered. "Why the fuck couldn't you stay retired?" Regaining his balance, Riley stepped forward; he couldn't afford to be afraid of Carlo's fists.

Carlo shrugged and offered a wry smile. "Sean Delafield is about to fuck up our island, Tom, *somebody* has to do something." Jumping toward Riley, Carlo launched a flurry of punches around the cop's face and shoulders. Riley deflected the blows the best he could and backed away toward the door.

"*Carlo!*" Angela Donato's voice startled Riley; it was sudden, shrill, and filled with panic. It also distracted Carlo and, just for a second, there was a pause in his attack as his eyes met his wife's across the projector room.

Riley charged into Carlo, using his weight advantage to shove him up against the wall, twisting him around as he did so. With his arms pinned against the wall, Carlo could do nothing more than kick out his feet which, in such close proximity, were all but useless. Riley swung an arm around Carlo's neck and began applying pressure.

Nine seconds and it would all be over.

"It's not just me . . . you have to stop . . ." Carlo gasped as Riley choked the life from him.

"Save it, asshole," Riley growled in Carlo's ear and squashed his broken nose harder into the damp wall.

Carlo opened his mouth again, either to say something or gasp for breath, but then his body went limp against the cop's, his legs buckling. Only Riley's weight pinning him to the wall kept Carlo Donato from slumping to the bare concrete floor.

Carlo was unconscious, but Riley kept up the pressure on his neck, starving the man's brain of oxygen. Nine seconds was all it took to shut Carlo down, but Riley reckoned another twenty, maybe thirty for good luck; the sick bastard would either slip away quietly or be left with irreparable brain damage.

Either way, it would give the detective plenty of leeway to pin the latest rapes on the copycat nerdy guy from the Historical Society who took the Rock's history far too seriously.

A noise from the doorway sounded like a quiet sob.

Shit. He'd forgotten about Angela.

Finally relinquishing his grip on Carlo's neck, Riley let the guy slide to the floor. He twisted his head around to see Angela Donato. She stood stock-still, framed by the doorway, eyes wide, her face a blank mask.

CHAPTER SEVENTY-SIX

TWO WEEKS LATER, SATURDAY, ST. GEORGE FERRY TERMINAL

THE HEAVY RAIN PELTED DAVINA'S CAR ALL THE WAY TO THE
St. George Ferry Terminal. Her bags were packed in the back seat—all four
of them. It was everything she was going to need; the apartment in the
East Village was small and wouldn't hold all that much. Charlene had
helped her find it and had arranged a part-time paid position for Davina as
a counselor's assistant at a Narcotics Anonymous halfway program.

Davina had transferred her credits to John Jay College, and once she
was settled in, she planned to find a position at a health club or gym doing
what she did best. Gerry had left Dobson's Gym to Davina in her will, but
she had little desire to set foot in the place—too many memories, too
much pain. She'd put the Florczak sisters in as joint managers and planned
to swing by once a month or so. The place would do just fine without her,
and she was content to leave it at that for the foreseeable future.

Why did making a fresh start feel so much like she'd failed? Not just
herself, but her fellow victims. She'd so desperately wanted to bring Son of
Cropsey to justice, look the guy straight in the eyes as they cuffed him and

had him face trial—maybe even get the chance to play hero and mete out a little justice of her own.

But no. The rapist had been caught by good, old-fashioned police work—the kind the likes of Detective Riley knew little about. And Carlo Donato was dead, the Son of Cropsey legacy along with him, and Davina and his other victims had been denied the closure they all so desperately needed. Of all the possible suspects, Davina would never have even considered Carlo in a million years. Sure, he was on the periphery of Sean Delafield's slippery circle, but he was a regular at Dobson's, he ran the Historical Society's ghost tours, and his wife was a wonderfully caring trauma counselor. Davina couldn't help but wonder how Angela was coping—not only with her beloved husband's death, but with finding out he'd kept such a dark secret from her and the patients she'd helped work through the trauma of being raped by Son of Cropsey. They were actually his victims. With no children to comfort Angela, Davina couldn't begin to imagine the poor woman's pain.

And, as if to stick a huge period at the end of it all, Ron Packer had been found dead in his retirement home. According to Geoff's intel, the cause had been a heart attack—possibly more genuine than those experienced by George Modica and Darren Rivers, but who knew with Riley, Sean Delafield, and the others with skin in the game? Geoff had hypothesized it might have been brought on by ten years of guilt, exacerbated by the stress of the rapist's case rearing its head again, which had done little to assuage Davina's conscience about causing yet another death.

All Davina could cling to was the hope Son of Cropsey's—*Carlo's*—victims would find some solace in their attacker's demise.

For her, it was an empty feeling, a vacuum of emotion, and the niggling sensation that something didn't quite add up.

Arriving at the ferry terminal parking lot, Davina took her two rolling bags, duffel, and backpack out of the back of the Jetta and locked the doors. The rain persisted, so Davina moved as fast as she could to find shelter. Once under the overhang, Davina checked around for Father Stephen. At Gerry's funeral he'd promised he'd be there to see Davina off when she left Staten Island. Considering she'd openly told him she'd turned her back on God years ago, she'd thought the gesture was a nice one, if somewhat odd. She thought maybe the rain had put him off—it wasn't as if they were close or anything.

But, instead of the priest, she spotted Joe making his way toward her. His hands were stuffed deep in his pockets, his face as colorless as the grim day.

"Hey," Davina greeted him.

"Hey."

Davina held out her car keys. He took them, briefly squeezing her hand.

"Thanks for this. Selling the car was just . . . I ran out of momentum packing up my apartment and saying goodbye to Millie." She tried to smile and found it impossible.

"I can't believe you're doing this, D."

"Me either." Davina studied the rain-slicked blacktop, unable to meet eyes with her lover. "But it was inevitable. I have to go. You know I do."

"Davina," Joe pleaded with her. "Can't we give it some more time?"

"Time won't help me, Joe." Davina tried to find the right words. "It's all still here on Staten Island. Riley—"

"Riley is on suspension, Davina." Joe sounded hopeful.

"They put him on suspension pending the inquiry into Carlo Donato's death, Joe," Davina said. "You know what that means? It means the police want to be seen to be doing something, and Riley will be back on the streets in a month or so. All the more reason for me to get the fuck out of Dodge." Her attempt at humor fell embarrassingly flat.

There was also Sean Delafield, plus the memories Son of Cropsey had indelibly left on her psyche and the sad reminders of Nick. Davina had been through her list of reasons to go so many times that she knew them by heart.

Tears formed in Joe's eyes. He spoke softly, "You could have a wonderful life here. With me."

Davina felt her chest tighten. "I could. And I *can't*. We talked about this, Joe. People have died around me. If I grab that life—as much as I want to—more people might die. You might even be one of them."

Joe put up a hand to stop her. "It's okay. I get it."

"You could always come with me. You'd easily walk into a job in Manhattan."

"You know I can't do that." Joe stared across the water. "I've just been promoted. I own a home. I love living on the Rock. I've never lived anywhere else. Nor have I wanted to. This is my home."

"Yeah, it is. Because your memories here are happy ones. At least, those not connected with me."

"Davina—"

"It's true and you know it. Your life got all complicated because of me. It got dangerous because of me. Understand, Joe—my memories of Staten Island are painful and scarring and deep. When I thought there was a chance I could fix that—that I could bring about some sort of justice and healing—I was prepared to be here. But I can't do that. I didn't solve anything with my poking around and my investigating. It only got people killed and hurt. People I loved. I'm glad you can salvage your happy life here. I can't." Sighing, Davina fought back tears. "So, this is where we are, Joe. I can't be here and you can't *not* be here."

Joe flushed red and lowered his gaze. "Can I at least help you with your bags?" Joe slipped Davina's car keys into his pocket.

"I think I got it."

Joe flung his arms around her and held her tightly. Relaxing in his embrace, she didn't feel the urge to pull away, and she recalled that one perfect night when she was able to give herself to Joe freely. She'd hoped then it was a sign of things to come. Instead, it embodied what she could not have.

"I'll always be here for you, you know?" Joe murmured in her ear, his breath warm against her cold skin. "I love you, Davina Speers."

Unable to stem the flow, Davina's tears began to fall. "I love you too, Joe. But I can't *live* here. I tried. I really, *really* did." What she didn't say was that he wasn't even willing to try life beyond this messed-up island. If he loved her as much as he claimed, wouldn't he at least have tried?

Joe released his grip on Davina's shoulders and wiped his nose with his hand. He glanced toward the ferry, which was already boarding passengers. The cacophonous blare of a boarding horn filled the air.

"That's my cue," Davina said.

Joe nodded.

Davina turned away and pulled her bags along toward the ramp, the rain cool and soft on her face. Checking back over her shoulder as she set foot on the ramp, she saw Joe was gone.

It was actually a relief.

Davina climbed to the second deck of the *Samuel I. Newhouse* and hauled her bags along to the stern of the boat. An empty bench beneath an overhang had a great view of the water; Davina positioned her bags there and sat. The damp bench soaked into her jeans. She dug out a rainproof jacket and laid it atop one of the rolling suitcases; she'd put it on if the rain became more insistent. The ferry's horn blew once again as the boat eased away from the dock.

I'm starting over with nothing but painful memories. Goodbye, Staten Island. All you did was take from me.

CHAPTER SEVENTY-SEVEN

SATURDAY, 4:30 P.M., OFFICES OF THE STATEN ISLAND ADVANCE

GEOFF WONG SAT AT HIS DESK MASSAGING HIS TEMPLES. HE'D been in the newsroom since 6:00 a.m. to write up his article on Sean Delafield's withdrawal from the city council race following the tragic suicide of his son. He'd found himself, instead, spending too much time in front of his laptop agonizing over a story that would probably never see the light of day.

As far as everyone at the paper knew—especially Stan, his editor—after Carlo Donato had been caught and killed and the story reported to exhaustion, often with Geoff's byline, the reporter had moved on from the Son of Cropsey case.

Geoff hadn't.

Starting with the press conference where the NYPD spokesperson and Staten Island DA proclaimed Carlo Donato a Son of Cropsey copycat, something seemed to stink, and it wasn't the Fresh Kills Landfill. Things didn't jive with what he and Davina had uncovered. With Donato conveniently killed by Detective Reilly, and the wife, Angela Donato, cleared of any involvement, there was no one to prove Riley had gotten it wrong this time—or the last time, a decade ago, when he fingered Rob Cox as Son of Cropsey. A frame-up, according to what retired cop Ron Packer down in Florida had told Davina and Joe.

The only clue left that might prove whether Cox was or was not Son of Cropsey was the theta, the enigmatic symbol the police withheld from the public that tied the original ten-year-old crimes to the recent ones. The symbol had appeared in enough of the cases before and then *after* Rob Cox's arrest to mean something. That it appeared on the recent Son of Cropsey victims could mean either Carlo *was* indeed the serial rapist who'd just happened to take a ten-year hiatus, or Carlo was Riley's fall guy who had been provided the inside information by the police department —just like Davina and, he suspected, Cox was. Either way, Geoff knew the 120th Precinct had some explaining to do, but that was never going to happen. No, for the moment he was at a dead end.

Stan broke into Geoff's musings when he dropped a heavy box on his desk. "Coffee?" He held up a plastic-capped paper cup that had been perched on the top of the box.

"Yeah, thanks."

Stan handed him the cup. "Fresh pot," he said.

"I hope you don't think this means we're going steady, boss." Geoff savored the brew. "What's in the box? Christmas come early?" It was a standard brown 12 x 16 x 10-inch-deep corrugated cardboard banker's box, the kind used for storing or shipping files.

"Actually, I spotted this in the mailroom," he said. "It's addressed to your buddy, Davina Speers, care of the *Staten Island Advance*. It's heavy, whatever it is."

Geoff's eyes went straight to the return address: Tina Packer, 15 S. Hummingbird Rd., Tampa, FL.

Packer.

Wife? Daughter?

Standing up, Geoff slit the shipping tape with a house key and opened the flap.

"*The* Packer?" Stan ventured.

Geoff nodded as he surveyed packed rows of well-worn letter-sized file folders. His gaze was immediately drawn to a single page of pink mono-grammed stationery and a handwritten note, which he read aloud for Stan's benefit.

Dear Ms. Speers.

My name is Tina Packer. I'm Ronald Packer's daughter. As you already know, he was, for many years, a detective with the NYPD on Staten Island. What you may not know is that he died unexpectedly a few days ago. As my sister and I were going through his effects I came upon this box of files addressed to you. I believe he intended to send you the package before he died. I hope this helps with whatever you are looking for.

Sincerely, Tina.

With interest piqued, Stan perched on the corner of the desk. "So, what's in there?"

As Geoff riffled through the folders, the enormity of what he held in his hands hit him. Grinning, he turned to his boss. "This is literally *deus ex machina*, Stan. Don't let anyone ever tell you there is no God."

"Stop with the suspense, Geoff."

"What we have before us are police reports on pretty much everyone who was anyone in the original Son of Cropsey case," he said. "Look at this," he said, extracting a few folders. "Sean Delafield and some of his cronies were persons of interest. Father Stephen—"

"Chapelle?" Stan cut in.

Geoff nodded. "The one and the same," he said with a wry smile. "Of course, the priest was a suspect! And you, Stan—you've got your very own folder in Packer's pile."

"I'm flattered. Probably after my sources. I wonder if we have to call in the lawyers."

Geoff plucked a rough, stained file from the box. "And look what we have here—Carlo Donato." He flipped the file open. "I guess Ron Packer had the sicko on his radar even way back then. Here's his note that Riley ruled him out, though.

"And that begs the question: If any of these guys, Carlo Donato included, was actually the original Son of Cropsey, why would Cox take the rap? Did Riley have something on him? What could possibly be so bad that you'd be willing to go to prison for something you didn't do?"

Immersed in the file, Geoff barely heard what his editor said. "Stan, get this. Donato was a suspect in a whole bunch of sex-based crimes in his youth—starting with voyeurism when he was thirteen."

"The kid was a Peeping Tom?" Stan let out a wry laugh. "What teenager doesn't like to sneak an eyeful when the opportunity presents itself?"

"His neighbors caught him hiding in their daughter's closet one night." Geoff frowned at his boss. "The girl was nine, Stan."

"Ah."

"All he got was a slap on the wrist, and nothing else stuck after that. In fact, everything in here is suspicion and psych reports—no arrests, no convictions, just a whole bunch of people saying what they *think* Carlo Donato is capable of. There's even a report from his own sister." Geoff skimmed the typewritten sheet. "She was fourteen, he was seventeen, and she claimed she was stoned when she woke up with him on top of her with his hand on her throat choking her out and his dick inside her. But she dropped the charges. Seems Carlo smooth-talked his way out of that one and his folks backed him up."

"I've interviewed plenty of criminals like him over the years," Stan said. "They could charm the panties off Mother Teresa. And those types have a real penchant for getting into—and then out of—jams. They live for it."

"You know, I can see why Riley went for Cox," Geoff ventured. "A guy with a rap sheet as long as his arm, a known criminal the cops could pin the Son of Cropsey attacks on with very little persuasion—he was a gift from God."

"Still doesn't explain why Cox took the fall."

Geoff put down the folder, which Stan picked up. "Maybe it does."

Turning his attention back to the banker box, he finger-walked his way through the labeled files until he came to the jacket he wanted. "Here it is, 'Cox, Robert Dennis.'" He flicked it open and eyed a handwritten notation. "Oh, you gotta love Detective Packer. This is what Packer told Davina when she met him down in Tampa, only here it is in his own handwriting dated around the time they announced Cox's arrest. Seems there were two homicides Cox was threatened with being accused of. Riley conveniently bargained a confession out of Cox, getting him to admit to being Son of Cropsey in exchange for a limited sentence based on his so-called cooperation. Of course, all this is according to Packer's suspicions."

"Exactly. It's all speculation. Nowhere is Packer stating that Cox was innocent. Nor is he saying Carlo or any of the others in your box was Son of Cropsey. Or for that matter that Carlo was the sick copycat Riley is making him out to be."

Geoff nodded his agreement.

"But I have a question. Why would there be a file on Angela included in Carlo's file?"

"What—?" Geoff grabbed the file out of his editor's hand. There, tucked into the back, was a separate folder. "Angela Donato," he read out loud. "She has her own jacket."

Geoff sat and a quick perusal had his brain reeling. "Near as I can make out at first glance, the reason Angela is in here is because of her father, Bill Jimenez. He was arrested for abusing Angela when she was a kid. Someone must have cross-referenced the names and pulled her file." Geoff kept on reading as he sipped his coffee.

"Listen to this, Stan," he said. "Angela's mother had been in Willowbrook as a seventeen-year-old. She was raped there and got pregnant with Angela. This was shortly before the place was finally closed. They believe the rapist, Angela's biological father, may have been another patient, diagnosed with paraphrenia, characterized by paranoid delusions."

"Let me see this," said Stan, taking the file. "The mother was given electroconvulsive therapy (ECT) several dozen times for depression before doctors even knew she was pregnant. The last one was given just a day before Angela was born. There's a note here that says the ECT would have retarded Angela's brain development. I quote, 'The late gestative period is when the inhibitory parts of the brain develop, that part which prevents the commitment of antisocial acts. Added to the fact that her father had a psychotic disorder and her mother was depressive and borderline, Angela is likely to endure severe mental dysfunction, including a lack of empathy.'"

Stan looked at Geoff. "Poor Angela didn't have a chance."

Geoff took the folder and began reading. "Angela was raised in the economically depressed section of Port Richmond where the family of nine lived in a four-room walk-up over a dry cleaners. Her father was a violent inebriate when he was home on shore leave from the Navy, and he was arrested for molesting Angela when she was just eight. It was discovered he was a diagnosed paranoid schizophrenic who never told anyone—it only came out after he was incarcerated for sexually torturing Angela's older sister, Margaret, during a psychotic episode. She was taken into foster care, where she was abused, and committed suicide jumping off the Verrazzano Narrows bridge a year later. Margaret was seventeen." Geoff swallowed hard; his mind was piecing together a puzzle he didn't much care for. "That's when Angela started in therapy."

"Seems like she was doomed before she even met Carlo," Stan stated the obvious.

"It gets worse." Geoff read on. "Angela and her father had a sexual relationship before and after he did his three-year sentence. An earlier report says Angela's father used all sorts of *happy toys* on her and loved to choke her while he had sex with her until she passed out. She didn't know any different and was caught in fourth grade strangling a first-grade girl and inserting pens into her. It happened again when she was in high school, and she was forced to go to psychiatric counseling."

"For every man there's a woman, isn't that what Frank Sinatra sang?" Stan put his coffee down onto Geoff's desk, his face pale.

Geoff was ghost white himself, not sure if Stan was joking. Geoff flicked up a couple pages. "She met her husband-to-be at the Richmond Historic Society. She was still only seventeen and he was fifteen years older. They bonded over a love of all things old and anything to do with the history of Staten Island. He was a guide, she volunteered after school —looks like they started having sex pretty quickly after that."

"Explains the ghost tours," Stan chipped in. "And their involvement in the Historic Society. They've always been vocal in anything to do with the island, especially any proposed real estate development. I always got the impression they saw it as a personal threat, but I always put that down to their passion for Staten Island."

"Fuck," Geoff gasped. "It goes deeper than *that*, Stan."

"How so?" Stan's forehead furrowed and his eyebrows met in the middle.

"Angela was accused by a fellow student of a serious sexual and physical assault. Packer managed to get hold of Angela's last psychiatrist report when she was sixteen, and he put a red flag on her."

"On *Angela?*"

"Yeah, it says here Angela is likely to be the enabler of extreme sexual behavior in a relationship, if not the instigator."

"Meaning?"

"Meaning they fed off each other—with Carlo's background and Angela's history of sexual abuse, it was the perfect storm. I read about a couple of cases like this a few years back—two troubled people who would likely otherwise lead relatively regular lives come together and create a kind of third personality."

"So, you're saying Angela drove her husband to rape all those girls?"

"No, Stan." Geoff put the folder down on his desk like it was something truly awful. "What I'm saying is Angela Donato is Son of Cropsey. She's the one who raped Davina and all those others. Shit, *Davina*." He grabbed his phone off the desk and began dialing. "I have to call Davina."

Geoff put the phone to his ear and listened to it ring.

CHAPTER SEVENTY-EIGHT

SATURDAY, 5:00 P.M., ST. GEORGE FERRY

THE BRIEF RAIN SHOWER HAD DRIVEN MANY COMMUTERS inside the ferry's passenger lounge, but Davina remained standing outside on the red-painted aft deck, leaning against the port taffrail. She was aboard the *Samuel I. Newhouse*, which was named appropriately for the publisher of the *Staten Island Advance*. A breeze off the dark-green waves of the Upper New York Bay carried with it the briny tang of sea air. She felt the light vibration of the three-thousand-ton ferry pushing through the chop, its powerful engines edging her closer to her new home. The ever-present boats, cargo ships, and ocean liners busied themselves in New York Harbor.

Staten Island receded four miles behind her as the boat plied its regular five-mile, thirty-minute scheduled run at a comfortable ten knots. She read on her phone there were actually four boats making more than a hundred crossings daily to ferry the seventy thousand mostly Staten Island passengers who worked and shopped in Manhattan. Davina purposely avoided looking back, preferring to set her sight on what lay to her sides and ahead of her. Less than a mile to her left was the Statue of Liberty, and a bit farther on, the Jersey City skyline. A thousand feet to her right was Governor's Island, once a military base, now a park she looked forward to visiting. She'd heard it was possible to rent bikes there, and it was only accessible by a little ferry. And there, a mile before her, just minutes away, was Manhattan with its skyscraper mélange of steel, bronze, concrete, and glass. Amazing she'd never been to *the City* as the Bridge and Tunnel crowd referred to Manhattan. There might be five boroughs, but Manhattan was what everyone thought of as New York. Davina was almost embarrassed having lived so apart, cloistered on the Rock. But now she'd truly be a New Yorker.

And finally, it was over.

She was about to restart her life on a different island: Manhattan Island.

Although Carlo Donato's death presented Davina a hollow victory, she felt finally free.

The ferry eventually closed in on the Whitehall Terminal, Lower Manhattan; Davina consulted the subway map on her iPhone to determine the best train to the East Village. Almost all her fellow ferry passengers were huddled toward what was now the bow of the boat in anticipation of disembarkation.

Thoughts of Joe suddenly popped into her head. Had she secretly wanted him to leave with her, or did she genuinely want the new beginning all to herself? Davina wasn't sure. But if he'd loved her as much as he claimed, he'd have been sitting there next to her on the boat; Davina knew in her heart they'd both made the right decision.

Davina's phone went off in her jeans pocket. She snatched it out and eyed the screen.

Geoff.

Do I even want to take that call?

A moment of hesitation passed before she answered it. "Hey, Geoff."

"Where are you?" Geoff's voice was sharp, urgent, strained.

"On the ferry. Arriving in Manhattan as we speak."

"It's Angela Donato, Davina! Son of Cropsey is Angela Donato."

"*What?*" The word came out as an airless whisper.

The ferry terminal was in sight; the few remaining seated passengers got off the benches and gravitated toward the bow. Davina found her voice. "That's crazy, Geoff. How do you—"

"Packer. Packer's daughter sent all his notes and files to me—well, to you, care of me. He died before he could send them. It's essentially an evidence trove."

"Of Angela. My trauma therapist?"

"She has a history of sexual abuse—both her and Carlo. They're as bad as each other, but according to what Packer sent, in my opinion, she's the one behind all the rapes . . . including yours."

The ferry's horn blared and drowned out Geoff's voice.

"Wait, I'm trying to hear you." To try for better reception, Davina crossed to the starboard side of the deserted aft deck. The horn quit blaring, but Davina's cell signal was breaking up.

"Geoff?"

"Davina, listen to me, this is *very* important."

Davina pressed the phone tight to her ear and paid close attention to everything the reporter was telling her.

"Hello, Davina. I came to say goodbye."

Startled by the voice, Davina turned to the woman who had appeared seemingly out of nowhere.

Angela? What the—?

Mind still reeling with the details Geoff had just shared, Davina fought to keep her voice steady, her every instinct imploring her to *run*. "Thank you, but you really didn't have to . . ." As Davina returned her phone to her pocket, she hit redial to Geoff, muted him, and began recording.

"Nonsense!" Angela beamed. "How could I let my favorite patient leave the Rock forever without saying goodbye?" She wore a wig, oversized plastic sunglasses, and had a bag slung over her shoulder.

Davina forced a smile for her former counselor; it seemed impossible to believe she had guided Davina through her darkest days following the rape. That Angela was Son of Cropsey. "We're about to dock . . . I-I need to go," Davina said as calmly as she could.

Angela gave Davina a quizzical glance, "You look frightened, Davina," Angela said. "I knew you'd remember me eventually—even with your memory." She tapped at her own temple with her forefinger.

"Of course, I remember you. How could I ever forget?" Davina's mind raced. "You were my therapist."

Angela tut-tutted and shook her head. "We don't have to pretend anymore, do we?"

Davina's brain skipped a beat. Nothing made sense.

Angela reached into her shoulder bag and grabbed something. Then, with a practiced rotation she tilted what looked like a metal cylinder just over the lip of the bag. It was a suppressor, a silencer, likely attached to a slim, subcompact semi-automatic pistol.

In her daze, Davina's brain was actually trying to figure out the exact model.

Angela reached across her chest and pulled the shoulder bag down; Davina saw it was a Glock G42, a so-called *women's gun* designed specifically for concealed carry. It was aimed discreetly at Davina's chest; they were not ten feet from each other.

Still staring at the muzzle, Davina struggled to form words. She looked around for someone, *anyone* she could call out to, but the deck was deserted. The ferry was only minutes from docking at the Whitehall terminal. Everyone was at the other end of the ferry, eager to disembark.

"It was Carlo, your husband. They killed him. It can't be you. You're . . . *him?*"

"That's me," Angela replied with a sage nod.

"It was you, you *raped* me?" Even as she said it, the idea sounded absurd to Davina.

Angela held up her left hand and wiggled her fingers. "One arm clamped around your throat, my free hand and my toys turning you on, making you mine. Making *all* of you mine. You still are." Angela edged forward. "I was angry with them. They were out to destroy Staten Island. *They* were the rapists, with their development plans. But I stopped them the best way I knew how: go after their daughters, the future. Show the island what a Delafield future would bring: more crime, rape, death. And it worked, slowed them down for years—until now, this election. Delafield wanted a second chance to destroy our island."

And then Davina saw it, the insight she was missing. "No, you got something out of this, Angela, something personal." She stepped back. "That's why you're really here. The first time wasn't enough. You're like a spider, hunting us down, wrapping us in your cocoon, then sucking us dry—reliving the nightmare you caused through our therapy sessions. You came here not to see me off but for another chance to feed. But now you're off the hook. Carlo is dead."

Angela gripped the pistol harder, the barrel of the gun pushing forward. "And it's your fault. If you'd just let things go, accepted the work I was doing, everything would have been fine." She paused. Her eyes bored into Davina. "I imagine you never once thought it was me who took your virginity—and then enjoyed reliving the moment over and over with you in our sessions together. I treasure those moments with you and my other girls."

Davina fought the urge to leap at the woman and beat the life from her with bare fists, but common sense held her back. One impulsive move would result in a bullet to the chest, and it would be game over. The ferry seemed to be slowing.

Time was almost up.

Standing on what now was the stern of the double-ended ferry, Angela faced west back toward Staten Island, where Davina faced east, ahead of her the Manhattan pier.

Angela peered over Davina's shoulder, into the passenger lounge, a feral smile appearing. She took another step closer to Davina. "But I can't forgive you for Carlo, Davina."

"Carlo did it for you, Angela," Davina lied. "He gave his life so you could just disappear. Why ruin that chance?" Please, come just a bit closer, Davina willed Angela.

Angela shifted foot-to-foot to keep her balance on the now gently rocking ferry. She kept the gun hip height, its muzzle trained on Davina. "I wanted to tell you one last thing before you . . . go. I saw you in that bachelor party video. I got a copy. It's everywhere, Davina. We have a network. Carlo and I spent a lot of time with you and that video. We came—"

There came a sudden, jostling bump when the three-thousand-ton ferry slowed into its berth between the dock's wooden pillars, hitting them hard. Angela took a step forward to counterbalance.

Taking advantage of the distraction, Davina spun to her left and kicked out at Angela's shoulder bag and gun. The toe of her boot connected with the revolver's handle and Angela's hand, making the gun clattered to the deck.

Davina kicked the gun out to the side as Angela cried out in pain and recoiled; her fingers reddened from the kick, she searched frantically for the gun. Then, she fixed her steely gaze upon Davina and her body tensed; Angela Donato was ready to attack.

Davina lashed out with her strong right leg, intending to catch Angela off guard and in the stomach. The woman was quicker than expected, and Davina's foot glanced off her hip, the blow muted by the coat. But she'd managed to knock the counselor off balance, and Davina made her decision.

She was not going to run—it all had to end right there, right then,

Davina slipped with ease into a fighting posture and attacked head-on.

Angela had staggered back a foot or two and had no chance of regaining her balance because Davina buried her shoulder in the soft part of her belly, driving with her legs.

Davina yelped as pain flared in her shoulder, and she imagined she felt the Steri-Strips tearing loose. But she'd caught Angela by surprise and she went down hard, rolling up like a pill bug to allow momentum to carry her into a backward shoulder roll.

Davina knew from bitter experience that Angela was stronger and more physically adept than she appeared. But seeing her collect that slight, soft-looking body into a practiced maneuver took her aback; Carlo really had taught his wife everything he'd picked up at the gym—some of them Davina's own moves. When Angela's feet shot out in an attempt to connect with Davina's forward knee, she was forced into a sideways leap and caught off balance.

Taking advantage, Angela leapt to her feet and charged at Davina like an enraged ram, her eyes glinting with murderous intent.

Deftly, Davina sidestepped her at the last moment. She flung herself onto the woman's back, legs wrapped around her torso, one arm around her neck. Angela's hooded jacket made the chokehold less effective than Davina had hoped, but she was able to hang on for several vital seconds as Angela bucked beneath her, fighting to wrench the choking arm from her neck. Davina's mind raced ahead as she hung on, knowing Angela would be losing vision, panicking, and more concerned about snatching a breath than anything else. Just a few seconds more and the counselor would hit the deck where Davina could finish her.

Angela staggered backward and rammed Davina hard into the ferry's rail.

Winded, blinded by white-hot pain, Davina let her legs drop from Angela's hips.

It was a reflex that saved Davina from tumbling overboard. But as Angela ground her lower back into the cold, hard steel, Davina roared in pain and loosened her grip just enough to allow Angela to twist in Davina's clutches until they were face-to-face. The counselor then forced herself between Davina's legs to crush her hips against the rail and bend her backward over it. Davina tried shoving her fists into Angela's throat. But Angela pinioned them with one arm, then snaked her free hand behind Davina's head to grab a handful of hair.

"You're going to die now, Davina Speers," Angela sneered, her voice low, rasping, *hateful*.

Davina shifted gears as she felt her hair torn out by its roots. She met her old counselor's eyes. "Go ahead, do it. Finish what you started when I was twelve, Angela. I spent ten years believing I'd be better off dead anyway."

With that, Davina relaxed completely to become a sudden dead weight. Angela was forced to adjust her grip, which meant letting go of Davina's hair. As she grasped under Davina's armpits to stop from falling, Davina kneed Angela hard in the groin, then, grasping the rail with both hands, she lashed out with her feet. Davina's blow caught Angela's upper torso and thrust her backward.

Angela Donato hit the deck in an ungainly sprawl, the wind knocked from her.

Fighting the temptation to run, Davina crouched slightly, one heel touching the base of the rail, raised her fists, and waited for Angela to clamber to her feet, using a stanchion for support. The once kind, caring face was twisted into an ugly mask of rage—one of pure, unadulterated hate.

"I'm going to finish you, Davina fucking Speers," Angela snarled as she clenched her fists into hard balls.

Then, she charged.

When Angela had almost reached her, Davina doubled over. She bulled into the woman's pelvis, grasped her thighs, and used the momentum to lift her just high enough to hit the rail. When Davina straightened, using all the power in her legs, Angela Donato, murderer and rapist, tilted headfirst over the rail and into the gap between the ferry and the dock. A beat later, Davina heard the splash of Angela hitting the water—heard it even over the dull thrum of the ship's idling engines.

Davina turned and peered down into the gloom. She thought she saw a face, pale in the shadow of the ship. She realized with a jolt that as strong as Angela was, she could likely swim to shore or pull herself up on the dock or even clamber back onto the ferry.

God, she thought, *this really has to end.*

The ferry vibrated beneath Davina's feet and she realized the engines had powered up for the return trip to Staten Island. Behind her, the passenger cabin was filling up with Saturday travelers, all excited, despite the rain, for their trip to the Rock.

Should she grab her things and try to get off the boat, or accept that she was going *back* to Staten Island? She spotted her phone lying on the deck—it was soaking wet. Fortunately, the device was water-resistant and sprang to life the moment she picked it up. Her mind went to poor Geoff sitting in his office wondering if the killer counselor had caught up with her. She wanted to tell him she was fine and that it was all over.

Except it wasn't.

Not while there was a chance Angela Donato was still alive.

Davina leaned over the rail and peered down into the water.

Nothing, nothing, and more nothing.

She was soaked through, exhausted, and shaking as the adrenaline that had driven her self-preservation leached from her body like water from a broken cup. She wanted to cry, to rage, to protest that God would have her go through all that and offer no closure. It was possible the East Village wasn't far enough from the island to keep her safe. Not if—

A flash of movement along the ferry's waterline, a vague blur just beneath the water . . .

Angela bobbed up almost directly below Davina, her panicked face ghostly white with a dark slash on one side of her forehead that could have been hair, a clump of seaweed, or a deep gash. She grasped desperately at the ferry's smooth hull, as if hoping to pull herself up. It wasn't possible. But if someone spotted the frantic figure, she'd be saved and Davina's nightmare would start all over again.

Davina's heart beat heavily in her throat as she scrabbled for something to do. What if she got one of her suitcases and . . .

She glanced up at the ferry's Staten Island bridge, wondering if she might draw the attention of one of the return crew. She could just go into the cabin and alert someone at the snack bar. But if the crew saved Angela, believing she'd simply fallen overboard, if they wouldn't listen to Davina's tale of attempted murder, her nightmare would live on.

The engines cranked with purpose, and the boat began moving. Davina stared back down at Angela, who was managing to keep herself afloat. She screamed something up at Davina, her voice a coarse shriek that blended in with the cries of the seagulls overhead; whatever the words, the meaning was clear—she wouldn't rest until Davina Speers was dead and in the ground.

Another voice, a young man's, this time from the shore. *"There's someone down there!"* The young man pointed down at Angela, and a small group formed around him. *"Somebody help her!"*

Davina's heart sank as she watched the sudden flurry of activity along the shoreline. The ferry slowed as the engines cut out and the propeller stopped; Angela was to be saved. But she seemed oblivious to that; her entire focus was on Davina. Her screams, now recognizable as profanities, could be clearly heard, rising even above the seabirds' cries.

What happened next wasn't something Davina could have explained. The *Samuel I. Newhouse* lurched inexplicably to port, pinning the murderous therapist between her hull and the dock. Blood spewed from Angela Donato's mouth, staining the water around her deep red. The screaming stopped, the ferry pulled away from the dock, and the nightmare face disappeared beneath the dark waters of the Upper Bay.

Davina hung on the railing for a moment, uncertain what to feel.

Son of Cropsey was gone. The legendary torturer of young girls was gone, and Davina Speers was still here. Still alive. Still standing. That was what she would tell Geoff and Joe and Charlie and the other thetas. And anyone who questioned or challenged her.

You are free, she would tell each of them. Then she would begin life anew in Manhattan. And maybe one day, when she was ready, she would return to the island, and settle the rest of her haunted past. For now, exorcising this one demon would do.

Strangely, the thought of going back no longer filled her with dread.

The rain was letting up as she went back into the passenger lounge. She found her belongings as she had left them and made her way to where the ferry crew was ushering passengers from the boat. Angela's gruesome death meant an inevitable delay to disembarking, and Davina could finally leave the Rock well and truly behind her.

Now, she thought, *I can leave without running away.*

THE END

Who am I? I sometimes find it hard to answer this question. It depends on what hat I'm wearing that day, what setting I'm in, or the venue I may be attending. I'm Dr. Vince. I'm an international financier, investing in stocks, real estate, people, and businesses. I was a CEO of a private equity fund in Hong Kong. I've operated my business throughout the Asia Pacific Region in amazing locations such as Indonesia, Singapore, Thailand, China, Japan, the Philippines, Hong Kong, and Korea. I helped executives and businesses raise billions of dollars in capital while making a small fortune for myself. But this is all the boring stuff I do. I am a Professor in the School of Business and Accounting at Monroe College. I love mentoring and teaching. Helping young people achieve their goals, and showing people how to make their own dreams a reality is what I'm meant to do with my life. This is the rewarding and satisfying stuff I do.

I have a Doctrate in Business Administration with an emphasis in Leadership, Decision Making, and Behavior. I also hold an MBA and a Master's degree in Innovation & Entrepreneurship. I'm passionate about writing, telling stories, and creating content. I want to bring a reader into a world that captivates them, makes them laugh, scares them, and gives them a brief moment to forget about everything else. I've always been enamored by great stories and even more so with great movies. Yes, I love Star Wars, The Lord of the Rings, The Matrix, and other great sci-fi movies. I'm a kid in an adult body. But agreat Suspense/Thriller, Mystery, or Drama also keeps me glued to the screen.

Yes, I cried during Charlotte's Web, The Notebook and so many other tear droppers. Who hasn't? Maybe I'm a hopeless romantic or just a sensitive soul. I guess you can say that I get moved by a great story. I am a member of the Writers Guild of the East. I'm passionate about film and attended the New York Film Academy as well as the Hollywood Film School to learn how to film my stories.

To sum me up, I'm a dreamer who never stops dreaming that the impossible is possible. I use my real-life experiences and adventures in all my novels. I've lived in 11 countries and 16 cities. I've interacted with gangsters, CEOs, scammers, and market manipulators as well as many wonderful people from beautiful cultures. I've loved, I've been heartbroken, I've climbed the mountain of success only to come tumbling down twice. I've learned a lot and experienced even more chaotic, often crazy things in my lifetime. I want to share these experiences with you. The good, the bad, the ugly. The full and very interesting me. Enjoy! For more information or to contact the author, go to: VincentdeFilippo.com

9 798988 342090